The Water Bearer

By Ken Himmelman

For Wendy –
To someone who in fact is doing
all she can to save the world.
with all my gratitude + appreciation.
Ken

"If the Modern Age began with the discovery of America, it also ended in America… We are going through a transitional period, when it seems that something is on the way out and something else is painfully being born. It is as if something were crumbling, decaying, and exhausting itself, while something else, still indistinct, were arising from the rubble."

— Vaclav Havel (1994)

"The power of erecting banks and corporations was not given to the general government. It remains then with the State itself. For any person to recognize the power of a foreign legislature [the US Congress], in a case belonging to the State itself, is an act of treason against the State. And whosoever shall do an act under cover of the authority of a foreign legislature, whether by signing notes or by passing them, acting as director, cashier, or any other office relating to it, shall be adjudged guilty of high treason and suffer death accordingly by the judgment of the state courts."

— Thomas Jefferson, letter to James Madison (1781)

"Thus in the beginning all the world was America."

— John Locke, *Two Treatises of Government* (1689)

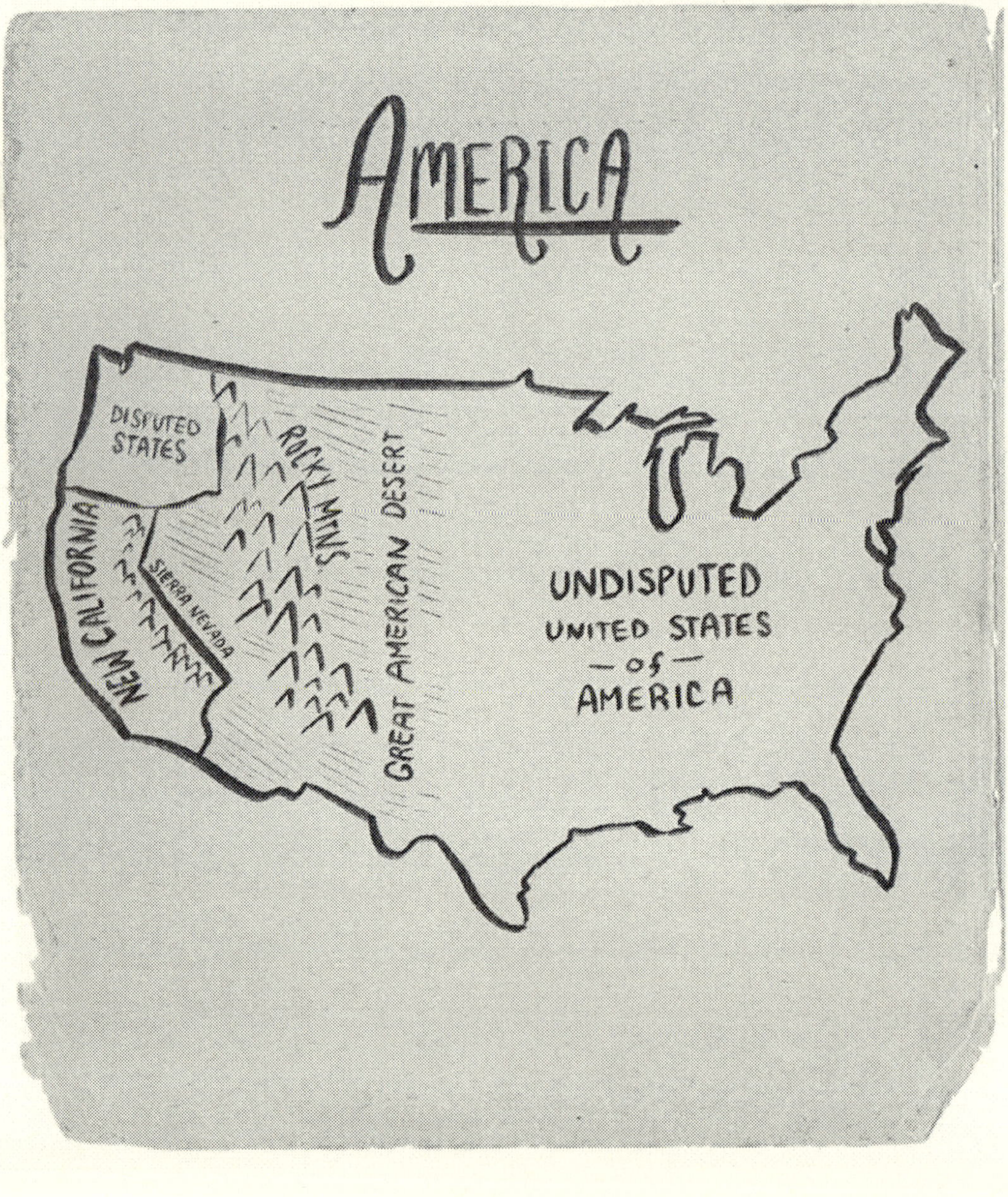
AMERICA
DISPUTED STATES
NEW CALIFORNIA
SIERRA NEVADA
ROCKY MTNS
GREAT AMERICAN DESERT
UNDISPUTED
UNITED STATES
—of—
AMERICA

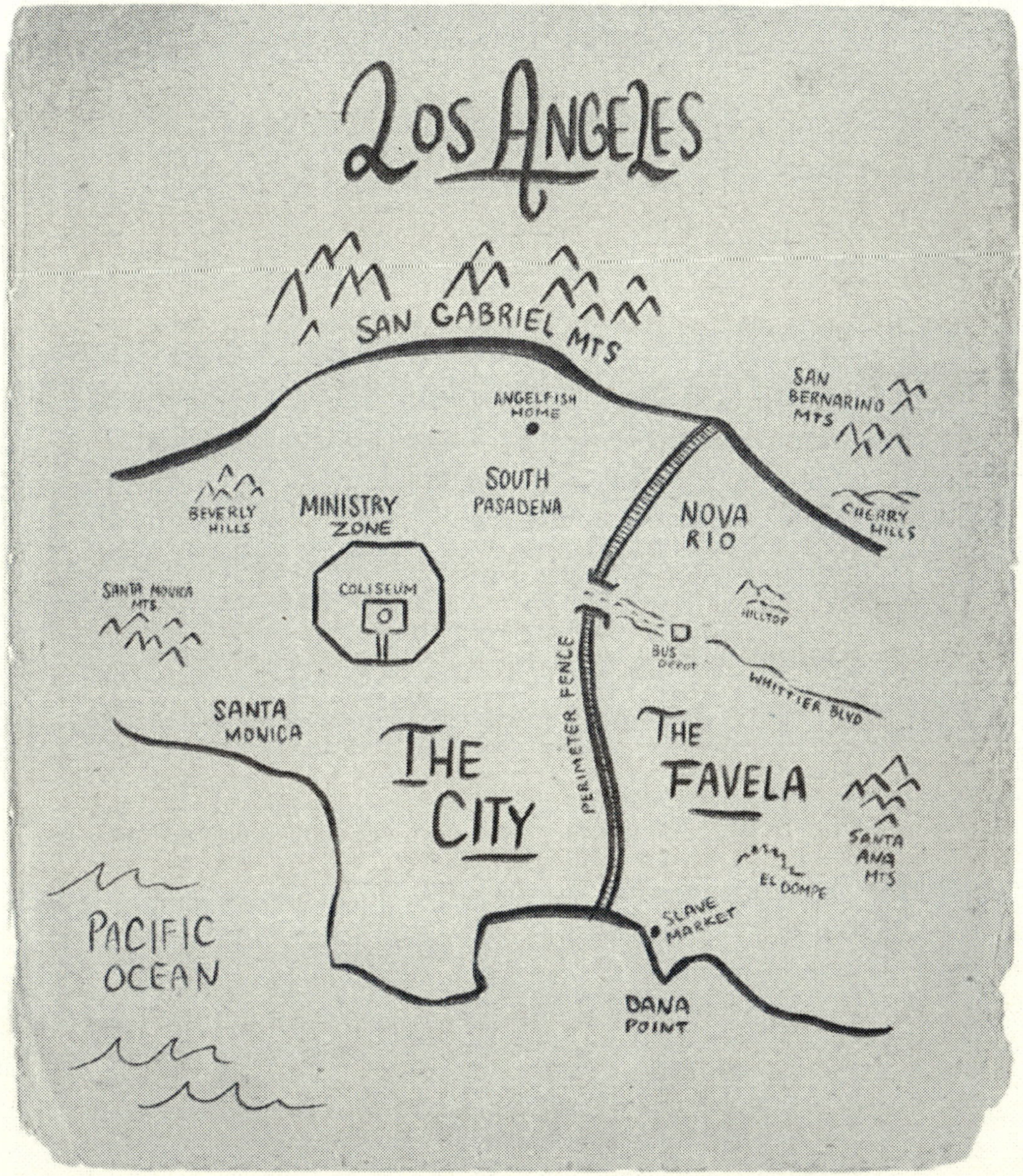
Los Angeles
SAN GABRIEL MTS
ANGELFISH HOME
SAN BERNARINO MTS
BEVERLY HILLS
MINISTRY ZONE
SOUTH PASADENA
NOVA RIO
CHERRY HILLS
SANTA MONICA MTS.
COLISEUM
HILLTOP
BUS DEPOT
WHITTIER BLVD
PERIMETER FENCE
SANTA MONICA
THE CITY
THE FAVELA
SANTA ANA MTS
EL DOMPE
SLAVE MARKET
PACIFIC OCEAN
DANA POINT

Ken Himmelman wrote his doctoral dissertation on the history of modern science fiction and co-wrote the original screenplay for the 2007 feature film *Gracie*. *The Water Bearer* is his first novel. He has worked in the non-profit sector on issues such as youth development, global health, and higher education for the last twenty years. He lives in Boston, MA.

For Caroline, Sam and Lily

Part I

Home

Kat

She sat upright in bed, eyes closed, ears attuned to everything around her. Grains of red dust pounded the windowpanes, a steady stream of tinseled chimes. In a slow crescendo, they blended with an onslaught of other sounds that threatened to overwhelm her: the high hum of electricity behind the walls; the steady beat of viscous drops of water falling into the basement storage tank; the thin whistling of the wind. Only one sound mattered to her just now: the hushed tones of her parents in the kitchen below. With her right hand, she rubbed the faded green blanket she had been given at birth against her cheek in a rhythmic motion. Otherwise, she remained perfectly still, straining to make out their words through the din in her head.

I don't know, she heard Mother say.

We can do this, Father replied.

Talking stopped. The kitchen door swished. Footsteps hesitated before mounting the stairs. Moments later, her bedroom door creaked open. Father's tall frame loomed in the doorway. He sat down next to her and tenderly brushed her cheek. Part of her brain registered love. Her eyes darted about Father's head, rapidly computing the shroud of anxious energy that radiated from his brow, jaw, and breath. In spite of the heat, she shuddered with chill.

"Hi, sweetie," he said, doing his best to sound upbeat. "I thought you might still be awake."

"What's happening?" she asked, averting her eyes, beginning ever so slightly to rock back and forth, folding and refolding her blanket.

"Nothing," he said with a limp smile. He attempted again to stroke her face. Almost imperceptibly, she twitched. He withdrew, not wanting to agitate her further. "I'm getting ready to leave for the conference. Joseph will be here in a few minutes to pick me up."

"Joseph drives you a lot."

"Yes, he's my favorite driver."

"I like him."

"He's a good friend. A good man."

"But you don't want to go," she murmured.

"Of course I want to go. I mean…I don't really want to go, you're right. I never like to be away from you guys. But I'm excited that you're all coming to meet me this weekend."

For a lingering moment, she lifted her eyes to meet his, seeking truth. Then, in a flash, she leapt to her knees and flung her arms around his neck, choking him with the ferocity of her embrace. Surprised, he pressed a cheek against her head, inhaling the sweet fragrance of her hair.

"I need to ask you a favor." He revealed a small leather notebook and turned it over in his hands. "I've been working on a puzzle."

She sat back, taking in the notebook's familiar brown cover, cracked and creased from its back-pocket life. Her memory quickly cycled through an inventory of images: Father stopping as they walked down the street to jot down an observation; laboring at the kitchen table to transcribe a quotation from a book he had been reading; scribbling chemical equations in bed in his striped pajamas. His notebook was as precious to him as her blanket was to her.

He gave her a restrained smile before moving through the murky light toward her desk. When he returned, his hands were empty.

"You know where I put it. I need you to keep it safe for me. Will you do that?"

Yes, she mouthed.

"Can I take this?" Pinched between thumb and forefinger, he displayed one of the United States pennies he had given her as a gift, and which he had just taken from the short, neat stacks lined up along the back of her desk. "For luck."

Although her face remained expressionless, a rare tear rimmed the edge of her eyelid.

"It'll be okay, honey. You have to be strong. You *are* strong. I'll see you in a few days, okay?" He kissed away the single drop that had commenced its slow tumble down her cheek.

"*Je t'aime*," he whispered huskily. "I love you."

She wanted to respond, but her tongue had turned to stone. Unsure how to read her silence, he leant down, kissed her again on the top of the head, then walked stoop-shouldered from the room.

"*Je t'aime*," said Kat, long after he had gone.

2

In her dream, she rode gentle currents of air that eddied between the soft cumulus above her and the thick smog that frosted the City below. Los Angeles lay dormant in the crepuscular light. Twin islands of skyscrapers – one in Century City, the other in the downtown Ministry Zone – towered over the precise geometric gridlines of an urban landscape reconstructed only a generation ago. In the distance, the great double fence, known as The Perimeter, curled around the City like a protective snake, its body battered from the north by the encroaching sands and from the south by the heaving chaos of the giant slum, the *favela grande*. To the east the mountains; to the west the sea. North, a lone black car sped along a ribbon of empty highway.

Father.

She willed herself on, flying through the air until she hovered directly over the car. She tried to descend through the smog, but the air resisted her, bouncing her back toward the sky.

A phone rang.

Crystal, she thought.

The car skidded to a halt, kicking up a cloud of dust. Father lurched out of the back seat, retching violently on the side of the road. Joseph emerged from behind the wheel, rushing over in concern to put a hand on Father's shoulder. Father rose unsteadily, head bowed, having regained some measure of composure. As he wiped his glasses clean with the hem of his shirt, he spoke to his friend in a low, urgent tone. Although Kat could not hear their exchange, she observed Joseph's face slacken in fear.

The two men argued briefly before Joseph pulled away to retrieve a crowbar from the trunk of the car. Kat could tell that he was trying to convince her father to take it – to hit him– but Father kept refusing. Finally, Joseph prevailed, clasping him reassuringly on the shoulder. As his faithful driver turned his back, Father took a deep breath and struck Joseph just hard enough on the side of the head to draw blood. Kat watched in horror as Joseph's knees buckled. Father was quick to lean down and check on him, but Joseph pushed him away, insisting that he go. Fear gripped Father fully. He scrambled behind the wheel of the sedan, floored the gas, and steered the car at breakneck speed off the main road to the east, spinning dust in his wake.

Kat raised her eyes toward the horizon, toward the mountains. From within the heart of the hillside, one tree began to move, tall and dark, slowly striding forward. A ghastly form, not quite man, not quite shadow, but something in between: something dark and menacing and terrifying. The form spread wide its arms, threw back its head, and began to laugh – quietly at first, then louder and louder and louder until the sound filled her with such intensity that she thought her entire body might explode.

Kat screamed.

3

She awoke with a start. Her breath cycled in short spurts. Clenching her eyes, she sought refuge in numbers. Cold, simple, clear, emotionless numbers. Using a trick her parents taught her years ago, she counted by threes as fast as she could, crowding out any other thought, until her anxiety began to subside. By the time she reached 408, her chest had loosened and her beating heart had slowed.

Gradually her room took shape. Her dresser, neatly arranged with pictures of her mother, father, and brother, stood against one wall. On her desk sat a perfectly laid miniature tea set; seven stacks of U.S. pennies, organized sequentially by year; and two boxes of flavored yogurt drops. In the corner by the closet door, her pet guinea pig, Meatball, rustled quietly in his box, squeaking pathetically for her company.

Standing on his hind legs, Meatball gripped the edge of his container as she approached. Stunted from his feral days before Kat rescued him, Meatball was exceptionally small, even for a guinea pig. His white and brown patches of fur spiked irregularly and in different directions, giving him a disheveled, vagabond look. She leant down to rub his nose. Meatball raised his snout eagerly, affectionately nibbling on the soft skin of her finger. She scratched the top of his head and base of his neck, prompting a songlike purr of pleasure in response. Stroking him, feeling his innocent and positive energy, Kat's anxiety diminished further.

It was a dream, she told herself. *Sometimes they're wrong.*

Kat walked to the window and wrapped the faded green baby blanket around her shoulders, stroking one cheek compulsively with the corner she had rendered almost transparent after so many years of use. Outside, drab houses lined the empty suburban street, each a pre-fabricated box, the signature architecture of post-earthquake reconstruction in Los Angeles. Kat's attention was drawn to a lonely street lamp halfway down the block. It flickered weakly in the soupy light. Even from such a distance, her acute hearing picked up the crackling of its weary exertions. At this early hour, the neighborhood would drink in the first rays of sunrise, hoping against hope that the sun might break through the unremitting dust. Today, like every day before it she could recall, the Los Angeles sky choked brown and thick.

At twelve years old, Kat was small for her age but not frail. Her hair was chestnut brown and straight, cut in a short bob around her ears. The almandine slope of her eyes and the length of her dark eyelashes complimented the hint of color in her complexion, but her limbs were muscular and lean. She moved with the erectness of a dancer, but Kat had never wanted to take a dance class or play the piano or participate in any social activities. Other people misunderstood her, or were afraid of her, and she had no real friends to speak of. So she preferred to follow the same, simple routine every day: go to school, come home, play with Meatball, walk in the woods behind her house, eat dinner with her family, do her homework, read her books, and go to bed.

"I'm going to the bunker," she said to Meatball. "Want to come? I'll read to you."

Meatball softly pleaded in protest.

"Fine. I'll get you one."

Kat fetched a yogurt drop and knelt close to Meatball's box. She dangled the treat in front of him. Elated, he snatched it with his little teeth.

"Now are you ready?"

Meatball chirruped contentedly and she scooped him up. From her closet, she removed the light, hooded trench coat that

Father bought her at a yard sale a few years ago. Despite the heat, she had worn it every day since. She slipped Meatball into one of the roomy pockets and padded softly down the stairs.

4

It took Kat only three guesses to crack the code for the bunker door. She knew that Father had recently started using the names of constellations to generate a password, that each letter in the name of the constellation would convert to its numeric position in the alphabet, and that the keypad could accept any combination of six to twelve two-digit numbers. After trying "Aquarius" and "Taurus," the red light turned to green when she punched in the numbers corresponding to "Gemini." She felt a pulse of satisfaction and pulled open the bulkhead doors.

The underground bunker into which Kat descended was mandated by the government for all houses built in Los Angeles after the Great Earthquake. Kat loved the cave-like feeling created by the low ceiling. Here, no electricity buzzed behind the walls, no bulbs crackled above her head. She would know the smells of this room anywhere: the faint whiff of leather from Father's reading chair, the dry sweetness of the packages of flavored oatmeal, the remnant trace of the last honey-scented candle that mother had burned. In the pitch black, Kat closed her eyes and began a ritual she liked to practice whenever she came down to this refuge. Rapidly, she clicked her tongue against the roof of her mouth. As the sound reverberated off the walls, it bent around the shape of objects in its path, creating shadowed forms in her mind: furniture, pantry, kitchen, water tanks, bookshelves. Gradually, a picture of the room emerged on the back of her eyelids, a ghostly projection in black and white so perfectly defined that she could move with ease through the dark.

Threading her way past the soft chairs of the living area, she arrived at her ultimate destination: the floor-to-ceiling bookshelf Father had built along the back wall. It held more than two hundred books her parents had secretly collected over the years – *real* books, books made with paper pages, the kind of books that people could not routinely find in New California. These volumes were all secondhand, either passed down from Kat's maternal grandparents (who had been able to collect them freely when California was still part of the United States) or picked up from dusty bookshops by Father on his business trips to Canada or the European Federation.

For most children at Kat's school, books existed almost exclusively on computer tablets, and the idea of sitting and reading a paper novel seemed distinctly strange. In fact, reading a novel at all, even on a tablet, would be considered odd. But for Kat, holding a physical book from her Father's collection constituted one of the deep pleasures of her life – a *connection*, she felt, to something meaningful and enduring, something ancient and wise. There were books that dated back to the eighteenth or nineteenth century. Books from this century and the last. Hardback and softback. Mottled and pristine. Heavy and light. She loved them all. When she held them in her hands, she absorbed their physical history, beyond the times and places of the stories being told, imagining the people who possessed the books before her – the other girls or women or men who, like her, sat quietly in the low light until they lost themselves in those very same pages.

Because clicking only allowed her to see objects in the dark, Kat had hung a penlight from a nail on the side of the bookshelf in order to read. Removing it now, she directed its narrow beam at the lower three shelves. These were *her* shelves, and she was zealous in taking responsibility for organizing them. Today, the shelves included texts devoted to marine creatures, a large volume of La Fontaine's *Fables* in the original French, and a book about Hopi culture. Next week she would exchange them for others in Father's collection. But the bottom shelf remained constant, filled only with her most treasured tales, arranged alphabetically by author: Richard Adams, Roald Dahl, Madeline L'Engle, Jean Craighead George, Phillip Pullman, J.K. Rowling, George Selden, Jonathan Stroud, J.R.R. Tolkien, E.B. White. Kat knew every character, every chapter, every line, in every book. Even when she played alone in her room aboveground, long after the storms had waned, the characters from those books remained her companions and her consolation. And whenever Kat felt particularly stressed or upset, Mother would acquiesce to open the bulkhead doors and let her descend to the bunker. Once there, Kat would gather several volumes from her shelf and stack them next to the old hamper where the extra blankets were stored. Penlight in hand, she would crawl inside the hamper, nestle down in the plush folds, and, securely compressed on all sides, lose herself in those extraordinary worlds.

Now Kat plucked one of the books off the shelf and climbed into the hamper. Burrowing warmly into the blankets, she touched the pages delicately to her nose and inhaled deeply. Meatball crept out of his pocket and settled in the nook of her lap.

"Ready?" she asked. Then she began to read aloud the opening lines. *"How could they sleep? All day on the radio there had been hurricane warnings. How could they leave her up in the attic in the rickety brass bed, knowing that the roof might be blown right off the house, and she tossed out into the wild night to land who knows where..."*

Jacob

"What's *wrong* with you?" Jacob asked his sister as they took a seat at the back of the monorail. "You almost made us miss the train."

Kat refused to look at him. Exasperated, Jacob turned away and stared out the window as the train slid along the rail high above the neighborhoods. Below, the residential districts in South Pasadena zipped past, their neat geometry and color coordination giving the appearance of a candy-coated world. In the distance and through the haze he could just discern the blinking crimson lights of the Perimeter watchtowers that kept constant vigilance over the boundary between City and slums. Jacob tapped his earpiece and started his playlist.

Every day with Kat was challenging, even when she wasn't in one of her moods. His parents knew that Jacob understood her better than anyone, and that Kat felt extremely connected to him. Which was why, like it or not, he was responsible for getting her to school, for getting her home, for making sure she got lunch, for watching out for her on the playground. When Mother told him at breakfast that Kat had slept in the bunker, he knew it would be a difficult day. On days like today, he wanted nothing more than to shed his fraternal responsibility and let her face the world on her own.

But as the music gradually soothed him, he glanced back at his sister. She looked fragile and vulnerable, rocking distractedly in the seat beside him. Her anxiety today was unusually elevated. In spite of his frustration, he resolved to stick with her more closely even than he normally would. He put a firm hand on her leg to calm her and she shot him a fast, grateful look.

I'm sorry, she said with her eyes.

It's ok, he nodded.

At the school station, a modest group of straggling latecomers emptied out of the train with Jacob and Kat. Hurriedly, they scampered across the yard to beat the morning bell. Jacob pulled Kat along and stopped in front of the middle school building.

"You have to go in, ok?" he insisted. "You can't stay out here. I'm already late. I can't come back for you. I have a big test tomorrow."

Reluctantly, Kat assented. He waited until she entered through the building door, then raced past the jungle gym and across the basketball court to the upper school. He skidded into his seat just as the bell finished its last chime.

"Nice," said the boy in the chair next to him. "Another fun morning with the Kat litter?"

"Shut up," Jacob replied, still breathing heavily and taking out his books.

David McCaw was Jacob's best friend. His bandy limbs and dreadful acne had kept him on the social margins through middle and now in high school. He was taller than Jacob by an inch but skinnier; he looked like a stork when he moved, awkward and halting. His friend group was small confined primarily to Jacob and one or two other boys from the cross-country team. The coach's praise for David mirrored the praise he most often received about anything: that he showed grit and determination more than innate talent. Girls tended to avoid him. But David had a wicked sense of humor, and he could make anyone laugh (including adults), which got him into, as well as out of, a fair amount of trouble.

By contrast, Jacob was tall and lean, with sandy colored hair, a much paler complexion than his sister and mother, and the ice blue eyes of his father. He wore his hair at a shaggy length, letting it fall over his brow, relishing the rebellious air it gave him. Over the last year, as he turned from fifteen to sixteen, he had grown a few inches and now stood almost five foot ten. His athletic frame and natural coordination helped him succeed at most of the sports he tried. His passion, however, was for California Rules Football – a popular version of the Australian game that, since coming to the U.S. West Coast forty years ago, had grown into the state's most popular professional sport. Athleticism leant Jacob some measure of social acceptance, allowing him to move across several different social circles and overcome the oddness people associated with both David and Kat. And lately, he even felt that girls paid attention to him.

Jacob and David had grown up a few blocks apart, their mothers having met in a babysitting co-op when they were only toddlers. As long as he could remember doing anything, Jacob had done it with David – going to parks, playing ball in the streets, joining the Junior Scouts, playing video games for hours on end. As they grew older, and Jacob's exposure widened, he sometimes wondered if he should have moved on from David. Already burdened socially by his association with Kat, Jacob at times regretted the additional weight of David's friendship. But David was like a brother to him; they shared a bond more powerful than the normative pressure of high school. And, without question, no one made him laugh the way David did.

"We barely caught the 7:50," Jacob said. "I was trying to get here early, too."

"So it *was* Kat."

"Of course."

"You gotta lose the babysitter thing, man," replied David.

"Tell me about it."

"Well, while I was waiting for you, it became very clear that Durfey forgot to take her valium today. So maybe you could wait at least five minutes before you piss her off."

"*Please rise for the morning recitation*," intoned a smooth electronic voice over the school loudspeaker. Dutifully, all the students rose and put their right hands over their hearts. Synthesized music echoed through the building in time with the chanting young voices.

We pledge allegiance to the flag, and to all of New California...

The students took their seats again after completing the pledge, while the teacher, Mrs. Adelia Durfey, squeezed down the rows of desks with a stern look on her face and a thin wooden rod in hand.

"The final exam is *tomorrow*," she bellowed, punctuating her sentences with special stress on certain words. "The primary subject will be the Founding. I'm *sure* you are *all* prepared for this and not thinking about summer vacation. Today is our last review. Take out your tablets. Chapter seven. The Founding. James Russell, summarize the three main points, if you *please*."

A small boy with oversized glasses near the front of the room smacked his lips nervously before answering.

"Was it..." James hesitated, "...the Recall, the Restoration, and the Proclamation of Defederation?"

"*Indeed*," proclaimed Mrs. Durfey. "And why is the Recall so important?"

More confident now, James continued. "The Recall was how the voters of the old state of California – in the early part of the century when California was still in the union with the United States of America – it was how they got rid of the old Governor and replaced him with our leader, President Malcolm Duke."

Mrs. Durfey's hawk-like eyes surveyed the classroom. They settled on Jacob as he and David whispered at the back of the room. "Mr. Angelfish… Maybe *you* would like to tell us about chapter nine. The Proclamation of Defederation."

"Oooh, so hosed," said David, covering his mouth with his hand and sliding down in his chair.

"Is there something you and Mr. McCaw would like to share with the rest of us?"

"Uh… no," Jacob mumbled. "I mean… no."

The entire class erupted in laughter, David most delightedly of all.

"Well then…" continued Mrs. Durfey stoically. "The Proclamation of Defederation?"

Swallowing hard, Jacob tried to focus. "It's the… the speech that President Duke gave declaring independence. For New California. For us."

David flashed him a furtive thumbs up. But Mrs. Durfey was unimpressed.

"Miss Appleton, *please*…" begged the teacher.

In her crisp manner, Julia Appleton sprang to the rescue. "The Proclamation of Defederation. Governor Duke's Second Inaugural address. Its major sources were the Declaration of Independence, Thomas Jefferson's 1781 letter to James Madison, and the Third Millennium Vision. The Governor – he didn't become President for another three years – he called for a validation of states' rights above federal power, just as the Founding Fathers originally intended. He declared that California was going to 'defederate', a way for a state to operate independent of federal control without needing a constitutional amendment. Governor Duke renamed our defederated state the New Republic of California and sought official recognition in the United Nations.

He said we have the right to a peaceful determination of our own future, just as the original Americans did when they declared independence from the British crown."

David leaned in close to Jacob. "That was a lot smarter than what you said."

"*Thank* you, Miss Appleton," sighed Mrs. Durfey with evident relief. "It is gratifying to know that at least *someone* will be ready for the examination tomorrow."

"Thanks for the moral support," Jacob said to David.

"I'm always here for you, bro," replied David with a wide grin.

2

As they waited outside the cafeteria to gel their hands at the disinfecting station, Jacob's attention was drawn to raised voices inside. Without hesitating, he rushed out of the line and into the teeming dining hall. Against the back wall, he saw a cluster of kids gathered in a circle around three tall boys who were laughing and taunting their victim. Bile rose in Jacob's throat as he tore across the room, already sure of what was happening. As he feared, in the center of the circle, hunched in a defensive crouch, was Kat. Her hands covered her ears, and her body rocked back and forth as she muttered nonsense words under her breath.

"Assholes!" he screamed, shoving and pushing aside the boys, placing himself between them and his sister.

"Whoa, look at that. It's Mr. Football Star," taunted the biggest of the boys.

More students joined the growing crowd now, eagerly anticipating the possibility of a fight. Jacob glared, fists clenched.

"Leave her alone," he said in a low voice.

"Or what?" responded the bully with half a smile, daring him to act.

Jacob knew he would lose, and lose badly, if they came to blows. But he did not back down.

"Just leave her alone," he repeated.

"Your sister…" the boy said, putting his face an inch from Jacob's, "is a *retard*."

He and Jacob continued to stare at each other. Finally, the bully stood up and called out to his friends. "Let's get outta here. These losers are a waste of time."

As the gang sauntered away, Jacob put his hands in his pockets to stop them from shaking. Kat continued to rock back and forth, eyes clenched, lost to her surroundings. A few curious students remained a short distance away, gawking at Jacob as he bundled his sister to her feet. David grabbed some pre-made sandwiches and followed them outside.

"Why did you come over to our cafeteria?" Jacob asked as he settled Kat down in the courtyard. She sat on the hard blacktop, knees to chest. He kept his voice steady and calm, knowing that his agitation would only make her more upset. "Those guys…You could've just sent me a message. I would've come over."

"Bad," Kat mumbled. She raised her eyes to his. "It's really bad, Jacob."

He softened at her intense vulnerability and felt the smallest prickle of concern. Over the years, he had learned that Kat's strongest feelings were often right. But his immediate priority was to get her through the rest of the day.

"Did they hurt you?" he asked quietly.

Kat shook her head no. "I'm scared."

"It's gonna be okay. You didn't have a good night's sleep. You know how you get when you're tired."

"This is different. It's…" Involuntarily, she started rocking back and forth again, shaking her head no, no, no. "I don't know."

He squatted down and put a firm hand on each of Kat's legs to convey his presence. In a stern voice, he commanded, "Kat! I said it's going to be okay. Should we count? Let's count."

Kat began counting by three, her lips moving rapidly as she worked her way higher and higher. Jacob kept his hands on her legs, trying to remain calm himself so that she would pick up on his quieter energy. Gradually, her rocking slowed and finally stopped.

"Better?"

"A little."

"Have you eaten anything?"

"I'm not hungry."

"You need to eat."

David, who had been watching this entire interaction from his perch on a wall a few feet away, picked up half a sandwich off the tray and offered it to them. Jacob placed it in his sister's hands.

"How about you sit over there by the tree," he said. "If you eat a little maybe you'll feel better."

"Man, I don't know what the hell her problem is today," Jacob said as he rejoined David.

"Those guys are just assholes," said David with his mouth full of sandwich. "They used to pick on me all the time in lower school. They know better now." He clenched a fist and showed a thin bicep to Jacob. Jacob grunted a reluctant laugh.

"Want the other half of your sandwich?" David asked him. Absentmindedly, Jacob began to eat.

"I'd love to beat the crap out of those guys," Jacob swore.

"Yeah, me too. Only problem is, they're stronger than us."

Jacob laughed. Pleased that his humor had lowered the tension, David reached into his backpack and removed his tablet.

"Check this out." Tapping a few times on the screen, he pulled up the image of an adolescent boy. About their age, his face painted in camouflage, the boy held a military knife triumphantly above his head. "I bought one."

"One what?" asked Jacob.

"A knife."

"You bought a *knife*? Like *that*? Why?"

"Standard issue for the Praetorian Guard," answered David, as if the answer were obvious. "Awesome, isn't it?"

"I guess," said Jacob. "Just don't cut your finger off. Or anything else."

"Ha, ha," replied David, tucking the tablet back into his bag. "Bet those jerks would be impressed if we pulled *that* sucker out the next time they picked on Kat."

"Don't be stupid," Jacob said, his mind returning to his sister. "I should walk her back over to the middle school before fifth period."

In a faint voice David said, "I'm gonna do it."

"Do what?"

"I'm going to sign up for the Youth Guard."

"What the hell are you talking about?"

"Do it with me!" David enthused. "How awesome would that be? You're a Rules football player. They'll love you. And I can run all day. *For God and Country!*"

Jacob stared at his friend. "But we still have two more years at school. It makes no sense. We can go in as officers after we turn eighteen."

"I don't want to stay around here another two years. Besides, they're going to start drafting sixteen-year-olds anyway. If we join on our own, we can still get on the officer track."

"You're serious?"

"I need the money," David said, resentment flashing. "Maybe that's something you can't relate to."

Jacob did not respond. David's father, an Army policeman, had been killed in a favela raid the previous year. David's mother had been in a fragile state ever since, struggling to hold a steady job. Jacob noticed subtle changes in David, too – that he was moodier, and just a little more easily offended. He had also become much more political. Jacob tried to reason with his friend.

"You're good at Spanish. They're always looking for interpreters. If you take the translator course next year you'll get paid more."

"I would still have to go through basic training and do a year of officer training before I could apply to be a translator," David said. "Besides, haven't you been listening to any of President Duke's speeches? The U.S. and Canada are blocking our water up north. They are going to cut us off. I want to fight for my country."

"There's not going to be a war with America," insisted Jacob. "Don't listen to that crap."

"It's not crap. If they block our water, there'll definitely be war."

"Whatever," Jacob huffed.

The two boys paused in sullen silence. Jacob looked over at his sister again, who was cupping a palm-sized brown sparrow in her hands. It had been pecking in the dirt around them, hovering for any crumbs that could be left behind. Kat had managed to coax it to her, and now the bird was happily sitting in her hands, nibbling the crust of bread from her uneaten sandwich. Jacob could see that the bird, more than anything, had calmed her down.

"Sorry," Jacob finally said. "I didn't mean to get angry about it. It's just this whole thing with Kat. She's kind of freaked out and it's got me on edge."

"No worries, man. Anyway, you need to know that I may not have a choice in the matter. The Praetorian Guard has already been recruiting *me*," David said in a falsely conspiratorial tone, trying to lighten the mood. Jacob raised an eyebrow. David plowed ahead with his game. "They heard about my unrivaled prowess. That behind my deep cover as a skinny, pimply high school kid, my true identity is the baddest-ass soldier this country has ever seen. I am… Secret Agent Man. Fighter. Lover. *Spy*."

"Oh my god," Jacob laughed in spite of himself. "You're such a loser."

Encouraged that he had broken through the stalemate, David crouched down low before continuing in a tone of false bravado, *"These hands have been registered as lethal weapons. These muscles are made of steel. I shoot to kill."* Taking on the character of every comic book soldier he had seen on TV, David looked around jerkily as if he heard a suspicious noise in the bushes and began speaking into his clenched fist. "*Chopper, chopper. Intruder level four. Bring in the beast.*"

Jacob laughed more fully now, shaking his head, unable to resist David's charm.

"You're such an idiot," he said to his friend, who beamed back a million-watt smile. "C'mon. Let's take Kat back."

3

After school, Jacob and Kat walked with a crowd of other students the quarter mile from the schoolyard to the monorail station on the main road. A large group of children bantered noisily on the platform overhead. On the road, a caravan of three dilapidated buses carrying workers from the slums sent skyward loose, rust-hued plumes of dust. These buses originated in the slums and were easy to distinguish from the electric, autonomous vehicles used by the City transport authority. They did not make regular stops along the streets, but rather brought their passengers – all migrants and slum dwellers – from the favela to a central depot each morning. There, they would be registered for the day. Only then could they continue on to the homes or small businesses where they performed the cheap labor they were brought in to provide.

As Kat and Jacob approached the corner, one of the buses backfired, its engine choking on a diet of recycled vegetable oil. The noise elicited a startled scream from many of the children on the platform above. Instinctively, Jacob turned to look for Kat, who he knew would react badly to the loud noise. Not seeing her at first, he panicked. Then he scanned more slowly; Kat could be hard to spot when she was scared. Finally, he saw her crouching by the side of the pavement. He knelt next to her and put his arm around her shoulders, his lips close to her ear, and whispered: *it's okay, it was just a bus, it's okay, just a bus, it's over.* He coaxed her back to her feet.

"It's been a bad day," he said. The monorail purred into the station above them. He tugged Kat to her feet. "C'mon. The train's coming. Let's catch it. We can get off early and go to the junkyard.

We can walk home from there. Through the woods. That'll make you feel better."

Kat nodded yes.

Twenty minutes later, they were walking through a quiet, slightly run-down area in northern Alhambra. A chain link fence marked the boundary of three square blocks that had been deliberately left untouched since the time of the earthquake. Compared to the neat and tidy rows of houses around it, the other side of the fence looked like a bizarre art installation. Some houses leaned precariously to one side; others had been reduced to little more than piles of stone, wood and glass; others remained miraculously intact. An explanatory plaque hung by metal clips to the fence.

> *These streets have been preserved in full and constant display to remind us of the horrors we have overcome, the sacrifices we have made, and the fortitude required to create The New Republic of California, greatest of nations.*

Jacob had heard different tales at school about why the government had cleared this neighborhood: because it had been a hotbed for the Emergence movement that opposed Malcolm Duke's rule in the early years of his regime; because it had been filled with illegal immigrants granted amnesty by the previous Governor; because it had been occupied by religious and ethnic minorities deemed a threat to the state. When Jacob asked his father what had happened to that neighborhood, he answered simply, and somewhat cryptically, "I'm not sure we'll ever know the whole truth."

The children slipped through a gap in the fence and proceeded down the ghostly pavement. At the end of the road ahead of them, a modest synagogue, ravaged by wind and vandals, stood eerie sentry. During their earliest visits, Jacob had explored the abandoned building, roaming its halls in genuine wonder. Although street children from the slums had picked the synagogue clean, Jacob liked to stare at the oddly formed Hebrew letters on the walls, which only added to the sense of inaccessibility and mystery he felt about the place. Kat refused to enter the synagogue altogether.

"Too much inside," she said.

The grounds behind the temple extended over an acre to some shabby woods on the edge of a park called Rocky Brook, which covered a thin strip of land that reached all the way to Jacob's and Kat's home a mile away in South Pasadena. Scattered across the grounds, furniture, appliances, books, old newspapers, and discarded food pitched and jumbled into a landscape of low hills, which in turn attracted a unique fauna of rodents, birds, and stray cats. Jacob had unearthed several treasures from the Old World at this ad hoc junkyard, like the metallic toy car that fit neatly into the palm of his hand, or the green plastic space-soldier with opposable joints missing its left arm and half its right leg. But Jacob looked forward most of all to a thing he could not carry home with him: the wreck of an old jalopy, a genuine Chevy station wagon. Wheelless and rusted, only the front half of the car remained visible; the back half receded under a hill of rubbish like a turtle's body in its shell. Immediately after discovering the car several years ago, Jacob had set to work fixing it up. First, he methodically removed all the garbage that had tumbled through the windows, excavating a cave in the hidden back seat. He used an old cushion to cover the sharp springs that poked through the front seats. Over the course of time, Jacob removed all the broken glass and hammered down jagged metal edges so that he and Kat would not cut themselves as they crawled into the rear of the car. The day he finished, he sat in the back seat with Kat, triumphant and proud, rejoicing in their creation of a secret hideout that felt as if it belonged, not to the beleaguered present, but rather to another time and place. And though he now felt in some ways too old to be playing imaginary games like he did as a child, bringing Kat here gave him permission to regress, to return to the refuge he had created for and with his sister.

As Jacob made his way over piles of garbage toward the old jalopy, he felt the device vibrate on his wrist.

Where r u? read the message from his mother. *I told u to come straight home today.*

He sighed and spoke his reply. "I'm just hanging out with Kat. She's been a total pain today. Trying to calm her down. Be home soon."

Come home now, read the reply.

OK.

"Kat!" Jacob called out. "We can't stay. Mom wants us to come home."

Kat was already waiting on the other side of the fence.

4

Just before dusk, the children emerged from the woods that abutted their house. As they started across the rough patch of dirt that constituted their backyard, they saw Clara Angelfish standing on the landing outside the back door. Their mother had been cooking and her apron was streaked with dirt from cleaning potatoes. Damp strands of black hair were matted to her brow from the heat, and Jacob was struck by the degree to which Kat increasingly looked like her as she aged. Now, Clara's eyes, which normally danced with playfulness, conveyed her alarm.

"Where have you been?"

"I told you, playing at the junkyard," Jacob replied, chasing one of the chickens back toward the small coop they kept for eggs. Kat mounted the back stairs and hurriedly made her way into the house without acknowledging her mother.

"She's still upset?" his mother asked.

"Oh my god. Seriously? I thought I was gonna kill her today. She came over to our lunchroom. And of course she got picked on. I almost got my ass kicked – sorry, my butt," Jacob corrected at his mother's scolding look. "Anyway, I decided to take her to the junkyard so we could walk home through the woods. The trees always calm her down."

"You're a good brother, Jacob," his mother said, ruffling his hair as he made his way tiredly inside. Her anxiety seemed to lessen slightly now that they were home.

"Yeah, right," he grumbled. "I wish someone else could be a good brother for a while. It's exhausting."

Jacob slung his backpack into the corner of the kitchen. He slumped down in a chair at the table by the window and began reading the news about his favorite Rules Football team, the California Grays.

Clara placed a helping of leftover pie in front of him and gave him a playful wink. Jacob smiled thinly. Clara returned to the sink, picked up a potato, peeled it, cored out the patches of black, rinsed it in the shallow pool of precious water in a pot in the sink, and placed the finished product on a dish. After several potatoes had been cleaned, she carefully picked up the pot of dirty water and poured it into a large receptacle built into the sink's basin. From there, the water would flow to the City's central filtration system. Decades of living in drought-plagued southern California had drilled into her this careful routine of conservation.

"I know you went to the junkyard because you were thinking of Kat. I appreciate that. I do. But you know I don't like you to stay after school when your father's away."

"I know," Jacob grunted, fiddling with his device, which he'd removed from his wrist and unfolded into a full screen.

"How was school, anyway?"

"You know what David told me today?" Jacob remained fixated on his screen as he spoke. "That he's going to join the military. He wants to take early entry so he can join the Youth Brigade. He wants to leave school at the end of the year. Like in two weeks."

"It seems silly not to finish school," Clara replied, glad to be engaged.

"That's what I told him. But he keeps talking about war with America."

Clara paused her peeling. Quietly, she said, "No one wants war."

"That's exactly what I said!" replied Jacob with enthusiasm. "I mean: we have nukes, they have nukes. It's crazy. I'll talk him out of it tomorrow."

Kat returned to the kitchen with Meatball in the pocket of her trench coat and dropped cross-legged onto the floor.

"How's he doing, sweetheart?" Clara asked.

"Hungry," Kat replied.

"Well, I'm sure he is. Here." Clara bent over to hand Kat a few of the wet potato shavings from the strainer. She tried to brush Kat's cheek with her hand, but Kat recoiled ever so slightly.

"Jacob said the boys were mean to you today. You doing okay?"

"I don't know," Kat said without meeting her mother's gaze.

"Did Dad get the tickets for the Grays' game next weekend?" Jacob called, still preoccupied with his device. "He said he was gonna get them before he left. If he waits too long there won't be any good seats left."

Kat abruptly stood up. "The phone."

A second later Clara's phone rang. Drying her hands on her apron, she picked up the device from the counter.

"Hello? What's…Oh, god, Crystal…" Her voice trailed off as she wandered almost mindlessly into the back hallway. Jacob looked over at Kat.

What? he asked with his eyes.

Bad, she replied silently. *Father.*

"Go home, Crystal," their mother said assertively. "Right now. Don't worry about the lab. Don't talk to anybody. The less you know the safer you'll be."

Clara returned, walking swiftly past them and through the other doorway into the living room. Pulling aside the long cotton drapes at the front window, she watched the street intently.

"Oh, no," she cried softly.

She braced herself against the windowsill with both hands, took steady, deep breaths, and bowed her head. Jacob and Kat had followed behind and now stood apprehensively in the doorway.

"What's going on?" Jacob asked.

"Quiet," Clara snapped, uncharacteristically harshly. "I need to think."

Her breath had shortened, coming now in shallow bursts, making her sound as if someone were sitting on her chest. Kat started shaking her head back and forth while chewing ferociously on her already tattered fingernails. Clara turned to face them both.

"You have to hide," she commanded, her voice resolute.

"What? Why?" Jacob asked.

"I don't have time to explain." Hurrying over to them, she put a hand on each of their shoulders. She lowered her voice to convey as much certainty as she could.

"The Praetorian Guard are coming. A car just turned the corner. I..."

She hesitated, trying to decide what to say and what to leave out.

"I don't know what they want," she finally continued, "but I don't want you here. You have to hide, okay? Just for a little while. Do you understand?"

"Is it Dad?" Jacob asked.

"I'm sure he's fine," his mother responded unconvincingly. "I'll talk to them. When they're gone, I'll put the back-porch light on. Then you'll know it's safe. *Don't* come back in until you see the porch light on. Do you understand?"

"But..." Jacob began to protest.

"No buts," his mother interrupted sternly. "Right now, I just need you to do what I tell you." She looked hard at him. "Ok?"

Clara hugged Jacob tightly, which scared him as much or more than her words. She knelt and held Kat's face in her hands with the kind of authority that calmed Kat in moments of stress. Lip trembling, Clara tried once more to sound reassuring.

"Kat, darling, I need you to go with Jacob. He'll take care of you for a little bit, then you'll come back and we'll figure out what's going on. It's going to be okay, I promise."

Kat remained entirely frozen in place.

"*Please?*" Mother pleaded.

Kat's head moved imperceptibly, but it was all the permission her mother needed. She took them both by the hand and hustled them through the kitchen toward the back door. Pausing one last time on the threshold, she desperately embraced her two terrified children.

"I love you very much. Your father and I both do. Now run."

Part II

Nova Rio

Kat

Daylight filtered through the front window of the old jalopy. Meatball, who had been sleeping in Kat's trench coat pocket, crawled onto her chest and nudged her under the chin.

"I'm scared, too," Kat said, stroking him.

She glanced over at Jacob, who lay with his head against an old sweatshirt that he had left in the car, and which he had balled into a makeshift pillow. They had been up most of the night, agreeing to wait until morning to go back, speaking little, each in their own world of imagined horrors and wishful thinking. Exhaustion had finally overpowered Jacob about an hour before dawn and he had dropped into a heavy slumber. Now his long hair covered his face in a tangled mess and his mouth hung open. Deep heavy breaths filled his chest. A thread of drool trickled down his cheek. For Kat, sleep had never come.

She tucked Meatball in her pocket and crept silently out of the car. Although dense summer air would soon choke the day, the early light mercifully retained a hint of freshness from the night, a gift from the stars to the parched earth. Cascades of soft sunshine sifted through the haze. Kat had never seen the junkyard at this time of day. Her senses absorbed everything: the fractured light, chipmunks scampering under the garbage, the scent of rotten fruit, the distant hum of military drones in endless patrol above the City. She stared again at the synagogue in the distance. Even in the forgiving light of dawn its stoicism made her shudder.

Tiptoeing through the scattered debris, she found an old cement block to sit on while Meatball scavenged at her feet. Her mind cycled through the events of the previous night. When they first left the house, they ran part way into the woods, hiding among the bushes but staying close and watching, hoping that the interrogation would be brief so they could return to their mother quickly. While they waited, Kat focused on the house, straining to hear the voices inside. Although she hadn't been able to make out the dialogue, she absorbed the tension of the soldiers' aggressive questions and her mother's quiet answers. At one point, Jacob pressed her slightly with his elbow. When she opened her eyes, a soldier emerged onto the back porch, scanning the tree line. Neither of them dared to breathe. As soon as he turned back into the house, they fled down the path to the junkyard.

For weeks, Kat had been suffering a deep foreboding. The looks her parents exchanged, the quality of their embraces, their hushed voices behind the bedroom door – all of it alerted her to their heightened anxiety, a feeling which, despite their efforts at secrecy, she had immediately begun to share. When Father came into her bedroom, she knew for sure that something dark and terrible would happen. The precise nature of that something she could not guess. But one phrase had repeated itself in her mind all day: *I need you to keep it safe for me.*

A dark-eyed Junco alighted nearby and tilted its head to look at Kat. She admired the sharp delineation between the black of the bird's head and the paler shades of gray and brown that marked its body. It looked quickly down at the ground, then back at Kat, down at the ground, then back at Kat. With one brisk turn, it sailed off in the direction of the woods, up over the trees, toward where Kat knew her house to be.

Kat stood, scooping Meatball under his little round belly and, ignoring his squeaking objections, made her way back to the car. She crawled into the rear seat next to Jacob. Gently she tapped him on the shoulder and he jumped awake.

"We need to go back," she said.

2

The children peered through the trees from the edge of the woods. The porch light remained dark. Kat closed her eyes and concentrated her senses toward the house.

"Someone's there," she said with certainty, opening her eyes again. "It's not Mother."

"The soldiers," whispered Jacob frantically. "They must be waiting for us. Let's get out of here."

"Not the soldiers," replied Kat firmly.

"Mom said we shouldn't go in unless the porch light was on."

"I need to get something."

"Don't be stupid. You can't go in there. We have no idea..."

Before Jacob could complete his sentence, Kat rose from the bushes and started for the house.

"Kat!" Jacob hissed desperately.

But she had already cleared the trees and strode purposefully past the chicken coop and up the back stairs. Cursing under his breath, Jacob hustled after her. He caught up with her just as she entered the rear kitchen door. The house was eerily quiet. Total wreckage greeted them: kitchen drawers pulled open; silverware strewn across the floor; sofa cut apart; chairs and tables overturned. No one in sight.

"What the…" declared Jacob, thunderstruck.

Kat hardly noticed the chaos as she made her way to the stairs. Her bedroom, like every other room in the house, had been ransacked. The main drawer of the desk was halfway open, its contents flung around the room. Her heart pounded as she furiously scooped the remains of the drawer onto the floor.

"What the hell are you *doing*?" Jacob asked as he arrived in the doorway, nervously glancing back over his shoulder.

Leveraging the desk against her hips, Kat pushed both drawer knobs at the same time with her thumbs to spring open the lining of the drawer. From a hidden compartment underneath, Kat wriggled out Father's leather notebook, which had been tightly wedged inside.

Exhaling in relief, she turned it over in her hands. She felt it breathe, intimate and alive: a piece of him. She thumbed through the pages, not reading, just absorbing the patterns of his handwriting, running the sensitive skin of her fingertips over the soft pulp. Some entries were numeric, scribbled formulae Father had been working out. Others contained snippets of poetry or personal observations about history or literature. In the upper right corner of the page she had settled upon, she noticed a strange notation:

5R

Before she had time to consider it more fully, a sound from downstairs caused Kat to cock her head.

"He's here," she said quietly, slipping the book into the empty pocket of her trench coat opposite Meatball. Jacob stared back at her with wild eyes.

"He is? Are you serious? Who is it? Oh my god."

A voice called to them from the bottom of the stairs. "I know you're up there. You better come down. They'll be coming back soon."

Jacob arched both eyebrows at his sister in desperation: *What should we do?*

Let's see who it is, Kat nodded in return.

Kat grasped Jacob's hand tightly. Peering over the bannister, they discerned below a lanky teenage boy, about the same age as Jacob, with light brown skin and jet-black hair pulled back into a short ponytail. He wore ragged clothes and carried a small pack slung over his shoulder. Both of them had heard stories of the street urchins from the slums who snuck into the City to commit petty crimes. But neither had ever seen one face to face. Kat took him in. Warm flushes of energy danced around his head. Unfamiliar, but not frightening.

"I can get you out," said the young man calmly. "But we have to leave now."

"Who are you?" Jacob asked nervously from the top of the stairs.

"*Approaching*," Kat said under her breath, squeezing Jacob's hand.

A second later a small device in the slum boy's hands crackled its message: "Approaching the Angelfish house now."

Without a second glance, the boy tucked the radio into his pack and glided noiselessly toward the back door. The sound of a car door slamming jolted them into action, and for the second time in as many days the children fled their home.

Jacob

The young man from the slums was familiar with the area, moving through backyards, over fences, and down quiet side streets. Once or twice, when residents took notice of them, he quickly diverted their course to move immediately out of view so that there would be no way for the person to describe where they'd gone. With feline grace, he slithered through the landscape without a sound, alert to all possible dangers, able to disappear in a blink. From time to time he would pause to raise a small handheld in the air above his head for several seconds. Then he would carry on, never speaking, only occasionally looking back over his shoulder, compelling his companions to keep up by virtue of his own quiet urgency.

After hours of walking, Jacob's feet ached. He could see that Kat, too, was growing tired. When at times the boy wandered far ahead of them, Jacob pulled Kat along at a slow jog to close the distance. When the three of them at last reached the edge of the City in Poco Rivera, they turned a corner and found themselves staring at the great Perimeter fence.

Jacob had never been this close to it before. An ambient feature of the L.A. landscape, he had never given the fence much thought. It was massive. The fifteen-foot high, heavy-duty iron barrier was topped with masses of razor wire, and it extended in either direction, east or west, as far as he could see. Guard towers on the City side punctuated the structure at regular intervals. On the turrets above, Jacob could make out soldiers, guns slung over their shoulders, staring through high-powered binoculars into a patch of wasted earth between the City and the slums. For the first time, Jacob realized that the Perimeter was a double fence, made up of the one before them and another closer to the slums: two parallel lines a half-mile apart on either side of the wizened San Gabriel river. Between the fences lay an open no-man's land. Any soul brave enough to venture across would surely be shot. Beyond it sprawled the massive favela. Jacob swallowed down the creeping nausea that bubbled in his gut.

The slum boy led them down a dirt path that ran between the Perimeter and the row of cheap houses that backed up to the fence. A stray dog wandered the no-man's land. Its ribs exposed with hunger, it ran toward them, sniffing for scraps amongst the discarded plastic bottles and windswept trash against the other side of the fence. Between the dirt and the fence and the dog and the trash, Jacob had the impression of the slums themselves extending an exploratory tendril toward the City, patiently seeking out any crevice that might allow them to transgress the barrier.

After another half hour, they arrived at what remained of a wide, stone support that had once held up the Whittier Boulevard Bridge. Jacob had seen pictures of Los Angeles before the earthquake, with its spider web of highways linking Santa Monica in the northwest, Pasadena in the east, and Long Beach in the southwest. Here, at the Perimeter juncture, the freeways still looked as if they had been bombed in an act of war. Huge slabs of concrete, broken urban bones, lay cracked across the no-man's land, rebar jutting out like rusted tendons. Further south, he could see the bright floodlights of the single bridge that connected City and slums. Known as the Southern Freeway, this highway now served as the only official route in or out of the City from the south.

As much as Jacob had heard and read about the natural disaster that devastated his hometown thirty years before, the sight of the broken Whittier Street bridge somehow made that time more immediate for him than anything he had experienced in his short life. This jumbled pile of concrete and steel evoked a vivid sense of the terror and panic that raged as the earth shook and the history of North America changed course. In his mind's eye, he saw the foundations of the bridge trembling, the thundering collapse of the highway. He pictured the nearby residents, screaming as they fled in front of the giant tsunami, knowing that the end of the world for them had come. Involuntarily, he shuddered at the enormity of it all.

Their teenage escort checked his handheld and looked up at the sky.

"We'll rest here," he said.

Jacob and Kat sat down, relieved to be off their feet. The slum boy reached into his sack, which Jacob could now see was embroidered with the emblem of a hummingbird, delicately designed in luminescent blue and green. From it the boy pulled a pliable leather canteen, a stumpy-shaped loaf of bread, and a plastic bag of Phoenix Water. Breaking the bread into three hunks with his hands, he offered one to each of them along with the bag of water. Suddenly aware of how little they had eaten in the last day, they gratefully accepted the nourishment.

"I'll be right back," the boy said.

Putting in an earpiece, he took out his old-fashioned handheld and walked several meters off. Jacob could hear only his side of the conversation.

"I know it's risky, but I couldn't just leave them there...Tina, there's no way they could make it back. They're not…I'm telling you, they could be valuable. The PG really wanted to find them…I don't know. Just look into it. Angelfish is the name."

The boy glanced back in their direction and Jacob suddenly felt self-conscious about how pathetic and helpless they must have seemed.

"Hector," whispered Kat, nodding toward the slum boy.

"What?" Jacob asked.

"Him. She called him Hector."

"Who did?"

"The girl he's talking to."

They broke off their exchange as Hector returned. He scrutinized them with suspicion as he sipped water from his canteen.

"Where are you taking us?" Jacob asked, finally mustering the courage. When Hector didn't respond, Jacob continued, "Our mother…"

"Your mother's gone," Hector interrupted. "The PG have her. She's not coming home. You can't go back. Unless you want them to take you, too."

Trying to appear stronger than he felt, Jacob asked, "What were you doing at our house?"

"Taking food," Hector replied candidly, holding up the hard cheese that Jacob recognized as having come from their refrigerator. He cut the cheese into pieces with his pocket knife. "And looking around for stuff."

"Did you make that mess? In our house?" Jacob asked.

Hector gazed steadily at him. "Do you *think* I made that mess?"

"Well, you're obviously a thief," said Jacob. The vague hostility that rose in his breast felt good, soothing and displacing his fear, and he let it expand and fill him.

"I guess you could say that," Hector replied. "You're a thief, too, you know. Just like everyone on this side of the fence.

You steal from the top, we steal from the bottom. And round and round we go."

Jacob moved to object to this analysis, but his momentary anger gave way to uncertainty. His words came out tinny and plaintive. "How do *you* know what happened to my mother?"

Reaching back into his bag, Hector pulled out his handheld. The device, which appeared to be almost homemade, had a simple LED display on one side; on the other, three thin heat arrays. Hector laid it on the ground with the heat panels upturned. Jacob watched the green light flicker as it quickly charged. Hector spun a thumb-sized dial on the side to wade through the static. Eventually he picked up a radio signal with the sound of a dispatcher.

"It connects to the City's security frequency," Hector explained. "That's how we know when a house has been raided by the PG. Those houses are usually empty for a while after a raid, so if you're nearby you can find some good stuff to resell in the favela. I was nearby when I heard they were coming to your street. So I hid in the bushes. I watched them take your mom away. That's how I know."

"Why did you help us?" Kat asked softly, eyes averted.

It was the first time that Hector had heard Kat speak, and he took her in for a long moment before responding.

"Honestly, I'm not sure. I figured your dad must be some important guy. And the PG are…" his voice trailed off. "I don't like the PG."

"If we get caught with you, we'll be arrested," Jacob said.

Hector laughed. "It looks like they don't need to find you with a slum rat to have a reason to arrest you, does it? I can leave you here if you want. But they'll catch you. I think you know that. I have friends in the favela who might be able to help."

"Tina," muttered Kat.

Hector frowned in confusion. “What did you say?”

Kat looked at his handheld device. A second later it buzzed. He stared uneasily at Kat while he listened to the voice on the other end of the line. He grumbled a response and hung up.

“How did you…?” he asked Kat in wonder.

“She has really good hearing,” Jacob offered quickly.

Hector eyed Kat curiously as he bundled up his pack. “We’d better get going.”

Tracker

Dressed in black, the tall figure crouched close to the ground, looking for signs: an unusual swirl of dirt, a loose thread of clothing that had fallen free, the imprint of a shoe. Unfurling himself like a prehistoric bird, the man stood to his full height. He had lean, wiry arms and skin the color of honey, his salt and pepper hair cut close to his head. His angular face was grooved with lines made deeper by the sun. From a distance, his agile movements made him appear to be young and athletic; but close up, one became aware of his age. A scar ran in a jagged cut from below his left ear to the top of his chin. The side of his neck displayed a dark tattoo in the form of a cross. His eyes were black and impenetrable.

The only name anyone ever heard him called was Tracker.

As soon as he had been briefed on the situation, Tracker went straight to the Angelfish house, expecting that the children would come back to find their mother. When he found the secret compartment in the drawer of the girl's desk, he knew that he had missed his opportunity. He examined the drawer for several minutes, admiring the cleverness of its construction. Tracing his fingers over the wooden interior, he felt the slight impression in the soft balsa made by the weight of the object it had hidden. Flecks of material, stuck to the wood, came up as he rubbed it with his forefinger. Examining the fragments closely, he held them just below his nose and breathed deeply. Beneath the pine scent, he detected the faintest traces of ink and leather.

A diary, he reasoned to himself. *The children ran when they heard the Guard coming. When they came back, their mother was gone. They grabbed a few personal things. Went stay with a friend or family member. Somewhere close, somewhere they could walk.*

A soldier emerged from the Angelfish house and approached Tracker with trepidation. "We've reviewed the surveillance tapes, sir," he stammered. "No activity on the street. I'm afraid the cameras don't have coverage behind the house, so we're not really sure…"

Tracker looked away from the soldier with total disregard. Surveying every detail of the backyard and the forest that abutted it, he slowly inhaled through his nostrils and closed his eyes. The soldier waited anxiously for several minutes until at last he felt compelled to break the silence.

"Maybe they'll come back again, sir," the soldier ventured. "Should we position some night wires? They're only kids, so they're bound to…"

The soldier's voice trailed off in fear as Tracker re-opened his eyes and glared at him. The young man retreated several steps.

"They're not coming back," growled Tracker. "Burn it to the ground."

Kat

Hector pulled open the heavy iron door, roughly four feet high, which had been built into the side of the wide column that had once held up the bridge. Jacob hadn't noticed it when they first sat down, but it had clearly been built into the column to allow servicemen to ascend to the bridge itself. Kat stayed close behind Jacob as they followed Hector into the small chamber inside the column. An iron ladder was bolted to the interior wall across from them. At their feet, a makeshift hole fell into utter blackness.

"Down there?" Jacob asked incredulously.

"There are handles on the side," Hector said.

It did not take long to reach the bottom. They could see nothing against the curtain of absolute blackness around them until Hector turned on a three-inch flashlight he pulled from his bag.

"This is the only light I have," he said apologetically. "I wasn't planning on having company."

As he shined the thin beam in wide circles, Jacob and Kat discerned the opening of a narrow smuggling tunnel to their left, which they had to crouch down to enter. Every fiber of Kat's body yearned for light. With each step forward, her body felt heavier, until she simply stopped and sat down. Wrapping her arms around her knees, she began to rock slowly, her head bowed and ears covered with her hands. Jacob returned to her side, feeling for her in the dark, and coaxed her back to her feet.

"It's okay. Hold my hand. We'll count the steps. One, two, three…."

Trudging through the chalky, stifling air, Kat became so disconnected from reality that her mind began to conjure hallucinations of snakes and centipedes swarming from the walls. Jacob held her tightly, compelling her forward. After what seemed an eternity, a variegated pool of light appeared. When they reached it, Hector removed a long, thin wire from a crevice in the wall and threaded it through one of the apertures in a manhole cover above them. Within an instant, a great scuffling started and the manhole cover slid noisily to the side. Kat felt the rush of air down the drainpipe. Light poured onto her face. She drank it in with relief.

A visage appeared, disembodied and framed in the circular opening. It was the filthy, dusty face of a young tan-skinned boy with an exuberant smile and ears that stuck out almost horizontally from his head.

"Whoa!" exclaimed the boy upon spotting Jacob and Kat, dirty and huddling in the shadows behind Hector. "Tina said you got some *pequeños. Hola, pequeños. Me llamo Pepe*! Welcome to…"

"Pepito!" interrupted Hector impatiently. "The ladder?"

"*Claro, claro*," said Pepe.

The street boy scrambled away and mumbled to himself as he worked. A moment later, a homemade rope ladder tumbled down the side of the drainpipe. Quickly, as if escaping from hell, Kat and Jacob climbed out of the darkness and into the light.

Jacob

The manhole was set back from the main street by fifty yards. In the unpaved alley, Jacob could stand in one place, spread his arms, and touch the crumbling walls of the dilapidated buildings on either side at the same time. In single file, the four began to move toward the hum of the busy road ahead.

"Stay close," Hector ordered.

"Stay close," Pepe repeated with a stern, authoritative look.

Jacob had a hard time guessing Pepe's age. He wore a pair of cheap blue flip-flops, a ragged t-shirt, and pants several sizes too large in the waist. The pants had been patched with irregular cuts of colored cloth and were cinched at the waist with a length of thin, white cord. Hardened calluses encrusted the soles of his feet, their talcum color contrasting with the skin on top, and they curled around the edges of his foot like a sandal of elephant skin. Minute scars, flecks of white, nicked the back of his neck. The tattoo of a snake wrapped around his left forearm, from his wrist to his elbow.

Hector led them down the short passage to the bustling thoroughfare. The effect was immediate and overwhelming. Assaulted by the sounds, smells, colors, and chaos of the street, both he and Kat swooned. Never in their lives had they seen anything like it. No matter how much he had read, or seen on TV or the internet, nothing prepared him for the reality of the favela. Dogs, cats, chickens, and goats all roamed freely, dodging the humans and cars and stones of little boys. Men waved frustrated arms out of open car windows in the standstill traffic. Mopeds, most carrying two or three people at a time, weaved in and out. Jacob noticed several brightly colored minibuses so loaded with passengers that they looked as if they would topple onto their sides. Two boys raced past them to jump on the nearest bus, which featured a garish portrait of Jesus, his arms open in beneficence, with the words *He will save us* scrawled in elegant cursive script beneath him.

Some of the buildings along the road had been rebuilt, but they stood in stark contrast to the cracked and ruined remains of much of the architecture. At one point, they passed an entire block where a large bank, several stories high, had fallen and crushed the single-story buildings beside it, like a row of monstrous concrete dominoes. Jacob watched small children, most of them half-clothed, as they ran in and out of the ruins, over rocks and broken glass and trash. He realized that amidst this rubble, under the ruins of these buildings, the children's families had created makeshift shanties they now called home. And everywhere Jacob looked there was garbage.

As they approached a major intersection, Jacob observed the massive transport depot that served the favela. Hundreds of people milled about, waiting to board the monorail line that terminated here, or to board the large idling buses run by private companies that brought legally credentialed workers or other travelers into the City. Patrols from the Favela Police walked up and down the loading platforms in their brown uniforms, checking the identification papers of the workers as they entered the terminal, pulling aside anyone they found to be suspicious.

He bore witness to the long shadow of the world his parents in which his parents had grown up. Their stories about the terror of the Quake, the loss of their own parents, the looting, the violence – Jacob saw their remnants here. In the City, buildings had been repaired, streets were kept clean, life was orderly. There existed rules and laws and institutions. Society functioned. But here…

Hector and Pepe turned in the direction opposite the transport depot. The older boy's demeanor had visibly relaxed since they arrived. People waved to him and shouted playfully from the windows above the street in the mixture of Spanish and English that characterized favela slang. Jacob held Kat tightly as they walked, clutching her under his arm and pressing her to his body. Her head was buried in his side. He knew how overstimulated and exhausted she was. She would need to be in a quiet place soon.

As they made their way down Whittier Boulevard, Pepe chattered incessantly to Hector, asking him questions, telling him about the goings on in the favela. Suddenly, Hector covered Pepe's mouth and pulled them all into the shadow of an alley.

"Shut it, Pepito. Look over there."

A cluster of teenage boys lurked ahead of them. Jacob watched a young man in a sleeveless shirt stride across the street. Two huge men, each with the massive face of a bear tattooed on their upper arms, stood on either side of him, AK-47s slung over their shoulders.

"Three more girls got stolen this week," hissed Pepe with great agitation.

"I know," Hector replied, looking back at Kat and Jacob protectively. "These guys are animals."

"Especially that *pendejo*," seethed Pepe.

"Wh…Who is that," stammered Jacob.

"Rat," said Hector. "He's the head of Bear Clan. The biggest gang in the neighborhood. He took over last year. Killed the guy who used to run it. Put his head on a stake in the middle of the Boulevard."

"Oh god," gulped Jacob. He watched Rat banter with a few people on the street. And he noticed how almost everybody moved respectfully out of his way.

"Yeah," agreed Hector. "He's a total monster."

By now, Rat had passed out of view and the boys led them across the Boulevard into a maze of alleys as tight as Venetian canals. They weaved this way and that, until Jacob could no longer tell from which direction they had first entered. They stopped in front of a battered old building, the word *Taqueria* barely legible on its crumbling façade. Iron bars covered the darkened windows. Two teenage boys sat on plastic folding chairs outside the door. Jacob noticed tattoos of snakes on their forearms – the same as Pepe's. One young man leaned on the barrel of a machine gun; the other boy casually rested his hand on the pistol in his lap. They stood at Hector's arrival and exchanged a complicated ritual handshake.

"Is Renard here?" Hector asked.

"Only for a few hours," one of the young men replied.

"We won't be long," Hector said.

The main floor of the restaurant remained in a permanent state of closure. Chairs had been flipped and stacked on the tables by their seats. Behind the old oak bar, a large, ornate mirror, broken in several places, extended the length of the wall. Dust covered everything in a thick gray blanket. Hector walked them past the bar and through a swinging door into the kitchen. After descending a set of stairs, they finally stopped at a metal door in a dimly lit hallway.

"Wait here," Hector said. He rapped on the door.

"Hector?" Jacob called. Hector turned. "My sister really needs to rest."

By now, Kat was shaking almost uncontrollably, her face still buried against Jacob's arm. Hector nodded his understanding before disappearing through the doorway, leaving them alone in the relative quiet of the hallway.

"Shhh," Jacob repeated over and over to his sister. Crouched against the wall, he wrapped his arms tightly around Kat's shoulders, rocking in time with her, trying to reassure her. Jacob knew it would take her much longer than normal to find her equilibrium in this alien place.

Hector returned. "Renard wants to talk to you."

Cushioned chairs surrounded a low coffee table. A group of men, some old, some young, stood at a round table in the corner looking over paper maps spread out across the surface. Near the tops of the walls, the old basement well windows had been reinforced with bricks, allowing the room no natural light. Several teenage boys lined the perimeter. All of them carried guns.

Behind a wide oak desk at the back of the room, a weathered old man sipped thoughtfully from a tin mug. Even through the weak orange light, Jacob could make out the pockmarks on his face. One eye drooped slightly beneath his bald pate. He wore a faded green camouflage jacket open at the collar.

"Sit," said the man, gesturing at the two chairs opposite his desk. His presence emanated authority.

Jacob felt mildly hopeful: perhaps they had finally met an adult who could help them. A young man entered the room with two bags of Phoenix Water. Jacob gratefully put a bag to Kat's lips before taking a long drink for himself.

"Hector tells me the PG took your parents," said Renard.

"Yes," answered Jacob.

"Can you tell me what happened?"

"Well," Jacob began slowly. Everything had happened so quickly that now he struggled to remember the sequence of events. "My father left for a business trip the day before…yesterday? I don't know when. The day before they came for us. We were supposed to go see him for a family vacation in Canada after his conference."

"So your father and mother were not together? He was not taken by the PG?" Renard clarified.

"No," said Jacob. "I don't know what happened to him. I'm not sure. He left and we haven't seen him since."

"But they took your mother."

"Yes. The next day, after my father left. My sister and I came home from school, like any other day, and then the PG were coming and my mom… She told us to run. So we did." He brushed his sweaty, dirty hair out of his eyes, feeling all the eyes in the room upon him. Weakly, he concluded, "I'm not really sure why."

"It's curious that the PG would be so… aggressive. Your father works for the government?" Renard prompted.

"He's a water scientist. For the Ministry of the Interior."

"And how did you two manage to escape? I don't get the sense you're in the habit of running from the police."

"Uh, not exactly." Jacob offered a limp smile. "Someone called my mom to warn us – my dad's lab assistant, Crystal. After that, my mom was really scared. She told us to run. We stayed out all night. The next day we went back to the house. That's when we met Hector."

"You were right to come," said Renard calmly. "And lucky Hector found you."

"Can you help us?" Jacob pleaded. "I'm sure this is all a big mistake. We just need to get home. My sister, she…" He looked down at Kat, who still trembled and had her head buried against him. He couldn't even be sure that she was conscious of all that was happening. "She needs to get home. To my mom and dad."

“Yes. She’s not doing so well,” Renard said. Jacob could see his mind working through the situation as his gaze shifted back and forth between them. Then he asked, “Can I have a look at your right arm?”

“What?” Jacob was confused.

“Your arm. Hold it out. I want to look at your wrist.” Renard tapped his own right forearm in demonstration.

Jacob extended his arm. Renard took hold of it and ran his finger lightly over a patch of raised skin.

“It’s my ID implant,” Jacob explained. “For the City.”

“Yes, I know,” Renard said. “Unregistered?”

Jacob furrowed his brow, unsure why Renard would ask the obvious. “We register when we’re eighteen.”

“Or if you join the military. You haven’t done a youth camp?”

“No.”

Leaning back in his chair, Renard clasped his hands behind his head. For several minutes he sat in deep thought. Finally, he said, “I think for now the best thing is to get you somewhere quiet and safe where you can have some food, water, and get some rest. As you say, your sister really needs that.”

Jacob nodded. “And then we can figure out how to get back home?”

“We can try,” reassured Renard. Turning to Pepe, he said, “Little one. Run and tell Agnes she will have guests.”

“*La vieja*?” Pepe wondered.

“They’ll be safe there,” replied Renard. “Now go, before I think you’re questioning my authority.”

“No sir!” Pepe said as he raced out of the room in a flip-flop sprint.

Renard turned to Hector. "Take them the back way to Hilltop. I think it's probably wise to keep their presence here quiet until we learn a bit more. I'll talk to Bettina while you're gone. Come to me when they're settled."

"Of course," agreed Hector. He nodded his head in the direction of the door, and Jacob rose, pulling Kat up with him.

"Thank you, sir," Jacob said.

"Call me Renard," replied the old man.

David

David McCaw had been mildly surprised when Jacob did not show up at school. He sent messages to his friend, but when he didn't hear back he assumed that Jacob must have been ill. When he returned home later that day, however, his mother met him at the door in an agitated state. Hustling David inside, she hurriedly lowered the shades and pulled him over to the couch.

"What're you doing, Ma?"

"You didn't hear anything at school today?" his mother whispered.

"About what? Why are you being so weird?"

"Jacob Angelfish?"

"What about him? Is he okay?"

"They've been *arrested*," his mother said, her eyes wild with fear. "The whole family. The Praetorian Guard took them away yesterday."

"*What*?"

"No one knows what happened. Sandra Jenkins told me about it this morning. She saw the whole thing from her front window." David's mother began pacing nervously, talking to herself as much as to her son. "I've been hearing rumors about their family for a while, but I didn't believe them. Jacob is your friend, such a nice boy, but that father, I always wondered about him. I certainly did. He's very high up, an important scientist; he must have done something terrible. Terrible!" She tugged nervously at the shawl around her bony shoulders. David had never seen her quite this unhinged. In a rush, she came back to the couch and clasped both David's hands in hers. In a low, conspiratorial tone she repeated, "I always had my suspicions about them."

David hardly knew what to say. The entire situation seemed absurd. Jacob and his family arrested by the PG? He supposed it was possible that Mr. Angelfish had done something wrong in his job. It was true that he held a prominent position in the government – he knew from Jacob that his father held a top level security clearance due to his water research. But David always felt comfortable and welcome at the Angelfish home. They had been so good to him in the aftermath of his father's death. He found it impossible to imagine that they would break the law.

"I don't know," he said, trying to soothe his anxious mother. "Mr. Angelfish just doesn't seem like he would do anything that bad. Maybe it's just a mistake."

"David, darling, listen to me," his mother began again. "It's been a hard year…"

"I know, Ma."

Regaining her composure, she continued, "Did Jacob say *anything* to you? Is there *anything* you know about what that family was up to?"

David recalled that Jacob had mentioned that he, his mother, and sister would be traveling to Canada this weekend to meet up with his father for a short holiday. He hadn't thought much of it before, but it occurred to him now that this was indeed an unusual thing for a family to do before the summer began. A sliver of doubt crept into his mind.

"No," David insisted, unsure if the trip to Canada qualified.

"If you think of anything, you come and tell me. They'll be watching his friends. Until we know what's happened, we have to be very careful. Okay?"

To himself, David wondered: *What on earth have you done, Jacob?*

Jacob

By the time they left Renard's room at the *Taqueria*, Kat was limp with exhaustion and Jacob had resorted to carrying her on his back. Hector avoided contact with the crowded main streets and squares, which in the approaching night surged with activity. Rolling blackouts meant the alleys were only illuminated by the pale flickering of kerosene lamps, or by the fires of burning trash – flaming oil drums around which clusters of men, faces darkened in shadow, barely glanced at them as they slid by.

"Don't walk there," Hector said at one point, putting his arm out to stop Jacob from stepping onto a barely discernable depression in the compressed trash that covered the alley floor. "It's a sinkhole."

"A sinkhole?" Jacob worried, unsure what that meant.

"You can tell from the depression there that it's going to cave in soon. When that hole opens up, if you fall in, we might not get you out."

Jacob shuddered and strained his eyes in the poor light to be sure he was following exactly in Hector's footsteps. Eventually they reached a set of narrow stairs that rose almost directly upwards between two dilapidated buildings. After strenuous effort, they emerged onto a plateau of rooftops: an extended manmade balcony that overlooked the teeming slums below. Here, Hector finally allowed Jacob to rest. The combination of heat, smog, fatigue and hunger caused Jacob to feel faint. Carefully lowering Kat to the ground, he regained his breath and tried to focus on the view rather than the trembling in his legs. Below them lay a stunning urban sprawl, more like an insect colony than a community of human beings. In the distance, beyond the Perimeter and through the scrim of dust, Jacob could just discern the faint outline of the City from whence they'd come. He stifled a powerful urge to cry.

"We're almost there," Hector encouraged.

Without asking, Hector picked up Kat and cradled her in his arms, concerned more now with reaching their destination than with concealment. Nervous as he felt to let Hector carry Kat, Jacob gratefully accepted the help. They walked to the far side of the balcony and approached two youths holding semi-automatic weapons. A ten-foot iron fence loomed above them and extended in either direction, encircling the peak of the hill. Inside this gated community rose newer and cleaner concrete homes, terraced neatly up the slope and painted in bright colors – an oasis of sanity floating atop the tumult of the crumbling alleys. Designed with the advantage of the hillside in mind, this neighborhood commanded a view of the favela such that it would have been difficult for anyone to approach from below.

Climbing steeply up the narrow passage from the gate, his legs still wobbling, Jacob prayed for respite with every step. After several minutes, they turned into a quiet lane. An ancient-looking woman with a slight hunch in her back waited in front of a modest shanty. Pepe stood at her side. The woman couldn't have been more than five feet tall, even at full height. A long silver braid hung down her side. Her eyes radiated a magnetic, pearled green, beautiful against her weathered, olive-colored skin.

Saying nothing, the woman led them inside the shanty. The single room had a kitchen on one side, a bed and side table on the other, and a rectangular dining table in the center. The floors were made of packed earth. Behind the kitchen table, a thick cloth curtain separated out a depression in the wall that served as a pantry and food closet. A heap of old woolen blankets lay piled in one corner. The woman held the curtain back for them. Jacob looked quizzically at Hector.

"Your room," Hector explained. "Get some rest."

At his elbow, Pepe echoed: "You stay here. You rest."

"Agnes will take care of you," Hector said upon seeing Jacob's skeptical look. "It's safe."

Again, Pepe repeated, "Agnes will take care of you. It's safe."

"I'll be back soon," Hector said, placing a reassuring hand on Jacob's shoulder. Then, pinching Pepe by the ear, he dragged him out of the shanty.

2

Kat lay in a fetal ball, her head on Jacob's lap, legs tucked tightly to her chest. Each minute her breathing grew shallower. She was entering a state of withdrawal – a defense mechanism she used to disengage from the overwhelming sensory world. Jacob had seen her do this many times, but he was less afraid for her now that she was nestled in the blankets. If he left her alone for a while, she would gradually come back to herself.

Meatball's twitching nose appeared from the pocket of Kat's coat. Jacob held out a finger to him.

"Hey little fella," he laughed in spite of himself. "I can't believe you've been stashed away in there this whole time. Kat will be glad you're with us."

The guinea pig chirruped quietly. Making his way out of Kat's pocket, the scrawny but ever-resourceful rodent rummaged in the blankets in search of food. Finding nothing, he approached Jacob and nibbled on his finger – then huffed in disgust. Agitated and hungry but reluctant to venture any further, he crawled up under Kat's chin and promptly fell asleep.

Beyond the curtain, Jacob could hear the muffled sounds of Agnes' footsteps and smell the aroma of her cooking. His stomach groaned in anticipation. He couldn't remember when he had last eaten anything substantial. Noticing bags of water in the corner of the pantry, he grabbed one without disturbing Kat. He closed his eyes and tipped his head back against the wall. For the first time since the mad dash from their house, the truth seeped into his consciousness: *His mother and father were gone.*

How could this be happening? How could it be that one day he had a family and a normal life in the City, and the next day he was running from the Praetorian Guard, hiding in a pantry in a shanty in the slums? Surely, they would wake up and realize this had all been a terrible nightmare. He found himself getting angry at his parents, who had obviously been planning something but had neglected to tell him about it. How could they have been so stupid? And now here he was, trying to look after his sister, with all her challenges, while figuring out how to get back home.

Abruptly the curtain drew back and broke his reverie. Agnes flashed her green gaze at him. Then she furrowed her brow in confusion.

"Where's the girl?" she asked in a strange, lilting accent.

"Kat?" answered Jacob, nodding down at his sister and stroking her hair. "Right here. She's resting."

Agnes took a step back, staring intently at Kat. After a moment, she cautiously entered the pantry. Closing her eyes in concentration, she passed her hands a few inches above Kat's body. Suddenly her eyes opened, and she gave Jacob what felt like an accusatorial look, as if she believed he had been hiding something from her.

"Always like this?" Agnes asked sharply.

"Kat? Like…" Jacob realized she was asking about Kat's low-energy state of withdrawal. "No, not always. When she's really scared or stressed."

Muttering indecipherably to herself, Agnes abruptly exited the pantry. The curtain swished closed behind her.

Home tomorrow, Jacob resolved. *We are definitely going home tomorrow.*

Kat

"Where are we?" Kat asked, curling upright as she woke.

"The slums," Jacob said, handing her a bag of water.

"We need to find Mother," Kat declared.

"What?"

"We have to find her."

"What the hell are you talking about, Kat?!"

The explosion of frustration caught her off-guard, but Jacob carried on.

"Do you have any idea where we are? What we had to do to get here? I mean, I *carried* you here –on my back! We followed that *kid* all the way through this disgusting, filthy…I don't know. And then some guy, some old guy, says he can help us. Then – oh yeah, we get up here to this…whatever this is. It's not even a house. A hut? We get up here and there's this crazy woman. She comes in here when you're asleep and waves her hands around like some kind of witch doctor or something. And I'm sitting here on my own trying to figure things out while you're sleeping, or withdrawing, or whatever you call it. And I'm trying to come up with a plan. Then you just wake up and say we need to go find mom? Jesus, Kat!"

His voice had risen in a crescendo, and he stood up, towering over her. She had never seen him become so mad with her before.

"You have a plan?!" he shouted. "Huh? Do you?!"

"No," Kat said almost inaudibly.

"Well then don't tell me what we need to do! I have to try to figure out how to get us home, and I don't need you acting crazy while I do it. Do you understand that?"

"Yes."

"Oh…my…*God*! This is a total nightmare!"

Just then, the curtain pulled back and Agnes appeared, disrupting the tension. Kat recoiled – not in fear, but in awe. Never in her life had she seen an energy like the one that enveloped this woman. Vibrant, colorful spasms of light and heat, like a human-scale solar storm, encircled her. Agnes locked eyes with her, filling Kat with sound and light, stretching her like the skin of a balloon, until Kat felt she might rise up off the floor and burst into a thousand pieces.

"You come," said Agnes abruptly, turning on her heels. "Come eat."

2

The smell of spiced fish drew out Jacob and Kat and distracted them from their misery. Sitting at the table in the center of the room, they hungrily spooned a thin but tasty stew into their mouths. From a wooden perch in the opposite corner of the room, a gray parrot flew to the back of an empty chair. Kat had never seen a bird like it before and was mesmerized. The bird cast a wary, imperious eye upon them.

"What happens now?" Jacob asked Agnes when they had finished their second helping of stew. "Are we going to be able to go back home?"

"You wait for Hector," she said in her odd accent.

"We need to see that old guy again. What's his name? Renard? We have to go back home. To the City. Our parents are going to be worried."

"Hector will come back soon," Agnes reiterated.

Meatball sat in Kat's lap as she handed down small lumps of cooked peas and carrots, which he nibbled greedily. Feeling daring, Meatball stood on his hind legs and put his foreclaws on the table's edge to gain easier access to Kat's food. He wasn't quite close enough, however. He tried to pull himself up onto the table but, struggling to maintain his foothold, almost fell out of Kat's lap. Kat gave him a little boost and Meatball hoisted himself proudly onto the tabletop, ready to tuck into more of Kat's meal.

Suddenly there was a great flap of wings and a flurry of feathers. The gray parrot, who had been watching Meatball suspiciously, was obviously upset by the guinea pig's aggressive move to the table. The parrot screeched repeatedly as he raced back to his perch. Meatball shot like a bullet back to Kat. She tucked her petrified friend into the safety of her trench coat pocket, where he shook like a leaf.

Without raising her eyes to Agnes, Kat asked under her breath, "What's his name?"

"Quito," responded Agnes. "You can go over."

Kat rose from the table and approached the bird. Agitated, Quito paced back and forth.

"Don't worry," said Kat, patting the pocket in which Meatball still shook. "He's more scared than you."

The bird was about the size of a pigeon, solid gray except for circles of white around each black marble eye and the dull reddish tinge of his tail feathers. Making low, cooing noises deep in his throat, he fluffed out his neck feathers to look as menacing as possible. Slowly, Kat extended her left hand to stroke Quito. At first, he resisted, scurrying to the opposite end of his perch: but then he let her touch him gently. A moment later, he maneuvered to give Kat better access to the most scratchable areas behind his head and down his back. Kat could sense that Agnes was watching every move she made.

That night, as Kat lay sleepless on the pile of blankets, she heard a whispered exchange on the other side of the curtain.

Are you sure? asked a man with a deep voice.

I am, Agnes responded.

The following afternoon the electricity went out, part of the unpredictable rolling blackouts that affected the slums each day. Agnes dozed on her cot in the corner of the room. Jacob curled on the blankets in the pantry. Next to him, Kat played with Meatball, enjoying the subtle light of the oil lamp Agnes had given her. As she shifted to make room for a tunnel that Meatball had burrowed in the blankets, Kat became aware of an unfamiliar weight in her pocket. Removing it carefully, she stared at her father's notebook. She opened the book to Father's familiar, slanted handwriting. Without reading anything, she flipped delicately through the pages, wanting simply to touch them, to feel connected to him.

Sitting now in the hushed seclusion of their favela cave, Kat turned to a random page and read a short excerpt:

> A beautiful day with Clara and the children. Bright sunshine, so unusual, and the dust in retreat for a day. As if God had found his breath, shown us again what the world could be.

His voice resonated so clearly, even on paper. Tenderness and caring sang out to her, made her adore him, reminded her of the French lullabies he would sing to her before bed at night, or the math games they would play, or the books he would read aloud to them from his big chair in the bunker. She pressed the notebook hard to her body, wanting to incorporate it into herself. Until they were together again, she would protect the notebook with her life.

For the next hour she read, slowly, purposefully, struggling to understand the cadence and flow of her father's thoughts, the impossibly complex formulae of chemical compounds, or entries that showed growing frustration with his work:

Another failure. The ecosystem I'm developing for the filter still can't sustain the microbes. I'm beyond frustrated. I suppose I will have to reconsider the chemistry one more time...

Other times she stumbled upon philosophical reflections, scraps of poetry, or excerpts from literature he had read:

As a flame grows the more, the more the wind

Attacks it, every virtue Heaven exalts

Will shine the more, the more it is withstood.

- Michelangelo

At one point, she paused over a strange verse that Father had penciled in the corner of one page otherwise filled with mathematical formulae:

The Pyramids, Parthenon, and Taj Majal,

Like lilies, bananas, and sunflower seeds,

Like dolphins and tigers and ants.

Five, the first five, in verse.

Repeatedly she read the lines, sensing a deeper pattern but unable to identify the connecting factor. Then it occurred to her: the manmade structures were perfectly symmetrical, as were the animals and plants. All of them exemplified the Golden Mean – the ancient measure of perfection. 1.618. She knew it must be part of what he wanted her to figure out, part of the puzzle he had mentioned the night he left. But why? Why would she need this number? Again and again her attention was drawn to a different series of ciphers scrawled in pencil in the upper right-hand corner of several random pages. She jotted them down in a neat row at the back of the notebook:

 Instr. OrPH. (f.) CW 5R A

Two thirds of the way through she came to an entry that made her stop. The frustration with his research he'd expressed in earlier pages now gave way to a tone of incredulity:

Even in my wildest dreams I couldn't have imagined such a result...

She read the totality of the passage with great care, struggling to understand the importance of what he had found. With extraordinary speed, she calculated the number of days since she first noticed the change in her parents' behavior. Quickly, she determined that the date of the entry marked the beginning of that change. Of one thing she now felt sure: this was what had caused her family to be blown apart.

Kat heard voices approaching the shanty. She closed the notebook and stuffed it back into her coat pocket. Moments later the curtain swung back.

"Renard is ready to see you," Hector said.

The Notebook

Lake Powell is dry. Lake Mead is dry. The Colorado River, artery of the west, is little more than sludge by the time it reaches the Pacific Ocean...

Almost one half of humanity has no access to clean water. World population has exploded in the last few generations. Most of that growth has been in countries that were already water poor...

Of all the water on the planet less than 0.5% of it is usable by humans. Most of the fresh water on earth is locked up in what's left of the ice caps. The rest is in the oceans...

Tracker

Following the footprints and broken branches through the woods behind the house, it had not taken him long to arrive at the junkyard. For some time, Tracker walked methodically around the abandoned memorial neighborhood, examining the streets, peering into the vacant buildings, absorbing what he presumed would have been the children's juvenile fascination. When he found the car buried halfway under a hill of trash, he knew that it was where the children had been hiding.

He leaned down and peered into the dark cavern of the old jalopy. Delicately, he traced his fingers along the wooden frame that had been crafted to reinforce the rotting front seat, sensing the love and attention the boy had devoted to his manufactured playground.

He's a teenager, thought Tracker, *but he's young.*

Squeezing himself into the car, he noticed the crumpled sweatshirt Jacob had slept on. He lifted it to his nose and breathed deeply, memorizing its scent. Licking his thumb, he scraped it along the cracked vinyl back seat and pinched together several hairs and fibers, which he tucked carefully into the front pocket of his shirt. Satisfied, Tracker slid back into the open air. He carefully studied the footprints in the dirt.

Boy, size eight sneaker. Same as in the backyard of the house. He's at least five foot eight – tall for his age. The girl is small. Flat-soled shoes, size four.

Reaching into his breast pocket, he removed the fibers he had picked up off the seat to view them more clearly in the daylight. A few were short and dark, threads from a coat or sweater. Mixed in with them was a golden-brown hair the length of his pinky. Upon close inspection, he realized that it was not a human hair, but that of an animal. He pictured the litter box in the girl's room. She must have taken her pet with her.

Yes, he said to himself. *This will be quick.*

Jacob

Kat and Jacob sat opposite Renard on the weathered sofa. Placed on the low table between them were a plate of dry biscuits and a clay teapot. In the shadows behind the old man, Hector stood next to a teenage girl. Trying not to stare, Jacob took in her desert brown skin, her fine features, her intense eyes. The odd crook in her nose and short hair gave her the aura of a street fighter. She wore a tight, khaki-colored, sleeveless t-shirt and a pair of loose cargo pants with oversized pockets halfway down each leg. A bronze snake bracelet curled around her bicep. Jacob felt her scrutiny like a laser through his skull.

"Tea?" Renard offered, gesturing to the pot on the table. Without waiting for a response, he began to pour the steaming liquid into three separate cups.

Jacob glanced over at his sister, who sat beside him, eyes averted. Although she barely moved, Jacob knew that she was highly attuned to everything in the room.

Renard sipped his tea, then sat back and exhaled deeply. "They burned down your house."

"W-what?" Jacob sputtered.

Kat raised her head and for a moment looked directly at Renard. When he stared back, she reverted her gaze. Renard waved a hand to beckon the girl standing behind him.

"Bettina. Show them."

Bettina stepped from the shadows into the shallow pool of light around the desk and slipped a handheld device off her wrist. Jacob and Kat watched the small screen as a video scanned the smoldering embers of their former home. Jacob recognized immediately the charred furniture, the backyard coop, and even his

Rules football in the smoky ruins. Kat turned away, mumbling softly to herself.

"I don't understand," said Jacob, shaking his head. "Why would they do that?"

"We have a permanent hack on the PG patrol network – what they use to communicate when they are out on the street," said Bettina in a business-like voice. "We picked up chatter about your father. Seems like maybe he was trying to leave the country. There've been a lot of defections recently. The government is clamping down pretty hard. I guess he was gonna leave you guys behind."

"NO!" blurted Kat.

"It's okay, Kat," Jacob soothed. "They don't know. It's okay."

"Bettina," Renard admonished.

"I'm just saying." Bettina shrugged and sauntered back to her spot next to Hector.

"I'm sure he was planning to take you with him, Kat," said Renard comfortingly. "He would have been smart to get his whole family out of the country if he could. These are terrible times. And they are about to get worse."

"Do you know what happened to him? Is he okay?" Jacob asked.

"We don't know. We would have heard something if they'd captured him. So he's probably hiding somewhere. But it won't be long before they find him. The Preaetorian Guard are good at that sort of thing, unfortunately."

"What about my mother?" Jacob asked.

"She's in the Keep – the prison at the Coliseum. Where they take political prisoners. I'm guessing they'll leave her there until they find your father. Or you."

"Us?"

A wan smile creased Renard's face. "You surprised them when you ran off and didn't return to the house. I don't think they were expecting that. They haven't officially put your names out for arrest. They don't want anyone to think they don't have the situation under control. But they've started to spread the word in the underground networks that they're looking for two children that fit your description. You're going to have to be extremely careful. The regime has many eyes in the favela. Many eyes."

"This is…unbelievable," Jacob stammered. "I thought today we could just, you know, go home. That this was all a mistake of some kind…"

"I'm afraid it's not a mistake," Renard said.

"What are we going to do?" Jacob asked, his voice cracking.

Renard furrowed his brow as if considering Jacob's options for the first time. "Well… you have a few choices, I suppose. Naturally, you could go back to the City and turn yourself in. This is one way to reunite with your mother, probably the easiest. Join her in the Keep until they find your father. A second option would be that we could take you to the southern side of the favela, to the foothills of the Santa Ana. We know some Coyotes who could get you over the Mexican border. Of course, after that you'd be on your own."

He paused as Jacob's complexion blanched.

"Or," Renard casually sipped his tea. "There's another option."

"Renard," Bettina objected through clenched teeth. "We did *not* agree on that."

But Renard held up his hand to silence her, his eyes never leaving Jacob's. Lowering his voice, the old man leaned forward and said in a whispered crescendo, "You could *fight back*."

"I don't understand," Jacob said, trying his best to avoid looking at Bettina.

Renard stood. With a slight limp, he made his way toward the wall to the left of his desk. He stopped in front of a framed portrait of a Native American man, noble and austere in bearing, with a high forehead and prominent nose. Penetrating, defiant eyes peered out from under a ceremonial headpiece. In the background, red hills stood in sharp outline against an indigo sky.

"Have you ever heard of the Anasazi?" Renard asked.

"No," replied Jacob.

"Yes," said Kat quietly.

"Oh?" said Renard with a tone of pleasant surprise. "And what do you know about them, little one?"

Kat continued mechanically, speaking rapid-fire, not raising her eyes and rocking slightly as she spoke. "I read about them in my books. They were an indigenous tribe of the Southwest, part of the Hopi nation. They lived in the southwestern deserts of North America for thousands of years before the Europeans arrived."

"At least twelve thousand years," Renard corroborated. "Probably more. The United States has existed for less than three hundred years. New California for less than thirty. Both are a grain of sand in the hourglass by comparison. Do you know what happened to the Anasazi?"

"Their society collapsed," Kat replied.

"Why?"

"Because of water."

"Yes," Renard sighed heavily. "Because of water. The Anasazi carved beautiful buildings into the red Arizona cliffs, created vast networks of agriculture and trade that extended south to Mexico and west to the Pacific Ocean. As part of the Hopi nation, they were like the Maya or the Inca – one of the truly great American civilizations. But toward the end they made the same mistake that many great civilizations make. The same mistake we are making now."

He shook his head sadly as he straightened the portrait.

"Greed, war, famine, drought. After thousands of years of building their great society, it only took decades for it to fall apart. In the end, only a small band of Anasazi remained in the Longhouse Valley, a few hundred of them. They were called the Kayenta. For several generations they survived in the desert, holding onto their old ways. There is evidence of their fires, their pottery. But then suddenly they disappeared without a trace. Gone. Those history books of yours, Kat, probably say that they died off from disease or famine, unable to adapt. But there is another history, passed down through the generations. A legend that says they have lived on into our times. That they are here, somewhere among us, waiting."

"Renard…" Bettina muttered in frustration.

"Waiting for what?" Jacob asked.

"Maybe for us," Renard said.

Fatigue overcame him, and Renard returned to the chair across from Jacob and Kat. He massaged his eyes, pressing the skin back and forth with thick hands.

"I don't know which history is true. But I can tell you what I do know. There are ten billion people on the planet and there's not enough water to go around. The Water Wars that started years ago in Africa and the Middle East have spread now to Asia and

Europe. The same is happening here in North America. The skirmishes between New California, Canada and the U.S – it won't be long before they turn into a fully-fledged war. Malcolm Duke craves war. He's a very bad man, Jacob. The future will either be his new world, or ours."

Jacob felt a deep sense of dismay. Conversations in the City about war always portrayed the conflict as necessary to protect the fragile independence of a new country. America was the corrupt power, not New California. The occasional fighting that took place now in the north wasn't a pretense for war, just defensive action to protect the country and ensure access to water for its people. The entire southern half of the state depended upon water that originated in the Cascades across the northern border. Surely Renard understood that.

"President Duke isn't a dictator," Jacob offered self-consciously. "He saved the country."

Bettina couldn't contain herself. Stepping forward, she spat her words at him. "Malcom Duke is a monster."

"He made things better." Jacob tried to hold his ground.

"Really? Better for who? Did you even look at the streets you walked down in this stinking slum? Did you see how we're living here? You know it's illegal to collect rainwater in the favela? *Illegal*. People get arrested by the water police. I've watched them haul off mothers who were just trying to make sure their babies had clean water. You live over there, with your school uniforms and running water, and you think that means life is good for everyone? Well, guess what: there's no running water here. We buy it in bags delivered by the Phoenix Water Company. Guess who owns Phoenix Water? Your savior, Malcolm Duke."

By now Bettina had moved within inches of Jacob, her dazzling eyes alight with flecks of brown and gold. He leaned away from the heat of their intensity. Renard put his hand on Bettina's shoulder, rupturing the moment.

"I'm telling you, this is a terrible idea," she said to Renard without taking her eyes off Jacob. Pivoting abruptly, she said, "C'mon, Hector. I need some air."

Hector shrugged apologetically at Jacob and followed her out. Renard sat forward with a resigned smile.

"I love Bettina. She's…a very passionate person. Like a daughter to me. The best I've ever trained in Snake Clan."

At the mention of Snake Clan, it dawned on Jacob that all the snake tattoos he'd seen must be symbols of the Clan.

"Snake Clan? But that's a group of…"

"Terrorists?" Renard prompted when Jacob's voice trailed off. "Is that what you were going to say? That's how they refer to us, I think. But we're freedom fighters, not terrorists. We're part of the Emergence."

"You've killed people," Jacob accused.

"People have died for the cause, yes. It's unfortunate. But lives are being lost here every day, Jacob. Bettina is right about that. On this side of the fence, a different kind of terrorism kills people: silent, hard to see, but very real. And the only way to change it is to fight. I've dedicated my life to stopping Malcolm Duke and everything he stands for. It seems to me like your father was trying to do the same."

"My father?"

"Why else would he be trying to get you out of the country?"

"I… I'm not sure."

A heavy silence hung between them as Jacob wrestled with the magnitude of the question for the first time.

"I think you can help us Jacob," Renard finally said.

"Me?" Jacob was incredulous.

"I'll make you a deal. I'll help you find your mother. But I need something in return." Renard leaned forward. "I want you to become a spy."

2

That evening, Jacob slipped out of Agnes' shanty and climbed a homemade ladder onto the rooftop. He leaned back against the large plastic water tank, pulled his knees into his chest, and stared out over the favela. In spite of the heat, he shivered with chill. From somewhere in the alleys below, the thin echo of a drum reached his ears.

This can't be happening, he thought.

Tears broke against his will, cascading down his face. Deep sobs rose from his gut, through his chest, and crested in heaving groans. For several minutes, he cried in a way he had not since before he was old enough to remember crying. Any reserve he had left, any appearances that he managed to preserve in the face of these strangers, or for the benefit of his sister, finally fell away. For several days he had deluded himself, telling himself that this was all a mistake, that if they could just find their way back to the City, to their house, to their parents, then things would return to normal. He could go back to school. David and he could hang out together. Kat could read her books and play with Meatball. Father could take him to the Grays game, just like they had planned. But now the truth hit hard.

How could you have done this to me? he silently berated his parents. *How could you possibly have done this to me?*

Taking long, deep breaths, he slowly regained his composure. Brushing the hair out of his eyes, he sat up straight. Then he wiped his running nose with his shirt and took a final decisive breath to pull himself together. Maybe he couldn't go back home, but there had to be a way out of this mess. His mind wandered back to all that Renard had told them.

His entire life Jacob had been taught to fear everything the Emergence stood for. Any time he bothered to pay attention to the news, or to listen to things adults said, he heard a similar storyline: The Emergence was a terrorist organization. They were criminals. They killed innocent people. They threatened the security of the country. How could he even consider joining such a group? And how on earth would a teenager like him – who had lived in the City his whole life – ever do something that would help the Emergence?

A few weeks ago, he would have shrugged off Renard's version of history as the rantings of a fanatic. But as he thought back on his parents' behavior, it seemed likely that they *were* trying to get the family out of the country. Which could only mean that Father had been doing something with his work that the government wouldn't like. Which meant that in some sense he was oddly aligned with the Emergence, even if that wasn't his intention. And hadn't Hector – a slum dweller himself, a member of the Emergence – helped him and Kat escape? Wouldn't they also be in the Keep with their mother – or worse – if Hector hadn't intervened? It was possible that Hector was a terrorist, but he certainly didn't act like one. On top of everything, the PG had arrested his innocent mother and then burned his house to the ground.

Weak lights, powered by old generators, flickered dimly in the windows below. In the distance, the infamous Torre Maria – a half-built high rise taken over by squatters – loomed like the mast of a lost ghost ship through the haze. A slight breeze touched his cheek. The wind peeled back a patch of the oppressive sky. For a moment, Jacob glimpsed the infinite and glorious array of stars beyond, twinkling in mirrored opposition to the firefly lights of the slums below, triggering a memory of his father. They had been camping together and had gone up just high enough to have a view of the stars. He remembered his father's explanation of starlight.

That light has been traveling for millions of years. The stars we are looking at now, Jacob, might not even exist today. They might have collapsed or exploded. But we'll never know because it takes so long for the light from those stars to reach us.

Such mysteries intrigued his father, but Jacob had always dismissed them as boring and academic, the kinds of things only adults would care about. But now, alone on the rooftop, feeling lost and desperate, Jacob was seized by a deep desire – a desire to reach through that celestial opening, to touch the clean air of that sky, to surrender himself to that fragment of universe, that place devoid of good and evil, that world composed only of cold, hard blackness.

When Jacob returned to the shanty, Agnes was sitting on her bed fingering the charms of a bracelet she held in her hands. She seemed lost in thought and did not acknowledge his presence as he walked across the room. When he pulled back the pantry curtain, Kat sat upright and alert. Jacob dropped onto the blankets beside her. He wanted to explain to her the desperation of their situation, while somehow reassuring her that things would be okay so that she would not panic any more than she already had. As he opened his mouth to speak, he noticed a curious expression on her face.

"Are you okay?" he asked.

"Father came into my room the night before he left." She held up a small leather notebook that he recognized as Father's. "He left me this. He told me I needed to keep it safe for him. I already knew something bad was going to happen, even before he came into my room. I knew for a long time."

Kat made eye contact with people infrequently, but when she did she would stare with an almost aggressive intensity. As she locked eyes with him now, Jacob struggled not to turn away.

"I've been reading it. While you were gone. He figured it out."

"Figured out what?" Jacob was confused.

"How to drink the oceans."

Kat became more animated now, excited to share. She opened the notebook and flipped through the pages until she came to the passage she wanted. She began to read:

Crystal and I have been working on refining the water filtration system based on the strand of halophilic archaebacteria I bio-engineered. As I was moving the ecosystem solution into the filter environment, a small drop fell directly into the beaker of heavily salinated water. Miraculously, when the biogel entered the water, within seconds the entire beaker was clear of NaCl. The salt content was reduced from almost 5% ions/sodium chloride to 0.001%. I tasted the water. It was perfect.

This result is beyond anything we could have imagined. No filters will be needed. No machines. No desalination plants. Water will be free for everyone. It could mean peace around the world. I think this might be the most important scientific discovery in the last hundred years.

Malcolm Duke must never find out about this.

"I don't understand," Jacob said after she finished.

"Father's been researching specialized water filters—"

"I got that part," Jacob interrupted, trying to regain some credibility.

"Well, most of the research in the field – Israeli, Chinese, American – has been focused on using technology or advanced chemical processes to remove the salt. But Father was working on a system using bacteria – bacteria that eat the salt and eject pure water. He created a biogel that can sustain halophilic bacteria. You can see from these earlier entries how he's trying to work it all out but he can't quite get it. He thinks they need to be put into the filter he created, but they didn't need to be. All his formulas are off. He's very frustrated. But then here—"

Jacob interrupted her. "Kat!"

She stopped, suddenly aware again of his presence.

"Slow down," Jacob pleaded. "I don't understand! What is 'halo'…? What are you talking about?"

"He made a special gel," she explained. "Inside the gel are bacteria that eat salt. When he put a drop of it in very salty water, the bacteria made the salt disappear completely. You could drink it right away. It was perfect. Perfect water."

"So you could drink the oceans," Jacob said softly, realizing now what she had been saying.

"Yes," she replied. "With this, anyone could turn sea water into drinking water. Or water for agriculture. Drought around the world would be over."

"And no need to go to war," continued Jacob.

"As long as people everywhere have access to the biogel," Kat said.

"Which is what Father was trying to do."

"They risked everything," said Kat.

"Including us."

They sat in silence, trying to take it all in.

"What are we going to do?" Jacob asked, painfully aware that it was she, not he, who seemed more likely to know.

"Tell Renard that we will help him," she said.

3

A ruckus from the room outside stirred them from their discussion. Kat quickly tucked the notebook away in one pocket. Meatball dove back into the other.

A rowdy group of boys had entered the shanty. As they emerged from the pantry, Jacob noticed that Agnes had risen from her bed and was now putting some nuts and berries into dishes in the small kitchen. The boys crowded around a wooden tray they had placed on top of the central table, into which two of them were throwing dice. With each throw, the group bellowed with laughter or derision, gesticulating animatedly, scolding, teasing. The intimate room suddenly felt vibrant and alive.

Pepe presided like a dealer at a craps table. Hector and a few older boys Jacob didn't recognize lounged around the periphery, leaning against the wall or sitting on upturned plastic drums. A few of the young boys around the table turned upon their arrival. Pepe leapt up happily.

"Jakey! *Gatterina*!" he shouted. "You come meet the boys!" He grabbed Jacob by the arm, though Kat slipped away, retreating from the boisterousness. Pepe dragged Jacob forward to introduce him.

"Beany," began Pepe, yanking a boy no older than six or seven by the collar. He had a hard look about him, like he was ready for a fight.

"Pinocchio," said Pepe, continuing around the table. He smacked a slight, slender boy on the back of the head. "Show him your nose, Pino."

"Wow," said Jacob as the boy turned.

"Big one, huh?" laughed Pepe.

"Hi," said Pinocchio, clearly used to his nose being a subject of amusement.

"And this is Trashcan," Pepe continued. To Jacob he said in an understated whisper, "Very stinky. But a big boy. Good fighter."

"Hullo," said the boy in a dull voice. He was thick set and taller than the rest by at least a head. His shoulders were broad and his hands massive. Jacob noticed how quick his eyes were, and how mistrustful.

Pepe came to the last boy around the table. "And this is Mouse," he announced with fraternal pride. Mouse possessed a sweet, angelic face. With wide eyes, he smiled and nodded vigorously at Jacob.

"*No puede espiquear*," said Pepe in favela slang. "Can't speak. He got no tongue." Jacob recoiled slightly. But Pepe put his arm around Mouse's shoulder and patted him hard. "Bear Clan left him for dead but we found him and we take care of him. Didn't we? He's like my own baby brother, right little *mousito*?" Mouse gazed back at Pepe adoringly and nodded shyly.

"You wanna play dice?" Pepe asked. "I can teach you. It's a game called *bananas*."

"That's okay," said Jacob. "I'll just watch for now."

As Pepe returned to the table, Jacob looked for Kat. She was sitting with her back against Agnes' chair, where the old woman had returned to attend to her needlework after laying out some food for the boys. She paid little mind to Kat, as if it were natural to have her at her feet. Jacob suspected quickly that this hands-off approach by Agnes put Kat at ease, and he felt a strange pleasure seeing her there. His sister sensed his gaze and looked up from Meatball, who had ventured out onto her lap to observe the commotion.

He perked up both eyebrows: *Are you okay?*

She blinked: *I'm fine.*

Jacob joined Hector against the back wall opposite the door.

"Impressive group, no?" said Hector, nodding at the raucous boys.

"Very," Jacob laughed.

"They're all *orfanos*," he explained. "We call them the *culebras* – the little snakes. They live in the Torre Maria. You know it?"

"I've seen it," Jacob replied. "It was supposed to be a bank or something, right? They never finished building it."

"Yeah, that's right," Hector said. "They started building it before the earthquake. They got one side of windows finished, but the other three are still just concrete. I don't know how it never fell down. Eventually the squatters started taking it over. I think there's a few thousand people who live there now."

"That must be pretty scary," Jacob said. "With half the building open like that."

"Yeah, of course," Hector said. "It's also pretty violent. Some floors and hallways you try to avoid at all costs. Most of the kids living there end up joining the clans, selling drugs, stealing…."

Jacob tried to imagine little Mouse navigating crumbling hallways, picking his way past unconscious drug users, on his way to some shabby room he shared with dozens of other boys. The incongruity of this small boy in that environment was hard to reconcile

"What about Renard?" Jacob asked. "And Snake Clan? Are they involved in the drugs and stuff?"

"Snake Clan's different," Hector explained. "It's a small clan. More like a family than a street gang. Renard and Agnes lead it. But they almost got wiped out about ten years ago.

"What happened?"

"In the beginning, when Duke was still getting his grip on power, he went after the Emergence," Hector continued. "Most senior members of Snake Clan were killed. By the Tracker."

"The Tracker?"

"Duke's assassin. He sent Tracker in to hunt them down one by one." Hector held his finger up and slid it across his throat.

"But he never got Renard?" Jacob asked.

"Renard and a few others managed to get out of the country, down to Mexico. Duke became so powerful that he forgot about Snake Clan. Tracker started doing other stuff for him. Then one day, Renard and Agnes came back. Together they restarted Snake Clan. But they didn't make any trouble for Duke. Mainly, they focused on helping people around here: especially the kids. Agnes loves the kids. Most of them don't go to school, so Snake Clan provides basic education. We give them small jobs so they don't turn to drugs for money. We even have a little network of nurses and health workers. Like I said, it's a family."

Jacob looked over at the silent old woman in her chair next to Kat. "Agnes is a leader of Snake Clan?"

Hector could see Jacob's skepticism. "I know she doesn't look like it. But people say she's the real leader."

After a moment's hesitation, Jacob asked, "Why does Renard want me to help you guys? I don't understand what he thinks I can do. I mean, I'm just a kid from the City. I don't know the first thing about politics."

Hector looked hard at Jacob. "To be honest, I'm not really sure."

"That girl definitely seemed pretty against it," Jacob said.

"Bettina?" Hector laughed. "Yeah. She thinks it's a terrible idea."

"She made that pretty clear. Who is she?"

"Renard's deputy. Runs operations."

"She's so young," Jacob wondered.

"Renard found her when she was about six. Out on the streets. He raised her. Now she manages the day to day. She's unbelievably smart. And really tough. A lot of the guys don't like her. They're mad that Renard puts so much responsibility in her hands. But she doesn't take any crap. She can fight the toughest guys, survive in the woods; she can design software better than anyone I've ever seen. And she can actually be pretty nice – if she likes you."

"She obviously didn't like *me*," Jacob said.

"Yeah," Hector chuckled. "You got a little work to do on that front. But if Renard says you can help, you can help. Bettina may not like it. But if Renard says it, she'll support it. Mostly."

Just then, a boy raced breathless into the room. "*El Capitán*. He's coming!"

"Get Kat," ordered Hector. "Into the pantry."

4

Through the slit between the pantry curtain and the wall, Jacob saw a short, fat man enter the shanty. He wore a beige khaki uniform and a black beret on his head. Dark sweat stains circled out from under his armpits and his shirt hung untucked at the place where his belly bulged and spilled over the crest of his pants. Although he wore a holster, it was unclasped and empty.

The Captain surveyed the room with narrowed eyes. The *culebras* had suspended their game upon his arrival and they watched him with equal anticipation. Agnes remained seated in her chair by the foot of her bed. Silence hung over the room.

"*Fatty!*" shrieked Quito.

A flurry of giggles erupted from the *culebras*. Hector stepped around the table and greeted the Captain in a cold tone.

"To what do we owe this honor?"

"You know why I'm here," snarled the Captain.

"I'm not sure I do," responded Hector evenly.

"The gringo," the Captain said, still scanning the room.

"Gringo?"

"You were seen bringing a gringo up to Hilltop a few days ago."

"You don't believe rumors in Nova Rio, do you Captain?"

"I don't believe anything that comes out of your *ratón* mouth," hissed the Captain venomously. Taking a step closer, he continued. "Are you saying you know nothing about any gringos?"

"I'm saying rumors are rumors."

The Captain, though several inches shorter than Hector, weighed considerably more. It was clear that he did not fear facing all of them alone.

"Don't play games with me, *boy*. Supreme General Duke – the President's *son* – called me himself when he heard the report of a gringo boy in the favela. You know what that means as well as I do. So if you *happen* to see two gringo children wandering around in the favela, I'm the first person you call. *Comprende*?"

"We're just simple *ratones*, playing a game of bananas," replied Hector.

"We have our understanding, Hector. I left my gun at the gate of Hilltop. Live and let live. But we both know the Supreme General. You better watch your back."

The Captain took a few slow steps backward. He surveyed the room again, letting his eyes pore over every detail before casually turning to leave.

David

David McCaw made his way down the empty hallway toward the school exit. At the top of the granite stairs, he paused, taking in the stream of students weaving past the rusted metal jungle gym. How he had fantasized about leaving this place, about putting behind him the tortuous days of being bored and bullied, about finally doing something meaningful with his life. For the tenth time that day, he read through the official notification he had received that morning on his handheld: *Congratulations! You have been accepted for basic training in the Praetorian Youth Guard.* He still had trouble believing it had happened.

As he descended the steps towards the blacktop, a movement caught his attention amidst the ebbing crowd. A tall man dressed in black walked toward him against the tide. David joined the flow of departing students but the man materialized almost magically in front of him, stopping David in his tracks.

"David McCaw?"

David looked up. The man towered over him. David could not take his eyes off the long, jagged scar that swept across the man's face.

"Yes?" David gulped.

"You know Jacob Angelfish."

It was a statement, not a question. Fear crept along David's scalp. With as much composure as he could muster, David said, "Sure…"

"You know where he is?"

"No," David replied truthfully. "He hasn't been in school all week. I thought he'd…" David hesitated. "I heard he was arrested."

"He and his sister are missing."

"Missing?" David was genuinely surprised.

"We're trying to find them. Has he tried to contact you?"

"No," David replied hurriedly, wanting to be clear about his own innocence. "Really. I mean, I swear, I thought he was in jail or something."

"If you hear from him, I want you to call this number," said Tracker, handing him a white business card with only a phone number printed on it.

"Sure. Totally," David confirmed.

Tracker glanced at the vibrating device on his wrist. As he walked away, he paused and said, "By the way, congratulations on the Youth Guard. I'm sure you'll make a fine soldier."

Tracker

Tracker stopped at the end of the blacktop, away from the stream of departing students, and unfolded his device. An image of President Malcolm Duke appeared.

"Sir," Tracker said.

"We have a problem," growled the leader of New California. He was sitting in a deep leather chair Tracker recognized from the President's home office.

"Do we?" asked Tracker curiously.

"An American spy." The President hesitated only briefly before confirming the gravity of the situation. "He was high up."

"How high?" inquired Tracker.

"Cabinet level."

"Your man's? Or Erik's?"

"Don't make this about him," warned the President darkly, sitting forward.

Erik Duke was the President's son and the Supreme General of the New California Armed Forces. The heir apparent of the country. He hated Tracker. Tracker hated him more – and the President knew it. On a different day, in a more generous moment, Tracker would admit that Erik Duke had some positive qualities – at least from the President's perspective. He had risen through the ranks of his father's corporate empire, The Phoenix Company, by building out its global paramilitary division, the Praetorian Guard. It was a mercenary operation, contracting with governments that could not afford to build significant armies of their own, or with major powers who did not want to send their own citizens into battle. By his late twenties, Erik Duke had built the greatest non-state army in the history of the world. After the recall election, the Praetorian Guard were given total control over the recovery efforts.

And Erik Duke excelled. He was tactically and operationally brilliant, ruthless in his decision-making and exacting in his standards. While no one thought Los Angeles could be rebuilt in a generation, he did it in less than ten years: putting up the Perimeter fence, pushing out the immigrants, rebuilding infrastructure on the City side, and establishing a robust technological platform so that Los Angeles could emerge as a paragon of power and excellence. In the process, he became a hero across the state – and while he had no stomach for the political stage like his father did, he was equally revered by the people. So when Malcolm Duke declared independence for New California and pronounced himself President of the Republic, there were only hosannas when he put his son Erik in charge of the newly formed military.

Now, thirty years after the earthquake and the formation of the Republic, the President was getting older. Erik Duke had consolidated power. Tracker was one of the few to escape his control. Reporting directly to the President, Tracker represented a throwback to the early days of the state, when the President needed non-conventional ways to battle the Emergence. Tracker was not a military man. He was unlike anything or anyone. And he alone had been responsible for bringing down the majority of the leadership of the Emergence. Erik Duke, Tracker knew, could scarcely hide his impatience for reaching the moment when, finally taking over for his father, he would eliminate Tracker once and for all.

"I knew the Americans had someone inside," Tracker snarled. "We can't afford this right now."

"I've deliberately kept the Cabinet in the dark about our plans," replied the President, trying to downplay the importance of it, sitting back again in his chair and picking up a glass of red wine from the side table. "Whatever information this man stole, it won't tell the Americans anything they don't already know. Even so, I need you to get on top of this."

"Why don't you let the Supreme General clean up his own mess?"

"He wants to, of course. And he could. But I need him to focus on other things. Besides, his anger would get in the way. This is a *delicate* moment. If handled right, this incident could provide us…leverage with the Americans." Duke waited for a moment. "It requires discretion rather than force. That's what I have you for."

"Where is he?" asked Tracker quietly, satisfied by the acknowledgement that he would be more capable at handling this matter than the General would.

"The spy? He's in the San Gabriel range. He has special forces training so he's probably holed up somewhere above 8,000 feet."

"How long has he been up there?" Tracker asked.

"Since yesterday. They lost him about twenty-four hours ago. We can tell you where."

"What about Angelfish?" Tracker asked. "We still don't have him. And we're going to need that filter. We can find the children in a few days. If we do, we can force the father out of hiding."

"They'll turn up. We don't need your considerable skills just to find a couple of kids. Some dumb cop somewhere will stumble on them and then we'll deal with it."

"What about Angelfish?"

"He's in the country somewhere, running around in his bare feet." President Duke was getting impatient. "We're looking for him. If he's dead, we'll kill the wife. If he's alive, we'll find him and then we'll kill both of them. Either way, we can leave the children to the slave catchers."

Tracker let his silence speak for him.

"Come down to the Coliseum," Duke said tersely, annoyed by Tracker's doubts. "We'll get you what we have on the American."

"I'll be there in twenty minutes," Tracker said.

"Make it ten," said the President.

Tracker tapped his wrist and the image dissolved. Rationally, he agreed with Duke: the children couldn't stay hidden for long on their own, and their only purpose was to serve as bait. If the father was dead, they were irrelevant.

Still, Tracker wondered if it was a mistake to let them go.

Part III

War

The warm Santa Ana winds rise from the sea, migrating gently but purposefully inland. Cooled and compressed by the early summer air of the Mojave Desert, the winds build gradually but steadily, until they roar with hurricane force into the open lowlands. In the best of times, the Santa Ana winds are menacing. In the days of unending drought, they are catastrophic. The parched earth rises thousands of feet into the air, whorling into blinding columns of sand. Air snaps and crackles with a dry electric charge. Fires spark at the slightest provocation.

In the City, sophisticated weather systems monitor the coastal winds. Early warning sirens scream with ululating urgency, giving families precious time to take refuge. Drilled in emergency procedures, residents insulate their homes with specially manufactured, triple-layered plastic sheeting designed to capture the infiltrating dust. As the unforgiving winds roar, steady waves of grit lash the houses like a malevolent rain. Locked safely with food and fresh water in their bunkers underground, the citizens wait for the storm to pass.

In the favela, the sirens taunt the helpless. Protected behind flimsy construction, or raw and exposed in the open air, the poor cower in the face of nature's howl. Mothers call children into makeshift shelters. Desperate shouts ring out then dissipate, swallowed up by the winds. Men frantically hammer sheets of tin or plastic in front of crumbling windows and doors. Feral dogs bark and whine. For the street children, wrapped in garbage bags, or hiding in tunnels, or exposed in the Torre Maria, their only protection is the will to survive.

And everywhere there is dust, caked upon the countertops and rooftops and eyelashes until all color is washed from the landscape and the entire world fades at the mercy of the brown summer snow.

Kat

Kat listened to the low groan of the afterwinds as the storm receded. Alone in the pantry, she heard the brisk scraping of Agnes' broom in the kitchen and the fluttering of Quito's wings as he washed. From her shoulders, she brushed a layer of dust that topped her like a frosting. Grit caked the contours of her ears and the corners of her eyes. Her hair was a thick matte, her throat parched and raw. All she could think about was water.

Carefully, she untacked the sheeting and stepped out of the pantry. Agnes waited with a bag of Phoenix Water. Kat took it gratefully. Sip by small sip the pollen and the spores, the dust and the grime, washed down her throat until she could swallow without feeling like a dry riverbed. Meatball squeaked pathetically from her pocket. Kat put drops of water on her finger again and again until Meatball, too, regained his equilibrium. Beginning to feel human once more, Kat thanked Agnes with her eyes.

Kat had been on her own with Agnes for several days. After endless hours of debate with his sister, Jacob had finally agreed to help Renard. In return for his service, Jacob made Renard swear that Snake Clan would do everything they could to help them find and free their mother. Kat assured him she would be both safe and happy staying with Agnes. Worried and scared, Jacob at last departed with Bettina and Hector to begin his training.

Kat struggled to articulate to Jacob precisely why she felt so strongly that he needed to go with Hector and Bettina. Or why she would be okay remaining behind with Agnes. In her mind, the certainty felt geometric and clear. Yet all she could find to say to Jacob was, "I know it's going to be okay."

For her part, Agnes took Jacob's departure entirely in stride. She did nothing to make Kat comfortable. In fact, she largely left her alone while she cooked or cleaned or sat in her tattered chair stitching the bags and clothing that were her trade. Such deliberate inattention had the effect of relaxing Kat, opening her up gradually to the old woman, who seemed not to need to talk. Kat observed how Agnes tidied the shanty, moving about with a purposeful if slightly unbalanced gait, one hip marginally higher than the other, accentuated by her bad back. When Agnes washed, Kat stared entranced as she unashamedly removed her clothes and stood naked in the center of the room, filling a thin aluminum basin with water that had been boiled and strained. Her brown skin loose and sagging with age, Agnes rubbed herself vigorously with an old rag lathered with homemade soap. She unbound her braided ponytail, letting the thickly tangled hair fall free, pouring just enough water on her head to create a lather. The remaining hot water she used to rinse the soap from her hair and body. Finally, a homemade hairbrush in her hand, she brushed and brushed and brushed until her long, wet hair loosened and flowed dark silver.

Most of all, Kat had become obsessed by Agnes' hands. The tips of Agnes' fingers were hard and smooth, the lines of her palms etched deep by time. The hard outer layer of skin formed a protective glove that allowed the old woman to grasp hot pans without fear of pain. Her hands resembled gnarled mandrake roots in their deformity, but to Kat they glowed with warmth and tenderness. And yet as Kat watched them fly through the intricate and delicate stitching of a bag, she was overwhelmed by their paradoxical grace and agility. In the text of Agnes' hands, Kat read a mysterious spiritual life and began to trust her.

One day Agnes simply handed cloth, needle and thread to Kat. Without needing to discuss it, Agnes patiently and silently showed Kat a simple pattern of stitching to get her started. Kat took to the activity quickly. She was hypnotized by its simplicity and repetition. Her body swayed gently with the rhythm of each stitch. Up, down, under; left, right, back, forth. Often Agnes would sing softly as they worked, rocking in her chair, Kat at her feet sitting cross legged, Meatball hiding under the tent-cave created by Kat's trench coat. Sometimes Agnes would correct Kat's technique by simply shaking her head, clucking her tongue, and placing her hands on Kat's to show her the proper pattern.

"Like this," she would say.

Kat relished these moments when Agnes' hands touched her own. Thick, honeyed calm flowed from them into Kat's veins. Each day, Kat grew closer to Agnes and began to anticipate her company. Words almost never passed between them, yet there was a harmony and seamlessness to the way in which they interacted.

Kat fretted about her new friend, however. Lying in the pantry at night, she listened to Agnes coughing in her bed. Shallow at first, more wheezing than coughing, it built gradually toward a crescendo until, at its peak, Kat had to cover her ears. And in those moments, Kat could smell the sickness in the air.

How does a desert come to be?

Vast sands now divide North America in half. The Great American Desert.

Long ago, the Bearpaw Sea ran north from Canada to the southern US, separating East from West, just as the desert does now. On the eastern half of the continent the geology was stable. The Appalachian Mountains, which formed 450 million years ago, are the oldest range on the planet. They give way to a gentle shelf, formed by the slow, endless process of erosion, that eases gradually into the Atlantic Ocean. The western half of the continent was always restless — volcanic, violent, tumultuous. The two landmasses united when the great asteroid hit the Yucatan 65 million years ago, draining the Bearpaw in the process.

Just under three million years ago, the Panamanian bridge emerged, connecting North and South America, creating a passageway for flora and fauna that would transform the continents in both directions as animals that had evolved separately over millions of years could now interact. Some have referred to this ecosystem exchange as "the most extraordinary event in the whole history of life."

For two and a half million years, the Pleistocene Megafauna reigned over this vast, singular continent: giant sloths, short-faced bears, saber-toothed cats, giant beavers, peccaries and tapirs, mastodons and mammoths, American lions, even cheetahs. Two and a half million years. We can't conceive of time like that.

When the Bearpaw disappeared, it left behind a remarkable legacy: a gargantuan reservoir of fresh, drinkable, underground water, called the Oligalla Aquifer, that spread across the continent. Unimaginably vast, it seemed at one time to be an endless inheritance to God's chosen country.

But of course nothing on this earth is endless, and none of it is given to anyone. Fifteen to twenty thousand years ago the first humans arrived in North America. For the next ten thousand years they hunted the megafauna to extinction, slowly staking their territorial claim. In that time, great human civilizations rose and fell – the Inca, the Maya, the Aztec, the Hopi. And then the Europeans arrived a little over 500 years ago and the pace of destruction quickened. Like a virus, humans spread over the land, clearing it, choking it, bending it to their will.

Once they began to mine it for water, it only took several hundred years to drain the entire Oligalla Aquifer. And so now the Bearpaw is a sea again – a sea of sand.

It is a curious thing, this geology, this other scale of time. Perhaps one day this sea of sand will give way in turn and become fertile prairie. Perhaps there is another iteration of the earth's mysterious self-generative power in store for North America. Perhaps, on a geological scale, there is another age to come of water and life and short-faced bears. Perhaps the despair we are living through now will one day pass and be the stuff of legends and myths for some future, happier world.

Jacob

A dilapidated, retrofitted, mid-century Chevy carried Jacob, Hector and Bettina out of Nova Rio. They left before dawn, chugging and sputtering east along the Perimeter in the direction of Whittier. There, they changed both vehicles and drivers, waiting several hours to be sure they had not been followed. Around midday, they continued to Hacienda Heights and then further into La Puente, where they were hustled into a basement hideout to wait for the arrival of yet a third car. The routes they drove were almost impossible to navigate. Gaping potholes and deep troughs of dirt pitted the roads. Cars drove fast for a few dozen yards, then had to come to an almost complete stop before easing through the hole or over the bump to avoid breaking an axel or losing a tire. In the City, Jacob was used to the autonomous cars that moved predictably down their side of the road, speeds regulated, traffic orderly in almost every way. The notion of crossing the street at the wrong time would have felt surprising and strange. Yet here, cars respected no side of the road at all. The only lane to drive was the singular path through the hazards, and cars in both directions jockeyed to take it. With all the speeding and slowing, the bumps and the potholes, the interweaving of traffic in both directions, Jacob felt like he had been riding a mechanical bull all day.

As they passed out of the busy heart of Nova Rio and into these gradually more forlorn favela towns, Jacob noticed the crowds of men languishing next to idle motorcycle taxis at the main intersections, waiting quixotically for a fare. He wondered how on earth any of them could make money, how they found a way to survive. As they drove through one suburb, Jacob observed a mother and daughter laboring to shovel out the endless sand that the winds swept into the abandoned swimming pool they now called home. And everywhere, desolate men, young and old, unemployed or unemployable, hunched in doorways spitting indifferently on the dusty ground.

"Is that tobacco they're chewing?" Jacob asked.

"It's *khat*," Bettina explained from the front seat. "It's a hallucinogenic. Bear Clan started importing it from the Middle East about ten years ago. Half the favela is hooked on it."

"Bear Clan doesn't import it, they just sell it," Hector corrected, turning to Jacob in the rear of the car. "The PG import it."

"The PG?" asked Jacob, confused. "Why would they do that?"

By now, the light was fading and the winds had picked up suddenly with the drop in temperature. In the front seat, Bettina pressed her forehead against the glass to peer up at the threatening sky.

"We'll get out here," she pronounced. "It's gonna get worse and we don't want to get caught in it."

"Are you sure?" the driver asked, pulling over to the side of the road. "We still have another few miles to go. We could probably make it."

"I don't want to take the chance," Bettina said. "Plus, it's good to be unpredictable. You keep going. We'll meet you there tomorrow if it's all clear."

As soon as Jacob stepped out of the car the wind whipped dust off the hardscrabble road and into his face. He grabbed his bag, pulled the front collar of his shirt over his mouth, squinted to protect his eyes and ran, head down, behind Bettina and Hector into an abandoned building. Once inside, Bettina led them up a stairwell to an empty room on the second floor. There was a single window that had been patched over with cardboard. Bettina punched a small opening into a corner of it to enable a view of the street below. Their car was gone. The street seemed quiet. Satisfied, she turned and threw her bag onto the floor.

"We're good," she said.

Jacob watched his two companions as they pulled out their supplies. Hector removed a small contraption from his pack and popped it into a standing position.

"You ever used one?" he asked Jacob.

"Why would he ever have used something like that?" Bettina asked scornfully. "He's probably had dinner served to him every night."

"That's not true," Jacob said quietly, though he struggled to think of a time when he had made dinner for himself. "I've camped. With my dad."

It sounded pitiful even to his own ears. She laughed and carried her supplies to the corner to set up her bedding.

"She'll warm up," Hector said sympathetically as he unpacked. Jacob grunted his doubt, but Hector persisted. "She was pretty tough on me, too. When I first joined."

"She joined Snake Clan before you?"

"She was really young when she met Renard, way younger than I was. Maybe seven or eight. She'd already been with him for a while when I joined. We became friends after a few years."

Hector smiled kindly at Jacob's forlorn look and patted him reassuringly.

"C'mon, let's make dinner."

"You asked a question in the car," Bettina said while she slowly chewed the meager stew that Hector had prepared from a freeze-dried pack. Jacob could feel the heat of her scrutiny and he tried not to betray his feeling of inadequacy.

"I did?"

"Right before we got out. You asked why the PG import drugs. The answer is: because they want us to be addicts, to waste our lives, to not care. And then there's the fact that they get rich by doing it."

"But they're the government. That doesn't make any sense."

"Strange, huh? The government importing drugs so that clans can sell them in the slums to poor people who get addicted because what else do they have worth living for?"

"I just can't believe…" Jacob started. "I mean, before all this happened, I thought they were the good guys. There to protect us."

"Yeah," Bettina scoffed. "Well, now you're starting to see the truth."

"The difference between the favela and the City is that no one in the favela pretends to be a good guy," Hector said, with a humorous grunt. "Here, it's every man for himself."

After they finished, Bettina retrieved three paper-thin fiber jumpsuits from her pack. As she handed one to Jacob, the tone of her voice softened just a little.

"Personal protective equipment. PPE. We don't have any fancy bunkers in the favela."

"Thanks," Jacob responded grimly.

By now darkness had fallen and Jacob was exhausted. Hector and Bettina slipped quickly into their PPE, rolled their bags under their heads, and promptly fell asleep. Jacob tried to do the same. But every movement generated a new discomfort in his hips, his shoulders, his back. Small whorls of sand kicked up off the floor and whipped against him. He had hoped to keep his nose and mouth exposed enough to breathe, but the prickling dust made it impossible. Eventually, in spite of the heat and the wind and the fear and the utter sense of loss, he fell into a fitful slumber.

When he woke, the sun had barely shifted the thick air from black to brown. Jacob felt almost delirious with fatigue, but he struggled to pull himself up. Hector and Bettina were already packing their bags and talking quietly on the other side of the room. Hector noticed that he had awakened and came over with an energy bar in his hand.

"It tastes terrible, but it's got a lot of calories. It'll fill you up."

Jacob forced the disgusting food into his mouth and tried to swallow fast, without tasting. He didn't ask where they were going, or what the plan was. Dejection ran through his every vein, though he tried his best not to show it. Keeping his head down and his mouth shut, he followed along behind them, one foot in front of the other, turning over and over in his mind an endless stream of second guesses. Why had he let Kat talk him into this? The idea that he might be able to help the Emergence against the President and the PG – how was that even *potentially* a good idea? Bettina's hostility towards him no longer seemed so unjustified. Surely, he would feel the same in her place. What good would come of relying on Jacob to do anything for them? He was a soft, and – as he now realized, all too painfully – fairly spoiled City kid who'd had everything he ever needed given to him or done for him. Like the other boys he grew up with, Jacob could complain about school or about not getting the latest immersive game for the fancy holographic system he had received for Christmas last year. But compared to this? Compared to the life he saw around him here in the favela?

For the first time since he'd run from home, his thoughts turned to David. What was he up to? What did he think about Jacob's disappearance? He consoled himself marginally by imagining the two of them reunited, back at school, telling wild stories about what had happened. They would laugh and shake their heads and exaggerate everything and Jacob would feel heroic as his friend told him how amazing it was that he had survived it all. A phantom smile creased Jacob's lips as he contemplated David's good humor and the comforts of home.

They walked in silence throughout the day, keeping largely off the main roads. Jacob lagged badly behind. Hector did his best to encourage Jacob along and even hung back and waited for him when necessary, but Bettina never turned to check on him. Towards the end of the day, they arrived in a tightly packed village in Bloomington. Rundown storefronts lined one side of the central square. A bright portrait of Mickey Mouse was painted on the side of a dilapidated two-story building – a strange and incongruous sight. In the square itself, barefoot boys kicked a California Rules football made of plastic bags tied tight with twine. Jacob felt no urge to join them.

Bettina led them up a steep incline to a small cluster of shanties along the side of the road. Each was modest but clean, with hedges of bee brush forming garden walls around them, separating them from their neighbors. Bettina approached the house at the end of the row and rapped three times on the metal door. A tall man in his mid-twenties greeted them.

"Tina!" said the man with visible pleasure, exchanging a ritual handshake and pulling her close. He had a wide face, with close-cropped brown hair and a bent nose that looked like it had been broken a few times. His eyes were small and sharp, keenly taking in each of his three visitors. He exuded an easy confidence.

"Hector!" he bellowed with pleasure. "A nice surprise. How are ya, man?" He embraced Hector warmly. "What took you guys?"

"Hi, Leo. Just being extra careful," explained Bettina. Then, nodding in Jacob's direction, she added, "We had a few…complications."

"Ah, I see," said Leo, glancing over at Jacob, who shaded red at being the cause of their delay. "Well come in, come in."

Jacob followed Hector and Bettina into the house. The main room was illuminated by two solar flashlights that dangled from the ceiling, a parody of a chandelier. Over a wood stove in the corner a woman prepared dinner, a child tied securely to her back with a dirty towel. She was a petite woman, her hair kept off her face by a bandana. Two boys, who could only be twins, chased a terrified, squawking hen across the packed dirt floor behind her.

"Cut it out!" shouted the woman at the boys. "You're going to knock over the water. Get out!"

Fleeing her swatting hands, the boys ducked and raced past Jacob into the street.

"Tina!" said the woman upon seeing them. With a beleaguered smile, she wiped her hands on the towel as she approached.

"Hi, Lindy," Bettina said, giving her a hug. "We're just passing through. I hope we're not causing too much trouble showing up a day late."

"You're always welcome," insisted Lindy. "Hello, Hector. So good to see you. And…who do we have here?" she asked, looking kindly at Jacob.

"This is a new friend of ours," said Bettina quickly. "He just arrived in Nova Rio. We're taking him up to Cherry Hills for a little visit."

"Really?" asked Leo, interested. Jacob found it odd that Bettina had not told them his name, but it seemed to be understood that they should not ask.

"Can I get you some water?" asked Lindy with warm eyes.

"Yes, please," Jacob replied.

"Tea would be safest, I think," Hector suggested.

"Right. Tea it is. I've got a pot boiling on the stove. It'll just be a second."

While Lindy returned to the kitchen, Leo ushered them to the cozy seating area opposite. "I have what you came for, Tina. Just give me a second."

Hector and Jacob plunked down on the ragged couch. Bettina remained standing, positioning herself so she could still see the door they had entered. A moment later, Lindy brought over a pot of tea. Soon, Leo reemerged and handed Bettina a brown manila envelope that had been folded over and bound several times with rubber bands. Bettina tucked the envelope deep into her hummingbird bag without looking at its contents.

"It took us several tries to pick it up," said Leo. "Our guy kept calling off the drops. He was very, very cautious." Leo sat down and poured himself some tea. "It's getting harder to move around the City. There're rumors that Duke is up to something big."

"Yeah, I've been hearing that, too," Bettina replied.

"They're saying he's planning for all-out war."

"That's his dream," Bettina said. "To take the water at its source, up north. We've always presumed that's where it would start."

"Yeah, but now he might actually be trying to do it. I mean, the propaganda that's coming out now. It's nuts."

"As long as the UN is still involved we have some time," Bettina said.

"You sure about that?" Leo emphasized the words to express his obvious skepticism. "You and Renard are betting pretty big on that."

"Renard knows what he's doing, Leo," Bettina said, more aggressively. "You and your buddies need to back off."

"Hey," said Leo, holding up his hands defensively. "It's not me you gotta worry about. Or my *buddies*. I'm telling you this because I care about the Emergence, Tina. You know I'm a loyal soldier. But a lot of the young guys, they're getting restless. Renard's a legend. But he's old. They think maybe he's lost his nerve."

"Yeah," said Bettina belligerently, "well, these young guys don't know crap about crap. They're a bunch of impatient brats who think revolutions happen on the internet."

"Okay," Leo smiled, backing down. "You're the boss."

"Our plan will be worth the wait. You find a way to keep 'em quiet until we can get it rolling. A month or two at the most."

"I'll do what I can," Leo reassured.

Catching Jacob stifling a yawn, Leo laughed. "Come on, my young friend. I'll set you up in the boys' room. They can sleep in with us tonight, God help me."

The light blankets Leo gave him, though coarse and stiff, felt almost like silk to Jacob after his hellish night in the abandoned house. The small child's bed, with its worn mattress, cushioned his body like the softest of pillows. Every muscle melted. In all his life to this point, Jacob never slept harder than he did that night.

Kat

On the fifth day after Jacob's departure, Kat sat quietly at the foot of Agnes' chair. With careful precision, she threaded a needle through the bag that Agnes had given her, stitching tiny beads onto its side. That morning, Agnes had produced the bag, with the penciled outline of an owl sketched lightly on its rough surface. Next to her, the pile of multicolored beads glistened in the low light. As they worked, Kat heard the rambunctious joking of the *culebras* in the distance as they made their way up the hill. Uncertain, she glanced up at Agnes.

"It's okay," said the woman quietly. "They're nice boys. You just stay over here with me."

Bursting through the door, Pepe jolted the room to life

"Agnes! Where's..." he started as he entered. But he pulled up short when he saw Kat sitting out in the open room.

"*Gatterina, mi amiga!*" he cried exuberantly.

Agnes interrupted him immediately with a swift wag of her finger.

"Tch!" she said. "You leave her alone, you hear? She comes to you when she's ready. Go play. Leave us be."

Admonished, Pepe turned and whacked Beany, who had sidled up beside him. "You heard Agnes! Leave Gatterina alone!" Then he dragged Beany over to the table and the boys gathered round with their cups and dice.

Kat closed her eyes. A gentle breeze curled through the open window. She let the wash of air cross her face, enter her nostrils, fill her lungs. She could still taste the brief hint of rain from the spasm that had cooled the dust off earlier in the day. Keeping her eyes closed, she listened to the back and forth of the *culebras* as they recounted their adventures of the day.

"How much did you make today, Pepe?" asked Pinocchio.

"Twelve caldos. I did my trick rolling on broken glass in the street. When I came to the window of one car, the man, he got pretty scared. He offered me two dollars! 'American money!' he says, shoving it in my face. 'American money! Take it! Take it!' I know he thinks I'm a killer!"

"Maybe you scare him cuz you're so ugly," said Beany, sniggering. Pepe gave him a reproachful slap on the back of the head.

"You could be a businessman with all your American money," Pinocchio offered.

"Yeah, a banker," Pepe beamed. "Pepe's Favela Bank. Put your money in, never get it out!"

All the children laughed.

"I want to be rich," said Trashcan in a sullen monotone.

"You can't just *be* rich, Trashy. You gotta do something to *get* rich," Beany said.

"Then I could be a boss," Trashcan ventured. "A *gerente*. They're rich."

"You're too stupid for a boss," said Pepe.

"I want to get out of the slums," said Pinocchio quietly.

"No one gets out of the slums," said Pepe.

Kat opened her eyes again. Each of the boys conveyed a different aura, a distinct mix of arrogance and innocence, fear and openness. But it was Pepe who captivated her. Especially in Jacob's absence, she found herself drawn to him, charmed by his exuberance, warmed by his kindness. Most children at home avoided her, afraid of her strange behaviors. They opted to ignore her at best, torment her at worst. From the moment she met him, however, Pepe made her feel comfortable and welcome. Kat might be a child of misfortune, but from Pepe's perspective so were all the *culebras*. In his worldview, misfortune was not something to be regretted or held over someone else like a club, but rather to be accepted as a fact of life. Deformity, injury, loss – all were nothing more than cruel inevitabilities, the random chance of an unfeeling world. To him, Kat was not short or strange or weird or quiet or compulsive – she was just a girl. Her differences were to be accepted as another of life's mysteries, not to be solved or corrected but to be assumed into the manufactured family of the clan simply because Renard had said it should be so.

As the boys clamored and objected to each other's cheating ways, Pepe glanced furtively in her direction. Kat met his gaze and smiled. A huge grin spread across his face, the light of it filling the room.

First the Hopi tried to tame the desert, but the mesas finally won. Then came the first wave of American settlers – "homesteaders", they called them, thinking they had some god-given right to the land. But the great Dust Bowl of the 20th century drove them away. After that, science and technology let us beat back Mother Nature for almost another century. We built cities on sand, grew grass in the desert, and drank all the water. And all that time She waited. Mother Nature. Patient, scornful of our self-delusion, knowing that ultimately we would defeat ourselves, and that when we did She would be there to take the land back to herself.

What is it that DH Lawrence once wrote?

"Oh, America,

The sun sets in you.

Are you not the grave of our day?"

Kat

"Oh, Meatball, I still don't understand."

Kat held the guinea pig in her lap as they nestled in the tight space of the pantry. Knees pulled to her chest, she held Father's notebook in one hand; with the other she scratched Meatball gently under the chin with a single finger. He purred with pleasure.

"It's on the tip of my tongue. I feel it, but I can't say it."

The *culebras* had long since gone. Kat heard only Agnes' labored breathing in the main room. Occasionally, the old woman would cough heavily before settling back down into slumber. Kat curled further into her pile of blankets. The surface of the warm wall behind her had baked hard, cracks threading like veins in multiple directions. But the material also breathed with the changes in temperature, cooler in the heat of day, warmer as the night descended. Kat cherished the close feel of the room.

Toward the end of the notebook, Kat had transcribed the five different symbols. While she had no idea what they meant, she felt certain that they represented the code she had to break. She focused on the first one: 5R.

Maybe there are five different things that start with "R", she thought. *Red, ruby, rose...*

But where would that lead her? Not to anything she could quickly ascertain – and she couldn't find a way to make those words connect with the other clues. She tried another tack, playing numerically with the symbol, since often Father used numbers in his codes. "R" is the eighteenth letter of the alphabet, so she tried adding five to it. Then she tried multiplying it by five. She wrote those numbers down, then turned her attention to the other images. The fern Father had drawn had seven tips, so perhaps the number seven came into play. Instinctively, she knew that her attempts were not quite right, and fatigue gradually took hold of her. Over her shoulder, the dim solar flashlight began to falter, as if signaling that the time had come to give up for the day.

"This is the hardest one he's ever given us, Meatball," she said.

But the little guinea pig was already fast asleep.

Jacob

Two days after leaving Leo's, Jacob, Bettina and Hector arrived in a remote section of the favela at the edge of the San Bernardino Forest. From this point, they made the journey on foot, walking along a dilapidated road that ran from the last significant slum in Yucaipa to the outlying squatter villages dotting Potato Canyon. Occasionally an army helicopter, guns hanging from its underbelly, swept overhead on patrol and Hector would pull Jacob off the road until the machine had flown past. Children jogged beside them as they left Yucaipa, begging for food, trying to sell them filthy water in used plastic bottles until Bettina successfully shooed them away.

After completing a long stretch of lonely road, alongside which the turf had baked to concrete and dust devils bounced on the low running swirls of wind, they arrived at a remote shantytown called Cherry Hills. Jacob had the sensation of walking into a forgotten, old-world village on the American frontier. With its abandoned shops and lethargic men sitting in doorways, skinny dogs sleeping listlessly at their feet, Cherry Hills had neither the vibrant energy of Nova Rio nor its implicit threat of violence. It just felt poor and hopeless.

They passed along the main thoroughfare, halting in front of an old church. A neat spire rose in front, extending at its zenith into a majestic cross. But the exterior walls had been repaired many times over with makeshift sheets of plywood and metal. Above the door, Jacob could barely discern the faded outline of letters that had long since fallen away: *St. Anselm's Catholic Church.* Scarred and battered, the church nevertheless retained a sense of obdurate pride, refusing to submit entirely to the wasteland surrounding it.

Bettina climbed the steps and punched in numbers on the electronic keypad. They pushed into the dark entryway.

"Julius will be excited to see you," she said to Hector, grabbing his hand and pulling him into the church.

As they walked down the central aisle, Jacob stared up at the window wells that lined the walls high above their heads. The glass from virtually every window had broken long ago; now plywood and plastic sheeting guarded against animals and dust. Even still, evidence of the recent storm lay in a thick crust atop the pews. Down one of the transepts, Jacob noticed a single window, its panes of stained glass miraculously still in place. A soft flux of kaleidoscopic light filtered gently through it, meager rays of heavenly color hinting at the awe that must have once showered the congregation. For a moment, Jacob imagined every window streaming forth with equal brilliance under the powerful Californian sun, the dance of color enveloping the singing masses, an honest, fervent celebration of life, joy and resurrection. But now this solitary window did little more than reinforce the profoundest sense of loss.

Bettina led them up a few steps past the altar to the sacristy door. From inside, they could hear a creaky voice, colored by the hint of an Irish accent.

"Is that you, Bet?" the man asked in response to Bettina's knock.

"We're back, Jules," replied Bettina.

"Well come in. I'm just sitting here alone with all me pals."

At one end of the room stood a desk piled high with papers. In the corner of the room an old brown leather chair, its skin pale from wear, was flanked on either side by tables, which labored under precariously balanced stacks of books. A diminutive old man stepped spryly from behind the desk.

"Bettina!" he cried. "And Hector, my boy!"

The man had a trim gray beard, a thin nose, and a rounded belly disproportionate to his narrow shoulders. A wild shock of white hair flew in every direction. Doughy bags of flesh puffed out from beneath his watery eyes.

"How'd you get on?" the old man asked, patting the much taller Hector.

"No problems," said Hector.

"Renard still making trouble?" They all laughed knowingly. Julius turned his attention to Jacob. "So, this is the boy?"

Bettina snorted. "I've got to go take care of a few things in the batcave. Jules, you know I love Renard, but honestly…"

"Ok, right!" piped Julius after Bettina had gone. "Seems like there's only one thing to do. Tea!" With that, he picked up a small bell from his desk, jingling it a few times. A handsome, middle-aged woman already stood, waiting patiently in a service doorway adjacent to Julius' desk.

"Marta!" Julius called, before realizing that she had already appeared. "Oh, you're already there. We have a guest. You know I can't even entertain the idea of conversation without a pot of tea."

"You didn't think I would leave you without tea, did you?" asked the woman indulgently. A few moments later, Marta returned to place a tray of tea and biscuits on the low coffee table in the center of the room.

"Ah, Marta, you're a pet," said Julius to the woman, taking a seat in his high-backed leather chair as she passed him his cup of tea. "Nothing like a good cuppa."

As Marta retired discreetly to the kitchen, Hector and Jacob took a seat on the couch opposite Julius.

"Marta's biscuits," said Julius, crumbs tumbling from his lips as he spoke. He playfully patted his belly. "They'll be the end of me!"

They drank their tea in silence and Hector waited respectfully for the older man to pick up the conversation.

"What's the plan, then?" asked ulius.

"To take him into the forest, up the Dragon's Head," Hector said.

"You or Bettina?"

"We haven't discussed that yet."

"It'll have to be her," said Julius decisively. "She won't want to do it, but we don't have much time and she's the best. No offense meant, of course."

"I don't know if that's such a great idea…" Hector hesitated.

"Oh, she'll get over it," said Julius knowingly.

"Well, anyway, we thought he should spend a few weeks in the mountains. We can train him in the lab after that," said Hector.

"Alright," concurred Julius. "Renard wants to have him in place in the City as soon as possible, but you can't rush these things. I'll let him know what we've discussed. Do you mind setting up my video link? It's been very cranky lately."

"Of course," Hector said.

Julius turned to Jacob, who squirmed uncomfortably in his seat. "Do you understand what you're fighting for, son?"

"Against Malcolm Duke?"

"I didn't ask who you're fighting *against*. I asked what you're fighting *for*."

Jacob thought for a long moment, then said with more conviction, "My mother and father."

"Ah. I see."

“I want to help Hector and Renard, too” Jacob added. “I think that’s what my parents would want.”

“You’re going to need more than a big heart. There’re only a few of us left, you know. Only a few who remember the terror of those early years. Malcolm Duke and his man, Tracker. They almost destroyed us.”

Julius put down his teacup and gazed hard at Jacob, taking stock of him.

“I don’t know the first thing about you, my boy. And lucky for you I’ve learned that first impressions don’t tell a person much. But I’ve been with Renard for over thirty years. He’s the cagiest fighter I’ve ever known. We don’t always agree, me and him. But there’s one thing I’m certain of. If he thinks you can do it, you can do it.”

David

In the rear of the transport bus sat the boys with bravado. Their fathers or brothers or uncles had fought at the Battle of Reno, or had taken part in the Oregon Border Wars, or had been part of the Phoenix militia that had rebuilt southern California during the Restoration. They laughed and joked and relished the privilege of inherited glory.

David sat towards the front. Next to him, an overweight boy, nursing a swollen lip from the bullying he had suffered before they boarded, pretended to cough as he stifled tears. David pitied him, wondering how on earth he had ever been admitted to the PG boot camp in the first place. As shameful as it felt to admit, he preferred not to be associated with the boy, lest the bullies transfer their attention to him.

So instead of making conversation or trying to cheer the boy up, David stared out the window as they drove through the desert scrub toward Fort Irwin. He listened to the braggarts behind him boast in overly loud voices about their experiences at the Phoenix Summer Institutes – the youth military camps they had attended for several years in order to prepare for their eventual enrollment in the Praetorian Guard. He recalled the confidence he'd felt upon showing Jacob that image of a knife. An ironic smile fleetingly pursed his lips. His mind replayed Jacob's skeptical words about the war and his insistence that David stay in school. A pit of doubt and insecurity opened wide in his stomach. What did he think he was doing trying to become a PG Youth?

The bus passed through the entrance to the gigantic military base at Fort Irwin. Since Defederation, it had become a sprawling martial city in the desert. Army jeeps whizzed past them in every direction. In the distance, David could make out the airstrip where a steady stream of cargo planes, fighter jets and helicopters flew in and out.

"Hey, how many kids are on this bus?" shouted one of the boys in the back, clearly aiming to be heard by the less confident boys in the front.

"Fifty!" answered his seatmate.

"How many you think'll make it through basic?" asked the first boy.

"Maybe twenty. If they're lucky," said the other.

"I heard that last time the training was so tough that almost the entire group got sent home."

"Yeah," his partner laughed. "I heard they were puking their guts out for two weeks straight."

David closed his eyes and tried to tune them out. No matter how much he rationalized to himself that they must be exaggerating, their words still had their intended effect: He wanted to go home.

The bus jolted to a stop. All the boys disembarked in front of the barracks. A weary soldier with a clipboard checked their names off a list and lethargically directed them toward a hanger across the courtyard. The recruits carried nothing with them, only the shirts on their backs.

David was surprised to see a group of boys already gathered inside. Some sat on folding chairs, others lounged on the floor along the wall. It was clear many had been there for hours.

"If you're coming off the buses, you need to get in the line on the left to pick up your gear!" shouted a young MP. David found himself standing next to a boy who looked just as frightened has he did.

"Hey," David tried.

"Hey," replied the boy.

"I just got here."

"Me, too."

"Where're you from?"

"San Diego."

"Really? I didn't know people came here from so far," David said.

"Yeah, lots of kids come from San Diego. Some from the Central Valley. Most are from LA, though."

"I'm David."

"Rafe."

For the next several hours the boys endured the tedium of waiting – in groups, in lines, sitting on the floor, napping against the wall. When he finally made it to the front of the line, David was sized for boots, pants and shirts, all of which he stuffed into the green canvas bag he had been allotted. Unexpectedly, and most humiliatingly, they passed through the health clinic, where the on-duty sergeant screamed at all the recruits to strip naked for their inspection. Bigger boys whooped it up, making fun of the younger boys.

Later, skin itching under his uniform in the heat, David followed his unit to the barracks. The aggressive boys in the group moved quickly to claim the beds they wanted. David ended up in a corner on a bottom bunk. The heavy boy who had sat next to him on the bus came in last. He tentatively made his way down the line of beds.

"Keep it moving, Fatty," one boy shouted. Others laughed.

When the bullied boy finally arrived at David's bunk, David's sense of compassion finally overrode his pride. Nodding his tacit approval, David watched as his expression transformed from terror to gratitude. In vain, he attempted to pull his heft onto the top bunk.

"Here, wait," said David. "I'd rather have the top. You take this one."

The boy muttered an embarrassed "thank you" and David swung himself onto the top bed. Stuffing his canvas bag under his head, David lay down and faced the wall, trying his best to block out the quiet sobs from the bunk below.

2

They lined up in rows of ten in the courtyard – legs apart, hands behind their backs, caps on heads – and stared straight ahead, sweat soaking into their new uniforms as they waited motionless for the sergeant to arrive. For more than two hours, they had been standing in place. And it was only 7:00 a.m. They had been given nothing to eat, nothing to drink. It took all of David's concentration to keep from fainting in the heat. When the sergeant appeared at last, he stopped to chat with the other officers, in no hurry to relieve the boys from their suffering. Turning his attention to them at last, he strolled leisurely up and down the rows of shaking recruits, taking in their sorry, reddened faces.

"You're all *pathetic*. You think you miss your mommies now? You'll be *begging* for them to pick you up by the time I'm done with you. Does anyone think they're good enough for the Youth Guard? You?!" he shouted at David's unfortunate bunkmate, placing his face just inches from the boy's. In a low, derisive tone, he said, "You think you can even make it two days, son? Do you?"

"*Yes sir*," the boy whimpered.

"I can't hear you!" shouted the sergeant.

"YESSIR!" shouted the boy manically.

"Drop and give me 20," sneered the sergeant.

As the blubbering boy strained to complete even a few pushups, the sergeant turned his attention to the rest of the group, many of whom stifled laughter.

"You think it's funny? To the stacks!" he commanded. "Nothing to eat for anyone until they're done."

The cadets trudged to a cordoned-off section of tarmac littered with tires. As they had done yesterday, and the day before that, they stacked the tires into six towers of equal height. It was grueling work, made all the more so given the knowledge that tomorrow the tires would be scattered on the ground again. When they finished, they were given ten minutes to wolf down the most disgusting gruel David had ever eaten. Then back outside, they did push-ups and sit-ups until their arms shook and their stomachs ached. Several boys threw up breakfast; others passed out and were carried away by the medical staff. Somehow, in spite of – or perhaps because of – his fear of failure, David managed to survive the day, crawling into bed in a virtually catatonic state. Every part of his body hurt.

The bunk below him remained empty.

His friend Rafe had said something to him earlier in the day over lunch, and his words replayed now through David's head.

"It's all a test," Rafe said. "They don't care who's the strongest or the fastest. They want to see who's the toughest. Cuz in the battle all you gotta do is survive."

Lying now in his bed, David thought of his mother, alone in their house, needing him to succeed. As he drifted down past the pain, past the pity for his unfortunate bunkmate, who he knew he would never see again, and into the welcome forgetfulness of sleep, he vowed that he would work harder at this than at anything he had ever done.

Tracker

From the rocky overhang, Tracker took in every detail of the area outside the cave: the position of the trees, the slope of the hillside, the size and shape of the rocks. No drone technology could detect such subtleties; only human observation could.

He's good, Tracker thought. *Just not good enough.*

After two days of meticulous work, Tracker picked up the trail of the American spy in a remote area of the San Gabriel Forest. At the base of the hill, he noticed a thread of fabric caught on the branches of a redberry shrub. Certain of his discovery, he moved swiftly up the slope, feeling his way along the path the man had taken, registering the slightest disturbances in the landscape. As soon as he arrived at the cave, just before dusk, he could smell the man's presence: an unmistakable aroma of stress.

The entrance was hidden behind a boulder. A logical choice. It would take only minimal effort to conceal it further. Tracker had noticed a small mountain stream on his way up, which meant that the man would be able to rest here for days – weeks if necessary – to recover his strength. A reasonable plan – to lay low until the scrutiny passed, to scavenge for food only at night, to sneak over the mountain to be picked up by U.S. special forces. All very reasonable. Except for one small detail. The American didn't know about Tracker.

Kat

On the plate in front of her were several thumbnail-sized balls of homemade nut butter covered with seeds. Quito stood on the back of the chair next to her, bobbing up and down in anticipation. Kat sorted a cluster of pebbles into different quantities. "How many?" she asked the bird.

Excitedly, Quito responded, "Five!"

"Good boy," praised Kat, rubbing his nose. She had been working with Quito for several days now, teaching him new words and concepts, amazed at the speed of his intelligence. Agnes observed the bond that seemed to be forming between bird and girl with pleasure.

The soft clip of flip-flops reached Kat's ears. She turned in anticipation.

"*Hola, amigas*," Pepe announced, entering the shanty with bravado. Seeing Kat with Quito, he approached. "Watcha doing?"

Kat did not respond. She put a treat between her teeth to give the bird. The grey parrot carefully took it in his beak.

"Good boy!" he congratulated himself.

"Yes," Kat agreed.

Pepe stepped closer, trying to command her attention. "Why do you talk to that dumb bird?"

"Gray parrots are highly intelligent," Kat said defensively. Clicking her tongue to get Quito's attention, Kat made an abrupt motion with her hand, pointing toward the corner of the room. "Get your toy," she commanded.

"*Treat, please. Pretty pleeeease*," pleaded the bird in his sweet voice.

"Get your toy," repeated Kat. "Then a treat."

With a quick movement, the parrot fluttered over to the corner of the shanty. From the floor, he retrieved a small cloth mouse that Kat had sewn for him. Clutching it in his right claw, he flew back to the table.

Kat gave him another handful of seeds.

"It's like a dog," said Pepe, mildly disgusted. "Anyway, you have to stop playing with Quito, *Gatterina.* Agnes said you have to go into the alleys, get used to the favela. I came to take you out. That's my job."

Kat turned toward Pepe but did not meet his eyes. Instead, she focused on his cheap flip-flops. The blue rubber had worn thin, drained of color. Kat could see the outline of his foot impressed into the sole of the sandal, darkly stained and smooth.

"It's okay," Pepe tried to reassure her. "We'll go see my friend, Buster. You'll like him. He has a teashop in Alexandria Square. Not far."

Kat held out her arm, allowing Quito to scamper up and settle on her shoulder, his red tail feathers fanning out to help him maintain his balance as he moved. She walked him over to his perch and shrugged her shoulder so that he could scamper up onto the bar.

"*Poor Quito*," whined the bird.

Then, as if Pepe had mentioned nothing about leaving the shanty, Kat walked to her embroidery chair, which she had set up next to Agnes. But the work she had left on the seat was gone. Agnes held it securely in her lap and appeared to have no intention of relinquishing it.

"Later," said Agnes sternly to Kat. "Now you go with Pepe. Outside."

Kat felt the pressure begin to rise around her ears and through her chest. A loud humming noise filled her head. Her breath came shallow and fast. She wandered to the corner of the room in a slight daze. Squatting on the floor, she clasped her arms around her legs, covered her ears, and rocked gently to and fro. Although Kat had grown increasingly comfortable in her new surroundings over the last week, she remained confined to Agnes' shanty. The thought of venturing beyond the safety of Hilltop into the chaos of the alleys crashed around her shoulders like a waterfall, drowning out any ability to think. Unsettled, Pepe took a step back, staring wide-eyed at Agnes in an appeal for help.

Agnes rose from her seat and dropped to the floor next to Kat. Picking up the cadence of Kat's rocking, she moved in synchronicity, such that they appeared to be performing a ritual dance. Agnes raised her hands into the air, turned her face toward the ceiling, and in a quiet voice began to chant rhythmically in time with their movement.

Gradually Kat slowed her rocking. Agnes slowed with her, always in time with the girl, softening but continuing her recitation, until Kat had stilled completely. With Kat now calm, Agnes touched her firmly, moving her hands steadily around Kat's face and shoulders. Then she clasped Kat's head and pulled her forward so that their foreheads and the bridges of their noses touched while she continued to speak rapidly to her in a whisper.

"You remember the first day?" Agnes asked softly "You slept a long time."

"I was scared."

"I could not see you there. I come in and I ask, 'Where is the girl?' And you are so quiet, so still, that I don't even see you. You remember?"

"I withdraw," Kat explained. "Go inside myself. When I get nervous or scared or…too much is happening. I kind of…shut down."

Agnes took in every word. She began to mumble to herself, as if having a debate with an invisible alter ego.

"I can teach you," she said at last.

"Teach me?"

"Teach you to do this… this…"

"Withdrawing?"

"Withdrawing, yes. I can teach you how. Without sleeping. In the streets. Then you can go outside. Any time. Be there – but not there."

"I don't…" Kat hesitated. Even the thought of going out in the streets alone started to initiate another wave of panic.

"Trust me?" Agnes held out her hand. Kat stared at her, and the old woman's eyes danced with surprise. Kat took her hand. The warmth of the smooth, polished skin radiated through her.

"Yes," Kat affirmed.

2

Several days later, Pepe led Kat into Alexandria Square. In front of the crumbling three-story buildings that lined the square stood homemade storefronts cobbled together with wood and tin. In the center of the plaza, the empty basin of a fountain peeled in the heat. Men lingered outside the teashops, squatting in small groups; some smoked hand-rolled cigarettes while others chewed *khat*, periodically spitting onto the street. A group of women sat on blankets near the fountain and displayed homemade jewelry and bags they hoped to sell.

Pepe strode diagonally across the plaza toward one of the several teashops on the other side. The *culebras* sat at one of the plastic tables in the meager shade provided by the shop's stained and tattered awning. Recessed in the shadows, a tall dark-skinned man with a perfectly rounded belly hummed to himself as he diligently dried ceramic cups with a filthy rag. Meat and onions sizzled on the grill behind him next to a tub of boiling oil that held a straining basket of fried dough. Two vats of tea steamed over the low-burning embers of a wood fire.

"Hey, Buster!" Pepe shouted as they approached.

The man's face was round and expressive under his shining pate. His huge smile revealed a large gap between two buck teeth. The front of his gray t-shirt, stained with sweat and grease, had been pried loose from his belt by his overhanging midsection, revealing a sliver of brown, stretched skin beneath.

"Well now, Mister Pepe!" replied Buster with a funny, high-pitched laugh. "What kind of trouble you bringin' with you today?"

"This is my friend, *Gatterina*," said Pepe, proudly showing Kat off. She stood shyly, her head bowed.

"She's new in Nova Rio… an *orfano*, like us. She, uh," Pepe paused mid-sentence, realizing he should not be saying too much about Kat. "She got lost in the last storm. Doesn't talk too much."

"Well now, that's okay," laughed Buster giving Kat a knowing wink as she glanced up cautiously. "Because ol' Pepe here, he does enough talkin' for everybody!"

"Hey!" protested Pepe as Buster burst into gales of high-pitched laughter at his own joke. The *culebras* joined in until Pepe threatened to smack them. Kat couldn't help but smile.

"Now, lemme get you both somethin' to drink," said Buster.

"Pino, do you have money?" asked Pepe as he and Kat pulled two chairs over to the table. Pinocchio pulled a few coins from his pocket.

"That's all I got," he said.

"I thought I sent you down to wash car windows on the Boulevard today."

"You did! I made ten caldos. But then some guys in Bear Clan made me pay them. *Taxes*, they said. They took seven caldos! Seven!" Pinocchio spit on the ground in disgust.

"Seein' as *Gatterina's* new 'round here," said Buster, "we'll give her the first-time special. Favela tea with a slice of Buster's world-famous coconut bread."

"Thanks, Buster!" beamed Pepe. To Kat he added in a serious tone, "His coconut bread is *loco bueno*."

Behind the counter, Buster cut two thick slices of bread and placed them in a greasy pan, which he held briefly over the fire. Once he had lightly grilled each side, he flipped them onto a plate, coated each with a thin scraping of soy butter, and served them alongside two steaming mugs of sweet milk tea.

"Thank you," said Kat softly.

She sank her teeth into the doughy bread, feeling flakes of coconut catch between her teeth. Near her, the *culebras* bantered and joked; Buster filled the shop with jovial laughter. Out in the square, the bustle of people in the heat and dust and smoke took on an abstract beauty she could never have perceived even a week ago. A strange feeling of contentment settled down through her bones.

"You okay?" Pepe whispered to her while the others carried on.

"Yes," she replied quietly. "And…"

"And?"

"Thank you."

"Thank *me*? For what?"

"For bringing me here."

"I told you Buster's the best," he beamed.

"*You're* the best, Pepe," she said, as her friend turned a deep shade of red.

Jacob

They moved briskly through the woods, pacing themselves at a steady run. Jacob's t-shirt was stained with sweat. On his back, he carried a special pack that hugged his body, double-strapped across his chest. Scratches covered his arms, legs and face; the crust of a black scab stretched from just below his right kneecap to the top of his shin.

Jacob thought only of each step, scanning the terrain constantly for where to place his feet, while keeping Bettina in sight. Just two weeks earlier Jacob could hardly breathe during these runs. Bettina, already resentful at having drawn this assignment, pushed him the harder for it. Their exchanges amounted largely to orders from her, or the motivational derision he needed to keep putting one foot in front of the other.

After the first painful days of waking up aching and exhausted, Jacob's fitness rapidly improved. As he began to keep pace with the tireless Bettina, Jacob sensed a thaw in her attitude. His dual desires – to prove her wrong and to demonstrate his strength – pushed him in equal measure. Each day they rose before dawn. After a threadbare breakfast of herbal tea and dry biscuits, they would depart from their dugout base camp and set out for various parts of the forest. Sometimes Bettina would lead Jacob on long runs to build his endurance, sometimes on shorter runs to build speed, and sometimes on no runs at all to practice stillness for hours on end. Bettina exhorted Jacob through an endless series of push-ups, sit-ups, and pull-ups. He performed squats with a heavy rock in each hand, or held the same rocks out at arm's length for increasingly longer periods of time. He climbed trees with his feet tied together, so that he was forced to rely almost entirely on the strength of his arms and shoulders to pull his weight upward through the branches. He carried heavy loads up and down steep inclines – up and back, up and back – until his legs shook with exertion. But he never gave up, and he never said no.

Physical training comprised only part of what Jacob learned in the forest. Bettina taught him how to camouflage himself by spitting into a mixture of dirt and crushed dry leaves, creating a brown paste that he could rub on his face, arms and legs to render himself practically invisible as he lay in the sandy turf. In the evenings, by the burnt orange hue of the setting sun, Jacob studied a botany pamphlet they had brought from Julius' library. Using the bark of a birch tree, Bettina showed him how to create a grass mesh water filter by shaping the bark into a cone and piling sand and gravel atop the grass, alternating fine and coarse layers until the water ran through clear and sweet. They spent countless hours building a figure-four trap to catch small mammals – a delicate mechanism of sticks that held up a heavy, leaning stone. Upon the slightest touch, the trigger that held the bait would release the stone, causing it to fall upon the unsuspecting animal. Jacob's hands were sore, his knuckles scraped and bruised from constantly setting and resetting the stone until it balanced perfectly. It would be a long time before he forgot the mixed feeling of exultation and disgust when they returned to the trap one evening to find a young yellow-bellied marmot crushed beneath the heavy rock.

Although he still had no idea what kind of assignment lay in store for him, Bettina's urgency fed his own competitive desire. Over those first two weeks in the woods, silence dominated their interactions, their conversations consisting essentially of instruction and response. But her hostility had started to diminish. From time to time, Jacob perceived a shift in her voice, a slight hint of encouragement, an appreciative if fleeting smile. Once, he caught her staring at him in the dark.

2

Bettina brought them to a stop. Jacob's chest heaved. A stomach cramp just above his left hip split him in half. Standing upright, he tried his best not to let the discomfort show.

"You gonna make it?" Bettina asked.

"Definitely," he replied with restrained cheerfulness.

Daylight had begun to wane and they had only an hour of visibility left. At least fifteen miles from their base camp, and in an unfamiliar section of the forest, they would not make it home tonight.

"I'll look for the main beam, you collect the sticks," Bettina instructed.

When Jacob returned, his arms laden with branches and twigs, Bettina had already positioned a fallen sapling into the Y branch of a black cottonwood four feet off the ground. Together they layered the sticks against the main beam, covering it with leaves and debris to create a lean-to just wide and tall enough for one of them to lie down out of sight. The shelter built, Bettina prepared the meat from two ground squirrels they had snared earlier that day. She skinned the animals with amazing dexterity, cutting the flesh into thin strips, separating the bones and sinews to save for fishing hooks and thread. In the meantime, Jacob gathered flat stones and kindling for a fire. He dug a small pit in the earth and carefully laid some of the stones in the base of the depression. Others he placed in a ring around the pit to contain the fire and guard against its spread, which would be deadly in the arid heat. Taking the flint that Bettina had given him, he lit the tinder with a few quick strokes. By the time Bettina finished butchering the squirrels, the fire had heated the stones to a pulsing glow. With great care, they smothered the flames, watching always to ensure that no embers floated away on the breeze, careful to keep the smoke low to avoid detection. They placed the thin strips onto the hot stones and listened eagerly to the hiss of cooking meat.

While they waited for the meat to brown, Bettina took a selection of various plants they had collected from her bag and spread them out in front of the fire pit.

"Okay," she said. "What are these?"

"Snow plant. Mountain sorrel. Cow parsnip. Phlox. Sneezeweed – I like that one."

Bettina did not smile. "Which one do you eat if you have a choice?"

"The sorrel. It has a lot of vitamin C. But you can only eat what's above ground."

"What about the cow parsnip? What do you do with that?"

"If I eat it, I have to make sure to peel off the outer stem. I can use it to treat sores and bruises, or I can make a lotion out of it to keep away the mosquitoes."

Jacob thought he detected a fleeting glint of approval in her eyes. The quick surge of happiness he felt discomfited him. He was grateful when she quickly suggested that they prepare for dinner.

Jacob fetched the canteen full of water he had collected from a barely trickling stream, and filtered out the mud and debris before boiling it for ten minutes in preparation for their precious cup of coffee. Bettina roasted some berries and nuts. While they cooked, she stabbed a string of meat straight from the rocks with a knife and handed it to Jacob. The meat was tough and leathery, hot on his tongue, and finer than any filet. When they finished the meat, they ate the berries for dessert. Savoring the final pleasure of bitter coffee from tin mugs, they listened to the pop and crackle of the dry wood. Thin smoke from the fire whisked like cream into the darkness.

"Can I ask you something?" Jacob said, keeping his eyes on the embers. Bettina arched an eyebrow. "Are you ever going to tell me why we're up here? I mean, I thought Renard wanted me to be a spy in the City."

Bettina flicked the coals with a stick. Then she said simply, "The forest is the best teacher."

As she spoke, she looked up at him, squinting her eyes in an expression that suggested both close examination and detached curiosity. Like he wasn't there. Like he was nothing more than a stone on the trail. Embarrassed by the intense scrutiny, he looked away. For a long while they sat in silence, playing with the coals, absorbing the night sounds: an owl hooting in the distance, the leaves whispering in the breeze. Jacob straightened up to indicate he was ready to sleep. Before he could stand, Bettina spoke.

"I was ten when Renard found me. I'd prob'ly be dead if he didn't. I'd been on the streets my whole life, just trying to survive…"

Jacob froze, head down, afraid that any further movement that might stop her from talking. He dared not look at her.

"Renard's like a father to me. More. He was the one who first brought me up here. I was wild. No one could make me do anything. We spent I don't know how many weeks in these woods together. Like he had nothing else to do, except just be here with me." She laughed to herself, lost in the memory. "He taught me to see things. In the favela, suffering was just the way it was. Hopelessness was everywhere, in everything, like air. It's so easy to give up, you know? Most people do. I kind of did. Then I came up here. Up here, you see something totally different. You see the world. The actual world. Trees. Animals. The air is so different in your lungs. And you realize that things don't have to be the way they are down there. You can imagine that it used to be that way, a long time ago, even in Los Angeles. That's what Renard was trying to show me. That the world of people can change. We make it the way it is. So we can make it different. He taught me that some things are actually worth fighting for, even when it seems hopeless. Especially when it seems hopeless."

The curtain had been drawn back, and he was amazed. He tried to imagine her at eight or nine years old, wandering the favela alleys, alone, fighting every day to survive. Until now, he had only seen Bettina the warrior, a partial view, a fragment of the whole person. He took a chance.

"Those scars," he said, nodding at her arm.

"These?" She fingered the puckered skin that ran from elbow to wrist on her right forearm. Then she emitted a quick, ironic grunt. "Yeah, I almost died with that one. Blood everywhere. It was pretty gross. Put my fist through a window during a fight." She looked at Jacob unflinchingly. "Let's just say the guy didn't bother me after that."

Jacob shook his head with awe and respect. "And now you're Renard's number two."

"Yeah. And everyone ain't so happy about that."

"Like Leo?" ventured Jacob.

"Yeah, like Leo. Renard holds everything together because we all revere him. He's a legend. But he's not getting any younger, and he knows it. Julius is barely involved anymore. He backed out after Tracker hunted them all down."

"Julius and Hector both mentioned Tracker. Who is he?"

"Hard to describe him. An assassin? A special agent? He finds people in…quiet ways. I don't know the whole story, but I know he goes way back with Renard and Agnes. Renard doesn't talk very much about the past, but I've picked up a few details along the way. Tracker definitely wants to kill Renard. We're always on the lookout for him. Luckily, he's been distracted by other things the last few years."

She shook her head as if to rid her mind's eye of an unpleasant vision.

"Anyway, Leo and the young guys in the Emergence all want bolder action – like back in the beginning, when Renard was young. They've heard all the stories of those early days. Guerilla warfare. Sounds very romantic to them. Typical guys. They don't understand that times are different. My generation isn't as unified as Renard's. We don't agree on the best way forward. That's why my plan has to work. It's probably our last chance to bring Duke down before the Emergence falls apart."

"Your plan? The one I'm supposed to help with." She squinted at him again, but he persisted. "I know you don't agree with Renard about me."

Even as he spoke, he could feel the stage lights dimming and the curtain drawing closed. In a flat tone, she said, "It doesn't matter what I think."

Later, lying alone beneath the lean-to, Jacob found himself unable to stop thinking about her. Straining his eyes, he watched her set up her bedroll further down the hill, trying to imagine what she was thinking, how she was feeling. Did she share his excitement at their most intimate conversation? Or did she regret it? Or was she not thinking about it at all? Having seen a fuller picture of her, he tortured himself with the possibilities, greedy for more.

You're an idiot, he said to himself, rolling over aggressively and fixating on a pile of rocks by his head. It took him a long time to fall asleep.

The Notebook

It began with frogs. In the late 20th century, scientists started to notice that frogs were mutating and dying out, but they didn't understand why. Then they discovered the chytrid fungus, older even than the earliest amphibians – 600 million years old – but co-existent until the present day. A particular genus of this fungus evolved – *Batrachochytrium dendrobatidis* –the first of that fungus ever known to attack vertebrates. It kills frogs within 3 weeks.

How did a fungus that had been innocuous for hundreds of millions of years suddenly spread to vertebrates? Humans transported it, that's how. In our cars, our boats, our planes; on our clothes, in our pet shops, in our polluted water. It turns out that we were the perfect delivery mechanism.

The frogs are not alone. Species all over the world are disappearing at rapid and alarming rates. A "sixth wave" of extinction, as catastrophic as the great meteorite that plunged into the Mexican peninsula more than 40 million years ago. Now, for the first time in the four-billion-year history of the earth, a planetary extermination is being caused by a single living species.

We are the sixth wave.

Tracker

Slouched in a metal chair, hands bound with plastic straps, the American looked utterly defeated. Dirt stained his shirt, his pants, his face. His head sagged forward. Blood flowed from his nose and upper lip.

Tracker leaned against the doorframe. In front of him, Erik Duke paced back and forth, a hungry leopard sizing up his prey. Duke's hair was cut to his scalp in military fashion. Short and stocky, his blunt features were dominated centrally by his eyes – one pale blue, the other green, both penetrating in their sharp intensity.

"So…" Duke intoned. "A spy. And after all I did for you…"

Duke's voice implied both vile hatred and grudging respect for the man who had betrayed his trust. For it was Duke who had advocated putting this man in the cabinet after a distinguished military career; it was he who had brushed aside Tracker's concerns about the man's character. Now the thing he hated most had happened: his judgment had been proven wrong. In the eyes of his father, and publicly before the cabinet, he had been made to look a fool. Duke leaned in, put both hands on the arms of the American's chair and spoke with slow precision.

"You're *pathetic*."

Tracker slipped from the shadows. "Are you working with Renard?"

The General turned venomously on Tracker. Duke was not accustomed to being interrupted, and Tracker could smell the resentment on his breath.

"Go back to your corner," hissed General Duke. "You did your job. Now let me do mine."

As the two adversaries resolutely stared each other down, the American raised his head, mumbling incoherently.

"Shut up!" raged Duke, striking the man. The prisoner coughed wildly, spitting blood. "Now tell me what I want to know! Who are you working with?"

"Rrr…" the broken diplomat stuttered.

"What?" asked Duke, crouching down and leaning in close.

The American surged quickly and unexpectedly forward, ferociously clenching the General's ear between his teeth. Caught off guard, Duke had no time to react. He screamed out in pain. Tracker had guessed the spy's intention and with one swift gesture smashed the man at the base of his skull, knocking him instantly unconscious. Duke rose, face flushed. Blood poured between the fingers he held to the side of his head. When he removed them, Tracker could see that the bottom part of his earlobe was gone. With frightening calm, Duke stared at the unconscious traitor slumped in the chair. Methodically, unhurriedly, he slapped the spy several times until he woke up. Placing his shredded ear directly in the man's sight, he said, "You belong with those filthy slum terrorists. Dogs, all of you. Nothing but scavenging dogs with dull teeth."

Then he stood up straight and removed the gun from his holster.

"No!" shouted Tracker.

One, two, three shots echoed off the walls.

David

After weeks of training, David felt exhausted but exhilarated. In the early stages of boot camp, he routinely finished at the back of the pack. But he kept Rafe's advice in mind and focused simply on making sure he always finished, that he never gave up. Over time, he noticed that the sergeants began to encourage him more, that they no longer berated him for being last but rather supported him for being tough enough to fight through his own pain. They shouted and cajoled and intimidated him into believing that he possessed an undiscovered inner strength. Soon he began to outperform many of the more boisterous and confident boys who, at the beginning of camp, had felt so certain of their superiority. On the last day, when the sergeant read out the list of those who had been selected, David's name was there – the last name called, but called nonetheless.

Now he sat on a luxury bus that traveled through the late afternoon heat toward the City, feeling not like a schoolboy but a soldier. Adolescent adrenaline ran high among the group. A natural fraternity of survival and success had formed, and David relished the deep sense of belonging he felt. He would do anything for them. After everything they'd been through, they were his brothers now.

The bus wheezed to a stop in a town a few miles outside L.A. and the cadets disembarked in front of a nondescript building. Entering a large hall on the ground floor, they whooped and applauded at the sight of a cornucopian dinner buffet. Meats, vegetables, pies and cakes crowded serving tables along the back wall. Greedily they lined up and piled their plates high. When they had finished, an officer silenced the room.

"I need you all to line up," he commanded. "Baker is standing in front of the doorway there – say hello, Baker." A menacing, heavily tattooed soldier stood in stony silence. "He has something…special for you."

One by one, the boys passed in front of Officer Baker on the way into the auditorium.

"What is it?" David asked as he stepped to the front of the line.

Baker smiled a fierce, gap-toothed grin. "Magic," he said, placing the pill on David's tongue.

On massive screens on either side of the stage, high definition videos showcased Phoenix paramilitary forces parachuting from helicopters into desert sands and raging oceans, or carrying out bold urban raids against overmatched, unsophisticated terrorists. As more and more boys filed in, packing the room, the collective energy began to rise. David's senses tingled. He felt alert and alive, strong and invulnerable. Without realizing it, he had started to bounce on the balls of his feet in sync with the others around him.

Once the last boy entered, the lights went out and the screens went dark. Everything stilled. Gradually, suspenseful music began to play and an image appeared on the screen: an alley seen through the lens of night vision goggles. The sound of breath filled the speakers. Unbearable anticipation gripped the cadets. Quietly, the soldier spoke into his headset, counted to three, and kicked in a door. In a flash of light, the screen filled with elite Phoenix soldiers dropping from the sky, swinging from the rooftops on ropes, spraying bullets and eliminating the terrorists holed up inside. The room erupted in glorious cheers. David's voice felt raw as he screamed his excitement into the crowd

When the lights came up, the commanding officer for their elite unit, Major Stevenson, took the stage. David joined his peers in a spontaneous cry of the commando call they had learned at boot camp: "Hoo-hah!" followed immediately by five foot-stomps in unison against the wood floor.

"You know why you're here," shouted the Major.

"Hoo-hah!" Stomp, stomp, stomp, stomp, stomp.

"I said, you *know* why you're here," the Major repeated, raising his voice.

"HOO-HA!" shouted the boys at the top of their lungs, their faces flushed, their clapping thundering off the walls.

"You have all excelled in basic training," continued Stevenson. "Tonight, you join the Praetorian brotherhood."

"HOO-HA!" screamed the rabid crowd.

"We have a special guest here to conduct the final part of your initiation. Chief Military Officer for all Phoenix operations worldwide. Commander of the Praetorian Guard and the Army of New California." He stood aside and gestured deferentially to the wings of the stage. "Supreme General Erik Duke."

The national anthem, *New Cal Undying*, blared over the loudspeaker. On the video screens behind the stage, the grizzly bear and lone star of Republic flag waved in an invisible breeze. Before them, a squat, powerfully built man made his way to center stage, his right ear bandaged with tape. The young soldiers surged forward, clapping their hands above their heads, facing their palms toward the General in a gesture of military reverence. To David, General Duke appeared almost supernatural in his presence. Never had he seen a man exude such effortless power.

Duke smiled almost imperceptibly and held up both hands, palms outward, in acknowledgement of their adoration. A hush fell over the room.

"In the months ahead we will face great challenges as a nation," began General Duke, surveying them with his intense glare. "Most of your compatriots will sit at home and wait for others to determine their fate. It is *you* they will be waiting for."

"HOO-HA!!" Stomp, stomp, stomp, stomp, stomp.

"It will not be easy. Sacrifice will be required. Your friends, your family, your boyhood games. They're gone now. They don't exist. Look around this room. *This* is your family now. *These* are your brothers. *They* are the ones who will give their lives for you. And you for them."

One boy at the front of the crowd put his arms around the shoulders of the boys on either side of him and spontaneously began to sing the Youth Corps hymn. Immediately, the rest joined him, arms over shoulders, until the room boomed with intoxicated passion.

"You'll do things you never thought you could!" Duke continued forcefully when the singing subsided. "Things you only do for love of God and country." He lowered his voice for effect. "And you will have to be strong. Praetorian strong."

Duke looked offstage and nodded. Two soldiers dragged out a half-naked slum boy, his hands tied behind his back.

"This rat was caught sneaking across the Perimeter into the City today. He had a weapon with him and the materials needed to make an improvised explosive device. What does that make him?"

"A terrorist!!" several of the boys shouted separately.

"That's right," said Duke calmly. "A terrorist. And there's only one way we deal with terrorists, isn't there?"

The cadets jeered and whistled their agreement. Duke's eyes scanned the crowd and somehow, unimaginably, found David.

"You," said the mighty General, pointing directly at him. "Front and center."

The crowd parted, all eyes glued to him with a mixture of horror and glee. David could not feel his body, and moved as if in a dream. Duke beckoned him onto the stage. Placing a hand on David's shoulder, he said quietly, "Are you ready?"

"Yes sir!" David replied with frantic energy.

"Ready to show them what it takes? To be a Praetorian?"

"Yes sir!" David responded, his head filling with white noise, his vision blurring. He was prepared to do anything for this great man.

"Are you READY?!" the General cried.

"YESSIR!!"

"Are YOU ready?!" the General shouted, turning to the crowd of frothing boys.

"YESSIR!!" they all cried in ecstatic response. Collectively, they commenced a slow stomping, which built in intensity until the room shook.

Duke removed the pistol from his holster and extended it. Then, in a voice only David could hear, he said, "For God and Country."

Jacob

The trail steepened considerably by the time Jacob passed 9,000 feet and emerged above the tree line. His breathing now came shallow and hard, echoing through his skull. Leaning into the slope so that he would not slide back on the loose scree, he dug his hands into the baked earth, clawing for any rock or root to steady him. The skin around his fingernails was cracked and bloody, his body frosted by the ghostly powder kicked up by his climb.

He had parted from Bettina two days ago for this final stage of training: time alone to ascend the peak. He'd never been so grateful for solitude. As if to make up for the vulnerability she revealed by the fire, Bettina worked him harder in the days that followed than she had at any other point during their time in the woods. He could tell she was trying to break him, to push him so hard that he would be forced to admit he couldn't do it. So he would just give up and go home. But he refused to concede.

When they parted, she handed him a two-way handheld. "The summit shouldn't take you more than two days. It'll be one coming down. Use this to call me if you're afraid you're gonna die. Otherwise, don't. We'll meet you in the little village along the road south of Cherry Hills. There's a small teahouse there called *Mi Casa*. You can't miss it."

The sheer physicality of the climb required his full focus, and he was grateful for the release from thoughts of Bettina. The final thousand feet had been grueling, but when at long last he clambered wearily into the flat, open clearing at the top, he could taste the purity of the thin evening air. At the opposite side of the clearing, alone on the barren peak, a twisted and mangled Jeffrey pine drew Jacob's attention. He had identified the Jeffrey thousands of feet further down the slope. There, each tree rose perfectly erect into the canopy, tall and majestic, princes of the forest. But this particular tree, alone on the bare summit, exposed constantly to the whipping north winds, was unrecognizable. Bent at the midsection, it gave the impression of wet clay that had sagged under its own weight before drying. Jacob approached the tree with a mixture of fascination and pity. He ran his palm along the trunk. Smooth as glass. His fingers traced the intersection of two giant, interlocking strands of trunk that formed the base of the tree. They twisted together in thick braids before arching elegantly southward and separating, flowing like a dancer's arms behind her in mid-flight. The tree had adapted to the shearing winds, learned to endure the torturous assault of sand and grit, given up its northern branches and focused only on preserving what it could on its southern side. It was simultaneously the saddest and most beautiful thing that Jacob had ever seen.

Turning in a slow circle, Jacob surveyed the horizon in the fading light. To the north and east, as far as he could see, the vast expanse of the Sierra Nevada unfolded: undulating slopes, rippled like hardpacked, wave-carved sand on a tidal beach; deep valleys pocketed with patches of green amongst the vast brown expanse; majestic mountains dusted with a faint white fringe. To the south and west, toward the Los Angeles basin, the land gradually submerged under a creamy foam of smog. The winds had temporarily beaten back the thickest layers so that the polluted air, ever-present and at times impenetrable, stretched translucent thin, allowing Jacob to take in the entirety of the coastal plain.

Looking out toward the sea, a band of turquoise sparkled in the sunlight where the Pacific Ocean met the sky, a bold stroke of watercolor on an otherwise gray-washed canvas. Beyond, bloodstained clouds hung heavy, beyond reach, saturated with the unfulfilled promise of glorious, fresh water.

Jacob pulled his hunting knife from his pack. Slowly and deliberately, he cut his hair, feeding the clippings to the wind.

2

Two days later, Jacob walked the long, straight, dusty road into town. Up ahead he discerned a smattering of buildings. Tables and chairs stood in front of a dilapidated structure, the words *Mi Casa* painted inelegantly on a slab of wood that leaned against the stand. Jacob strained to see who might be there to meet him. All he could make out were three mongrel dogs, prostrate and panting in the oppressive heat. Concerned that he had gotten the meeting point wrong, he double-checked his map. A familiar voice rang out.

"You're late!" Hector laughed sardonically, approaching with easy strides and a wide smile. Looking Jacob up and down, he added, "And skinny!"

"Couldn't get a decent cheeseburger anywhere up there," Jacob joked, taking the bag of water Hector handed him and gulping it down gratefully.

"And what the hell did you do to your hair?" Hector asked.

"Oh, yeah. I don't know. It felt like it was time to cut it, I guess."

"It looks…good? I think? Makes you look older, anyway."

Jacob laughed. Then, in the most casual voice he could muster, he inquired, "Where's Bettina? I thought she was going to meet me."

"Yeah, well, she had a few things to take care of after being away for so long, you know? So she sent me. You're probably glad not to have to deal with *her* another day!"

"Yeah," agreed Jacob, trying his best to hide his disappointment. "Yeah, of course. It's great to see you, Hec."

"You definitely look different. How was it up there?"

"It was great. Hard, but great. Kat? Have you heard anything? Is she okay?"

"She's fine. No need to worry. Agnes is taking care of her. I spoke with Renard this morning. He said she's doing well. Apparently she gets along great with the old lady."

"Really?" Jacob wondered, relieved.

"Agnes has a way about her," said Hector. "When we get back to Cherry Hills we'll set up a link so you can talk to her. But first, let's get you cleaned up. Damn, you stink!"

Tracker

Tracker gazed out the window as his driver turned off the Hollywood Freeway and headed toward Beverly Hills. From downtown, they had driven north toward Griffith Park before beginning the winding route along Sunset at the base of the canyons. Unlike the planned housing estates south of the Municipal Zone, where most of the government workers lived, the area north and west of the downtown core had been beautifully reconstructed to evoke the glory of old LA. Here, the elite of modern Los Angeles made their homes – top government officials, wealthy businessmen, celebrities. During the Restoration, President Duke insisted that the rebuilt houses in West Hollywood, Beverly Hills and Santa Monica rival those of the greatest cities of the greatest civilizations. At a time of despair and desperation, declared Duke at his second inauguration, such majesty did not represent disparity. It represented hope, something for the people to aspire to. It was, he assured his audience, the harbinger of a better future for all.

The driver slowed as he reached their destination, turning off Sunset Boulevard through massive iron gates. The mansion at the far end of the drive, known as Beverly House, had once been owned by a publishing magnate in the twentieth century. When Malcolm Duke decided to make Los Angeles the capital of New California, he commissioned the rebuilding of the house as the official state mansion. No cost had been spared; the restored house and grounds more than equaled their original splendor. Much to the Governor's satisfaction, many said that the new mansion rivaled the palaces of the great European monarchs of the past – a twenty-first century Versailles. Towering trees arced over their path as they progressed up the long brick driveway. Sculptures commissioned from top New Californian artists dotted a lush green lawn that carpeted the mansion's foreground. In the distance, an enclosure held exotic animals; Tracker could just make out the bobbing neck of a giraffe as it loped toward a feeding pole. Along the tops of the fifteen-foot high security fences, specially designed industrial fans circulated the air with stunning silence and opened a blue window to the sky. From the dust and haze of the rest of LA, here one entered into a small piece of heaven.

The car slowed as it pulled in front of the mansion. One of two soldiers who stood rigidly at the base of the stairs stepped forward to open Tracker's door. Tracker slid past the man's crisp salute without acknowledgement and up the wide marble staircase.

"His Excellency is expecting you," said the Head Houseman with an ingratiating nod of the head.

He led Tracker through the main foyer with its vaulted fifty-foot ceiling and down the grand hallway into the center of the house. Tracker caught a glimpse of the library, adorned with hand-carved woodwork and a second story wrap-around balcony with bookshelves. They passed the billiard room with its herringbone parquet floors and immense stone fireplace mantle. Tracker had heard the President boast to top military officers and visiting foreign dignitaries about some of the mansion's other signature features: spas, dining rooms fit to seat 500 people, cinemas, and wine cellars.

Passing through the French doors at the rear of the mansion, Tracker stood on a veranda overlooking a series of three swimming pools, each larger than the next, cascading in waterfall fashion toward the huge main pool. Alongside each of the pools tropical plants fluoresced vibrantly. Beside the pool, two beautiful women sat under an umbrella in sun loungers watching a lone figure swim in a vigorous freestyle.

"Something to drink, sir, before you head down to the pool?" asked the Houseman. "We've just received a shipment of outstanding iceberg water. Twelve thousand years old. Very refreshing."

"I'm fine," replied Tracker.

"Very good, sir," said the Houseman, bowing and retreating indoors. Tracker made his way down the terraced steps as Malcolm Duke finished his swim. At 72 years old, Duke's tanned flesh had loosened, but his physical prowess remained evident. A full head of silver hair had been slicked back by the water, accentuating his angular, handsome features. One of the women stepped forward with a towel, which the President used to mop his face, while the other woman draped a thick robe of Egyptian cotton around his shoulders.

"You did well," said Duke, gesturing for Tracker to sit with him at the patio table. He picked up a bottle filled with rich amber liquid. "I know you don't drink, but you might change your mind after you try this."

Tracker demurred. The President sat in a wide reclining chair while one of the attendant women poured the syrupy liquid over several perfectly formed cubes of ice and handed it to him. They tinkled when the President swirled the glass.

"I know what you're thinking," said Duke before taking a sip of his drink. "Ah, that's special." He put the glass down and savored the aftertaste. "You're thinking my son shouldn't have killed the American. Of course you're right. But what's done is done. There *is* justice in it. After all, it was *his* man."

Tracker said nothing.

"Erik doesn't often make mistakes," the President continued, less with paternal pride than simple objectivity. "But then neither do you."

Tracker raised his chin slightly in acknowledgement and paused. "The American was working with Renard. I think he would have told us more about what Renard is planning if your son had shown some restraint."

"Renard is an old fool. He's already lost his fight and now he's flailing in the wind. He's no threat to us," continued Duke, with a slight tone of irritation.

"You underestimate him," Tracker said.

"And you *overestimate* him." For a brief moment the President's eyes flashed. Tracker could see the violence that raged just beneath his superficial decorum. Tracker did not exactly fear the President, but he came closer to fearing him than he did any other man. It was for this reason that he respected him. The shadow passed from Duke's face as quickly as it had surfaced, but his eyes did not soften.

Indicating an envelope on the table, Duke added, "I've wired you something for catching the spy. A small token of my appreciation. The details are there."

Tracker picked up the envelope and slipped it into his pocket without examining the contents.

"The American changes nothing," Duke said. "As far as we can tell, he got no essential information – only what they already know. What we want them to know. Everything is still on track. The Phoenix mercenaries are mobilizing. They'll be arriving soon." The President considered for a moment, calculating. "But there is one loose end I would like you to take care of."

"Sir?" inquired Tracker.

"Paul Angelfish, the water researcher. They found the car he was driving the day he disappeared. Crashed into a dry riverbed. Over a cliff. Burned out chassis. But no body."

"You think he's still alive?"

"We have to assume so."

"Does it matter?"

"Treason always matters," the President said icily.

Tracker considered for a moment. "Find the children. That will flush him out."

"Whatever it takes," said Duke.

"I'll take care of it," replied Tracker coolly.

"I know you will. You always do."

Part IV

El Dompe

Jacob

Jacob startled awake at Hector's rough touch.

"We're gonna be late," Hector said. "She won't like that."

The loft where he and Hector slept in the old church annex had just enough room for two mattresses, with the slope of the ceiling dropping so steeply that they could do no more than stand on their knees without striking their heads. Beside his bedroll, a small hand-powered lamp made it possible for Jacob to write in his journal and to begin reading one of the books Julius had loaned him from his library. It was a history of America – but not the history he had learned. Even after reading only the first few chapters, Jacob swelled with feelings of confusion, anger, and shame.

Emerging through a narrow door into the main body of the church, Jacob took in the vaulted ceiling before bringing his gaze to rest on a wooden sculpture of the limp Christ above the altar. The agony seemed to him not holy at all, but rather an honest account of what he had come to learn about the way human beings treat one another, and always have.

Hector's voice roused him from his reverie.

"C'mon. Bettina will kick our asses if we don't get down there," Hector said. "Oh, and your shirt's on backwards," he added.

Embarrassed, Jacob swiveled his t-shirt around as he followed Hector through a hidden doorway behind the altar and down a narrow set of dimly lit, winding stairs to the church basement. Feeling along the cracked grout between the cinder blocks that made up the foundation of the church, Hector found the desired spot and pressed a heavy block in the wall. The wall in front of him lifted, sighed, and receded half an inch. He leaned his shoulder against the wall and swung open a massive, vault-like door.

Squinting at the bright light that now flooded over him, Jacob entered a huge, open space. A bank of computers lined one wall, in front of which boys and girls, young men and women busily typed streams of computer code. In different areas of the lab, teams of people soldered, hammered, or talked over blueprints spread out on wide tables. Jacob observed two boys who could not have been much older than six or seven pushing a cart across the floor from which they distributed tools, electrical wire, and other items to the various teams of workers. On an unattended workbench, half-built devices lay split open like steamed clamshells.

"We run all of the e-ops from here," Hector said, surveying the room.

"*E-ops*?" asked Jacob, bewildered.

"Electronic Operations. It all happens here. We call this place the Batcave."

As they spoke, Bettina caught sight of them from across the room and walked quickly in their direction.

"'Bout time you got here," she said impatiently. Jacob wondered if she would say something about the way he looked, about his hair. But she said nothing.

"Bettina built this whole thing," Hector explained. "You should've seen it before she took over. It was pathetic."

"You were here at the beginning, too," Bettina said to Hector.

"C'mon," Hector objected. "I'm just here to serve. One of your many minions." He smiled playfully at her. She punched him in the shoulder.

"Ouch!" he protested. They both laughed. Jacob felt a mild surge of resentment at the ease of their exchange.

"This room was half the size when we got here, remember?" Bettina continued, addressing Hector. "They had a couple of crappy two-gig desktops running some kind of ancient code I could barely read."

"What was that guy's name?" Hector asked. "The guy who was running it before you?"

"Antonio," Bettina replied.

"Antonio! That's right. God, he was a dinosaur. I can't believe they ever thought he'd be able to do anything."

"Anyway, enough of all that," Bettina said. "We've got work to do. C'mon."

She led them over to one of the workstations where an eleven-year-old boy was typing code faster than Jacob's eye could follow. Bettina tapped the boy on the shoulder.

"Hey, give it a rest," she commanded. The boy immediately jumped up and vacated his seat. Bettina slid into the chair and tapped in a string of short commands.

"This is our standard interface," Bettina explained, calling up a new screen. "I designed a platform that allows us to work across multiple code profiles at once. My program translates real time so that no matter what coding language you're fluent in, you can hack any system."

"Cool," Jacob responded somewhat uncertainly, given that he had not really understood anything she said.

"We had to upgrade like crazy – I mean, like crazy. It was ridiculous how old this stuff was. But of course we couldn't just go and buy a new high-end computer off the shelf in the City. All that stuff is so tightly controlled. So I built the processors from scratch. I got a lot of the parts from car circuit boards that we stole from the

City – you'd be amazed how advanced they are in the self-driving cars. Some of our *mousitos* – those are the kids we send into the City – they stole cheap laptops from people on buses and in restaurants, then I jerry-rigged the hard drives to boost their processing power. These babies may look like crap, but they're as good as anything you can buy. And faster."

A young girl came running up to Bettina with a tablet in her hand.

"Look at this, Bettina," she said excitedly, flicking through a series of screens with her finger. "I got inside the Glendale power grid!"

Bettina took the tablet and tapped at fantastic speeds with one hand as she checked the girl's work.

"Pretty good. But see this line here? It's a dead giveaway to their security bots. So we can't activate it. Still, I like how you got around the firewall. I haven't seen anyone use that approach before. Why don't you upload the protocol to the shared server so that everyone can see how you did it? Hector, will you go with her and check on the dailies?"

"Sure," Hector agreed amiably, putting a kind hand on the girl's shoulder. "Good luck!" he said to Jacob as he left.

"We found that little girl in a factory out at Mahatshula Textile in Riverside," Bettina explained as Hector led her away. "They had her fixing the operating systems there. Only twelve years old, but a coding whiz. Lots of potential."

"I guess the government doesn't have any idea about this place?" Jacob asked.

"Of course not," Bettina replied, offended. "Duke's geeks have been hunting us for a long time – right now they think we're in Brazil. Or Uzbekistan!" She allowed herself a moment of pleasure at the thought.

"Am I going to have to do code?" Jacob asked, trying to sound indifferent.

Bettina responded with her characteristic squint. Then, trying to reassure herself as much as him, she said, "I hope not."

Kat

"Water delivery today?" Pepe asked Buster.

Kat sat at the teashop with Pepe and a few of the other *culebras*. A growing crowd of women and children carrying buckets and plastic containers of assorted sizes filled the square. Kat normally enjoyed the general hum of the market, but today she sensed tension. Agitated women pushed and shoved to position themselves for the arrival of the water truck. Two young women had started shouting at each other, one accusing the other of trying to cut the line. A few older men tried ineffectively to quiet and organize the crowd. Kat sat uncomfortably in her chair, rigid and attentive to the hostile energy in the square.

"Since they been having problems with that big desal plant down in Malibu," Buster explained, "there ain't been no regular clean water deliveries. Used to be every week, but they ain't come for the last two. People are startin' to get pretty desperate."

"We got nothing in the favela – nothing! And they make us buy our own water!" Pepe spat on the ground in disgust.

Just then, several jeeps with mounted guns swept at speed into the square, scattering the crowd. Armed young men leapt out, drawing weapons and waving them menacingly. Moments later, a large tanker truck rolled in behind them, the red Phoenix logo emblazoned on its side. The agitated crowd pressed forward, abandoning any pretense to a line, wanting only to ensure they received their share. As they jostled for position, a black armored Mercedes skidded to a stop. Shots fired in the air. People fell to the ground or covered their heads somewhat comically with their buckets. Emerging from the car, semi-automatic pistol held aloft, stood Rat, the local Bear Clan *gerente*.

"You want water?!" shouted Rat.

Kat had never seen energy so malicious around a person as she did around this man. Rat approached the tanker truck, grabbing one of the women at random by the hair. He dragged her behind him while she scrambled awkwardly to maintain her balance, her arms flailing backwards above her head. While the woman screamed for mercy, her young child ran after her, blubbering and terrified.

"You want to be treated like dogs?" he shouted to the crowd. He held a gun to the woman's head. People gasped and looked away.

"Mommy!" bleated the little girl. Rat looked down at the sobbing creature.

"Is this your mommy?" he said. "Well, you better tell her to stop acting like a dog or I shoot her dead like I shoot a crazy old dog dead! You hear me?!" The little girl nodded and blubbered *yes, yes, yes*. Rat glanced from the child to the woman then back again. He surveyed the terror of those cowering in the square. Abruptly, he released the woman with a shove and gave a wide, magnanimous smile, opening his arms.

"You see?" he cried to the traumatized crowd. "See how good I am? But you don't want to see me get angry. Now line up and no one gets hurt!"

The crowd organized itself in almost total silence, forming an orderly line along the back side of the square. Rat cavalierly tucked his gun into his waistband and ambled toward Buster's teashop, followed closely by two thick-cut bodyguards. Kat pulled her hood down over her face. Mercifully, the *gerente* appeared not to notice her.

In his early twenties, Rat had pale skin, a compact build, and short, curly hair. He wore a sleeveless Rules football jersey which put his rich array of tattoos on full display. A massive gold cross hung around his neck. Oversized rings adorned most of his fingers, each of them sparkling with diamonds. Buster poured him a shot glass of *weezo*, the raw vegetable vodka that he preferred. Rat offered no money and Buster asked for none.

"What're you staring at?" Rat glared at Pepe, who had been fixated on Rat.

"I'm not scared of you," Pepe said defiantly. Rat exchanged an appreciative laugh with his two bodyguards, flashing the gold that rimmed his teeth.

"No?" he said.

"Not scared," repeated Pepe quietly. Rat laughed again, but this time in a forced, artificial way. Then, like a cat, he leapt across the tables and, pulling his gun, shoved Pepe's face to the ground, opening a cut across his cheekbone. With his left hand firmly around Pepe's neck and his knees pinning Pepe's stick-thin body to the ground, Rat lowered the barrel of the gun to the spot between Pepe's eyes.

"How about now?" he whispered menacingly.

"I'm… not… scared," croaked Pepe through the chokehold.

"Stop!" Kat yelled, standing up.

Rat turned slowly to face the girl. Everyone at the teashop froze. Rat released Pepe's throat and the small *culebra* rolled onto his side, coughing breath back into his lungs. Rat approached Kat, cocking his head to one side as if having come upon a strange, exotic bird. Placing his hand under her chin, he lifted it up gently. Kat's skin burned at his touch, but she dared not flinch.

In a low voice, Rat said, "Did somebody leave you by the side of the road, little girl? Like a piece of trash?"

He knelt down so that his face was only inches from hers, his gaze shifting rapidly from one of her eyes to the other, making inscrutable, terrifying calculations. The menacing energy surrounding his head made Kat feel faint.

"Slave traders pay good money for little girls, you know," he said.

The *culebras* and other patrons of Buster's teashop all watched in horror, but none dared move. Even Pepe realized that a false move now, with Rat in such an agitated state, could mean a bullet in Kat's head.

"Take her to *el dompe*," commanded Rat.

As a bodyguard shoved Kat into the Mercedes, Pepe leapt to his feet. Buster grabbed him and enveloped him in a tight embrace.

"No!" screamed Pepe, struggling to free himself. "*Gatterina*!"

"Let 'em go, Pep," Buster soothed quietly, tightening his grip. "Let 'em go. Ain't nothin' you gonna do against him. Ain't nothin' you gonna do."

The Aztecs built Tenochtitlan – what is now known as Mexico City – on an island in the middle of a group of shallow lakes. They regulated the flow of water by building dykes and canals. When the Spanish conquerors arrived in the sixteenth century, they drained the lakes to expand the city, unconcerned with depleting what must have seemed to them abundant water resources. Hundreds of years later, in the early 1900s, the city began to extract water from wells drilled to the water table below. And all the time the city kept growing in size as the poor abandoned their meager lives in the country for the promise of work and a future for their children.

At the time of the Aztecs there were probably only a million people in all of North and South America combined.

Today, 25 million people live in Mexico City.

And all the water is gone.

Jacob

Jacob followed Bettina to the rear of the lab. A long table had been set up against the wall. Several objects were carefully laid out like an exhibition of surgeons' instruments.

"We've been preparing your cover," Bettina explained, picking up a pile of clothing. "This is the PG youth guard uniform you'll be wearing. And this," she continued, holding up a sleek palm-sized device with a touch-screen, "is a Janus phone. Looks like a regular mobile gaming unit, but when you pop off the back it has a quantum phone interface. Pretty cool, huh?"

Jacob took the device in his hand, puzzled by how to "pop off the back". Bettina smiled in satisfaction, pleased by his confusion, then took the phone from him. With a sleight of hand that preserved the mystery, she slid off the rear plastic shell to reveal a digital keypad.

"Amazing," Jacob said.

"If you use the front like normal, it still plays games. Music, too. Make sure to use it that way – it'll seem much less likely to be anything else."

Jacob only half listened to her as she explained the mechanics of the device. Alone with her again for the first time since the mountains, Jacob furtively read her expressions, searching for any indication of their fireside intimacy. But she remained distant and business-like. With some dismay, Jacob guessed that his obvious lack of coding skills had only reanimated her anxiety, erasing whatever confidence his physical abilities in the woods had inspired. Resentment crept in. He felt he had proved himself, that he had surmounted at least her fundamental opposition to his involvement in their scheme. He was annoyed at the prospect of having to do that all over again.

"Since you'll be working down here for the next few weeks," Bettina continued, returning the phone to the table, "I'd better show you something else." Leading him along the back wall to the corner where the ceiling sloped to such a degree that they both had to squat down, she gestured into the semi-darkness. "Can you see that door? In the corner?" Jacob discerned the faint outline of a small door cut into the wall. It was extremely hard to see because of the heavy shadows. "Everyone who works down here has to know about that," Bettina continued. "It's an escape route. You push hard on the right side for ten seconds, then a spring mechanism automatically swivels it open. It stays shut if you push any less than that. A tunnel runs from here out to the road about a half mile away. We have motorcycles waiting at the other end in case we need to make a fast getaway. And this…" Bettina indicated on her right to what looked like a fire alarm on the wall. "This is the self-destruct latch. If government troops ever show up at the church, you break the glass and pull the handle down. Then you have three minutes to get the hell out of here before it blows. That's how long it takes to get down that tunnel if you run. You can always pick the handle back up again to stop the timer, in case you make a mistake."

She took in his wide-eyed, bewildered expression. "God help us, you'll never have to use it," she muttered, standing and walking back toward the table.

Bettina picked up what looked like a battered passport next to the folded uniform as Hector casually rejoined them. Flipping the book open, she turned it toward Jacob to reveal a picture of himself. Beneath the picture, he read a name: Jake Samuels.

"We backloaded you a transfer from a Youth Guard unit in San Diego. Here's the full dossier." Bettina grabbed a tablet off the table. "You can't take this with you into the City. You'll have to memorize it. His life is your life now."

Jacob scrolled through the documents on the screen, all of which laid out the life story of the fictional Jake Samuels.

"I'm going to load this same data into your sub-cutaneous ID," she said. "That means under your skin."

"Uh, yeah, I got that. Thanks," he tried to control his mounting irritation.

"We can do it before you go back upstairs. Right?" she asked, looking at Hector.

"We have everything ready," Hector confirmed.

"You're going to operate on me here?" he asked skeptically.

"It'll only take a minute. And it has to be done soon. Your digital ID has to match the documents exactly. Transfers only last a month. We need to get you into the Coliseum as soon as possible. To give us time." Then she said what by now had become clear to him. "That digital ID is what we need you for."

"For my citizenship," he said.

"Yes."

It made sense, of course, that there would be a very concrete, tactical reason why Renard felt that Jacob could become a spy. Jacob felt foolish for believing that Renard might have perceived something unique in him. Oblivious to his inner ruminations, Bettina picked up a thumbnail-sized lapel pin in the shape of the New California flag and continued to deliver her instructions.

"Most important of all, when you get inside the Coliseum, you'll need this."

"It looks like a pin," remarked Jacob sourly.

"It *is* a pin," said Bettina, trying to contain her own irritation. "And it's gonna bring down the whole damn government." She snatched the pin back from him. Winding the needle in a clockwise direction, she revealed a universal connector that emerged from the edge of the flag. "I equipped it with a password accelerator – that's a program I designed that rapidly scans recent activity from a given keyboard and uses a special algorithm to decode passwords. The accelerator will allow you to hack the system from someone's personal computer. Once you actually get into the system, the worm launches a program that infiltrates their entire network while constantly linking back to ours. I'm beta testing one last piece of code before we go operational."

"So what am I supposed to do with it?" Jacob asked.

"The New Cal military network – it's called CalNet – is totally isolated from the public internet," Bettina explained rapidly. "So the program will have to be manually loaded. Until a few weeks ago, we had an American spy inside Duke's government. He confirmed our suspicion – that Duke is planning an attack in the north – the start of a wider war for North America. All those troops that are coming in – that's not for self-defense. It's for an invasion. That's the information we got at Leo's. Our original plan was to have the spy plant the worm, but… that won't be possible now."

"Why? What happened to the spy?" Jacob asked.

Bettina paused before responding. The she said simply, "Tracker."

She scrutinized his reaction, but Jacob strained every nerve to remain impassive, determined not to give her any further reason to doubt him. "So now you want me to plant the virus instead?" he said matter-of-factly.

"You can see why I wasn't crazy about the idea," mumbled Bettina.

Jacob tried to ignore the insult. "What'll the worm do?"

"Once it's on their network, I can signal a program that'll knock out their entire command capabilities, and the launch controls for their nukes. They won't be able to access satellite data. They'll be totally incapacitated. And the US can march right in. That's what we've been coordinating with the Americans."

"I don't know…" Jacob fretted, unwittingly reverting to self-doubt.

"*Look*," seethed Bettina, taking a quick, forceful step toward Jacob. He stumbled backward in surprise at her sudden aggression. But she was within inches of him and he could feel the breath on his face, see the wild intensity in her eyes. "You *better* start understanding how serious this job is! I've been busting my ass for the last two years to develop this thing. The future of the Emergence – of our country – depends on it. I'm doing what Renard wants me to do, even though every bone in my body tells me this plan is totally nuts. Everything we've been fighting for, all the suffering we've put up with. You understand what happens if Duke wins a war with America, right?" Her voice rose in a crescendo. "A *goddamn psychopath* will dominate half the globe!!"

"Back off!" Jacob exploded back, breathing heavily, letting go of his own tidal wave of feeling. Exhausted by the revival of her petty badgering, all Jacob wanted to do was to scream back in her face, to swear at her, to say anything he could that would be hurtful. The angry flush that rose along his neck and into his face prickled his skin. Rage emboldened him and he did not back down.

"We've been working on this for two years." Bettina repeated in a more controlled voice. "Two years. Every day.

Everything is riding on this, Jacob. There's no room for doubt. No room for being a boy. You gotta grow up. Right now. Right here. This war isn't about your mom, or your sister, or you. You showed me in the woods that you can be strong physically. But physical strength won't be enough. You get that?"

"Yeah, I get that," Jacob replied determinedly.

"We'll see," she said. As she turned on her heels, she fumed at the wide-eyed Hector. "I can't do the ID right now. Bring him back in an hour. Jesus, this is insane!"

Kat

The black car barreled through the crowded alleys. Kat heard the *thump thump* of the tires as they ended the life of a dog that made an ill-fated attempt to dash across the road in front of them. She curled herself against the door, knees to chest, eyes clenched, lips moving silently as she recited Agnes' incantations. The mixture of fear and instinct that had driven her to rise in Pepe's defense in Alexandria Square had gradually given way to waves of panic as they drove through the packed favela streets. Desolation filled her. She wanted nothing more than to withdraw, to open a hole in the fabric of the world and slip through it. But she knew that she could not. She knew that only if she remained present and aware would she stand any chance of surviving whatever ordeal awaited her.

Rat sat in the front passenger seat of the sedan. Next to her in the back seat, smelling like rotten cheese, sat one of Rat's hooligans.

"Yo, what's wrong with her?" said the Bear Clan henchman observing Kat as she rocked back and forth and muttered incomprehensibly. "She's kinda freaking me out here. Look at her."

Rat leaned back over the front seat to take in Kat's strange behavior. He shrugged dismissively. "I bet they let her out of the loony bin in the City and dumped her. I know a guy who'll pay a lot of money for someone like her. A lot of money."

Rat flashed his sidekick a golden, toothy grin.

Kat smelled the dump long before she saw it. Dense, acrid fumes carried the stench of burning trash and cremated corpses. The fetid air lay low in thick, swirling clouds. From a distance and through the haze, the great mountain of trash blended with the natural landscape of the valley and could easily be mistaken for part of the southern range that encircled the City. Close up, it resembled an entrance to hell.

Kat stared out the window. Gaunt, hopeless faces peered back at her from the doorways and windows of squalid cardboard dwellings. Oil drums filled with paper, twigs and dried dung burned along the road, adding their smoky breath to the polluted sky. Above the looming garbage mountain hordes of seagulls swarmed, screeching their wretched calls as they fought in mid-air for their bounty. Periodically, a Phoenix tanker sold bags of water to an endless line of women and girls. Kat locked eyes with a young girl, perhaps sixteen years old. One infant slung carelessly on her hip, a toddler clasped shyly to her leg, the girl stared expressionlessly back at Kat. Flies crawled unmolested over the baby's half-closed, crusted eyelids, his belly distended beneath his filthy t-shirt. The young woman herself was covered in scabs that had been scratched raw.

The car came to a stop. Rat opened the rear door and pulled Kat out into the humidity, which hit her like a drum. She broke into a fit of coughing.

"Don't worry," Rat said. "You won't be here long."

Rat took Kat by the back of her shirt and directed her toward a chain link fence that marked the official boundary of El

Dompe. An endless row of peddlers and entrepreneurs had constructed makeshift stands of wood and tin along the fence. From these small huts and shelters, they sold assorted treasures recovered from the mountain, each shop specializing in some arcane item: tools, tire rims, electrical wire, plastic containers. Up the hill, amid swarms of black flies, teams of boys shouldered long poles, at the ends of which were hooks made of bent nails. The boys thrust their poles deep into the flesh of the mountain to snare otherwise unreachable scraps of tin, wood and plastic. Sacks full, the scavengers descended to the market where they stood in line to show their wares to a boy no older than ten who sat atop a large barrel, cross-legged like a young Siddhartha. With electrifying speed, he tossed the goods into different piles – metal, glass, and plastic – sometimes biting an object to make his final, mystical determination of its value. Then he gestured silently to an elderly man with a purse full of coins who dispensed the fee and shooed the scavenger away.

"I got a good one," Rat bragged to a guard outside a dilapidated concrete shed tucked against the hillside. Listlessly, the guard waved them through.

They passed through a long hallway that penetrated deep into the heart of the mountain. After walking for a good while, they at last emerged into a wide cavern carved from the mountain's interior. A weak electrical current powered sputtering lights that cast macabre shadows in all directions. Kat gazed up at the domed ceiling, amazed that the garbage had compacted so completely that it could be sculpted like marble. She had seen pictures in her books of the natural caves in southern France where long ago early man had miraculously painted lifelike images on ancient stone walls. Now she stood in a most unnatural cave, hewn from thousands of tons of manmade waste, where the writing on the walls came not from the inspiration of sacred animal spirits but rather from the faded images on discarded packaging.

Kat's attention turned to the room itself. Along the wall to the left stood a series of gated iron enclosures, each filled with sad-eyed children. The holding cells – for that's what they were – had no beds: only floors of compacted trash and metal basins for toilets. Kat made quick calculations: six cells, forty-eight children total.

In the center of the room, writing fastidiously in a notebook at his wide desk, sat a mousy man with wide, yellow eyes that glowed behind his half-moon spectacles. Next to him, a curved metal bar gleamed dully in the flickering light. From the steel rings that hung at regular intervals, Kat guessed that the children from the cells were brought out here and chained to the rail before being sold as slaves.

Rat made his way over to the bureaucrat. Slowly, the man registered Kat's presence. He smelled like a decaying fish.

"I talked to Tang," Rat said. "He's interested. But he wants her clean. Big money."

"Big money?" purred the bureaucrat.

"She's a gringo," explained Rat.

"Seems a little dark to me."

"She's a gringo," insisted Rat belligerently, taking hold of the man's collar.

"Gringo it is," concurred the bureaucrat smoothly.

Kat wondered how frequently the man rose from his desk, or whether he had, like Gollum, become addicted to the dark. The bureaucrat handed one of Rat's henchmen a tag with the number eight on it.

"Attach this to her shirt. On the back. Cell number three. It's the cleanest."

Rat turned to his bodyguard. “You stay here. I’ll bring Tang in the morning. Make sure no one messes with the girl.”

2

As the bodyguard thrust Kat into the one of the cells, her heel caught on a protruding edge of the floor and she lost her balance. Swiveling to break her fall, she skidded to her knees and felt a sharp pain as the skin broke. She retreated to a corner, rolled up her pant leg, and pulled her knee to her mouth to lick the wound. Watching with fascination as the line of blood turned from red to white under the rough care of her tongue, she soothed herself with this feline ministration until the bleeding slowed.

A soft touch on her shoulder drew her back. Kat blinked up at a petite girl with jet black hair that framed a round, sweet face. One of her eyes was missing, revealing an empty socket.

"Are you okay?" the girl asked kindly. "I brought you something."

In the center of her palm was an insect. Silver strips on the black shell shined dully in the poor light. The creature moved with deliberate lethargy. Kat turned the bug over, marveling at the beauty of its shell and smiling at the pathetic way it wiggled its legs helplessly in the air.

"June beetle," Kat reported.

"Right," said the girl. "They know when the storms are coming."

"They do?"

"They sing before the winds come. Before the warning sirens even start. So if I have one with me, it gives me time to find shelter. You can keep this one if you want. I'm good at finding them."

"Thanks," said Kat, gently cupping the insect in her hand.

"I'm Jo Lin. Where did they get you?"

"Alexandria Square. On water day. A man called Rat took me."

"*El gerente*," Jo Lin said quietly. "He's crazy. You're lucky to be alive."

"He said he wants to give me to a man named Tang."

"Oh..." Jo Lin's voice trailed off. "Did he say when Tang is coming?"

"Tomorrow."

Jo Lin looked like she wanted to say more, but she bit her lip and just stared at Kat sympathetically.

"Did Rat get you, too?" Kat asked.

"Not Rat. But Bear Clan, yes. They're always looking for kids on the street. I had to go to the clinic for my mother. She has TB really bad. The health worker never came that day – you need to take the pills twice a day – and I didn't want her to miss her medication. It was late, but I knew the Phoenix truck was in the area and we needed water. I thought I could do it quickly, stay on the main streets. But it didn't matter. I was on the main road and someone came up behind me while I was walking. Threw a sack over my head and grabbed me. No one did anything to stop them."

"What's going to happen to us?"

"You're not from the favela," Jo Lin observed.

"No."

Jo Lin looked around the cell at the other children. For the first time, Kat took real notice of them. Three small girls were huddled in the opposite corner, trying to sleep, their bodies clustered together more out of fear than for comfort. A tall, emaciated girl stood alone, eyeing them suspiciously as she leaned against the bars of the cell. Lanky hair fell in greasy strings down to her shoulders. Her cynical smile revealed several missing teeth.

"Slaves," said Jo Lin quietly. "That's what Bear Clan does with kids. Sells them as slaves. There's a market at Dana Point – a big one. I have a friend who escaped from there. Traders come in from Asia, South America. But also from here, in New California. People working the mines up north, or the farms in the Central Valley. The healthier ones sometimes go into the City as servants, but that's pretty rare. If they go to Asia it's to work on the fishing boats or in the factories." Lowering her voice, she added, "No matter what, it's never good."

Kat did not ask her why.

3

Awake far into the night, the two girls shared whispered stories from their childhood. Kat learned about Jo Lin's difficult life with her sick mother; about her mother's violent boyfriend who caused her to lose her eye; about her dream to become a nurse. For her part, Kat explained to Jo Lin how differently she sensed the world. She talked about school and being bullied – not to inspire pity, but merely as a matter of fact. And although she might normally have been reticent to describe the recent events surrounding her family's arrest and flight, she found that she trusted Jo Lin and wanted to tell her everything. It all came tumbling out – about her father, his notebook, his great discovery, Agnes, Renard. Jo Lin never interrupted.

"So Renard needs you?" she affirmed. "He thinks you can help?"

"That's what he wants Jacob to do. To help them with their plan."

"What about you?"

"Me?"

"Of course *you*!" Jo Lin kept her voice low. "Listen to everything you just told me. Your Father gave you the notebook. He trusted you with his secret, a secret so important that he risked his own life for it. And Agnes. Everyone in this part of the favela knows Agnes. She's a saint. *She* believes in you. Why do you think she taught you? So you could help! All that stuff about how to turn down your energy while staying awake – you couldn't do that before, right?"

"No."

“See? Agnes sees something special in you, Kat. You have to find your father’s invention. That’s what you have to do to help.”

“Yes,” Kat responded quietly, as if she had always known.

“So then we have to get you out of here. If they sell you tomorrow, you’ll never have the chance.” Jo Lin lowered her voice. “Not many people get the chance to do something really important, Kat. Most of us are too poor, too sick, too busy surviving. But everyone hopes their life will change somehow, get better some way. If I can help you, and you can make a difference…” Jo Lin’s voice trailed off. “Right?”

“Right,” Kat agreed.

Throughout the night, Jo Lin worked to convince Kat that she could do it – that she could intentionally lower her energy to such a level that the guards would fail to see her if they were not really looking for her. She could willingly become invisible. Kat argued that Jo Lin had to come with her, that she couldn’t leave her behind.

“My whole life is invisible,” said Jo Lin with more resignation than bitterness. “I’m just a poor slum girl with one eye. It won’t matter what happens to me.”

“No!” Kat objected.

“It’s ok,” Jo Lin reassured her. “My life will have meaning if I help you, Kat. I’m going to suffer one way or the other. If you escape, I’ll suffer just a little bit less. So please. Do it for me.”

Jo Lin’s smile practically broke Kat’s heart. Not because it was a sad smile, but because it was such a kind one.

The Notebook

So much of science is achieved by accident. You think you are doing one thing, when really you are doing another. The real art of science is not in choosing, but in noticing.

In the 3rd Century B.C., Archimedes settled into his bath. As he did, he noticed the water level rising. He famously ran naked through the streets yelling, "Eureka!" His insight: water displacement is related to volume.

In 1928, the Scottish biologist Alexander Fleming failed to clean up the workstation in his lab at the end of a busy day. After returning from a family vacation, he noticed a strange fungus growing on a stack of cultures he'd shoved into a corner of the lab. Curiously, he saw that bacteria nearest the fungus failed to grow. This was the origin of Penicillin and all subsequent antibiotics.

As Louis Pasteur said, "Chance favors the prepared mind."

For ten years I have been working on my research. One dead end after another. Then tonight I spill a drop of liquid by accident and I make a breakthrough that could literally change the world...

David

David sat dejectedly on his bunk and stared at the deployment notification on his handheld. Through weeks of excruciating hardship in basic training, he'd more than kept up physically with the bigger boys. His commanding officer appeared to like him enough to recommend him for a favorable posting. So why had he not been sent to the Oregon border? Everyone knew that's where the action would be. All the boys in his squad were talking about it – they all wanted to go. But the note on his device was short and clear. He was to report at 0800 for a southern deployment.

"McCaw?" It was a young military policeman who approached him. David stood to attention. "Major Stevenson wants to see you. Follow me."

David followed the young MP out of the barracks toward the main administrative building. As they crossed the tarmac, the heat was almost unbearable. It radiated off the asphalt in waves, intensifying the natural humidity of the day. When they entered the small office complex, David was self-conscious of the stains under his arms and at the base of his neck, and never more grateful for the gentle flow of air conditioning that prickled his skin. The MP knocked briskly on Major Stevenson's door.

"Come!" shouted a voice from inside.

They entered the Major's office and David stood stiffly at attention while Stevenson finished signing forms on his tablet. When he signed the last of them, Stevenson handed it to the MP, who saluted and scurried away.

"At ease, soldier," the Major said. "Have a seat."

David saluted crisply and did as he was told. David liked his commanding officer very much, though he still felt nervous in his presence. They did not interact often, since the drill sergeants ran most of the daily training. But Stevenson would come by every day at some point to observe the young recruits, talking quietly with the sergeants or other senior officers who might be with him. Occasionally he would shout an encouraging word or issue a sharp rebuke. But unlike many of the officers David had met, Major Stevenson displayed an even temper and a natural authority that came from confidence rather than intimidation. Above all, he was deemed by the cadets to be fair – the greatest of compliments among teenage boys.

"So, you're not going to the front lines," the Major stated, tapping leftover tobacco from a pipe he kept on a little rack at the edge of his desk. A neat, conical pile of ashes had accumulated in the oriental ashtray that he used. "And you're disappointed."

"Did I do something wrong, sir?" David inquired.

"On the contrary," replied the officer. "You've done extremely well, McCaw. Better than most, in fact." From a drawer in his desk the Major pulled out a worn leather pouch. As soon as he opened it, the room filled with a sweet aroma. Dipping the pipe into the pouch, he stuffed the bowl full as he continued. "With each new group of cadets we keep our eyes open for boys we think have some promise. What you did on that stage..."

David's throat clenched. Since that wild evening in the auditorium, he had been having terrible dreams. In them, he was always walking through the crowd of boys, all of them shouting, jeering, egging him on. The fear rose in a crescendo as he walked, until he arrived on stage and stood face-to-face with Erik Duke. Duke's bi-colored eyes shone demonically as he handed David his gun and whispered, "For God and Country." Always at that moment, David bolted awake drenched in sweat. Now, he unconsciously fingered the pills in his pocket that he had started to depend on to calm his nerves. He would be taking one as soon as he got outside.

"What I mean to say," Stevenson continued, clenching the pipe between his back teeth, "is that we think you have the potential to play a bigger role in the organization."

"Yes, sir?"

Stevenson took a moment to light his pipe again, using a silver lighter that popped pleasantly when he opened it. Puffing several times to make sure the bowl had caught, the Major filled the air around his head with a shroud of sweet-scented smoke.

"You'll spend the next several months on what we call Rotation," explained the Major when the smoke around his face had cleared. "Patrols in the slums and along the borders east and south. Every few weeks you'll rotate back to the City. I'm currently posted at the Navy Yard, so you'll spend a week or two at a time with me there before going on to your next posting. You'll take a military tactics class when you're there, and serve as a personal assistant to me to gain practical experience. If you continue to learn quickly, you have a very bright future in the Praetorian Guard."

David hardly knew what to say. The Major leaned forward and removed the pipe from his mouth.

"This is a critical time for the country, David. You need to see it all, so you can understand what's at stake. Believe me, there's no better way to see how important the PG is in maintaining order than to spend a few weeks in the slums or on the borders."

"Yes, Sir!" David replied, hoping his enthusiasm did not come across as naive.

"Report tomorrow to the office of Central Command here on the base," said Stevenson. "They should have everything you need for your first assignment."

David immediately stood to attention and saluted again.

"Welcome aboard, Sergeant McCaw."

"Thank you, sir," said David. "Thank you *so* much."

Jacob

"Jacob," a voice whispered. "Wake up, Jacob."

Jacob swam from the depths of sleep and gazed through the semi-darkness at the half-formed figure. Bettina's eyes expressed an uncharacteristic softness.

"What's wrong?" Jacob asked, sitting upright in alarm.

"I just got a message…" said Bettina. "From Renard."

"Kat?" He threw back the covers without waiting for an answer. "What happened?"

"Bear Clan. They took her."

Jacob shook his head wildly. All he could say was, "no, no, no." It was impossible. Not Kat. Not his baby sister. He had just spoken to her a few days ago. She was with Agnes. Safe. Fine.

"What happened?"

"They took her from the market."

"I don't… It's not…" His mind raced. "They sell them, don't they?"

Bettina grimaced and looked away.

"Don't they?!" Jacob shouted.

Hector sat groggily up in his bed. "What the…?"

"Where?" Jacob pressed.

"Dana Point is the main market. But Jacob, you'll never be able to..."

"I gotta go," he said, pushing her aside.

"Jacob, stop!" Bettina cried as Jacob stuffed clothes into his mountain traveling bag. Just as he reached down to pick up the knife she had given him in the woods, Bettina's vice-like grip came down on Jacob's wrist.

"Stop!" she seethed. Her eyes were angry and flaring. Jacob stared back at her stonily. "I know you're scared for her. I am, too. But we have to be smart."

"Smart?" He was incredulous.

"There's a bigger picture here," Bettina warned.

"She's my *sister*," he said with emphasis. "For me that's the *only* picture."

"You can't leave!" Bettina insisted as Jacob tucked his knife into his belt and slung a bag over his shoulder. "You need more time. You're not ready."

"It doesn't matter. If I don't find her…" he trailed off. "She's all I have, Bettina. Please."

Their eyes locked and he felt her will concede to his. Turning to Hector, she said, "Grab his stuff from the Batcave. Meet us at the end of the tunnel."

"Us?" Jacob cocked his head as Hector scrambled out of bed.

"Damn it, Jacob," she said. "It'll be faster if I come. Let's go."

Tracker

He stood perfectly still in Crystal Barrington's living room. The young scientist had worked for Paul Angelfish as his senior lab technician for five years. Her telephone call alerted Angelfish's wife the night of his disappearance. If there were something to know, she would know it. And if she knew it, he would find it.

Behind the kitchen door, he could hear the sound of Crystal's video feed streaming the day's news. A fork and knife scraped against a plate as she ate.

She always watches the news in her kitchen, he thought. *I have fifteen minutes before she heads upstairs.*

Tracker had been watching Crystal, following her each day from the Ministry of Science in the Municipal Zone to her condominium in the academic housing district in South Gate. She was the easiest kind of mark to follow: all routine. Up at six. Exercise. Coffee and pastry at the corner café at 7:30. Long Beach Monorail line. In the lab by 8:15. Leave at 6:30. Simple dinner at home in front of the nightly news. Shower, paint, video, bed. The only suggestion of something more than a spartan, lonely life was the presence of her painting easel in the corner of the living room and a food dish for the gray tabby cat that Tracker had encountered briefly outside. It had only been a week and already Tracker was bored with her life.

He knew that neither Paul Angelfish nor his children had contacted Crystal since their flight. The Praetorian Guard had been monitoring her apartment, phone and computer intensely. They would not miss an attempt to connect with her electronically. Still, Tracker knew Crystal was the closest ally that Paul Angelfish had. Experience taught him that when people are close they share valuable information, even if you had to look in some strange places for it.

Twelve minutes, Tracker thought, pulling himself back to the task at hand.

He opened the front closet. Jackets. A few pairs of shoes. Nothing of interest. He walked over to the stack of paintings that leaned haphazardly against the wall in the corner of the room. He flipped through the canvases: She wasn't a terrible artist, but it was clear that painting was just a hobby. He made his way to her desk and opened the drawers. Detail-oriented, organized. Her screen was on. He sat down.

Ten minutes.

Quickly, he opened and closed several digital files – research notes, graphs, spreadsheets he couldn't understand. He found a folder of photographs and began scanning through them quickly. Family on a boat, on the coast, probably upstate. Then a series of work pictures. The lab. Paul.

Tracker paused.

Staring at this sequence of images, he could tell that Crystal felt something for the man. Each photograph – Paul at work, at his desk, leaning over his test tubes – conveyed a feeling. Not amorous, exactly. More like…admiration? Maybe envy? Paul had something Crystal wanted. Creativity? Genius? Family?

Five minutes, said his internal clock as he heard Crystal cleaning up in the kitchen.

Just as he was about to close the file of pictures and make his retreat, one photograph caught his attention. Paul at his desk. Smiling at the camera in good humor, as if he had been caught doing something mildly embarrassing. What was it about this photo? There. On the desk. A notebook. Leather. Brown. Paul's notebook. Wheels turned in Tracker's mind. Gears clicked into place.

It wasn't the girl's diary, Tracker realized in a flash, thinking back to the desk in Kat's room. *It was her father's. And the girl came back for it. She risked everything to get that book. Why on earth would she do that?*

When Crystal pushed open the swinging door to the kitchen, she hesitated for a moment, struck by a vague feeling of something being out of place. She pulled her cardigan a bit tighter around her shoulders and went to the front window. The empty street stared back at her. She opened the front door and called out for her cat, but it did not appear. Uneasily she double locked the door, then checked to make sure the cat flap on the back door worked well so the cat could come in during the night. She never liked it when he stayed out. As she made her way up the stairs, she wondered if there would ever come a day when she no longer felt like she was being watched.

David

The land rover bounced along the uneven terrain, clinging to one of the myriad paths worn into the parched earth by human traffickers. Hot air rippled through the porous cab. The driver, a young Guardsman named Elliot, had been on the Mexican border for over six months. For the last two weeks, David had been assigned to Elliot's patrol. Elliot was two years older and spoke perfect Spanish. David admired the ease with which he maneuvered the rover and navigated the practically invisible roads.

Through the open cab window, David took in the waste of scrubland that extended in every direction, marveling at the desolation. Saltbush, ash and desert lavender sprouted sporadically from a turf of crushed rock. Although drought ruled everyday existence in southern California, there was a dramatic difference between the City and this central border region. Here, homes had long ago been abandoned, ceded to the encroaching sands and crawling smugglers.

"Did you see that?" exclaimed Elliot suddenly, hunching over the wheel and staring intently through the windscreen. "Over there, four o'clock."

David strained his vision across the scrub, but everything blended into a two-dimensional, shimmering brown.

"I can't see anything," David confessed.

"I can." Elliot turned the wheel violently to the right, tilting the rover with such force that the boys had to lean their weight in the opposite direction, like sailors on a racing schooner. Elliot gunned the engine and sped across the chalky ground, kicking up clouds behind them. A minute later, a group of six children scattered in all directions like frightened rabbits.

Elliot skidded the car to a halt and the two young soldiers leapt out, guns drawn, shooting into the air. After securing the terrified children with cheap plastic cuffs, David and Elliot led them back to the rover. None of them was older than their early teens, and David wondered aloud to Elliot why they would be alone in the desert.

"Oh, they're not alone," Elliot replied. "The Coyotes knew we were coming. Left them to fend for themselves."

"How did they know?"

"Are you kidding? They see our dust cloud from miles away. They tell the kids to sit down and be quiet and don't move. Then they take off for their hiding places to sit tight until we pass through."

"They just hope we don't see the kids?"

"If the kids don't move, they're almost impossible to see. But most of them get spooked when the jeep gets near."

"Why are they trying to get into the country?"

"Get *in*?" Elliot laughed. "They're trying to get *out*! These are slum kids. Coyotes traffic them into Mexico for the cartels. The cartels use them as runners – drugs, but also guns. That's how weapons get into the slums. The government doesn't really care about the drugs, but they do care about the guns. So here we are."

"What are we going to do with them?"

"What are we *supposed* to do them?" asked Elliot with a mischievous grin. "Or what are we *gonna* do with them?"

Tracker

"Open it," Tracker instructed the guard.

The nervous soldier dried his hands on his shirt before releasing the gate to the long row of cells. Vacant faces barely acknowledged him as he passed. At the end of the block, he stopped in front of number seven. The woman inside was curled in a fetal position on the cell's hard bench, a ratty blanket bunched under head to form a makeshift pillow. Even in the low light, he could distinguish the angularity of her cheekbone and the jutting protrusion of her hip through the thin cotton of prison-issued pants. On her exposed ankle, the standard tracking device had rubbed her skin raw. Pus and scabs bordered the tight strap, suggesting infection. For a flickering moment, he felt compassion toward her. When he first encountered her after the arrest, he was struck by her natural beauty: the soft tapered ovals of her eyes; the two fine worry lines etched delicately between her eyebrows; her smooth, light brown complexion. Even more, he had been impressed by the depth of her strength. She remained undaunted in the face of her questioners; terrified by the uncertain fate of her children but resolved to confront her own. The source of her strength lay deep within: an aspect of her inherent character that predated and superseded marriage or motherhood, a natural fierceness that he could not help but admire.

As quickly as these feelings of sympathy coalesced, they dissipated. *We all make our choices,* he thought.

Even from the depths of dream, she sensed his presence. Smacking her dry, chapped lips, she sat up, groggy and disoriented. As her surroundings slowly took form, she recoiled toward the wall in one smooth motion.

"Did you find them?" she croaked, her voice choked with sleep and thirst.

"Not yet," he replied matter-of-factly. "But we will."

She started sobbing uncontrollably. Tracker waited patiently while she collected herself. With a flick of his left hand, he gestured toward the adolescent guard at the entrance. A second later the cell door slid open. Tracker stepped inside.

She wiped her nose with the sleeve of her loose cotton shirt and pulled her knees to her chest, the wall at her back preventing her from further retreat.

"Are they alive?" she asked quietly.

He hesitated, appearing to consider her question in earnest. "It's hard to say. If they are, they may not be for long. After all, children on the streets, in these times…" His voice trailed off menacingly, leaving her to draw an array of horrible conclusions.

"Kat," she gasped, tears welling. He wondered briefly if she would rather both children be dead instead of subjected to the fate of the world, abandoned and afraid. Whether or not she did, he could see that she would never forgive herself for what she had done.

"She's very young," he suggested.

"Yes, she…" But as she lifted her gaze, Tracker saw her instincts snap to attention, closing down her open brow, sealing him off from the transparency of her emotions, regaining her composure.

"Yes," she repeated, more authoritatively. "*Both* of them are young." He admired the speed of her recovery and the calculation of her words. "What do you want?" she asked defiantly.

"It's not the children we want. It's your husband. He discovered something very important." A glint of recognition flashed in her eyes. He pressed his advantage. "If you help me bring the children in, I can make sure they're safe. Then you can all be together. Just tell me where you think they are."

"If you harm either of my children, I'll…" she snarled.

For a brief moment, Tracker seriously contemplated the sincerity of her threat. Then he laughed – a full belly laugh, mirthless and cruel.

"You'll what?" In a softer tone, he said, "I told you, I don't want to hurt them. I want to help them."

"You people have no scruples," she spat back, "no respect for human life, no morals. You're butchers. Why should I believe you?"

"Because you don't have a choice," he said simply. Then raising his voice he commanded, "Door!" The door slid open and he exited the cell before turning back to face her through the bars.

"Let's not play games, Clara. Your husband's work belongs to us, not to him. I'm sure you are familiar with his notebook? The one your daughter came back to your house to get?" Her eyes widened, amazed and terrified. "That's right. She came back to the house to retrieve it from her desk. The desk with the special drawer. Quite a brave thing to do."

He gave her a moment to consider how much he knew, to let the fear soak through. "Now your daughter has that notebook… out there in the streets. We *will* find it, one way or another. So your choice is simple: your children's lives for a book. A balanced trade, all in all, wouldn't you say?"

She remained silent.

"So be it," said Tracker.

Kat

Kat awoke to a gentle touch. Jo Lin's hand was on her shoulder.

"It's time," her friend whispered, gesturing at the group of men gathered around the desk. "Now or never."

Kat closed her eyes. Breathing deeply, she began the ritual of lowering her bodily energy. Gradually, the sounds around her softened. She could feel herself losing heat, losing color, becoming shadow.

"We have traders from the Valley coming first," said the bureaucrat as he handed keys to Rat's henchman. "Let's make sure they're gone by the time Tang arrives. He likes to work alone."

Rat's bodyguard grabbed the key ring and made his way over to the cell. Without thinking, Kat rose in a smooth continuous motion, trying to avoid any reason for the man to look in her direction. He fiddled with the keys and finally found the one he was looking for. After he entered the cell, he called back to the bureaucrat.

"Which ones you want?"

"Number seven, fifteen, twelve, four."

The guard moved roughly among the whimpering children, cuffing the designated girls two at a time and bringing them out to the post. Almost trance-like, Kat drifted toward the cell door as he returned. Keeping her eyes locked with Jo Lin, she could see her friend holding her breath in fear and amazement as the henchman returned and walked straight past Kat as if she were not there – as if she were invisible. Jo Lin's eyes widened with excitement and she motioned with her head for Kat to go. Kat slipped quickly through the open door behind the bodyguard.

The big man paused, causing Kat to freeze. He looked over to the corner where Kat had been resting only moments before. He seemed puzzled, as if unable to put his finger on what had changed. Kat's heart rate ticked upward but she remained perfectly still. She knew that if the guard focused on finding her, he would be likely to see her.

"Hey," said the bodyguard, calling out to the bureaucrat to express his confusion. But just as he spoke, he was interrupted by shouting at the other end of the cell. Jo Lin had started pushing the tall, skinny girl with tattoos on her arms, accusing her of trying to steal her food. The two girls were shoving each other. Other girls gathered round to cheer on the conflict.

"Stop them!" shouted the bureaucrat. "No injuries! No bruises!"

The bodyguard slammed the cell door closed and locked it from inside so he could deal with the commotion. As he attended to the fight, Kat skirted unhurriedly along the wall toward the tunnel entrance. There she paused, looking back again at Jo Lin. The bodyguard had her in a bear hug and was carrying her toward the cell door. Girls in the cell were cat-calling their approval. Jo Lin began to laugh.

"You can't beat me!" she shouted at her captor. "I already won!"

As the henchman carried her to the stocks, Jo Lin began to sing a sweet, high tune that ricocheted off the walls. "*Swing low, sweet chariot!*"

"Shut your mouth, girl!" snapped the bureaucrat, while the men wrestled her into a chair. But Jo Lin kept singing.

"*Coming for to carry me home!*" Then, at the top of her voice, shouting to the ceiling, she cried, "Home! Run home!"

Kat slipped into the dark tunnel and ran.

Jacob

The motorcycle kicked up clouds of dust as they rode. Through the night, Bettina stormed along dilapidated roads, avoiding potholes and oncoming traffic with swerving grace. Jacob sat behind her, clinging to her waist. Twice they stopped at one of the low-grade slave markets Bettina had mentioned – dingy garages filled with a few truckloads of sorry, sick children. The sight of these sad bazaars made Jacob feel the urge to kill someone for the first time in his life. The slave traders here seemed to him among the most wretched and despicable characters on earth. How could they do this? What amount of money would convince someone to steal and sell a child? The thought of Kat being in a place like this tortured him almost as much as not finding her at all.

"It's getting late," Jacob fretted as they mounted the motorbike after the second market and no sign of Kat. "How far to go?"

"Still a ways. But the big market goes all night. It's huge. You'll see."

As they pulled into the town of Dana Point an hour later, Jacob could smell the salt coming off the ocean and hear the sound of waves on the shore. Bettina weaved carefully through a snarled intersection and down a side alley, where they dismounted and secured the bike. They took off at a jog. As they rounded a corner, Jacob made out the massive stone walls that enclosed the Dana Point trading post. Deep trenches had been carved between the fort and the sea, creating a semicircular waterway for speedboats that picked up loads of children and ferried them out to the waiting tankers and schooners that lingered offshore. Favela Police patrolled the docks – not to stop the illicit activity, but to ensure that this human economy functioned smoothly.

Jacob and Bettina plunged through the crowded boardwalk, with its tight clusters of bars, dance clubs and gun shops, and made their way to the main pedestrian entrance of the fort. Two thick-necked Bear Clan thugs barred their way as they tried to enter.

"What you need?" one of them asked gruffly.

"We're looking to buy," Bettina replied with authority.

"Yeah?" said the guard doubtfully, looking her up and down.

Bettina pulled out a thick wad of caldo notes from her pocket and shoved it into the hands of the beefy sentry. Slowly, he counted the bills.

"No drinking inside the post," said the guard, smiling grotesquely. He patted them both down – Bettina more slowly and thoroughly than Jacob – then waved them in.

A great courtyard opened up inside the high walls. At the back of the yard was a two-story building that clearly served as the primary office for the trading post. Large floor-to-ceiling windows on the second story revealed rows of desks from which men surveyed the market's activity and talked on phones to runners in the yard. Given the shady nature of the traders milling around him, Jacob surmised that, even with the security they had passed through, the glass must be bulletproof. Directly below the offices stood a great wooden stage, where an auctioneer manned a lectern with gavel and microphone. In front of him and fifteen feet off the ground, a cage hung from a cable above the crowd. Giant video screens along the outer walls flashed a live feed of the imprisoned children, along with a running digital ticker tape of vital statistics giving the gender, age, height, and weight of each child in the group. Above the head of each child flashed a set of letters – A, B, AA – which Jacob realized were grades they had been given by the market inspectors. From the stage, the auctioneer bellowed his pitch.

"This package is a good one! All of them over fourteen. Been examined by our doctors and approved to work the boats, the fields, AND the factory floor…"

"Two hundred!" offered a man in the crowd, waving an electronic paddle.

"Two hundred?" replied the auctioneer with perfectly feigned disdain. "This lot'll go for more than that! Do I hear five hundred?"

"Four!" someone shouted.

"Four hundred," echoed the auctioneer.

"Five hundred," said someone else.

"Now we're talking," smiled the auctioneer, picking up his banter. "Do I hear six? Six! Seven? That's my good man! One thousand! Gentlemen, we have a thousand for this fine group of workers. Going once, going twice – sold for a thousand!"

A runner, distinguished by his blue coat, approached the trader who had won the auction and scanned the electronic paddle with a handheld device. He pivoted and spoke in his earpiece to one of the men in the office building above to confirm the trade. The auctioneer pushed a button and the cage of children swung along its semi-circular rail and into the building. At the same time, a new cage, with another petrified group of children, emerged from behind the other side of the stage to hang above the crowd and begin the process again.

"Oh my god," Jacob said, horrorstruck.

"They load the cages in the back," Bettina said, grabbing his hand. "C'mon."

They slipped along the base of the wall, past the stalls selling greasy, deep fried pastries and found their way to the loading docks at the side of the fortress. A jagged line of flatbed trucks and rovers idled as they waited to deliver their goods. Up on the loading dock, huge Bear Clan henchmen sorted children, packed them into the cages, and sent the steel enclosures lurching along the automatic wire that pulled them into the office building, where they would be examined, graded, tagged and resorted.

"You take this side of the cars," said Bettina. "I'll go down the other."

"What if she's already been sold?" Jacob said desperately. "What if we're too late?"

"Don't think like that. We're gonna find her."

Jacob started down the row of vehicles, which bent around the corner of the fortress wall and out of sight. Some drivers stood outside chewing khat or smoking cigarettes; others stayed in their seats with the doors opened, talking or dozing while they waited. Jacob moved deliberately, looking at the chained groups of children cowering in the beds of the trucks. On a few occasions, he saw petite dark-haired girls from behind who he believed might be his sister, only to be crestfallen when they turned around.

Preoccupied with his search, Jacob rounded a corner and walked straight into a young Praetorian soldier. Both were knocked sideways and Jacob felt his shoulder slam painfully into one of the trucks.

"Hey, watch where you're going!" shouted the PG youth, putting a hand on Jacob and spinning him around to confront him. Both boys froze instantly.

"Jacob?"

It was David McCaw.

Jacob's first impulse was to embrace his best friend. Relief at seeing him, at the prospect of reconnecting with his old life, surged through him and overrode the urge to ask any questions. But as he took a half step toward him, Jacob could see David's eyes dart around manically, looking from the slave traders to Jacob and back again. He seemed jumpy and nervous. Jacob took a slight step back to create some distance between them.

"What are you doing here?" he asked in genuine wonder.

"I should be asking you that."

David's breath came quickly. His hand twitched toward a gun holstered on his hip. Silence hung between them.

"People are looking for you, Jacob. You're in a lot of trouble."

The skinny, goofy friend Jacob left behind months ago at school had become unrecognizable: skin darkened from days in the sun, eyes wild and distant, he seemed taller, bulkier and stronger.

"You did it, I guess?" Jacob said, trying on a charming smile.

"Did what?"

"Joined up. The army. Like you said you were going to."

The recognition of his military status seemed to soften David for a moment. "I just got promoted. I'm a sergeant now. I was one of the best in basic training, if you can believe that."

"That's great," Jacob enthused. "Congratulations."

"Come with me," David suggested hopefully, a hint of his old voice returning. "I can make sure that my commanding officers know that there was a misunderstanding. That you want to cooperate. They like me. You're my friend. I can protect you."

"They tried to kill my family, David. I don't think I can go back."

"They didn't…" David objected reflexively. "Of course they didn't! I'm sure it's all a big misunderstanding. If you come willingly, we can clear everything up."

David took a step toward him. Jacob backed away in equal measure. Now David's eyes, which had softened at the prospect of bringing Jacob back to the Coliseum, darkened with suspicion.

"Don't make me do this."

"I can't, David. Please…"

As David reached for his gun, a dark shape flew from between two cars and knocked him violently to the ground. David tumbled face-first into the dirt. As he rolled on the ground clutching his ribs, Bettina raised herself up.

"Let's get the hell out of here!" she shouted to Jacob. Without hesitating, they both disappeared between the cars.

David struggled to his feet, ashamed. He looked at the small crowd of traders that had gathered around him – all laughing, none eager to help. His veins seared with humiliation and rage.

"Bastard," he seethed. "Bastard!"

David reached inside his uniform, feeling with shaking hands for the crumpled white card he had been holding since that day long ago in the schoolyard. He took it out and looked at the telephone number inked in simple black writing. Slipping his device off his wrist, David didn't hesitate before dialing the number.

Kat

"Is she dead?"

Kat stood in the doorway, dusty faced, ragged from her long trek across the favela. Renard leapt up at the sound of her voice, startled both at the unexpected visit, and for that visitor to be, of all people, Kat.

"Child!" he said, leaping from the side of Agnes' bed, where he had been keeping solitary vigil. He bundled her in one swift motion into his arms.

"Is she dead?" Kat repeated.

"You're okay? Did they hurt you?" Renard held her at arm's length so he could examine her. His hands pressed the sides of her face so he could look into her eyes. But Kat's attention was singular.

"Is she dead?"

"She stopped eating a few days ago. It won't be long. I told her it's okay to let go. But she…" He paused. "She said she was waiting for you."

Agnes' translucent skin stretched thin over jaw and cheekbone. Her mouth gaped open and closed in a slow rhythm, like a fish sucking air for lack of water.

"I'm here, Agnes," Kat whispered, kneeling close. "I made it back."

Agnes slowly moved her lips in supplication. Kat scrambled to the kitchen, where she put a small amount of water on to boil. Taking two of the apples from a bowl by the side of the sink, she briskly peeled them and placed them in the water. After several minutes, she removed the softened fruit and crushed it into a warm sauce. With great tenderness, she spooned the mash to Agnes' lips, some of which reached her parched tongue while the remainder of which dribbled down the side of her cheek, the juice running in a thin rivulet along her jawbone to the back of her head. Kat touched Agnes' brow with a cool cloth that had been soaking in an aluminum pan beside the bed.

"Almost forty years we've been together," Renard said vacantly as he slumped back into his chair.

"Is she your wife?" Kat continued to mop the old woman's brow.

"We were… partners. We rebuilt Snake Clan together. It became our family." Renard reflected for a long time before speaking again. "I'd never met anyone like her. Not just physically beautiful, which she was, but spiritually beautiful. When we met it was a terrible time. The world had fallen to pieces. You didn't know if civilization would even continue. I only cared about stopping Malcolm Duke. It became personal to me. For Agnes, it was different. She never cared about Duke one way or the other. He was a distraction, a by-product rather than a cause. To her, there was always a bigger picture. It's taken me a long time to understand what she was talking about."

Agnes interrupted them with a violent bout of coughing. Kat slid her hand beneath the old woman's head to give the air a chance to pass into her lungs. When Agnes' fit subsided, Kat lay her head gently down.

"The world is full of tragedy, Kat," said Renard in barely a voice. "You see that in the favela, no? For all her gifts, Agnes was not immune to the world."

"I love her, too," Kat said. "Very much."

Renard smiled and reached out his hand. Kat extended hers in response and let him hold it while he wept.

2

While Agnes dozed, Kat and Renard sat at the table and talked. Renard insisted that Kat recount every detail of her ordeal.

"You walked right past them?"

"Yes."

"I don't understand. How did they let you do that?"

"Agnes taught me. I lower my energy and people don't really notice me. It makes me sort of invisible. My friend Jo Lin told me I could use that trick to escape. So I did."

"I see," said Renard, shaking his head in admiration and disbelief. "Your brother is looking all over the favela for you right now," he continued. "And Pepe – poor Pepe. He's been beside himself – inconsolable – saying that he didn't protect you in Alexandria Square. That he failed the Emergence. He hasn't come out of the Torre since you disappeared. I think he will be the happiest of all."

Kat smiled at the thought of her friend.

"I'll contact Jacob from a secure line as soon as I get back to my office," Renard went on. "Will you come with me?"

"I'll stay with Agnes," Kat said. "But I'll be very happy to see Jacob. And Pepe."

"I'm sure they'll feel the same."

They returned to Agnes' bedside. Renard looked down at his dear companion, dying before his eyes. He brushed stray strands of silver hair out of her eyes. Taking a deep breath, he touched his lips to her ear.

"Renard…" Agnes strained.

"I'm here my darling," he replied, crouching close.

"The girl…"

"Yes. She's with me."

Agnes nodded, her eyes still closed, summoning all the energy she had left in her body. Smacking her lips several times in the dry heat, she managed to push her words out through a thin smile: "She's the one."

3

In her dream, Kat had a vivid picture of Father walking slowly through a thick forest, high along a mountain trail. His face had turned gaunt. A ragged beard covered his face. The filthy shirt that hung loose on his shoulders looked like a sorry rag. In his eyes, she read a combination of despair and determination that broke her heart. Kat longed to speak to him, to hear his voice, even to let him hold her. But she could only float behind him like a shade, hovering, watching, listening.

He traveled with a family of four. For a while, Father walked at the front of the group with the other man, but turned when he sensed the man's daughter trailing behind. Waiting for her to catch up, he reached out to take the child's hand.

"I have a daughter like you," he said encouragingly to the girl. "She's very smart. And very pretty. Like you." The girl gazed up at him wearily but did not smile. Father continued on in a spirited voice. "She's very special, my daughter. She has the most amazing mind. She's much smarter than I am. One day I'm sure she'll be a better scientist, too. Her name is Kat. She loves to read. Do you like to read?"

"I can't read," confessed the girl in an almost inaudible voice.

"No? Well, shall I tell you one of Kat's favorite stories? She has a shelf in our library at home where she keeps all her books. Sometimes I think the characters in those books are more important to her than her own family!" Father laughed at the thought of it. "Charles Wallace, Fern, Fiver. They're all smart, sweet, quirky – just like her."

At this point, Father turned his eyes up to the trees, speaking to the girl, but seeming to look through Kat's dream directly at her. "I make puzzles for her, and she always figures them out. Don't you, darling?"

"Yes," whispered Kat in the dark. "I do."

4

A light touch grazed Kat's forehead.

"Agnes," she said, pulling herself out of her dream.

Agnes stood unsteadily above her, frail but alert. She stroked Kat's hair.

"I go now," said Agnes softly. "Time for me to go."

The old woman's face had recovered a bit of color, perhaps revitalized by the meager amount of applesauce she had managed to swallow.

Encouraged by her recovery, Kat scrambled to her feet and started for the kitchen. "Let me get you a drink."

Kat returned with a glass of cold tea. Grateful, Agnes drank, leaning precariously on her walking staff, trying to maintain her balance. She motioned for Kat to kneel so she could see her more easily.

"You… are… a… special girl," Agnes rasped. Reaching under her cloak, Agnes produced a necklace and extended it toward Kat. A bronze pendant in the shape of a jug dangled from a fine cord of leather. Kat recognized it as one of the charms from the prayer bracelet Agnes kept by her bedside. "You take it."

Kat accepted the gift without question, fastened it around her neck, and tucked it under her shirt, never taking her eyes off Agnes. The old woman tottered dizzily. Kat reached up to steady her.

"*Haliksa'i,*" Agnes croaked. "Listen to me. Very important. I have a brother. His name is Kikmongwe. We have been waiting for this time. For the End. My grandparents…they told us stories. How our people had to leave the Valley, centuries ago, to cross the hot sands, to start again. They passed the stories down, mother to daughter. My grandmother… she said, when the time comes, we will know. We will see the signs. Then Kikmongwe, he was to go to the mountains, to take the People with him, to go down into the earth until it was time. But I… I had to wait here…"

"Wait for what?"

"For you."

"Me?"

Agnes' body may have been giving out, but her spirit sang strong through her eyes. "Yes, you. I waited for you. That was my purpose, Kat. You need to find what your father left for you. When you do, then you must take it to Kikmongwe, on the mountain. We call the mountain *Chu'ovi*, but you call it Olancha. You will find him there. Show him my charm. He will know what it means."

"To the mountain…" Kat felt unsure.

"Can you do that? For the People? For me?"

"Yes," Kat replied.

"One more thing. Very important," labored Agnes. "*He* will come. *He* will try to stop you. He is filled with hatred now, very dark, very lost. But he was not always this way. Not at the beginning. Don't fight him. Help him remember who he is."

"Who is he?" Kat asked.

"Ask him what his name is. His real name. The name I told him was his own."

With that, Agnes clucked her tongue and Quito flew to her shoulder. Ruffling the feathers on his neck, she said, "And keep your eye on this troublemaker for me! Now, say goodbye, Quito."

"Goodbye Quito!" quipped the bird.

Agnes placed her hand on her own breast and took a long, slow inhalation. As she exhaled, she transferred her hand to Kat's breast. A hot, dry desert wind blew straight into Kat's heart.

Leaning heavily on her staff, without another word, Agnes turned her weary body toward the door. Kat followed to the threshold. Out in the ink-black lane, the woman's frame stumbled forward.

"Agnes," Kat called softly.

But the bent, ancient woman, this wise mother of the slums, this fighter and sage, friend and mentor, did not turn back. Gradually her silhouette melted forever into the night.

Tracker

Tracker stood on the veranda outside the Officer's Club at Fort Irwin. In the distance, networks of runways welcomed fighter jets and cargo planes that carried Phoenix mercenary units from all over the world. Below, swarms of Army vehicles churned up dust in their wake as they moved between buildings. A television behind him replayed Malcolm Duke's speech from earlier in the day.

My fellow New Californians. It is a grave and sad day for our country, the end of an era of unsteady, untenable peace...

Tracker marveled at the President's ability to convey, through his solemn, baritone voice, a sense of calm resolve in the face of great turmoil. All his guns and soldiers would be for naught if he did not bring that steady, trust-inducing oratory to the people.

After months of good faith negotiations with our American and Canadian neighbors, we have been betrayed...

Most of all, Duke possessed an uncanny ability to make complicated situations simple for the masses. People did not like messy things, Tracker had found. They preferred things to be simple, even if it meant believing a lie. The President knew this, of course, and he could paint in bold strokes on the moral canvas, always in primary colors.

Recently, the Praetorian Guard captured an American spy working at the highest levels of our government. This spy was planted for one reason only – to undermine New California and our aspiration for independence. We have legitimate political differences with the Americans and Canadians. But we have always played by the rules. After thorough interrogation, this spy revealed that our neighbors are enacting a plan to cut off our access to water in the Pacific Northwest. I hardly need to tell you that in this time of water scarcity, of drought throughout much of our state, this would be catastrophic.

Here was the artful play, thought Tracker. The Americans wouldn't be able to deny it – the spy was indeed theirs. The fact that he never revealed any such plan wouldn't matter. All Duke needed to do was show the spy's face and make his inflammatory claim on television. Then it would be reality, even if it wasn't true. In the minds of the majority, the coming war for water was justified now on the grounds of self-defense. How impossible it would be to go back, to be weak, not to fight.

Many of us still have family and friends in America. So the fact that our former countrymen would take this action hoping to use drought as a weapon – hoping to turn our own citizens against my government, the very government that brought stability and safety to the people of our great nation – when the spineless officials in Washington DC, sitting behind their big desks, did so little to help us in our hour of desperation thirty years ago. And now they seek to turn us against each other? Now they expect us to bend to their will? This cannot stand, my fellow citizens. This will not stand.

In light of these unconscionable acts, and in order to secure the safety and future of New California for our children and grandchildren, I am taking decisive measures.

Our right to water in the northwest has historic roots…

And here comes the appeal to nativism, thought Tracker. To "natural rights," whatever those may be. The people may not be interested in the legal particulars, but surely they would support the idea of fighting for something that belonged to them by right. Tracker smiled to think of the levers the President pulled with such ease.

This infringement of our natural rights amounts to more than an act of legal malfeasance. It is an act of aggression. It is, in short, an act of war.

How long had they discussed it, this justification for war? What basis could they use to warrant taking land from America and Canada? Religion? Trade? None of these would be enough. But everyone saw the dust and the winds. Everyone knew the legacy of drought. Water would do it. Water was how they would drive the world where they wanted. The rest could follow. In the coming era, New California would finally become the shining city on a hill that America once pretended to be.

I have ordered our ambassadors to return home from the negotiations at the United Nations. At the same time, I have asked Supreme General Duke, Commander of the Praetorian Guard and Armed Forces of New California, to make preparations to defend our great homeland. Let me remind all of my fellow citizens, and all countries of the world community – I did not initiate this conflict. I did not seek war. War is only ever a last resort. But We stand ready to defend our independence. We stand ready to fight for our rights. We stand ready to die for each other as brothers in arms, if that's what it takes to be free.

God bless you all, and God bless this chosen land of New California.

Tracker turned from the television and contemplated the vast mobilization of steel, guns and men taking place on the tarmac below.

His phone rang.

Part V

Hilltop

Jacob

Jacob dismounted and raced into the *taqueria*. From the moment Bettina received Renard's call, Jacob had been out of his mind with joy. Scarcely could he believe that after such a night of despair at Dana Point, Kat had somehow managed to make it home to Nova Rio. All thoughts of David, of Bettina, of his parents, of his mission as a spy – all of it became incidental now that his sister was safe.

He burst into Renard's office. Jacob almost didn't recognize his sister, so stunned was he by the steadiness of her gaze and the gauntness of her face. Crying out her name, he rushed to her as she stood up from her chair and hugged her with every ounce of his being. She laughed and gasped for breath as he swung her around.

"Let's give them some space," said Renard, gesturing to the others to follow him out.

"Yes, a little space," echoed Pepe, his lower lip quivering with sympathetic emotion. "Oh, *Gatterina*!" Unable to help himself, Pepe sobbed uncontrollably and flung his arms around Kat and Jacob.

"Pepito!" Bettina said, taking hold of Pepe's shirt. "Leave them."

"She came home, Tina," Pepe blubbered in explanation as he followed her out. "My *Gatterina*, she came home."

"Oh, god, Pepito. You're embarrassing all of us!"

"You cut your hair," Kat remarked when the room had cleared. Jacob ran his hand over his close-cropped scalp.

"Yeah," he laughed. "I did it myself. With a knife."

"I can tell," Kat said. "And you're tan – you look more like me now."

Jacob laughed. "I spent a lot of time outside. In the mountains. I have so much to tell you. You look different, too, you know. Really different. Not physically, but… I don't know. You just seem different."

"I am," replied Kat.

For the next hour, they talked without stopping. Kat listened intently as Jacob described Cherry Hills, his training in the mountains, and the plans for disrupting the government's computer network. She sensed ambivalence in him about Bettina, though she had no idea why. Sometimes he gushed with admiration, but other times he huffed in frustration at the way she treated him. Hardest of all for her to hear – and to understand – was Jacob's account of running into David at Dana Point.

"He started talking about bringing me in, Kat. How his commanding officers would be lenient with us if we cooperated. It was nuts."

"He told you he wanted to be a soldier," Kat reminded him.

"I know, but still… I'm his best friend. How could he do that?"

"You changed. I changed. Maybe he changed, too."

Jacob pressed Kat for details of her life with Agnes, how she gradually learned to walk out in the streets with Pepe. Her account of the abduction by Rat, of El Dompe, of Jo Lin, and of her unbelievable escape left him breathless. That she, of all people, had not only endured such hardship but navigated it successfully was beyond his comprehension.

"I saw so much suffering, Jacob. Jo Lin. The girl with the baby. It's too terrible."

"I know," Jacob replied solemnly. "When I saw those kids being sold in the market to be slaves... When I thought you might be one of them…"

"It shouldn't be like that," said Kat.

"I don't know if we can ever be apart again. I don't think I can do it. The thought of losing you…" His voice trailed off with emotion.

"I don't know why this is happening to us, Jacob. But it is. We have to be brave."

"You think I should still go into the City?"

"I do." She hesitated before confiding, "I had one of my dreams. I saw Father. He's still alive."

"Really?" Jacob was thrilled and excited. "Are you sure?"

"It's never totally sure. But I think so, yes. He's in the mountains somewhere. He gave me the key to the puzzle."

"The one in the notebook?"

"Yes. Those pictures he drew – they're the names of the characters in my books."

Jacob thought back to the pictures. "Fern!" he declared. "From Charlotte's Web."

"Fern, Charles Wallace, Fiver, Sam Grisby, and Lyra. I have to go back into the City. I have to find my books."

"What? Why?"

"The answer to the puzzle is in the books. It will tell me where to find the Ecosystem filter Father created. He said in his notebook, if we can get the filter out to the world, it could change everything. That's what he was trying to do, Jacob. That was his way to resist. Now it's up to us."

Just then, Bettina burst through the door. Renard and a few armed men followed.

"We have to leave!" Bettina cried urgently. "Now!"

"What's going on?" Jacob rose in alarm.

"They know you're here. We need to get to a more secure location – maybe even out of Nova Rio."

"I can't," said Kat.

Renard turned to Kat. "You can't what?"

"I can't go with you," she replied.

"Kat," stressed Bettina. "Tracker was seen entering Nova Rio only minutes ago. He must know you're here."

"Tracker…" Kat's voice trailed off with foreboding.

"If he finds you… Kat, he's going to be here any minute. Jacob, tell her."

"Kat…" Jacob started.

"I need to go back to the shanty," Kat insisted, coming back to herself.

"Kat!" Jacob interjected. "Listen to what they're saying. We can go back later."

"No," insisted Kat.

Renard spoke very deliberately, unrushed by the circumstances. "This is a serious situation, Kat. I know you understand that. We would need a very good reason not to leave for our secure bunker right this second."

Kat looked squarely at her brother. "I have to tell Renard."

"Tell me what?" Renard encouraged.

Jacob hesitated. But at Kat's determined expression, he began to explain. "A few weeks before my father disappeared, he made an important discovery. A discovery that could change everything. It's the reason he tried to get us out of New California. The reason the PG came to our house that day."

"He discovered the secret of water," said Kat.

Tracker

The helicopter left him at the edge of the slums. The young soldier, David, had managed to track the Angelfish boy to Nova Rio. When Tracker arrived at the precinct headquarters, the Captain sat behind his desk smoking a cigar, a self-satisfied smile on his face. Tracker found the man so loathsome it was all he could do not to kill him instantly.

"Where's the boy?" Tracker snarled.

"I've got some very interesting news about that," said the Captain. "Something I think you'll be quite eager to know."

Tracker glared impatiently.

"The boy is with his sister. They're *both* here. I found *two* of them. Left them both for you to have. How about *that*?" the Captain gloated. Tamping out his cigar, he continued, "*And…* guess who they're staying with?" The Captain leaned forward for effect. "Renard."

For several seconds the Captain looked with great anticipation at Tracker's face, convinced this news would pay off handsomely. Tracker's left eye twitched with impatience. He said nothing. Undeterred, the Captain carried on. "I seem to remember that you have a special interest in Renard, am I right? Isn't Renard the last of the great Emergence leaders? Haven't you killed all the others?"

"*Where… are… they*?" Tracker asked almost inaudibly.

"Well, now, that's another interesting thing," continued the Captain. "They were at an old *taqueria* down in little Chiapas. But they must have gotten wind that you were coming because they left in a big hurry. I thought they might flee Nova Rio, which would have been a problem. But for some crazy reason, they went to Hilltop. Too easy!"

"What's Hilltop?" Tracker asked.

"Renard built it with the old lady. Their little gang gets together in her shanty, with that group of scumbag street boys…"

"Old lady?" Tracker interrupted.

"I think they call her… Agnes."

At first, the Captain was unsure if Tracker had heard him. "*Entiendes*?"

Tracker closed his eyes and breathed deeply. Then like a coiled snake, he exploded toward the Captain and took him by the throat. Slowly, he raised the fat man up and pinned him to the wall.

"I'm going to ask you one more time. *Where… are… they*?"

"I…they…" the Captain choked. "I… show you."

Tracker released him and the Captain crumpled to the ground, gasping for air. Crawling away from Tracker, the Captain scrambled behind his desk and opened the drawer. Slowly pulling himself up, he reached in and procured his tablet.

"Here," he pointed on a map.

Tracker registered the location. For good measure, he hit the Captain on the back of the neck so that he crumpled to the floor like a rag doll.

Kat

The group huddled together in Agnes' shanty as Kat spread the notebook out on the table and opened it to a specific passage. Absentmindedly, she stroked Meatball, who cowered in her trench coat pocket. Renard read aloud:

... Water will be free for everyone. It could mean peace around the world. I think this could be the most important scientific discovery in the last hundred years. Malcolm Duke must never find out about this.

Renard's words hung in the air. All eyes were upon him. He stood up and paced toward Agnes' bed, as if seeking her spiritual counsel. Without turning back to face the children, he asked, "You think he hid it somewhere, this filter? And that you can find it?"

"Yes," Kat replied. "The symbols are the first part of the puzzle. The next part is in my books. That will tell me where to find it."

"And then what?"

"I'll do what Agnes asked me to do."

"The Mountain?"

"Yes."

Renard nodded with wry appreciation. "And so it goes. I have my plan, she has hers. And ours together…is the plan."

Bettina stepped forward. "They burned your house down, Kat. We can't be sure the books are even there."

"They were in the bunker," Kat replied. "They should be there. I have to try."

"Even if you find the filter, how will you get it up a mountain?" Bettina pressed.

Pepe stepped forward. "I'll take her. I'll protect her."

"Don't be ridiculous, Pep," Bettina said.

"You're a brave boy, Pepe," Renard admired. Then he turned to Jacob. "And what about you? You're prepared to do this? To risk your life to plant the computer virus? You may never see your sister again."

"I am," Jacob replied.

Gunshots rang out from the street. A moment later Beany tore into the shanty.

"He's coming!" Beany cried. "Up the hill! It's Tracker!"

Renard hardly seemed to hear him. To Bettina, he said calmly, "The final act. Are you ready?"

"Renard…" she replied in a pleading voice.

Ignoring her implicit objection, he said, "Take Kat to the safe house at Ernesto's in the City. Hector, you go to Cherry Hills. Tell Julius what happened. Pepe – you need to make sure the *culebras* all stay in the Torre and out of sight until Bettina returns."

"What about you…?" started Bettina.

"I must face him."

"No!" Bettina insisted.

"No more running, Tina." Reaching down, he took Bettina's face tenderly in his hands. "Agnes always told me it was about the children, not about us. I never understood how right she was." He kissed her gently on both cheeks. "It's up to you now."

Kat secured Meatball in one pocket, the notebook in the other, then followed Jacob, Hector and Pepe out the side window. Bettina took one long, sad glance back at her mentor before she too disappeared from the shanty. Renard lowered himself into a chair and faced the entry. No sooner had he done so, the tall man in black filled the doorway.

"It's been a long time, my brother," Renard said quietly.

Tracker

"Tea?" Renard asked, gesturing toward the kitchen.

Tracker's eyes darted around the room. "Put your hands on the table where I can see them."

"You look well."

"Where are they?" Tracker asked, ignoring Renard's provocation.

"Who?" Renard responded innocently.

"You know."

"How long has it been? Twenty years? Longer?"

"Does it matter?"

"To me it does. I've missed you."

"Then you're a sentimental fool."

"We're brothers," said Renard. "We're blood."

"We're enemies," responded Tracker stonily. "Tell me where the children are." As he spoke, his eyes continued to survey the room, landing finally on the pantry curtain.

"I don't know what you're talking about," Renard replied.

With a violent wheel of his arm, Tracker leapt toward Renard and struck him on the head with the butt of his knife. The elder man toppled backward and fell in a crumpled heap to the ground. Tracker strode to the pantry and flung back the curtain. Quickly he took in the contents: blankets piled on the floor, a small stack of clothes in a corner, a few childish sketches taped to the wall, a bed of straw for her pet.

The girl's room.

Slowly he returned to Renard, who had managed to pull himself into a sitting position on the floor, blood streaming down the side of his temple.

"Let's not play this cliché game of Cain and Abel," Renard said. "You've lost."

"*I've* lost?" Tracker laughed. "I don't think so. *Brother*. You were the only one left from your pathetic Emergence. I killed the rest of them. Your American spy is dead. The war is about to start. It seems, on the contrary, that *I've* won."

"Malcolm Duke is a tyrant. Tyrants always lose in the end."

"You were always the romantic."

"She's dead," Renard said quietly. "Agnes is dead."

Tracker stepped backward involuntarily. In spite of every mechanism of self-control he had put in place over a lifetime of emotional poverty, his heart clenched at this news. Just as quickly, however, he regained his composure. His eyes were blacker than they had ever been.

"She was already dead to me…"

"She loved you," Renard said. "You loved her."

"You *stole* her."

"We all made our choices – and she was always going to choose the world over either one of us. Somewhere in that frozen heart of yours you know that."

"She was a deceitful witch."

"We must forgive each other," Renard said. "She would have wanted it."

"I would no more forgive the two of you than I would cut off my own arm and feed it to the dogs."

"Well, I forgive *you*," Renard replied.

"Go to hell," Tracker said.

For a long time the two brothers stared at each other. Tracker saw Renard search for some shared relic in the distant history that once connected them – saw him mentally excavate their days in the orphanage as young children, their teenage years on the streets of LA, searching for any hint of a fraternal bond. But Tracker met his eyes with emptiness.

"To Hell?" Renard repeated. "Well, then. I'll see you there."

With a swift motion, he pulled something from his sleeve and popped it into his mouth. Almost instantly, his body went into spasmodic convulsions.

"No!" Tracker yelled as Renard's eyes rolled back in his head, foam collecting in the corners of his mouth. He grabbed Renard's hands and pulled them back, but Renard's body stiffened. Suddenly, he ceased to move, his wild eyes staring vacant at the sky.

As the sound of helicopter gunships thundered their arrival above Hilltop, the door to the shanty burst open and three Praetorian Guard commandos in full fatigues entered the room, guns drawn.

"Stand down," Tracker said. "Radio President Duke. Tell him Renard is dead."

Jacob

They moved silently and quickly, losing themselves in the alleys and side streets of the favela. When they arrived at last at the bus depot, they drifted apart without thinking, each lost in their own thoughts, numbed by the speed with which the ending had arrived – Renard, their mentor, their leader, the moral compass to a generation of freedom fighters, was gone. Bettina wandered a little distance off. Jacob knew she was crying and did not want anyone to see, that she wanted time to recover her composure before facing him. He wanted to go to her, to put his arm around her, comfort her. But he didn't dare. Hector and Pepe sat on the curb, Hector trying his best to console the sobbing boy. Kat crouched alone.

The depot buzzed with activity. Life did not stop for tragedy. Most of the people here, Jacob realized, would never know or care that Renard had passed away. This man, who had given his whole life to make theirs better, could never mean much to them. Each struggled in ways small and large every day – struggled for food, struggled with illness, struggled with loss as profound as Jacob's. Why would the death of an old man concern them? Hadn't this battle already been lost? Why should they suffer to lose it again? Jacob realized that being inured to death did not mean that life was cheap: no mother in the slums cared less for her son or daughter than his own mother cared for him. People here were simply resigned to the fact that life was inherently cruel and unfair. Growing up in the favela, you quickly accepted that Suffering slipped quietly through your home like a fog, hovering over you as you slept, following you down the street, watching, waiting, contemplating when to take you gently by the hand and pull you into her embrace. This was true for everyone, of course, not just those in the favela. But until the day he and Kat ran from their home, Jacob simply had not been aware of her proximity.

A burping bus pulled up to the parking bay where they waited. A heavyset driver, an unlit cigar between his teeth, pounded down the bus stairs and began heaving passengers' bags into the storage compartment. In block handwriting, a cardboard sign on the dashboard signaled the bus's destination: *City Municipal Zone.*

"This is your bus," Bettina said as she came up behind him. She had recovered herself and looked composed again, steely and defiant.

"You okay?" he asked apprehensively.

Ignoring his question, she continued in a mechanical voice, "You have everything you need in that pack. All your papers should be in order. You remember the protocols for using the gaming device to communicate with me?"

"I remember."

"You won't have much time. Maybe a few weeks. Tracker's on us now. We have to assume they'll figure out our plan."

"I know."

"Remember – they have cameras everywhere. If they find out you're in the City, they'll start looking for you with facial recognition software. The only head start we have is that they'll expect you to be hiding here in the favela, not right under their noses."

"I know, Tina. You told me all that." He was aware that this was the first time he had used her nickname.

She continued as if he hadn't interrupted. "As soon as the worm is in, then we can try to get your mother out. But not until the worm is in. Once it is, the Americans will invade right away.

It's gonna be chaos. Whether you find her or not, you have to get to the rendezvous point if you want to meet up with Kat. After that..."

"I know what Renard meant to you," Jacob said softly. "I'm really, really sorry."

She looked at him for a long time before responding. "We have to succeed, Jacob. It's our last chance."

The bus driver barked for the passengers to board. Jacob turned to Kat, who had approached quietly. Pepe, eyes red with tears, held her hand tightly in his own. Hector stood behind them both, as composed as he had been on that very first day they met.

"I don't want to leave you again," Jacob said to his sister.

"I can do it," she said. "We can both do it. I know we can."

"I love you, Kat," Jacob said.

"I love you, too, Jacob," she said, and she stepped forward to embrace him. Pepe started to cry again. Finally, unable to endure his own dolor, he rushed forward and flung his arms around Jacob and Kat, burying his head in Jacob's side, and burst into a full wail. Jacob pulled him closer. "You have to be the man now," he told his little friend. "The *culebras* need you. We're all going to need you. You promise you'll keep an eye on Kat for me?"

"I'll never let her down again," Pepe blubbered. "She's my sister. Like you're my brother." He wiped his runny nose with his t-shirt and stood up tall. Jacob gave him one last embrace. Then he did the same to Hector.

"Good luck, my friend," Hector said, clasping him firmly with the Snake Clan grip. "I know you can do it, too."

The bus driver made his final call. Jacob turned back to Bettina one last time, a determined expression on his face. She stepped toward him slowly, locking eyes with him. Then she held his face firmly and pulled him into a long, slow kiss. Warmth flowed through his body, dissolving muscle and flesh, spinning his brain into confusion. When she pulled away, Jacob could hardly move.

"You better make it back to me," she said quietly, still not taking her eyes from him.

"I will," he whispered. "I promise."

Part VI

The Keep

Tracker

They bundled the body onto a stretcher and carted it away. A single soldier paused at the door and waited for instruction.

"Leave me," Tracker growled. "Make sure I'm not disturbed."

Alone in the shanty, he gradually let his body descend until he sat cross-legged on the floor. Time disappeared into his breath. All that moved were his eyes. Every detail of the room came alive for him – the flimsy cot; the battered metal trunk; the empty birdcage; a single plate on the counter; the dirt floor stained with Renard's blood.

Feelings bubbled up as if from a dark well: anger, hate, resentment, and rage mingled with hints of sadness, loss, and regret. He fought against them all with his breathing, tried to banish them back to the deep, but he could not contain them. When he finally let his feelings flow, the room faded and his vision blurred. Two shapes appeared in his mind, ghostly and young. A man and a woman, holding hands, smiling benevolently at him. Crossed over from the dead. Coming for him. For a moment, he disconnected from time and space. A flicker of warmth kindled in his heart, awakening a hope he had not felt for many, many years. As if she might now, in death, be his at last. She electrified him, as she always had. He drew him toward her. Reaching out her hand, she beckoned him, encouraged him.

Please, she hushed, the palm of her right hand open and extended, her eyes warm and soft and full of love. She looked just as he remembered her – young and beautiful, in body and spirit. Every fiber in his body wanted to rush across the void to her, to take her in his arms, to envelop her and submit to her. Then he looked at her other hand, still holding firmly to Renard's.

"No!" he cried. It was a bestial sound, low, guttural and full. "I made my choice."

Agnes continued to hold out her hand, sorrow and remorse spilling tears down her cheek. Renard bowed his head. Gradually, like the dying smoke of a fire, they faded back into darkness. Tracker opened his eyes. His breath came in rapid spurts. With intense concentration, he slowed it down – in, out; in, out – until he had lowered his heart rate and the room came back into focus.

"I made my choice," he repeated quietly to himself.

When his breathing returned to normal, he rose from his sitting position. He felt totally in control again. He made his way over to the bed, tracing his fingertip over the mattress. Picking up the pillow, he touched it to his face, closed his eyes and inhaled. It smelled like death. He felt nothing. It was over. He had won. Carelessly, he tossed the pillow back onto the bed.

A bracelet on the bedside table caught his eye. It lay coiled in a dish like a serpent in its nest. Carefully, he pinched it between his fingers and let it unbundle as he picked it up. Three charms hung on the chain: a crow, a coyote, a snake. He recognized it in an instant, for he had given it to her when they first met, picking out the charms himself and clasping them with love to the thin silver chain. She had loved him in that moment, looking at him with a serenity beyond words. But that love had been a lie, like so much else in his life.

Part of him pitied Agnes and Renard. In the end, their idealism could not overcome the reality of human nature – the animal, tribal truth that the world is violent and unforgiving; that it favors the strong and the unsentimental; that optimism and hope are, in the end, different words for weakness. Malcolm Duke saw the world as it is, not as he wished it would be. That, in the end, was the reason Tracker believed in him as the more genuine prophet.

As he absent-mindedly fingered the bracelet, he found himself working an empty clasp. He scrutinized it closely. A single charm had been removed. He shook his head, surprising himself by laughing aloud. Agnes believed her stories to the very end. She had given the jar to the girl: the water jar. She thought the girl was the chosen one. But he would find the girl – and he would kill her. When they wrote the history of this time, no one would know who the girl was or what Agnes had asked her to do.

But they would remember him.

Kat

Bettina and Kat hunkered out of sight behind a dumpster at the dark end of the alley. For over an hour they had waited there, watching the road, waiting for daylight to recede before crossing the street to the safehouse. A light wind had picked up, and here and there twists of dust snaked into the air. Leaning back against the cool brick of the wall, Kat watched her companion intently. When she first met Bettina, Kat had not been able to judge her energy properly, still traumatized by her arrival in the favela. Without giving it much thought, she knew only that Bettina seemed hostile and antagonistic. Now, gazing at her profile, with her crooked nose and intense eyes, she saw that energy directed not at her but at the street ahead, calculating the risks and threats that lay before them. Rather than feeling intimidated or afraid, she felt grateful and protected.

And then there was the kiss.

Kat had been utterly shocked by it. She knew what love was, or at least understood the idea of it. But her perspective on love had been largely defined by the moments of tenderness she had witnessed between her parents: Father pulling Mother to him as music played in the kitchen; or Mother tousling his hair affectionately as she laughed about his absentmindedness. In such instances, she could see how their energy harmonized, revealing a depth of mutual understanding, care and dependence that had developed over time. Yet when Bettina held Jacob at his moment of departure, the honeyed plumes around them interwove more violently than her parents', charged and tentative, but with a comparable synergy that convinced Kat that Jacob loved her, and that Bettina loved him in return. It made her unexpectedly happy.

As the sun at last surrendered itself to the skyline, Bettina turned to Kat. “It’s time to…” She stopped mid-sentence, surprised to see Kat staring at her. “What’s wrong?”

“Nothing. I was just looking at you. Your nose is a funny shape. But I think you’re very beautiful.”

“Oh, boy,” Bettina scoffed, embarrassed and surprised, unconsciously putting her hand in front of her face. “We need to get moving.”

“I understand why Jacob wanted to kiss you.”

“Uh, okay,” Bettina said, shaking her head and narrowing her eyes. “Now we *really* have to go. C’mon.”

Bettina led Kat across the street. At first, Kat thought they would be going inside an Italian restaurant with fluorescent red letters flashing above the door. But Bettina led them instead into the tight passage between the restaurant and the adjacent apartment building. Along the side of the restaurant, a short flight of steps led down to an iron basement door. Aromas of onion, garlic, and baking bread streamed from a vent in the wall and out into the street. Kat’s stomach groaned audibly as the full force of hunger washed over her. Bettina tapped a code quickly into the keypad on the doorframe.

Automatic, motion-sensitive lights fluttered on as they crossed the threshold. The mixed scent of cured meat, mouse droppings and dust overtook the fresh cooking smells from above. Metal shelves stocked with canned tomatoes, beans, and pasta lined the back wall. From the ceiling hung dried sausages and hams. Against the wall to the right stood an industrial sink and a kitchen locker; on the opposite side a large overstuffed recliner crammed between two tall stacks of boxes. Bettina walked across the room and moved some cans stored on the middle shelf to reveal a green button that looked like a refashioned doorbell from fifty years ago. She pushed the button three times in quick succession, then held it twice for more than ten seconds. A hidden compartment in the wall sprung open at her touch; from it, she removed a handgun. Bettina examined the chamber to ensure it was loaded before slamming it back into place with her palm. Tucking the gun into the waist of her pants, she carefully replaced the cans.

"Now we wait," Bettina said.

2

Bettina pulled a shelf down from the back wall.

"You'll sleep here," she said to Kat, patting the shelf.

Kat dutifully folded her cloak into a makeshift pillow, creating a small nook in which Meatball could nest close to her face. He whimpered softly in her ear. She knew he was desperate to move around in search of food, but also that he was too afraid to do so without her reassurance. He nipped her nose to confirm his unhappy state.

"I'm hungry, too," Kat said, pushing him away. "Bettina said we'll get something to eat soon, so you're just going to have to wait with the rest of us." Meatball gave a small squeak of protest and buried his nose under the coat.

After traveling through the tunnel with Bettina to the City, Kat was struck by how different it seemed to her after several months away – too clean, too spare, too empty. The very things that at first had so frightened her in the favela – the clatter and hue, the filth and stench, the colors and crowds – had gradually become familiar. Moreover, she took unexpected pleasure in how alive it felt. There, life alternated between extremes: one moment full of creative energy, the next full of desperation and pain. For every broad smile of the street urchin entrepreneur, she saw the vacant eyes of the forlorn teenage mother near El Dompe. It felt vibrant, immediate, and real. Here, in the City, there were no such extremes. Life was predictable. Monochrome. Very little noise and smell. Nobody begged on the street, nor suffered from open wounds or obvious illness. But there were very few smiles. Very little joy.

She missed her parents desperately. And yet, without having the language to articulate it, she understood that she was meant to be where she was: sleeping on this shelf, listening to the quiet breathing of a young woman in a chair across a dark basement storeroom under a restaurant in the middle of the City. As lonely as she felt, there was no other place she could be, no other reality that might have been hers.

As she lay on her bunk, her mind drifted back to something Agnes had said to her not long after she had arrived in the shanty.

"You feel scared," confirmed the old woman. "Alone."

"Yes," replied Kat.

"You miss your mother. Your father."

"Yes."

Agnes nodded in understanding. She reflected on this fact for several minutes, and the two of them sat close to each other in comfortable silence.

"When I was a child," Agnes continued, "my brother and I also had to leave the home we knew. We left family, friends. We came here, to this City, before it fell. I was unhappy then. Like you. It took me a long time to accept. We all feel scared when we are alone, when we lose our connection to the people we love. But the thing about the deepest kind of love – the love your mother has for you – that I have for you – is it never really breaks. When those you love are not with you, *that* is when you feel them the most strongly. Their voices are there, in the air, on the wind, in the dust. You have the gift of hearing, Kat. Open your ears to them."

Now, in the dry, dim reality of the basement storeroom, she did what Agnes asked. She closed her eyes and concentrated. At first, she could hear only her own breath. Then, from somewhere on the other side of darkness, a faint sound reached her. Not words, but tones. Voices like the songs of whales, modulating and flowing, saying nothing but telling her everything. A deep calm settled over her.

Clutching Meatball closely, Kat drifted into sleep.

3

In her dream, she is above him. In the sky? On a tree branch? It's hard for her to tell. All she can feel is the sensation of height and distance. From her vantage point, he appears so fragile, curled on the ground, wedged into the crook of a large oak tree. The air around her bites with cold, metallic and sharp. Kat imagines each gust of wind raking his skin, aching his bones. But he seems to feel nothing. His breathing is shallow. He does not try to warm himself. Kat struggles to go to him, but she cannot move. Frozen in place, she can only observe. Just as she thinks she might burst, feathers rustle against her arm. A large gray bird has settled beside her. Their eyes meet. Easily, it lifts off, able to do what Kat cannot, curling on the downdraft through the maple and oak, coming to rest softly at the man's feet. He has drifted out of consciousness, but he senses the bird's presence and stirs into awareness. The bird stands directly in his line of sight, still and statuesque. Confusion smothers him. In spite of his grave condition and enfeebled mind, he still knows that gray parrots do not live in the Sierra Nevada. The bird's unexpected presence energizes him enough to lift his head for a moment.

"Kat?" he manages, his voice as cracked and broken as his body.

"Kat!" Quito responds in perfect imitation of the man's voice.

"I love you," he says, his eyes filling.

"I love you," repeats Quito quietly, this time in the tender voice of a girl.

Jacob

Jacob padded quietly past the cadets breathing heavily in their bunks. Having spent several nights in the Youth Guard dormitory after his arrival on the Coliseum campus, he knew that soon they would all rise at the sound of the pre-dawn reveille. Towel wrapped around his waist, Jacob stared at himself in the bathroom mirror. In the months he had lived in the favela, his complexion had darkened. His hair had lightened. Leaning in closely, he thought that even something about his eyes had changed. He ran his fingers over his chin, examining the traces of light stubble along his jawline. Stepping back a pace, he scrutinized his torso – the muscles in his arms, chest and stomach. He had always been lean, but it was the lankiness of a boy, wiry and undefined. Now, he thought proudly to himself, he looked strong: the pectoral muscles no longer lay flat against his rib cage but stood out, clearly defined; his biceps, while not huge, bulged naturally when he turned his wrist or flexed his elbow, which he did now repeatedly.

As he readied he razor that Bettina had included in his military pack, his thoughts turned to her. Ever since he felt the soft urgency of her lips against his own, he could think of little else. He relentlessly reviewed the timeline of their relationship, seeking out the signs of her affection in retrospect. Small moments began to filter through: the look she gave him the night they talked around the fire in the San Gabriels; the light brush of her hand as she leaned over his shoulder to examine the code he'd been writing. He tried to create a story in his mind that wove these small signs together. But somehow it all still seemed so implausible.

Although Bettina was not conventionally beautiful, he found even the thought of her intoxicating. The angular features of her face; her scarred arms; the intensity of her eyes; her close-cropped hair and baggy clothes: she was a wild mix of mystery and allure. Her kiss had carried him past the guards at the border, propelled him through the intake interviews when he arrived at the Coliseum, and filled him with confidence when he showed up on the first day at his assignment as an attaché to Major General John Brown on the twelfth floor. She, more than anyone, had brought about these changes in him. She was the one who trained him, berated him, exhorted him, demanded more from him. She had been the inspiration for him to cut his hair. She had left him alone on the mountain to find his inner strength. She had designed the worm to plant and trusted him to deliver it. Her life's work was in his hands. And she had sealed all of it with that final, wonderful, unforgettable kiss.

You better make it back to me.

"I'll make it back," he said quietly, leaning in towards the mirror.

2

Evelyn Frazier had worked with General Brown for over fifteen years. She could organize his messages knowing that, for the first hour of his day, he preferred to take care of the trivial things (the easy things), catch up on the news, or skim the latest deployment reports for the ground regiments in the north. If a matter were truly urgent, of course, she would bump it to the top of the list even before his cup of coffee had cooled. The coffee was critical in either case. Of course, she could do all this because she knew who was who. She knew who General Brown trusted and who he liked – though they were not always one and the same. She could delay meetings or expedite them without needing to ask. In many ways, she knew him better than his own wife, given how much more time he spent in his uniform than out of it.

From the first day, Evelyn had been kind and helpful to Jacob. She quickly read the dismay on his face when he realized that the General had already gone up to the council chambers, denying Jacob the chance to meet him. Quietly, she suggested that Jacob arrive before 7:00 am whenever he could. "The General will probably not pay any attention to you, but he will notice it if you're there." The next day, and every day since, Jacob stood at attention by the office door when Evelyn arrived. From the little twinkle in her eye, Jacob knew that she approved of his ambition.

"Good morning, Jake," Evelyn said pleasantly, fumbling in her bag for her security badge.

"Good morning, Ma'am," Jacob replied curtly.

"How many times have I told you? No need to 'ma'am' me," Evelyn laughed. "Now come in and let's see what we have to do today."

Jacob followed Evelyn through the doorway and into the windowless anteroom outside the General's door. Jacob watched her as she bustled around the office. She was efficient in every way – her size, her proportions, her movements. The style of her gray-streaked hair never changed: always pulled into the same nested bun at the back of her head. Glasses hung on a chain around her neck. Most of all, Jacob appreciated her laugh, which chimed musically and lit up her eyes.

"Are those your children?" Jacob asked, pointing to the picture on the shelf.

"Oh, yes, they are. That's my daughter, Shelly – Michelle, but we call her Shelly – and her husband Bob. Such a nice man. And they have two daughters themselves. In fact, I just became a grandmother again! The first boy in three generations – Patrick. Here he is." She walked over to the shelf and pulled down one of the pictures to show him a chubby little boy sitting forlornly on a swing.

"You said your grandmother came to California as a child?"

"She did, yes. It was a different time."

"So were you a child when the Quake hit?" Jacob took a chance to ask.

Evelyn paused before responding, hesitating in the way so many Californians did when thinking back to both the personal and shared horrors of that trauma.

"I was a young girl when it happened," she finally explained. "Of course, now, looking back, you can see that things had been getting bad for a while. The Quake was the last straw. California had been drifting apart from the rest of the country for many years. I guess it shouldn't have surprised anyone when it finally happened. I mean, what do we really have in common with those folks in the South, or even with the Original States in the East? They act more like Europe, anyway. We have to deal with Mexico and Asia. Then there's the drought, of course. And all the refugees from Arizona, New Mexico, and so on. And Mexico! Good Lord, what a mess that place is, with the drugs and the gangs. I mean, we have to look after ourselves, don't we? I may not always agree with President Duke about everything, but he has done remarkable things to keep New California safe. Some people don't like him, but they don't remember what it was like before he came along. It was terrible! So I find I usually end up agreeing with him on the most important things. You can't expect much more from a politician, can you now?"

"I guess if some people have to suffer, that's just a price that has to be paid," Jacob said. His tone of voice was neutral, but she looked at him, unsure of how he meant the comment. "I mean, we *have* to pay that price, I think," he added quickly, trying to be more assertive.

"Well, yes, unfortunately that's true. No one wants anyone to suffer – or to be discriminated against. Of course not. We're not racist. But the world is full of suffering. That's just the way it is. And we have to protect the country for the majority. The whole situation is very sad, really."

"President Duke has brought peace and stability. It's hard to argue against that," Jacob said, trying to sound like a patriot.

"That's right. It certainly is," she agreed readily. Looking at her screen, she said, "Oh dear, we let the time slip. We're going to have to hustle a bit now." She unlocked the top drawer of her desk and removed the tablet that she prepared every morning for the General.

"It looks like there's a package down in the mail room. He's been waiting for that one. They likely won't be able to deliver it up here until this afternoon, but I know he's eager to see it. Would you mind being a doll and fetching it for me?"

3

When Jacob returned with the large padded envelope, the Major General was at his desk. Jacob looked to Evelyn, and she nodded that he should proceed into the office. He took a deep breath, entered the room, and stood rigidly at attention. General Brown continued scrolling through his pad, seemingly unaware of Jacob's presence.

"Excuse me for interrupting, Sir," Jacob started hesitantly. "Ms. Frazier thought you would want to know that this had arrived."

He held out the envelope but did not dare approach the desk. Brown raised a languid eye. Lines etched deeply into a face baked by long days in sun and wind. Closely cropped hair, gray along the temples. The crisp uniform hugged shoulders taut and strong. On the desk to his left, his military cap displayed the symbol of New California: a Byzantine Cross with the small emblem of a bear in the center. Brown reached out a hand to receive the package, his calculating eyes never leaving Jacob's. Jacob approached the desk with one brisk stride and handed the envelope over.

Brown emptied the contents – an encrypted disk and a handwritten note, both intended to avoid the network. He scanned the note quickly before tearing it into pieces, then inserted the disk into his mainframe.

"Evelyn!" he called when he had verified the contents.

"Sir?" she replied alertly, appearing in the doorway.

"We're going to need to send back a confidential message. The Supreme General needs a response tonight."

"I'm sure Jake can handle it, sir," Evelyn said confidently. "I can send him today in the courier car over to Fort Irwin. After all, that's what he's here for."

"When did you start?" Brown asked, casting a skeptical eye.

"Two weeks ago, sir. The day before you left for the front."

"I remember. Remind me – before this you were stationed in…"

"San Diego, Sir. At the naval base."

"Was it with Colonel Thompson?"

Jacob could tell the General was testing him, and he was glad he had committed the file Bettina prepared to memory. "No sir, it was Colonel Ericson. Of the fifth division."

"Ericson, right," said Brown with a glimmer of approval. "I remember him now. He gave you strong reviews."

"I believe so, sir."

"I should give him a call. Find out a little more about you."

"I would be honored, sir." Jacob did his best to mask the rising anxiety. He knew that Bettina had picked this assignment with great care. But Jacob was unsure how much his cover would hold up under close scrutiny.

"Are you *from* San Diego?" the General continued.

Keep it simple, Jacob thought to himself. "Yes sir," he replied.

"You a surfer?"

"Not really, sir, no."

"From San Diego, and you don't surf?"

"Rules Football, sir. That's my sport."

"Ah, well that's something," the General said with genuine approval. "I prefer that to surfing myself. What do you play?"

"Center half-forward, sir," Jacob replied honestly. He felt on firmer ground now, able to draw from real experience.

"The key man, huh?"

"When I play well, yes sir."

Brown snorted. "Fair enough. If you're off your game, it's hard to be the key man. I'm a ruckman myself – or was, back in the day. Played amateur for a few years. That was a long time ago, though." Brown turned to Ms. Frazier. "Well, I already like this one better than the last. Keep him on his toes, will you, Evelyn."

"Oh, I will," Evelyn reassured him. "I've been very impressed so far. Jake has an excellent work ethic. He's here every morning waiting for me when I arrive. I think he has a wonderful future ahead of him."

"Evelyn's a tough sell," said the Major, softened by Evelyn's kind words and the conversation about football. "If you pass her test, then you're on the right track."

"Ms. Frazier's been very kind to me, sir."

Brown chuckled knowingly. "Yeah, well don't let her soften you up too much."

Brown took a key from a clip on his belt and unlocked the top drawer of his desk. He paused, realizing that Jacob and Ms. Frazier were still standing there looking at him.

"Dismissed," he said. "I'll call when the reply is ready. Then you can send the boy."

Jacob saluted and turned to leave the room. As he reached the door, he cast a quick glance back at the General, who was removing a small device from the drawer and plugging it into his computer. Standing once more at attention in the anteroom, he thought to himself, *That's a network drive.*

Ms. Frazier gave him a little pat on the shoulder as she walked past.

“Nice work!” she said, smiling broadly.

Kat

"Breakfast?"

Bettina held out a piece of bread and a hunk of cheese. Kat sat up in her makeshift bunk. The kettle next to Bettina's chair boiled water for tea.

"Ernesto will come down when it's safe," Bettina said. "That button I pushed behind the shelf lets him know we're here. He'll make sure no one followed us before he comes down."

"Who's Ernesto?"

"He runs the restaurant upstairs. Owned it since before Defederation. He's part of the Emergence, but he stayed in the City and set up this safe house. We've been using it for years."

They took a few bites of their food and ate in silence. Bettina's device buzzed and she glanced at it quickly before shaking her head.

"Just so you know, Pepe's been messaging me all morning. I made the mistake of letting Hector give him a two-way since he was so worried about you. I think he still hasn't recovered from your kidnapping! I can't wait to get home and take that damn thing away from him."

Towards evening, long after the bustle of the restaurant above them subsided, a dim yellow light snapped on above the door. Bettina pulled the gun from her waistband and beckoned to Kat; the two girls drew back out of sight into the small bathroom. Moments later, the locks tumbled open and an elderly man shuffled into the room. Head down, he carried a sack over his shoulder. Without bothering to look around, he made his way straight to the back shelves where he unloaded the goods in his bag and left. Bettina pressed down on Kat's shoulder, not allowing her to move. After several more minutes, the yellow light went out.

"All clear," said Bettina.

She approached the shelf where the man had emptied his sack. Turning, she extended a shiny red fruit in her hand.

"Apples," she said with a wide grin.

2

After they devoured the improvised meal Ernesto left them – apples, shelled walnuts, cold split pea soup, leftover pasta – the girls reclined on the floor, full and satisfied. Meatball, too, had binged himself into a stupor. Now he lazed in Kat's lap, purring as she stroked the fur at the base of his neck.

Bettina checked her device, flipping through screens of various kinds. "Jacob seems safe – everything is quiet." She closed her eyes and sighed deeply. "Now the clock's ticking. We have to get the worm in before they figure out he's there. Because they'll figure it out."

"Renard wanted to see him," Kat said.

"Who?" Bettina was confused.

"Tracker. He wasn't afraid of him."

"Renard's not afraid of anyone."

"They had a connection. With Agnes, too, I think. All of them."

Bettina scrutinized Kat. "How do you know these things?"

"I just know," Kat said. "Like with Jacob."

"What do you mean?" Bettina asked cautiously.

"He's different now," Kat stated.

Bettina concurred. "When I first took him out into the woods, I was so mad at Renard. I thought, 'Who *is* this kid?' Skinny, long hair, clueless. I couldn't believe Renard was gonna waste my time with him. It was when he came down from the mountain that I saw the change. It's like I really saw what he could be – as a man, you know?"

Kat considered this carefully, trying to think of Jacob as a man. It was difficult for her. She said, "I didn't like you very much when I first met you." Bettina burst out laughing, both in response to the comment and at Kat's unfiltered style. Kat continued. "Usually I'm not wrong about people. But I was wrong about you."

"I'm not sure you *were* wrong," said Bettina reflecting. "I *didn't* like you! At least not at first. I was pissed off because I thought you'd screw up our plans. We'd been working for years – I'd been working for years – and now these two kids from the City are gonna to be the key to the whole thing? I thought Renard finally lost his mind. But, you know, one of the things I learned from working with Renard --"

"Jacob loves you," Kat interrupted suddenly.

Bettina flushed involuntarily at Kat's words, emitting something between a laugh and a cough. "What…? No…"

"I can see it," said Kat. "He's very… I can just tell."

Bettina cocked her head and pursed her lips.

"Do *you* love *him*?" Kat pressed.

Bettina hesitated. She opened her mouth to speak, then closed it again. Kat could tell that Bettina didn't often talk to people about her feelings. She was practiced in protecting herself, especially her emotions. When Bettina finally spoke, it seemed to be as much to herself as to Kat.

"I care about him," she began, cautiously. "A lot more than I thought I ever would, that's for sure." A dismissive hardness returned to her face. "But how I feel, or how he feels – it doesn't matter right now. The only thing that matters is that he gets that worm in there. Until that happens, we don't have the luxury of thinking about anything else."

"And if he does that? Then what?"

Bettina stared at Kat for a long time before answering. "Then the country gets a chance to start again – not just California.

America. If the world stops fighting over water, if we have peace… That's what this is all about, Kat."

She picked up her bag and slung it over her shoulder. Carefully, she returned the loaded gun to the hidden compartment.

"I have to go back," she continued. "I have a lot to do to get ready for Jacob's drop. I don't know how much time we have, but it's not much. Days. Maybe a few weeks if we're lucky. Let's pray he doesn't fail."

"He won't," said Kat.

Bettina gently brushed a hair back off Kat's forehead. "I don't know where you came from, but I'm very grateful that Agnes helped us all see who you really are."

"Me, too," said Kat.

Bettina smiled. "Are you gonna be okay?"

"I have Meatball," Kat said, scooping up the little rodent, and rubbing him against her cheek. He chirped in solidarity.

Bettina laughed. "Yeah, he's a tough cookie, that's for sure."

She gave Meatball a scratch on the head, to which he responded with a loud trill. Then she reached into her bag and pulled out a battered, outdated handheld.

"I know you don't use these things, but this is an old one – simple to use. There's only one name programmed into it. Mine. It's practically useless except to message me. If you find the filter – sorry, *when* you find the filter – let me know right away. Once we've activated the worm I'll alert you, and when I do you have to go directly to the rendezvous."

"Will Mother be with him?" Kat asked.

"That's the plan," Bettina said.

David

The uncomfortable silence that had been hanging over the cramped police station office had become intolerable. Coupled with the body odor radiating from the sweating Captain – who continuously cast nervous glances at Tracker, who stood motionless against the back wall, David thought he might actually pass out. So when car doors slammed outside, both David and the Captain leapt up in grateful anticipation. Seconds later, Supreme General Erik Duke entered, ill temper spraying from his eyes as he surveyed the room.

"That the boy that called this in?" barked Duke, his eyes on Tracker. At first, David was unsure to whom the General addressed his question.

"Yes sir," David tried hesitantly.

In a growling voice, Duke spoke to directly to Tracker. "A goddamn cadet finds the kid faster than you. Losing your touch?" Tracker stared back with stony indifference. The General continued, "The President is starting to lose patience with this charade, and so am I. I have more important things to be doing than cleaning up your mess."

"Well," mused Tracker with slow effect, "since I work for the President and not for you, I'm sure he and I will have much to discuss."

General Duke grunted his disgust and turned his attention to David. "So, you knew this boy? Angelfish?"

"We were in school together, sir. Before I joined the service." David tried as hard as he could to keep his voice steady.

"And you just happened to bump into him in the slums? Odd."

David felt a flush of nerves. He did not want the Supreme General to think that he had conspired with Jacob in any way. "I was… it was a coincidence, sir. Honestly. I was assigned to a patrol along the southern border and..."

His voice trailed off as Duke took several steps toward him, scrutinizing him with narrowing eyes, placing his face directly in front of David's. David could feel the heat of his breath.

"I know you," he stated quietly. "How do I know you?"

David swallowed hard. "At the initiation ceremony, Sir."

"The initiation ceremony… That's right." The General's face relaxed, a wicked smile spreading across his face. "I called you out of the crowd. And you…" he lingered on the memory, his eyes sparkling with malevolent pleasure. "…you did your duty."

"I did, sir." David's throat was suddenly so dry he could barely swallow.

"And you did your duty again. Called us just like you were supposed to. Ratted out your friend." Duke's eyes roamed up and down David's body, examining his posture, his uniform, his hair. David exerted every ounce of willpower to still his shaking hands.

"For God and Country, sir," David said.

"For God and Country," repeated Duke quietly. Then he bellowed out a huge laugh and slapped David hard on the shoulder. Turning back to Tracker, he cried, "Now *that's* a soldier of mine!"

2

From the moment Duke had mentioned their first meeting, David's pulse raced. Breathing deeply, he fingered the packet of pills he always carried now in his pocket, dreaming up excuses to step outside so he could pop one in his mouth. But Duke commanded the room, pacing as he spoke, and David knew he would have to endure.

"Tell me again why you were in the slums?" Duke prompted.

As calmly as he could, David recounted the details of how he stumbled across Jacob: how they exchanged words, how David planned to bring Jacob into the City for questioning, how he'd been knocked down from behind; how Jacob had fled. Duke pressed him for details about his assailant.

"I didn't see the person, sir," David confessed. Although David had been hit from his blindside, he vaguely recalled that the voice he had heard from the dust after he fell was female. But since he never saw his attacker, he could not be sure – and he thought it might not place him in the best light with the General. So instead he equivocated. "Whoever it was came out of nowhere and knocked me down from behind. By the time I got up, they were gone."

Duke took this in thoughtfully. Walking over to the single, barred window next to the door, he stared out at the dusty road. Back and forth, the busy favela street hummed with unstoppable life.

"This place disgusts me," he said quietly, to no particular audience. "Look at this filth. People forget what we did. That's part of the problem. They forget what it was like after the Quake. If it wasn't for us..." Returning from his reverie, the General possessed the same steely resolve in his eyes that David remembered from that terrible moment on the stage many months prior. "Are you prepared to serve your country again, son? To do whatever it takes?"

"I am, sir."

"I know these Angelfish kids were your friends. But now they're your enemies. They stole something priceless from us, and we need it back. At all costs. Do you understand?"

"I do, sir."

Tracker stepped out of the shadows. "I want to know more about the girl. The sister. She's different."

"Kat?" David said, looking back and forth between the two men, as if they must be mistaken. "I'm not sure what you…"

"She's here," Tracker interjected. "In the slums. With her brother."

"Really?" David replied, shocked. "Here? She's so…"

"Different," prompted Tracker again when David seemed unable to complete his thought.

"Yeah," David concurred quickly. "Really different. Like kind of weird. She freaks out at sounds and smells and stuff. I never saw her without her parents or Jacob, except at school. But she was always getting picked on at school 'cause she's so weird. Are you sure it was her? I doubt she would last very long in a place like this."

"I'm sure," said Tracker. "Tell me about her."

David gathered himself. "Well, she's not very good at relating to other people. Jacob was one of the only people she was comfortable with." He cast a quick glance at Duke and then, as if to confirm his usefulness, added, "And me. She liked me too. I was kind of like a second brother to her."

"How is she different?" Tracker persisted.

"Uh, well… She doesn't really look you in the eye for one thing. Always looking down at her feet and stuff, and mumbling to herself. One thing that's kind of cool, though – she can hear things, stuff other people can't. One time when I was at their house she started talking about a radio show she could hear – and the radio wasn't even on! Jacob said she does that kind of thing all the time. It was nuts. The other thing – Jacob used to talk about how she sees people in colors, or something like that. I'm not exactly sure what that means, but he said she can tell a lot about people just by looking at them. She had a name for it. I forget what she called it."

"An aura," Tracker said quietly.

"Yeah, that's it. An aura. She can see those around people. Like some kind of mutant!" David blurted a nervous laugh.

"Renard is using them," Tracker stated. "I don't know how, but they're part of his plan."

"Don't start with your conspiracy crap," the General jeered.

"Don't underestimate Renard and Agnes. They're up to something."

"They're dead."

Tracker approached the police Captain, whose attention had wandered during this long exchange. He leaned forward, placing two fists on the desk that separated them. The Captain slid down slowly in his chair.

"If you wanted to find the children, where would you start?" Tracker pressed.

The Captain swallowed hard, his eyes flitting frantically from Tracker to Duke and back again. Clearing his throat, he replied dryly, "Bettina. Everyone knows she was closest to Renard. They say she'll take over operations now. With Renard dead, they'll be careful. She'll be hard to find, moving all the time. But she'll know, if you can find her."

"How do I find her?"

"Maybe..." he wracked his feeble brain, knowing he had to give Tracker something substantial. "The street kids? The *culebras*. Or Leo." He said this with conviction, as if he'd come up with the key to the whole problem. Relief flooded through his words. "*Si, si*. Leo. We've been keeping an eye on him. Bettina likes him."

"Where?" Tracker pressed.

"North. Bloomington."

"Show me," Tracker said. The Captain pulled out his device and with a few quick swipes produced an image that he shared with Tracker. Tracker stared intently at it, then handed back the device.

"And where are those street kids?" Tracker asked.

"In the Torre."

Tracker stood upright and turned to David. "Go to the Torre Maria. Get them to talk to you. I'll go look for Leo and Bettina."

To Duke, he said, "As you said, you have more important things to do. So go do them."

Kat

Dusk had settled by the time Kat found the entrance to the bunker. She had waited patiently in the woods behind the house, watching for hours before she felt comfortable approaching the wreckage. Glass and shards of wood had exploded from the intense heat of the fire, and she had to pick her way carefully through it. The house had collapsed in on itself, folded into the middle like a deflated pastry, making it extremely difficult to find her way around. After several hours of lifting and digging, her knuckles bled, lacerated by the charred wood, chunks of loose drywall, and slivers of glass.

She was surprised to find the door already loose on its hinges. For some reason, she had presumed that the bunker would be intact, that the Praetorian Guard would not have been able to crack Father's code and descend into their family retreat. But the twisted, scarred metal around the lock reminded her that the police had other means at their disposal. Gathering her will, she reached down with her toes until she felt the solid touch of the stairway. A moment later, she was totally submerged in darkness.

Raising her tongue against the roof of her mouth, she emitted a series of swift clicking noises. Gradually, a monochrome map of the room unfolded in her mind. Nothing had been left untouched. While the fire had not penetrated to this space, the PG had turned over every piece of furniture, scattering every loose article across the floor. Kat picked her way toward the kitchen. It took only a moment to find the flashlight under the sink. Dust, that unstoppable force, filled the narrow beam as she shone it around the room. Tentatively, she approached the bookshelves, her horror growing with each step. Most of the books had been pulled to the floor. Some appeared to be missing altogether. Rapidly, she took what inventory she could.

Scientific volumes: gone. American history: gone. Mythology: gone. Desperate, she pushed and pulled books aside as she searched. At last, beneath torn copies of some Greek and Roman tomes, she spied the blue edge of a familiar cover. Crouching low, she gently unearthed the slim novel, caressing it as she would an injured bird. One by one, she scavenged each of the books she sought. In a matter of minutes, she had laid out five books neatly by her side.

"We got them," she said to Meatball.

2

Kat sat on the floor, flashlight tucked under her arm. In the back of the notebook, she had transcribed Father's symbols.

5R Instr.Orph.(f.) CW  

Fiver, Lyra, Charles Wallace, Fern, and Sam Gribley. These had been her very best friends growing up. Their adventures had enraptured and transported her; their victories had uplifted her; their struggles had been her struggles. Father knew what they meant to her. He knew that only she would make the connection, that only she could decipher the special, secret code. If she could not crack it, no one would.

She picked up *Watership Down*, as its symbol was the first to show up in the notebook. Uncertain exactly how Father would take the puzzle from here, she flipped slowly through the pages. She paused over the opening chapters, when Fiver tries to alert the warren to impending disaster. Only Hazel trusts his strange visions, only he will listen to Fiver's prophecies, but only Hazel needed to believe. As she read, she came across a page that had the symbol "5R" in the upper right corner. On the page, a single word was boxed in red pen: "*What*". She jotted down the word and kept flipping through the pages. She found the symbol again later in the book. On that page, two consecutive words had been boxed: "*you seek*". Kat wrote these down next.

"*What. You seek.*" She smiled in pleasure. "Oh, I see! I see!"

Frantically, she combed through each of the books in order, writing down the words Father had boxed into the message he had constructed for her:

What. You seek.

Is. The treasure.

In. The gift.

I gave. To.

Crystal.

Tracker

Tracker lingered at the edge of the yard. Through the thin curtains, he could see dark outlines moving back and forth. Periodically, the voices of the children escalated to a heightened pitch, making him wince with aggravation. He flicked the shells of sunflower seeds from his mouth into the dirt with scrupulous efficiency.

I detest children, he thought.

While he waited for daylight to fade, the thought of children carried his memory back to the time just after the Quake, before Malcolm Duke had won the recall, when the City was still a chaotic mess. It was a cool November day. Renard had gone down to Santa Monica to meet with other activists, all of whom feared the popular support that seemed to be building for Duke's campaign. Tracker and Renard had argued about it that morning – Renard infuriated by Tracker's tolerance of Duke, by his cynicism towards politics, and by his increasingly missionary orientation. For his part, Tracker resented Renard's elitist disdain for the strong leader, a realist who knew that politics as usual would not suffice to address the problems of the world and who drew upon the strength of traditional American ideals in a time of moral relativism and social decay.

Alone with Agnes, Tracker abandoned his usual plan to flee the urban stench by hiking long hours up into the mountains. Instead, with Renard gone for the day, he promised to do whatever she wanted. Anything just to be with her. And when she smiled at him and took his hand and pulled him into the street with her, his heart felt full. Decades later, he could still picture how beautiful she looked that day, working humbly among the indigent and hungry, handing out packages of food. To him, the work of charity felt empty and pointless; to her, it meant everything. But if doing it allowed him to spend time with her, then he could swallow his cynicism for a few hours.

At dusk, as they returned to the squat, Agnes spied a young child darting between two fallen stone slabs. Climbing over the rubble to see if the child needed help, they noticed a pot simmering over a low fire. No doubt the girl feared that they had come to rob or kidnap or kill. Agnes crouched down by the entrance of the stone shelter but did not attempt to go in. She simply talked. For an hour, as darkness thickened around them and the temperature dropped, and as Tracker began to lose whatever small amount of sympathy he had managed to muster, Agnes talked. Into the mild evening breeze, she whispered tales about the old days in the red canyons, before cities and wars and drought had divided the people. Drawn in by her melodious voice and the romance of her tale, the child gradually inched toward the open air, until eventually she sat next to Agnes on the stone. Skinny beyond possibility, the fragile girl's innocent eyes stared from orbits carved abnormally deep from hunger and fatigue and fear. Before long, she was sitting in Agnes' lap. Tracker kept his distance in order not to frighten the girl away, but he took in everything.

Agnes asked the girl about her family. She replied that her parents had died in the Quake, along with two of her brothers. Another brother had died from cholera, which had recently been spreading across the city. Even in those days, Tracker had been leery of children, finding them unintelligible and uninteresting. But as he watched Agnes with this frail girl, so vulnerable and trusting, Agnes' tenderness sparked in Tracker something he had never felt before. A small part of him began to imagine them all together – in a better place, in the mountains, away from people, in a simple cabin built with his own hands. The child would be plump and happy, running through the trees; Agnes igniting the world around them with her joy.

Then the girl began to cough. All night they stayed with her. There was no point taking her to the hospital – they couldn't afford it even if a doctor agreed to see her. While they dozed, street children crept out of the shadows like a starving pack of hyenas and stole the remaining food from the fire. Tracker woke up to see them running off with the only possession the girl had in the world: the single pot that she used to cook her food. He chased after them, but they laughed and split in many directions, disappearing like insects under the rubble.

In the morning, he and Agnes carried the girl's lifeless body to a nearby hilltop where, in death at least, she might enjoy some separation from the terror of the streets. They buried her there, laying a stone to mark the spot. And while Agnes wept, he vowed never to let himself bring a child into this sick, broken world.

2

Through the thin curtain, he watched the wife give the man a kiss. Soon the bedroom light went out. The man remained alone downstairs. Tracker picked up a pebble from the ground and stepped closer to the house. He tossed the stone lightly against the pane. After a minute, the man pulled the curtains back to look outside. Tracker faded into the shadows. The curtains fell and the lights went dark. Tracker again picked up a small pebble and tossed it against the window. A moment later, he saw the figure of the man moving stealthily into the yard, gun drawn, pivoting and pointing in the direction of every sound. When the man felt sure that there was no one in the yard, he stood upright and lowered his gun.

And he never saw it coming.

Leo was a big man, and heavy. Tracker dragged him away from the house and up the hill, through the dirt, Leo's shirt rolling up underneath his limp body as they went. When they reached a spot secluded enough such that they would not be heard, Tracker bound Leo by his feet and hands, then leaned him up against the crumbling wall of an abandoned house. A small trickle of blood ran from his nose. His head lolled to one side. Tracker slapped Leo's face methodically until he regained consciousness. In a spasm of fear, Leo jerked his body in a vain attempt to escape, only managing to topple over in the dirt and to pull his bonds tighter. Leo looked frantically around to identify his attacker. His eyes widened in fear as Tracker's black boots entered his line of sight. Tracker pulled him upright again and sat him back against the wall. Long, thin fingers curled around the edge of the tape that covered Leo's mouth. With his other hand, Tracker raised a finger to his own lips, signaling *quiet.* Leo nodded, and Tracker removed the tape.

"I'm not gonna talk," Leo grimaced, keeping his voice low. "You can kill me if you want to. But I'm not gonna talk."

Tracker squatted down until their faces were level. His dark eyes bored cold into Leo's. Then he raised his long frame back into a standing position, and sighed sadly.

"Okay," Tracker said, starting for the house.

"Where're you going? What're you doing?"

Tracker turned back slowly. "Well, if you're not going to talk, I thought I'd see if maybe your wife or boys might be more inclined."

"You wouldn't…"

"Wouldn't I?"

Tracker could hear Leo's breath behind him as he rounded the corner of the abandoned house, disappearing from Leo's view. Suddenly desperate, Leo called out into the darkness.

"Wait!" he shouted. "Wait!"

Tracker held still, out of view, so that Leo had no idea where he might be.

"Not my boys," Leo panted. "My wife. Don't…"

Tracker still did not move.

"Oh, god, please. Please!"

Tracker could hear Leo squirm as he tried to break free of his bonds, toppling over again and writhing in the dust. Tracker reappeared. Leo had wriggled a few feet from the wall where Tracker had left him, dirt caked on his tear-stained face.

"Where are they?" Tracker asked simply, looking down on him with disdain. "The gringo kids from the City?"

"Gringos? I don't know what you're..."

Tracker kicked him violently in the stomach. Leo grunted and gasped for air.

"I know Renard is using them, so skip the bullshit."

Leo spat into the dust, trying to regain his voice. "I swear I don't know anything. I mean, I know they wanted to use the City boy… for something… I met him once… It was a crazy idea. Would never work, I said. But that's all I know, I swear."

"What about the girl?"

"I don't know anything about a girl. I didn't even know there *was* a girl. I'm telling you, only Renard and his people knew the plan. No one else. They kept it that way to protect the mission."

"Where's Bettina?"

Leo hesitated, unnerved by how much Tracker seemed to know already, calculating what he could reveal and what he could dissimulate. Tracker kicked him hard again. Leo cried out in pain.

"Where is she?" Tracker repeated calmly.

"Cherry Hills," Leo sputtered, blood trickling from his mouth. "Usually. At the church. In the basement. There's a door. Behind the pulpit."

"Traps? Locks?"

"A code for the cave. 1-9-9-0."

Tracker squatted down again in front of Leo. Calmly, he said, "Renard was smart not to tell you his plan. You're weak. Like all of them."

Leo's eyes widened, fear emanating from every pore. He started to shake his head. "I told you everything. I promise, that's all I know. Please. I have a family."

Tracker stood. Tears rolled involuntarily down Leo's face. Tracker sat him upright.

"So did I," he said quietly.

David

As the black armored car wound its way through the teeming streets, the Torre Maria grew taller and taller. Rising forty stories above the favela, its skeleton of steel and concrete haunted the skyline. Nothing within sight approached even half its height. A crowd of small children clustered immediately around the car when it came to a stop. David emerged into the thick heat, senses sharp, adrenaline pumping. The children instantly stepped back at the sight of his uniform, but they giggled shyly, wide-eyed at the rare sight of a PG officer in the slums.

"Wait here," David commanded the driver.

Residents ducked in and out of the window frames above him, open but for the colored curtains that waved lightly in the breeze. He read about the Torre on his way over – famous as the intended U.S. headquarters of the Red Star Bank, owned by a wealthy Chinese businessman and built to the highest earthquake-proof standards. Clearly, that fact was true, as somehow the building had remained standing while everything around it had been destroyed. As the slums filled up with the poor, the orphaned, the criminals, the refugees, and the mentally ill, the abandoned Torre had rapidly become home to a vibrant, eclectic and dangerous community of squatters.

David's nostrils flared as he stepped inside. Urine, tobacco, alcohol, dogs, bodies – the stench assaulted him. He covered his face with his arm in a vain attempt to fight it off. As he made his way to the stairs, empty bottles, used syringes, and garbage lay strewn everywhere. Two forlorn women cowered, each clutching a child so small and vacant that David wondered if they were still alive. Head down, he pushed past them.

The stairs ended at the 20th floor. To climb higher, he would have to lift himself up through holes in the ceiling on ropes that hung down to the floor. Only the nimble – mostly the young – lived above the twentieth floor. It was the most physically treacherous part of the building, with open walls exposed to wind and dust, and the threat of a fall ever-present. But with that danger came the benefit of safety from the gangs, which dominated the sturdier floors below. In a world of calculated risk, this is where Pepe and his band of *culebras* chose to live.

David tugged on the rope ladder in front of him a few times to make sure it felt secure. With his left hand, he touched the spot on his lower back where his military-issued revolver had been strapped. Then, with a deep breath, he hoisted himself up.

Wind whipped him through the gaping façade, scattering sand and piles of trash, and pushed him off-balance as he stood upright. With no wall to his left – just open air – he felt as though he was standing on an exposed beam, surrounded only by sky. Stumbling to his left, he crouched down to restore his equilibrium and instinctively drew his weapon as he gradually regained his bearings. He scanned the area around him. No people. Two rotting mattresses in the corner. A small gas stove, rusted and grease-caked, propped up by two cinder blocks. Slowly, he replaced the gun.

A crumbling interior stairway took him to the 22nd floor. But the entrance to the 23rd floor, where the *culebras* made their home, could be entered once more only through a hole in the ceiling. Here there was no rope.

"Hello!" David shouted up. "Is anybody there?" When no one responded, he tried again. "I'm here to see Pepe. It's about Jacob. And Kat. I'm a friend of theirs."

A face appeared in the gap. Just as quickly, it receded. He could hear children's voices talking excitedly. Then one of them called down: "Wadda you want?"

"Can I come up? I want to talk."

"Talk from down there."

"I'm a friend."

"Sit there. Where you are. And put your hands on your head."

David took a step back and sat cross-legged on the floor. He placed his hands on his head. A rope unbundled from above and a skinny, roguish boy dropped down in front of him. Dressed in ragged clothes, pants held up with a homemade belt, he stared with wily intensity at David. His ears stuck out at a significant angle. Behind him, a larger boy with dull eyes thudded to the floor.

"Are you Pepe?" David asked.

"How can you be a friend? You wear that uniform," Pepe said.

"Jacob and I went to school together," David explained. "We lived in the same neighborhood. I was his best friend. We talked about joining the Youth Guard together. That was our plan. But then Jacob's parents got into some kind of trouble and Jacob disappeared. No one knows what happened to him. So they asked me to help find him."

"Why?" Pepe asked curtly.

"We're all really worried about him. And Kat."

Pepe cocked his head in surprise.

"Really," protested David, proceeding with a line of reassurance that General Duke had suggested before he left for the

Torre. "The PG took Jacob's mother in for questioning, but she came back home and Jacob and Kat were gone. When we heard that Jacob had been spotted here in the slums, she was so relieved. She asked me to help. Of course I said I would. The army gave me permission to come here to look for him."

Pepe stared suspiciously. David pressed the advantage and modulated his voice to convey sincerity.

"Do you know where he is?"

"No!" Pepe blurted protectively.

"Oh, that's really… Damn. She'll be so sad. His mother, I mean." David gazed up at the hole in the ceiling above. A gaggle of faces gaped down at him. He made his play. As matter-of-factly as he could, he said, "How about a message? Do you think you could get a message to him? I'm pretty sure he would want to have this." From his inner pocket, he produced a square device no bigger than his palm. Pressing the screen, a picture of a pretty woman appeared, speaking in pleading tones to the camera.

"Jacob, honey," she said. "Please come in. Go with David. I'm here. I'm waiting for you. I need you and Kat with me. Please, sweetie. Come home."

The video went dark. David thought he saw a flicker of doubt cross Pepe's face, and he felt more confident that Pepe wouldn't know that this woman was not actually Jacob's mother.

"If you can't take me to where he is, maybe you can at least take this to him? Just to make sure he sees it. And when he does, he can call me – my number's written on the back there," he said, turning over the device. "I can come back to meet him. If he's with me, he'll be safe to go back into the City. I can protect him."

Pepe stared at David for a long time, and David maintained his expression of genuine concern. Pepe took the device.

David ducked past the crowd of children into the cool, conditioned air of the sedan, which still idled in front of the Torre. A self-congratulatory smile spread across his face. Slipping his wrist phone into call mode, he pulled up the number with his voice.

"Call General Duke," he commanded. Within seconds, the phone rang.

"Yes?" Duke said.

"He took the video," David said, triumphantly. "They just destroyed the device. But before they did I heard everything they said."

"And?"

"Jacob's in the City. They didn't say where, but there's a rendezvous point set up. So they plan to meet him somewhere."

"Well done, soldier. It won't take long now. Goddamn Tracker, running around doing his hocus-pocus. All it takes is a little military discipline. I'm up at Fort Irwin. You go to the Coliseum; I'll have someone meet you there. We'll track him down in no time. Then this whole ridiculous episode will be over."

David leaned back into the cool leather seat and pumped his fist into the air.

Jacob

Jacob passed through the main gate of the Coliseum along with a pack of fellow cadets. They were boisterous, excited to be heading out on the town for a few hours of leave.

"All right, boys, all right," bellowed the middle-aged officer who stood before them. "Settle down. Now listen. You may be off duty for a few hours, but you never stop representing this country and this army. You understand that?"

"Yes, Sir," came a disjointed response from the distracted group.

"I'm sorry. I didn't catch that," prodded the officer.

"Yes, Sir!" the group replied loudly, this time in unison.

"That's more like it."

"Back here at 2100. Understood?"

"Yes, Sir!" chorused the group.

From the Coliseum, Jacob separated from the rest of the young men, claiming he had to go meet an uncle and aunt for dinner, and walked up Thomas Jefferson St. toward the financial district. He turned right on West 6th and followed it all the way across Main St. until he found himself in a crowded commercial area filled with shops and cafes. During the school year, in what seemed like an utterly different life, he and his friends would take the monorail from South Pasadena to hang out in the coffee shops and the second-hand clothes stores before going to catch a 4-D movie near Duke Square. This side of Main St. also offered slightly more diverse food options, and he found himself craving a decent chalupa after weeks of eating cafeteria food in the mess. He knew a good place on Maple St. and headed in that direction.

The evening was pleasant, with the dust levels low and the air warm. Mindful that he might be followed, he sauntered slowly and stopped to look in a few shop windows, using the reflective glass to scan the streets behind him. He doubled back once or twice, as if suddenly remembering something he needed to go back for, just to see if anyone behind him seemed alarmed by his about-face. But the street that evening was filled with average citizens, most of them making their way home, some of the younger workers headed to a bar for a few drinks after work, none of them taking any notice of him.

After ordering two spicy beef chalupas from a cute girl who flirted with him while he waited, he walked to the public square between 5th and 6th, where he found a quiet place to sit alone on a low stone wall. Glancing casually around the square and surrounding streets, he eagerly unwrapped the greasy, fried tortilla.

Taking a deep breath while he savored his food, he removed the device from his wrist and opened it to the gaming screen. For a few minutes he looked like any teenage boy, mindlessly playing electronic war games. Subtly, he removed the back and revealed the secret Janus screen. This he tapped three times in quick succession, then swiped his thumbprint across. It began to dial. With each pulsating ring on the other end of the line, his heart jumped higher in his chest.

"Jacob?"

The sight of her face and the sound of her voice radiated beams of light down his arms and legs. He struggled to bring words to the surface.

"Hey," he said softly.

"Oh my god," she said in a rush. "How are you?"

The obvious concern in her tone, the lack of filter to keep him guessing about her feelings, opened a floodgate in his breast and allowed his breath to flow again, reassuring him that everything had not just been in his head. It was real. What they had was real. On the other end of this phone – with beautiful eyes and skin and teeth and hair and voice – was the girl he was rapidly falling in love with.

"I'm fine," he replied more confidently.

"Where are you? It looks like you're in a park or something. Is it safe?"

"Yeah. I'm in a public square. I finally got permission to go off campus. I have to be back in a couple of hours. But I'm alone."

"Good," she said, the relief in her voice giving way to the tension of the business before them. "Listen, we shouldn't stay on the phone for too long and there's a lot I gotta tell you."

"Is everything okay?"

"You remember Leo?"

"The guy we stayed with on our way to Cherry Hills?"

"He's dead. Tracker got to him."

"What?!"

"Lindy found his body. She was hysterical. It was awful. Those poor kids."

Silence hung between them as Bettina looked away to regain her composure. When she faced the screen again, steel had returned to her eyes.

"Why would he kill Leo…?" Jacob asked.

"He killed him because that's what he does. There's only one reason he went for Leo… He was looking for me."

"Jesus."

"How close are you to getting onto the network?"

"I... I don't know," Jacob hesitated, a familiar rush of inadequacy flooding over him. Before he came out this evening, he had felt confident in the trust he'd earned with Evelyn and General Brown, and that after a few more weeks he might be able to figure something out. But this conversation made it clear that he had made nowhere near enough progress for them to succeed. He tried not to sound discouraged. "I've just been getting my feet on the ground, you know. Trying to make sure people trust me. Scoping things out. But… I don't know… I thought we'd have more time."

"Think. Is there anything you've noticed? Any vulnerability?"

He wracked his brain. "I've been watching the General, but the problem is, I don't see him that much. He's always off in meetings or up at Fort Irwin. It seems like they're definitely getting ready for a big attack. There's Ms. Frazier – that's his secretary – she likes me. But I'm pretty sure her computer doesn't operate on the closed network." He paused again, then perked up slightly. "One thing I did notice – I saw the General use some kind of external drive that he plugs into his desk. I think he does it when he's working on classified stuff."

Bettina responded excitedly. "That's it, Jacob. They give each senior officer a specially encoded drive that gives them individualized access to the network. You have to get your hands on that drive somehow."

"Uh, no problem," Jacob joked weakly.

"I've sent a message to our contact in America. They know Renard's dead. They know we're playing our last card. We all heard President Duke's speech. The Americans are preparing for war, but they'll never attack first – not unless we can get the New Cal defenses down. Our contact said they can mobilize almost immediately if we get them down. But they have to know the nukes have been frozen. They won't risk it otherwise."

"So, all I have to do is…" he trailed off.

"Listen Jacob. There's another thing. I don't want to worry you more, but I don't know if we'll get the chance to talk again. We have to assume Tracker is also after Kat. I have a source in the favela police. He said Tracker was asking about her as well."

Jacob felt instantly nauseous. He bent over, afraid he would retch.

"Jacob?" Bettina's voice rang tinnily from the phone.

Not Kat, he thought.

"Jacob!" Bettina's stern voice wrenched him back into the moment.

"I'm here," he said weakly.

"Kat's okay. I just messaged with her before you called. The faster we do our part, the less chance there is that Tracker will find either of you. We have to get the worm onto their system. *You* have to."

"Oh, god," Jacob whispered, still feeling sick.

"Jacob – if they get their hands on that filter, if we can't plant the worm, the Dukes will rule for a long time. And America will be..."

"We have to protect Kat," Jacob interrupted. It was all he could think about.

"I'll make sure she's safe. I'll keep checking on her. If I get worried, I promise I'll send someone in to get her."

"If you *get* worried?" Jacob asked incredulously. "Jesus, Tina. Tracker is asking about her. He's hunting her, for Chrissake."

"Tracker's here in the slums. He must think you're still here. I don't want to do anything to attract his attention. If we start sending people into the City, it increases the chances that someone will get caught. And that would be a disaster."

"I don't know..." Jacob hedged.

"Look at me," she insisted. "You trust me?"

"Yes."

"I promise I'll keep an eye on her. Right now, we need to focus on what we can control."

"I just thought we'd have more time."

They knew they needed to hang up, that every moment they spent on the line – even a closed line – exposed them to risk. But they also knew that once they hung up, they might never speak to each other again.

"And what about us?" Jacob dared to ask. "What happens now?"

"We can't let ourselves think about that. We just have to do our jobs."

Silence hung oppressively between them. Jacob thought about his mother, somewhere deep beneath the Coliseum, so close to where he slept each night. He thought about Renard and Agnes, both of whom had died and passed on their legacy to Bettina – and to him and Kat. He thought of his sister, strong and certain about what they needed to do – transformed into someone he no longer recognized. He thought of his father, whose life's work had culminated in an invention over which so many people would fight and die, and from which millions of people around the world could derive salvation. And he thought of Bettina, there on the other end of the line, focused, determined, willing to die for the cause.

"I'll find a way," Jacob said.

Kat

Kat's hood obscured her face from the surveillance camera as she boarded the driverless bus. She entered the rear door and found an empty seat. The vehicle passed slowly through the downtown municipal zone. As it approached the Ministry, she sat up a bit straighter. How many times had she come here, to these drab stone buildings, to meet Father? Iconic bear statues rose on hind legs on either side of the plaza; between them, the towering bronze figure of Malcolm Duke pointed east with a single finger, an American version of Ivan the Terrible, towards a future that he alone could envision. Kat had never liked these statues; she found them to be aggressive and ugly. But now she shuddered involuntarily at their menace.

A young woman in a pretty dress boarded the bus, her head wrapped in a light scarf to protect herself from the dust. She took a seat a few rows ahead of Kat and unwrapped the scarf, shaking it free of particles. Kat stared at the strands of short, blond hair at the nape of her neck as the woman tapped her earpiece. Kat heard soft music begin to play as the woman stared blankly out the window at the passing City. After a few stops, Kat rose as if to disembark, but instead took the seat next to the woman.

"Hello," Kat said quietly, pulling her hood off her face.

Crystal Barrington turned in her direction.

"Don't say anything," said Kat, as Crystal's eyes widened in astonishment.

She stopped the music on her device and glanced nervously around the bus.

"I'm not being followed," Kat reassured her. "I picked the bus because it's the safest place. There are video cameras up there, but there's no audio. We shouldn't talk for too long now, though.

We need to pick a different place to meet. I think the library would be good. There are stacks below ground and you can get a carrel there. No one really goes there very much, and they don't have video cameras. So we can talk."

Crystal was taken aback by Kat's rapid-fire plan. Still trying to process Kat's presence, she said, "They told us you'd been arrested. The whole family."

Without trying to address the question Crystal implied, Kat responded, "My father sent mc to find you."

"Your father? I don't understand…"

Anxious to get off the bus, Kat asked, "Did my father give you a gift of any kind? Before he went away? Anything?"

"A gift? No. Not that I can think of."

Kat was perplexed. For a moment she wondered if she'd misinterpreted the message somehow.

"Wait," cried Crystal, suddenly remembering. "He did give me something. I mean it wasn't a gift – well, it was sort of a gift. The tank for the hermit crab. He said he really needed me to take it. That he only trusted me to take care of Jackson."

Jackson, the hermit crab, had been a favorite distraction of Kat's whenever she would spend summer hours in Father's lab while he worked. Kat's mind raced with possibilities. She filtered quickly through mental images of Jackson and his tank. In an instant, she knew what she was looking for.

"The treasure chest. In the tank. Is it still in there?"

"The little decoration?" Crystal asked. "Yes, I think so."

"Bring that with you to the library. Can you meet me tomorrow?" The bus slowed down for its next stop. "I need to get off. I'll explain everything when we meet. Six o'clock? Tomorrow? The library?"

"Yes," Crystal agreed.

“I’ll find a carrel in the history section. On the sixth floor underground. Row H, at the back.”

“Yes, fine.”

“Bring the chest?”

“I will,” replied Crystal, who sat in wonder as the young girl turned abruptly, stepped lightly down to the street, and seemed to vanish into thin air.

2

The majestic building in downtown Los Angeles had been badly damaged in the earthquake. One of Malcolm Duke's first signature public works projects, the new public library was constructed in just six months. Massive blocks of sandstone, separated by metal and glass, rose almost overnight on the same site between 5th and 6th streets. Its hard lines and massive base came together in a twisted central tower that rose several stories above the street, modern and historical elements interwoven in an expression of uniquely New Californian aspiration. At the top of the tower, the Virgin Mary stood, beneficent, mercifully holding out both hands to the suffering masses.

Inside the library, light billowed across a vast atrium. Video touchscreens lined the inner walls. The upper floors were composed of offices and viewing rooms, while the books, every one of them, were kept below ground. Ten stories of dark stacks descended into the earth, the figurative burial ground for the physical texts that had been digitized for modern access – made available via the screens and borrowable tablets kept aboveground. At the grand opening of the library, which took place on his first inauguration, the President decreed that this repository would be able to house a single copy of every printed book in the state, and that no personal paper copies of books would be necessary any longer. He ordered that all people donate their books to the library, where they would be scanned, catalogued and stored. In exchange, every citizen would be granted a tablet through which they would be able to access every volume the library possessed, free of charge. Millions of books poured into local town offices; a few made it here, to the capital. They were only selectively digitized. The vast majority were burned.

It was late in the afternoon when Kat slipped quietly past the central desk. The librarian behind the counter did not even lift her head as Kat walked by. She passed first through the grand atrium, staring at the large mural that covered the entire expanse of the north wall, which depicted Malcolm Duke's journey from childhood to the Presidency. It had been painted in an effusive, Baroque style, and represented Duke as an ancient warrior, riding majestically through battlefields on a tank surrounded by soldiers: a man both of the people and superior to them all. Eventually she made her way to the elevator and down to the sixth floor below ground.

Crystal arrived closer to seven than six. Kat had started to get nervous that she might not show up, but then the young woman appeared, flushed and distracted, at the far end of the stacks. As she approached, Kat could see the agitated energy around her, and the somewhat wild look on her face.

"Sorry I'm so late," she apologized, pulling out a chair and sitting down. Keeping her voice low, she said, "I had to make sure no one was following me. The PG don't really do that so much anymore. But I was a little paranoid, so I took extra precautions."

She reached into her bag and produced the treasure chest from the terrarium.

"I brought this, like you asked. But…" she seemed reluctant to finish her thought. "I'm sorry, Kat. There's nothing in it."

Kat picked up the chest. Carefully she turned it over in her hands, running her fingers over the surface, inspecting the exterior from every angle.

"There are some words on the top," Crystal remarked, trying to be helpful. "*Coenobita compressus.* Latin for something."

"It means 'Ecuadorean hermit crab'. What Jackson is."

"How strange."

"Ecuadorean hermit crabs metabolize salt."

"Like the filter," Crystal marveled.

Gently, Kat pried open the lid. The interior was designed to look as if it were filled with pirate's booty: a metallic surface molded in the shape of coins, goblets, lanterns and other assorted treasure. Kat quickly realized that this surface was a lid of some sort, one that covered the cavity of the chest below. On the interior face of the lid, Kat noticed an almost imperceptible digital screen about a quarter inch long. She pressed her thumb against it gently for five seconds. Gradually, a set of numbers appeared on the screen. 99999.

"Whoa," Crystal said.

"It's a combination," Kat replied. "Five numbers. 90,000 possibilities."

"Ninety thousand?" sighed Crystal, dismayed.

"But he left me the key," Kat said. She reached into the pocket of her coat and took out the notebook, placing it gently on the desk in front of them.

"That's your father's notebook!" Crystal recognized it instantly. Kat picked up the notebook and read aloud the lines:

The Pyramids, Parthenon, and Taj Majal,

Like lilies, bananas, and sunflower seeds,

Like Dolphins and tigers and ants.

Five, the first five, in verse.

"I figured out pretty quickly that it refers to the Fibonacci number. All these things in the poem are perfectly symmetrical."

"I remember the golden mean," said Crystal. "1.618. Right?"

"Yes," said Kat. "And the fifth number is zero." Carefully, Kat punched in: 16180. The light above the keypad flashed yellow.

"What does that mean?" groaned Crystal. "Why is it blinking?"

Kat furrowed her brow. She was genuinely confused. She had been certain that she had resolved the puzzle correctly.

"It's a safeguard," explained Kat, as much to herself as to Crystal. "He's done that because otherwise you could just run a computer program to try all possible combinations and it wouldn't take long to figure out, even with 90,000 possibilities. But if you only have a limited number of guesses, then you'd be highly unlikely to get it without knowing the combination. He's used one like this on me before. It will flash yellow again after my next try. If I don't get it right after the third try, it will either lock completely, or maybe…"

"Maybe what?"

"Maybe self-destruct."

"So you only have three guesses?"

"Two, now."

Kat looked again at the words on the page: *the first five, in verse*. Kat muttered the words under her breath. Then she sat back and smiled. "Oh, Father."

"What is it?" inquired Crystal.

“Look at this line. Five digits – *in verse*. The “inverse.” Which in this case means one divided by Phi. Which is also the golden proportion in geometry. And that number is 0.6180.”

Without hesitating, Kat punched in: 06180. A green light flashed three times, and with a little click, the metallic lid popped open. Thick black foam padded the interior of the box. In the upper right corner, a pin-sized red light pulsed in a rhythmic beat – part of the temperature control system Father had created to protect the biogel. At the very center, wedged deeply into the foam, gleamed four small vials. Crystal tapped the flashlight app on her wrist and turned it on the treasure chest. A blue-green viscous liquid in each of the vials sparkled back at them.

“You found it,” Crystal marveled.

3

They stared wordlessly at their treasure. So much had happened – so much pain, so much suffering, so much terror – because of these vials of precious liquid. Father had risked his own life and the safety of his family for it. Renard had died to protect the girl who could find it. A war was about to be fought over it. And now, here, in the bowels of the public library, they possessed it.

With great care, Kat closed the inner lid. The combination scrambled automatically. Kat punched in the code once more to make sure it re-opened. Then she slipped the chest into her dragonfly bag.

"What are you going to do now?" Crystal asked.

"I need to find a map of the mountains. Then I'm going to take this to someone who can help us."

"What can I do?"

Crystal's wide face and warm eyes exuded concern and hope and love. Kat watched the aura dance around her head, sparkling whites and pinks. It was an energy of friendship, and Kat could not resist the urge to reach out and touch Crystal's arm.

"You already helped," Kat said. "Twice. You called my mother the day the PG came to take us. And you helped me find this."

"I wish I could do more."

"It's safer if you don't know where I'm going. Do you have anyone you can stay with? Outside the City?"

"I have a sister up north," Crystal replied. "She lives by a lake. It's very beautiful there."

"Leave as soon as you can," Kat said as she stood. "It won't be safe here."

"I will," Crystal said.

"Thank you," Kat said.

"No, thank *you*, Kat," said Crystal. As she watched the small girl disappear around the towering shelf of books, she added, "Your father would be very proud of you."

When Kat returned to the safehouse, she carefully placed her dragonfly bag on a shelf behind the sacks of potatoes. Then she slipped the device Bettina had given her out of her pocket, flipped it open and typed in a simple message:

I have it. Am back at the safehouse now.

A moment later, the phone buzzed.

Amazing. Stay there. Will send a message when it's time to meet. Soon, I hope. Great job.

Kat looked at Meatball, who stared up at her from his box on the floor.

"Now it's up to Jacob," she said.

Tracker

Tracker approached the old church in Cherry Hills with caution. Once inside, he swiftly headed for the altar. After releasing the door mechanism, he kicked it open then pivoted away. An alarm sounded below; a bullet thunked into the doorframe beside him. Tracker lunged low across the doorway and released a dart into the dark passage. A second later, a body at the bottom of the stairwell hit the ground with a thud. Tracker descended in two quick bounds. A teenage boy lay on the floor. Tracker knelt down to retrieve the dart from his body.

"Where is she?" Tracker asked. "Bettina."

"C-can't move," Hector sputtered from the floor, his mouth drooping as he rapidly lost muscular control.

"Where is she?"

Hector said nothing. Stepping over him, Tracker kicked open the door to the batcave and stepped inside. Smashed computer equipment lay strewn across the floor. Surveying the mess, Tracker's eye caught sight of the escape tunnel in the back corner of the room.

"She went out that back door," Tracker declared as much to himself as to Hector.

Making his way across the room, Tracker noticed the emergency handle on the wall by the escape tunnel, and the timer above it: 3 minutes, 36 seconds, and counting. The boy must have been only seconds from running himself. It wouldn't be long until the whole place blew. Calmly, he pulled the handle down; the clock blinked three times, then went dark. Tracker guessed that he had missed Bettina by fifteen minutes at the most.

As Hector continued to spasm outside the batcave, Tracker walked the length of the north-facing wall, pausing to rummage through the scraps of paper and debris that littered the worktables. He picked up random objects, turning them over in his hands before tossing them on the floor. At the end of the long bench, a scrap of paper caught his attention. Tracker knelt down and picked it up, unfolding it carefully. Written in a barely legible scrawl were the words: *A-Fish RDV @ 19:00.*

The phone buzzed in his pocket.

"Where the hell are you?" the President raged into the phone.

"In the favela," Tracker replied, his attention still focused almost entirely on the paper in his hand.

"Do you have it?" the President. "The filter?"

"Not yet," Tracker replied, still distracted. Then, suddenly, he knew. "But I know where it will be."

"If that thing falls into American hands…" the President's rage was so intense that he found it almost impossible to speak. "Everything we've been working for is on the line, Tracker."

"I said I know where it will be," Tracker repeated with equanimity.

"We can't afford any more mistakes. I'm giving the order to attack by Friday, one way or the other."

"I should have the filter in a day or two."

"You better. Or it won't be pretty."

Tracker stood over Hector's twitching body. The young man stared back at him, defiant.

"I like your spirit," Tracker admired.

"R-r-renard…" struggled Hector through his immobile lips, "…has more character…"

"Than me?" Tracker knelt close to Hector's face. "Perhaps." Then, holding the piece of paper up in front of Hector's eyes, he said. "I'll tell your friends all about his character when I meet them at their rendezvous. Will that make you feel better?"

Hector's eyes widened in terror.

"Like I said, I admire your pluck," Tracker said. Then he sighed wearily before slowly pressing his boot onto Hector's neck.

David

The armored sedan passed through the gate without stopping. David smiled to himself as he watched the guards at the entrance to the Coliseum stand at attention. For all they knew, David thought, there could be a high-ranking General behind the vehicle's tinted windows. But it was just him – a skinny, pimply, newly promoted sergeant in the Youth Guard. Part of him wanted to howl in laughter at the thought of it.

The car came to a stop at the top of the circular driveway and a young soldier pulled the door open. David gazed across the expansive central courtyard, where uniformed men and women hurried from one side of the complex to the other along crisscrossing paths. He focused on the towering statue of Malcolm Duke in the center of the yard, massive bronze arms spread wide toward all below him. As David controlled the impulse to bow down before it, a middle-aged officer appeared by his side.

"David McCaw?"

David spun to face a short, trim man with a square face and broad shoulders. His eyes expressed of uncertainty, as though David's presence might be a mistake.

"That's right," David answered, straightening his back to convey confidence.

"First Lieutenant Reed," the man said curtly, extending his hand. David's knuckles compressed under the pressure of the man's grip. "If you'll follow me, please."

The Lieutenant led him at a brisk pace across the courtyard toward the main entrance to the administrative building. They passed through tall glass doors into a sealed vestibule, where Lt. Reed removed his cap and glasses before jets of air blasted them free of dirt and dust. In the corners of the chamber, vacuum-like vents sucked the particles off the floor and whisked them through giant tubes into the bowels of the building. After thirty seconds, the onslaught stopped and the interior doors slid open to allow them entry. As the Lieutenant presented their identification to the guards, David marveled at the pristine environment they had entered. The floors gleamed with polish. Digital screens lined the walls, projecting images of the President speaking before large, enthusiastic crowds about the looming threat of war. Small messenger drones scurried along the floor like vibrant electronic terriers. Closing his eyes and inhaling the cool, artificial air, David thought he could detect a faint scent of pine.

Elevators took them several floors below ground. Exiting into a long hallway, David admired the seemingly endless rows of black server columns on either side of the corridor's glass walls. A machine hum purred soothingly through the thick glass, green and red lights blinking on the towers as they processed endless amounts of data.

"I bet that glass is pretty thick," David ventured. The Lieutenant arched an eyebrow but said nothing.

Soon they came to a doorway on the left side of the hallway; as far as David could tell, it was the only doorway on the entire floor. Two guards stood at attention outside the doors. After a short interaction with Lieutenant Reed, they buzzed them through. Inside the office, soldiers of various ranks manned three banks of screens. Each of them wore headsets and computer glasses, issuing voice commands to their screens as they read the data presented to them. Lieutenant Reed gestured for David to follow him and they walked to the end of the first row of computers.

"Baker!" Reed commanded.

"Yes sir!" exclaimed a female cadet, caught off-guard by the unexpected approach from behind. She shot out of her seat and stood to attention.

"At ease," said Reed. The girl relaxed and flashed a quizzical look at David before returning her gaze to the rear wall. "This is David McCaw. He's also a cadet…"

"A sergeant, actually," David corrected proudly. "I just got promoted. Haven't got the ribbon yet, but…"

"He's working on a very important operation for us," Reed interrupted gently. "It's been given the highest security clearance – by the Supreme Commander himself. We are to make all resources available to him."

Lt. Reed punched a few icons on his wrist device and David's face popped onto Baker's screen. A green approval stamp appeared in the corner to confirm David's credentials.

"We're looking for a fugitive," Reed explained. "McCaw knows the suspect personally. He's here to provide visual verification if you can find him." Turning to David, the Lieutenant said, "Baker's one of our best spotters."

"I should be able to handle it, sir, if you'll send over the image," Baker said with evident pride.

"The fugitive was underage. He's not registered yet, so we don't have an official file on him. Like I said, McCaw knows him. The Supreme General asked us to do anything we can to locate him. Understood?"

"Yes sir," Baker responded.

Geraldine Baker smelled like hibiscus. She was plain looking and tall, with lanky brown hair pulled back in military style. Yet something about the combination of her uniform, her smell, and her posture intrigued David. At first, the two of them sat in awkward silence as she methodically plowed through video feed. But David's natural gregariousness eventually bubbled out.

"Seems like a fun job," he ventured. Geraldine just snorted. "Bet you see some pretty sketchy stuff," he tried again. "Looking in on people like that when they don't know."

She looked at him sideways, a conspiratorial smile creasing her mouth. This gave David a first full look at her eyes, which were soft brown and wider than he expected. He felt a little jolt of energy as their gazes met. Brusquely, attempting to assert a business-like attitude, David pulled the chair closer as if to make it easier to see the screen.

"Well, you better show me how you're doing this if we're ever going to find my friend." And though he looked directly at the computer monitor as he said this, he noticed that Geraldine held her position so that their shoulders brushed.

Their initial strategy for the search was to look at video feed from across the southern part of the City, starting from the day David first encountered Jacob in the slums. Geraldine explained that most illegal crossings into the City came through the tunnels, not through the controlled border. Since Jacob wouldn't have official papers, they assumed that this would be how he had entered. While they did not know where all the tunnels were, they began looking quadrant by quadrant at the southern border regions, where the tunnels seemed to terminate most frequently. It took hours to go through the video feed in this methodical way. By midday, they realized they would need to reconsider their approach.

"We need a specific location," Geraldine said. "Is there any way you can narrow down where you think he might be? Even if we knew the day he came across, that would help."

David thought for a moment, unsure. "Maybe we should look at South Pasadena." Geraldine looked at him quizzically. "It's our old neighborhood. I was just thinking, it's hard to know where he crossed over. But maybe once he was back he would want to go see his old house again. Or try to find his friends or family."

"I like it," Geraldine said, punching in coordinates. A long list of video monitors popped onto the screen: street corners, businesses, schools, churches. All of them had mounted cameras that constantly surveilled the surrounding streets.

"Try around the high school," David said. After browsing through several days of video, nothing suspicious appeared. "Maybe the area around their house?"

Geraldine pulled up a camera from the streetlight a few doors down from Jacob's house. Grainy footage showed people walking up and down the pavement past the cordoned-off ruins.

"Man," David marveled. "They left it all burned down. Can you zoom in at all?"

When Geraldine blew up the feed, David noticed a deflated, blackened football in the corner of the yard. A movement at the edge of the woods caught his eye.

"Stop!" he exclaimed. "Go back. Up there. Zoom in on the yard more."

Geraldine rewound the tape. The quality of the twilight and the graininess of the zoomed-in video made it difficult to discern specifics. But David did not doubt what he saw.

"Stop the tape…there," David commanded.

A small figure emerged from the bushes and crossed the yard toward the house.

"I thought your friend was a boy," said Geraldine, confused. "That's a girl."

"Yes," David replied with amazement. "It most definitely is."

2

David excused himself and stepped into the hallway. He slipped the device off his wrist and converted it to phone mode.

"Yes?" came Tracker's gravelly voice over the line.

"I found Kat," David said. "She's here. In the City."

He could almost hear Tracker thinking over the line. "Where is she?"

"I'm looking through security footage, trying to help the spotter find Jacob. I thought maybe he'd go back to his old house, so I had her zoom in on it. That's where I saw Kat. She was at their house."

Tracker digested this information. "Did you see her leave?"

"Yes," David said. "She was in there for about an hour. Then she left with – this is going to seem strange – with a bunch of books. It was hard to tell because of the quality of the video, but that's what it looked like. A pile of books."

"How long ago?"

"The date stamp is from three days ago."

"Have you told General Duke?"

"Not yet. I figured I should call you first."

"Keep looking for the boy. I'll be in the City in an hour."

Jacob

Jacob could not focus. On the screen in front of him, he had typed out the list of items that General Brown wanted him to research. Repeatedly he would look at the first topic, type it into the database search engine, and find that his mind had wandered back to his conversation with Bettina. If Tracker was asking about Kat, he must know that Jacob was in the City and that they were trying to locate their father's filter. Even under the best of circumstances, Jacob couldn't imagine how he would hack into the closed military network in any fewer than a couple of weeks, the time it would take to devise a reasonable plan. By then it would be too late.

"You seem very out of sorts today, Jake," said Evelyn, who had materialized behind him. "I think you've retyped that same phrase into the computer about twenty times! Is everything okay?"

"Oh, yeah," Jacob said, sitting up straight and struggling to regain his composure. "I'm a little spacey, I guess. I didn't sleep that well last night. I found out that my sister's, uh, really sick, so I guess I'm a bit worried about her."

"Oh, I'm sorry to hear that. I hope it's not too serious."

"No, no. Not too serious." Jacob tried to sound as nonchalant about it as he could. "She just… she's kind of a sickly kid, you know? So we all worry about her. I'm sure she'll be fine."

"Well, listen. I have to run downstairs. I can't find my tablet. I think I may have left it in the car. I don't want to disturb the General – he's on a call with the Chiefs. Some serious business going on. I should be back before he gets off. Do you think you can man the fort while I run down? I'll be back in a flash."

Jacob looked vacantly around the office after Evelyn departed. Desperation welled in his chest. He walked over to her desk. As he put his hand down on the surface, it brushed against some papers, revealing Evelyn's ID badge. Knowing that she would need the badge to reenter the building, he grabbed it in case he could catch her before she went downstairs. Hurriedly, he stepped out into the hallway, but Evelyn had already disappeared. As he returned to the office, the General stood expectantly in his office doorway.

"Sir!" Jacob said, surprised.

"Where the hell is everybody?" bellowed Brown.

"Ms. Frazier, she… I guess she left something in the car so she went down to get it. She said she'll be back in a few minutes."

"Damnit," cursed the General. "I have to go up to the war room. It's urgent. Do you think you can handle something for me?"

"Of course, sir!" Jacob replied.

"I need you to type in a set of codes. Encrypt them and forward them to me over the shared network. Normally I would have Evelyn do it, but I don't have time to wait. I need them for the meeting and I have to head up there now."

He handed Jacob a tablet with an extensive list of numbers on it. As Jacob looked them over, the General headed back towards his office. A crazy idea popped into Jacob's head. He acted before he knew what he was doing.

"Sir?" Jacob said, taking a firm stride in the General's direction. At the same time, the General swiveled to respond. He did not realize that Jacob was moving towards him and, as he turned, the two of them collided awkwardly, losing their balance and grabbing onto each other to keep from falling.

"Jesus, Samuels!" the General swore. "What the hell's your problem?"

“I’m so sorry, sir,” Jacob fumbled, as he quickly regained an upright posture and stepped back. “I just – oh my gosh, I’m so sorry – I just wanted to confirm that these are the numbers you want encrypted,” Jacob said, pointing to the tablet.

“Isn’t that what I just told you?”

“It is. It was. Yes. That’s what I thought. But I wanted to be sure… Thank you, sir!” Jacob turned fearfully and immediately sat down at his small desk to begin the encryption process.

The General mumbled something about the incompetence of cadets as he retrieved the briefcase from the floor next to his desk. Pulling his office door firmly behind him, he hovered over Jacob.

“I want those messages waiting for me by the time I get upstairs,” he declared.

“Yes sir,” Jacob said, without looking up.

As the General swept out of the room, Jacob waited for a full minute. Then he took a deep breath and opened his clenched fist. The General’s gold desk key gleamed in the palm of his hand.

2

Adrenaline fueled him now. Swiftly, he crossed to the General's office and swiped Evelyn's keycard. Jacob knew that cameras in the ceiling were recording his every move. No one would be looking at the tape in real time, but every move he made from here on would be recorded. If this crazy, impromptu plan didn't work, then he would likely be in a cell in the Keep by tomorrow. Rounding the desk, he sat in the General's chair and slid the gold key into the lock in the top right drawer. It tumbled easily and the drawer slid open. In the middle of a tray sat the disk drive that Jacob had seen the General use – the drive that would, he hoped, get him onto the closed military network. Heart thumping, he inserted the disk into a port in the mainframe beneath the desk. A monitor slowly emerged from the desk and a female AI announced itself as the screen came to life.

You are now logged into CalNet, Major Brown.

Suddenly parched, Jacob forced saliva down his throat and removed the pin that Bettina had given him from his lapel. Carefully, just as she had shown him, he wound the needle until the USB emerged. Kissing the disk for luck, he slipped it into an empty port next to the network drive and immediately turned his attention to the computer monitor, waiting to see what would happen. Nothing. He checked to make sure that he had pushed in the pin all the way. A full minute passed, but the screen remained dark. To Jacob, time felt suspended. Every sound – every sensation – was amplified. With each passing second, he felt increasingly sure that he had done something wrong, that he had failed to follow Bettina's instructions. At any moment, Evelyn, or General Brown, or the military police, or all of them together would come bursting through the door.

Uploading file now, said the AI as the screen popped to life.

Green bars gradually progressed in the center of the screen: 10%, 20%, 30%. He willed them forward – *faster, faster* – peering anxiously into the main office, sweat beading on his brow in spite of the cool temperature in the room.

"*C'mon*!" he urged under his breath.

60%. 70%. 80%.

A sound at the door startled him and he leapt back from the desk, irrationally looking around for somewhere to hide. Someone was fumbling with the handle, unable to enter. A knock. And then a voice.

"Jake? Are you there? I forgot my ID." It was Evelyn.

"C'mon, *c'mon*," he urged the screen.

90%.

A moment later, the outer office door opened.

Upload complete, the AI said, as the screen slowly retracted.

3

"Jake?" Evelyn stood in the doorway of General Brown's office with a look of genuine confusion. "What are you doing? Where's the General?"

Jacob stood behind the General's desk, his back to the door, the picture of the General's adult children in his hands. He tried to act surprised by Evelyn's sudden appearance.

"Oh, Ms. Frazier, I didn't hear you…" Hurriedly he replaced the picture in its spot and started around the desk. "He had to go upstairs to the war room. An emergency meeting. He needed me to encrypt a message to send up to him. He left the door open, so I came over to close it, and then… I've been curious about her for a while…" He indicated the framed picture of General Brown's adult daughter he had been holding when she entered. "I'm really embarrassed, but I just wanted to look."

"At Rachel?" Evelyn asked, confused.

"It's kind of embarrassing, but every time I come in here I see her picture behind the General, and I think she looks really beautiful and so, I don't know, I guess I just wanted to… I know it's wrong. I shouldn't have come in here."

He could tell from her unforgiving glare and rigid body that she did not believe him.

"Is that my ID?" she asked, indicating the badge Jacob held in his hands.

"You forgot it," he said, extending the ID toward her. "I tried to catch you in the hall, but you'd already gone down, and then the General came out, and…"

She scrutinized his face as she stepped forward to take back her badge. For the first time, he thought about the consequences of his actions for her. Evelyn had been nothing but kind to him since he arrived, taking him under her wing, promoting him to the General, giving him helpful advice – and even now she had unwittingly presented him with the very opportunity he needed to fulfill his mission. Her innocence in this situation and the stability of her own life were about to be sacrificed in the name of war. Although he could justify his actions to himself – as part of President Duke's regime, she was complicit in everything that had happened to Jacob's family by association – he could not help feeling some level of regret.

"I really am sorry," he said softly. "I never meant to cause any trouble for you, Ms. Frazier. Honestly. I just…"

"You just wanted to look at a pretty girl," she finished his excuse, a tinge of resignation in her voice.

"Yes," he replied, holding her gaze. "A pretty girl."

Evelyn made Jacob stand away from the door while she collected a few things from her desk that she needed before taking him down to the security station. For a crazy moment, he contemplated bolting out the door, but he knew he would not get far. It would only make things worse for him, anyway. He had been a pawn in this game all along, and now he was going to be sacrificed. He had no idea if Bettina's worm was successfully in place or not. For him, now, it hardly mattered. The dreams of saving his mother, of reuniting his family, of helping the Emergence – all of them seemed foolish and naïve now.

Evelyn slung her bag over her shoulder, the sense of betrayal still palpable in her body language. "Are you ready?"

"Yes," he said with as much fortitude as he could muster.

"Let's go, then," she said, indicating the door.

He took one step forward – then the alarms began to sound.

Tracker

The car that carried Tracker over the Whittier Bridge had just crossed into the City when the phone buzzed on his wrist. He looked down and saw the caller.

The final piece has been played, he thought.

As soon as he lifted his phone, the Supreme General's voice boomed over the line. "You goddamn piece of… Where the hell are you? There's been a breach. A hack on our system."

A knowing smile spread over Tracker's face – a chess master recognizing the brilliance of his rival's move.

"Renard," he said softly.

"Did you hear what I said?" raged the General. "This isn't about your stupid, goddamn, superstitious bullshit, you ass. There. Has. Been. A. Breach!"

"Where?" Tracker asked coldly.

"Inside the Coliseum. A virus. How the hell did they…"

"The boy," interrupted Tracker quietly.

"What are you talking about?"

"The Angelfish boy. They sent him into the City, to the Coliseum. That was their plan. An unregistered citizen. We would never suspect."

"There's no way some kid did this," Duke objected.

"Ah, but there is. And he did."

Kat

Kat sat up before the device even buzzed. Holding it in her hands, she waited for the message to appear on the screen.

Package delivered. Plan in motion. Go to RDV. Car arrives at 1900. Good luck.

— Tina.

Jacob

This is not a drill. Repeat, this is not a drill. Proceed to your dedicated emergency stations, announced the central AI.

Red lights in the ceiling flashed on and off. Evelyn stopped in her tracks. A look of terrible understanding spread slowly across her face.

"Jake…?"

Code red. Code red, screamed the AI through the hallways. *Report to your emergency stations immediately.*

"I'm sorry, Evelyn," Jacob said. He turned and ran out the door.

2

Disregard all previous announcements. All personnel, return to your posts.

Workers emerged from their offices and froze in the hallways, staring at each other in uncertainty as the video from the information panels on the walls blinked in and out of service. The AI had gone haywire, issuing new orders every few seconds:

Disregard all previous announcements. Report to your emergency stations.

Disregard all previous announcements. All Youth Guard please return to your barracks. Commissioned personnel, evacuate immediately.

Streams of men and women, in uniform and out, flowed in different directions, searching for the fastest way out. Confusion and fear dominated every face. Jacob lost himself in the tide. Armed soldiers had arrived at the far end of the hallway, bashing in doors, searching the quickly emptying offices. Jacob knew they were looking for him. He ducked inconspicuously down a side stairway that led to the lower floors. Once in the stairwell, he pulled up the digital map of the building he had uploaded onto his device during his first week in the Coliseum. At the back of building, three floors down from where he stood, he found his destination:

The Keep.

David

The alarms began to sound as David and Geraldine pored over video from the border crossing. They looked at each other in shock as the AI announcements came in rapid-fire.

"What's happening?" David asked.

"I don't know," she replied. She began typing madly into her console. "I think there's been a breach of our network. That's never happened before. It could only happen from inside the facility. No one can get to it unless they are here, or in Fort Irwin."

Dread began to spread through David's body. "Oh my god," he said quietly. "Can you pull up the register of youth guards assigned to the Coliseum? Run it from the date when I saw Jacob in the slums."

She looked at him curiously for a moment, then did as he asked. Six names appeared on the screen, with a picture next to each one.

"He's here," David said.

Jacob

The two young guards leapt up as Jacob passed through the outer gate and entered the prison complex. One of them pulled his gun and aimed it directly at Jacob's head. Jacob raised his hands in the air.

"It's okay! I'm not armed," Jacob shouted. "My boss – Major General Brown – he sent me down here. You can see my ID. In my pocket."

The other youth soldier jumped over the desk and pulled Jacob's ID from his pocket. He nodded back at his partner, who lowered his weapon.

"What the hell's going on up there?" the soldier with the gun yelled at Jacob. He was so jumpy that Jacob forced himself to remain overly calm.

"We're not sure," Jacob said. "We think there's been a breach of our firewall. The General sent me down. Since the network is malfunctioning, he needs visual confirmation that it's not a prison break. Let me do a quick check, and then I'll be out of your way."

"What're we gonna do, Carl?" asked the jumpy soldier.

"They're supposed to send down reinforcements during a code red. We need to lock down the cell blocks," Carl replied. To Jacob, he said, "I don't know if I can let you through until we get authorization from a commanding officer."

"Sure," agreed Jacob. "Of course. But I'm telling you, something crazy is going on up there. The whole system's gone nuts. The AI is changing its command every thirty seconds. I can help with the cellblock lockdown if you want to go up and talk to a commanding officer."

Carl looked at him for a long moment. "Yeah, okay. No one goes in or out until I come back."

"I don't like this," said the jumpy soldier. "I don't like it. We should lock up and get the hell out of here, Carl. What if we're under attack?!"

"Bev!" shouted Carl to his partner. "Focus, ok? This guy's gonna help. We gotta make sure no one gets outta here. I'm gonna go see what the hell's going on."

"Damn," muttered Bev after Carl had disappeared through the door. "Damn. Damn. Damn. I don't like this. Not at all. Where the hell's that manual? We should have a paper backup somewhere, since the system's all screwed up. Check the top drawer."

Jacob rifled through a clutter of junk in the desk, his mind scrambling with ways to get past Bev, when his eye settled on a baton hanging on a hook behind the desk.

"Here it is!" Bev shouted triumphantly, producing a browned, soiled manual and slamming it down on the desk and starting to flip through the pages. "I'm pretty sure the procedure is in here—"

He never finished his sentence. Jacob dropped the baton as Bev slumped to the floor. Grabbing him under the arms, he pulled the body into a corner before finding an old extension cord to tie his hands behind his back. Sweating profusely, Jacob returned to the desk and scanned through the prison roster screen. Block A. Block B. Block C – and there she was. *Angelfish, Clara.* Cell number 7. She was one hundred feet away. He pressed the red button and the gate to the cellblock slid open.

"Stop!" demanded a voice behind him.

Jacob turned to see David McCaw pointing a gun at his head.

2

"I knew you'd be down here," David said quietly. "Once I realized you were in the Coliseum. Came to find your mommy?"

"David, please," Jacob begged.

"You won't make it out of here," David gestured toward the flashing lights. "You caused all this. It's treason."

"I just came to get my mother out. That's all I want. I promise to just disappear after that."

"You're not going anywhere," David snorted. "You're a traitor. And I'm taking you in."

"Come with me," Jacob pleaded. "We can get out together. Away from all this. There's going to be a war, David. The City will burn."

"Yes, there will be a war," David seemed almost gleeful at the prospect. "But the only thing that will burn is you, and everyone like you."

"That virus… You don't understand… New California is going to lose. The Americans will be in control here in a few days. If you don't get out now…"

"We're not going to lose," David insisted.

"That computer virus is destroying CalNet. The country will be defenseless. The nukes won't work. The Americans can just march in. That's the whole plan." A trace of uncertainty flashed across David's face at Jacob's words. Jacob tried to capitalize. "Come with me," he repeated urgently. "I know this isn't who you are."

David's visage hardened. "It is who I am."

In a flash, Jacob lunged, throwing the full weight of his shoulder into David's midriff. The gun discharged and for a fraction of a second Jacob wondered if he'd been hit. He felt no pain, so he just kept driving his knees forward, following the good tackling technique he had learned on his Rules football team. David's back slammed against the door and Jacob heard the air rush out of his friend's lungs as he collapsed beneath him. The gun clattered to the floor. As David struggled for breath, Jacob grabbed the gun stepped back, pointing the weapon at his friend. David rose onto one elbow and massaged his throat, then tenderly touched his ribs. Pure hatred spilled from his eyes.

"You're gonna pay for this," he choked from the floor. "Favela scum."

"Yes, I am. And proud of it."

"Traitor!" David leapt off the floor in a surge of adrenaline, teeth bared, roaring like a cornered lion.

Jacob pulled the trigger.

Kat

Kat crawled through the fence just as she and her brother had done countless times before. The old synagogue hunched, tired and heavy, in the diminishing light. Meatball wriggled nervously in her pocket. Over her shoulder, the dragonfly bag held all that she now possessed in the world: the communication device Bettina had given her, father's notebook, the Genesis Ecosystem. Giving the synagogue a wide berth, she paused to scan the junkyard that sprawled behind it. In the distance, air raid alarms and emergency vehicle sirens wailed disharmoniously into the gray twilight. Meatball squeaked pathetically in her pocket.

"I know," she said, stroking his head reassuringly and keeping her eyes forebodingly on the dark woods. "I feel it, too."

Making her way down to the old jalopy, she placed her hand on its roof, the warm metal penetrating her skin and sending ripples of memory through her body. She peered inside. The seats gave off their familiar, fuggy smell. She resisted a powerful urge to curl up on the back seat and hide until Jacob arrived. Better to return to the hill where the synagogue stood, where she would have a more commanding view of the area. She could wait there until Jacob and Mother arrived.

Suddenly, the air around her felt colder. Her spine tingled as she felt a presence behind her.

"Hello, Kat."

Jacob

David's groans echoed off the walls. His shoulder had exploded from the gunshot, splattering blood and bone. Jacob dragged him across the floor, which only elicited more violent screams of pain. At the first vacant cell, Jacob deposited David inside and pulled the gate behind him. David moaned in agony. Jacob grabbed an old coat from the rack and a roll of tape from the drawer and shoved them through the bars.

"The bullet went through your shoulder. It didn't hit anything else. Tape it as tight as you can to stop the bleeding. If you do, you'll be okay until they find you."

Jacob took a long look at the writhing boy on the ground before him. Knowing he would likely never see his friend again, he finally said, "I'm really sorry, David. I'm really, really sorry."

Jacob made his way down cellblock C, carefully following the numbers above each door. By now, most of the prisoners had been aroused from their normal states of disregard and were standing at the bars of their cells. As he passed, a few of them stretched out their hands, urging him to open their doors. He kept to the middle of the corridor, only one thought on his mind.

Cell 10. Cell 9. Cell 8. Cell 7.

A frail, ragged creature lay curled in a fetal ball on the cell's metal bed – this could never be his mother. Dirty hair. Gaunt features. Barefoot. Weak. Choking on his voice, he spoke softly, unsure if she would be capable of responding.

"Mom?"

It took a moment for the sound of his voice to reach her through her clouded consciousness. Sitting up gradually, she looked confused, distrusting her own senses. For a terrifying moment, Jacob wondered if perhaps she had gone mad. He pushed the button for her cell and the gate slid open. At the sight of his uniform, she instinctively backed toward the wall, fear descending over her face, as if they were playing one last, cruel trick – sending a soldier resembling her son as her executioner. Jacob raised both hands, palms outward, and whispered quietly: *it's okay, it's okay*. Slowly he lowered himself into a crouching position by the bed so that he looked up at her like a supplicant.

"It's me," he reassured her. "It's Jacob. I came to get you out."

He took hold of her hand. The warmth of his touch began to dissipate the clouds in her eyes. Gradually, flecks of gold and green surfaced and recolored her bleached iris. Her body knew before her mind could process the thought: this was her son. Tears began to roll down her face.

"Mom?"

Clara reached out and touched his cheek with a bony forefinger, her voice cracked and weak. "Jacob?"

"It's me."

Jacob moved quickly to the bed. Clara's lower lip trembled. She took his face in both hands, still unable to fully comprehend his presence. Then, relenting to the truth at last, she let herself fall into him. Great heaves shook her body. Jacob wrapped his arms around her impossibly narrowed shoulders, shocked at the sharpness of bone against his chest and by how small she felt. Every ounce of strength she had summoned to get her through her captivity evaporated as she sobbed uncontrollably. Jacob simply held her. He had never embraced his mother in this way before – as a man, not a boy; comforting rather than seeking comfort. Suddenly she pulled back, her face slick with tears, wild desperation in her eyes.

"Kat?" she cried.

"She's waiting for us. Can you do it?"

A shot of strength jolted through Clara's body from some hidden maternal well. Wobbly at first on her feet, she held out her hand for his support. He grasped it firmly as she tested her legs. Then she stared at him with burning intensity.

"Let's go," she said.

2

Mayhem had broken out within the Coliseum. Guards at different checkpoints were overrun by the everyday workers who, confused by all the conflicting announcements and terrified that the alarms might mean an imminent attack, lost all discipline and ran for the exits. Jacob gave his mother a military jacket and cap that hung in the prison's outer office, which he thought would be enough to make her inconspicuous in the confusion. Jacob eased them into the flow of the crowd, letting the human current carry them toward a side exit. Pausing on a side street, Jacob scanned through his phone for the details of the self-driving car Bettina had arranged for him to pick up.

"You should eat something before we get in the car," he said.

"No," Clara insisted. "I want to see Kat."

"This way," said Jacob, taking hold of his mother's arm and guiding her up the street. "We'll find some food on the way."

The autonomous vehicle glided smoothly along the side roads towards the destination Jacob had punched into its navigation system. Clara chewed slowly on one of the nutra-bars Jacob had grabbed from a convenience store that had been abandoned by its owner. The physical movement and nourishment had returned color to his mother's face, and Jacob took pleasure in watching her eat. With small sips, she drank gratefully from one of the bottles of clean water Jacob had also grabbed. For the remainder of their journey, Jacob explained as best he could what had happened. Clara interrupted occasionally, unable to believe that her children had not only endured such hardship, but that they had the fortitude and cleverness to rescue her.

The sense of chaos around the Coliseum diminished as they passed further into the surrounding neighborhoods. For the final quarter of an hour, they sat together in an increasingly heavy silence, oppressed by the uncertainty they felt about whether Kat would be waiting for them. When the car pulled to the side of the road near the entrance to the memorial neighborhood, Clara took hold of Jacob's hand.

"You think she'll be there?" she asked in a tremulous voice.

"That's the plan," Jacob replied unsurely.

They approached the synagogue with caution, moving among shadows. When they circled around the dilapidated building and stepped onto the back veranda, Jacob immediately searched out the old jalopy among the piles of trash. Kat sat on the hood, staring back at them. Clara saw her, too, and, with a sharp inhalation of excitement and emotion, instinctively went to her.

"Wait!" Jacob said, grabbing her arm and holding her back.

Like a shadow, a man emerged from behind the car. He held a knife and placed it gingerly at Kat's throat.

"No!" Mother cried, freeing herself from Jacob's grasp and surging down the hill. "Not you!"

"Stop!" Tracker shouted. "Come down slowly. Together. Hands up. You don't want the little one to get hurt."

Jacob and Clara clambered down the hill of trash in as measured a way as they could, hands raised above their heads. Finally, they stood before him: this man, this murderer, their nemesis. Kat remained perfectly still, her eyes never leaving her mother's.

“Kat, darling,” Clara said, reaching out her hands. She begged Tracker, “Please.”

“Stay where you are,” Tracker ordered.

Clara began to sob. “Please,” she cried again. “Let me go to her.”

“Sit down where you are. Both of you.”

They did as he commanded. Tracker approached them cautiously, then checked to make sure they carried no weapons. Stepping back, he produced the small treasure chest that he had taken from Kat. He turned it over in his hands, marveling at it.

“All of this craziness,” he said quietly. “To think that this little object could end so much misery. Except…” He crouched down in front of Clara. “Except, I still have a problem. You see, I can’t open it. Only she,” he gestured toward Kat with his knife, “can help me. I think your husband gave her the code. I’ll confess, I’m impressed by her: that should could do all this even though she is so… abnormal.” Clara’s rage simmered, but she held her tongue. “I would just kill her, of course. But she confirmed that unless I open this box properly, the filter will self-destruct. And we don’t want that to happen, do we? Not after all we’ve been through to get it. So… I thought that if I waited for you, she might be more… motivated to help me.”

“You’re a monster,” Clara hissed.

“No,” Tracker replied. “I’m… a pragmatist.”

“Let us go to her,” Jacob pleaded.

Tracker considered his proposition carefully. Then he rose again to his full height and took a step back. Needing no further permission, Jacob and Clara scrambled madly across the short distance that separated them. Mother threw her arms around Kat and pulled her tight, kissing her face repeatedly.

"You're okay?" she asked, finally, pulling back to inspect her more closely.

"Yes, Mother," Kat replied calmly. "I missed you."

"Oh, god. I've thought about you every day, every minute, every second…"

"Very touching," interrupted Tracker. "Now, little girl, unless you want to watch me kill your brother and mother right here in front of you, you'll open this box like I asked you to."

Jacob never felt such pure hatred as he did right at that moment. He took one step toward Tracker, but Kat reached out and stopped him. She slid off the hood of the car and stepped in front of her brother. Undaunted, she addressed Tracker directly.

"Tracker is not your name," she said with quiet intensity. "What's your name?"

Tracker scrutinized her, the skin at the corners of his eyes contracting almost imperceptibly in both surprise and confusion. He sneered and held out the treasure chest. "Open the box."

"She loved you," Kat insisted, refusing to take the chest from him. "She told me she forgives you. She hopes you will forgive her."

Tracker cocked his head slightly, as if straining to hear a distant sound. Jacob had no idea what Kat was doing, or why, but she seemed to have touched a nerve in Tracker, forged the slightest crack in his otherwise impregnable carapace.

"She told you this day would come," Kat pressed, offering an upturned, open hand to him. "Can you do what she asked? Can you forgive?"

Tracker took half a step backward, making every effort to suppress his disorientation. Viciously, he asked, "What did she tell you? That you're *the one*? The *chosen* one? You're not the first she's said that to, you know. It was just one of her many delusions."

"It's not a delusion," Kat replied.

"You're not," Tracker insisted again, though this time his voice did not convey the same confidence.

"I am."

Tracker shook his head as if to clear his vision. "You're just a foolish little girl."

"Help us start again," Kat said, extending her other hand.

Her fearlessness had disarmed him, as if by submitting to him so willingly, she had paradoxically pierced his armor. His eyes searched hers, trying to verify a truth that descended upon him – one which he did not want to accept. Doubt germinated. Kat waited patiently.

"It can't be," he said. "I don't believe…"

"You know, don't you? In your heart. You can feel it. She was right. About me. About you."

They stared at each other in silence, and for longer than Jacob felt able to bear. Then, with his voice weakening, Tracker said, "It's too late for me."

"No," Kat insisted. "It's exactly the time."

Tracker bowed his head. When he raised it again, his eyes had gone completely dark. Taking a step toward Kat, he extended his left hand in almost slow motion, curling his long fingers around her throat. Just then, without warning, the crack of a gun split the air. Then another. And another. For a moment, Jacob was unsure where the shot had come from, who had fired it, or if anyone had been hit. Then, with agonizing lassitude, Tracker dropped to his knees. His grip on Kat's neck tightened, and he pulled her with him to the ground. Jacob spun around wildly to find the source of the gunshot.

From the top of the hill in front of the old synagogue strode Pepe, pistol in hand.

Tracker

His vision blurred as his body hit the ground. For a moment, everything went dark. When he opened his eyes, he felt strangely peaceful and calm.

Where am I? he wondered.

Around him, trees vaulted to the sky, endless in their appeal to the blue above. The air felt crisp and cold, stinging the back of his throat. Birdsong merged with the rustling leaves and he understood.

Redwoods, he thought.

Instinctively he rolled his head to face the edge of the copse. From among the broad, rust-colored trunks, a female figure approached him, eyes blazing in emerald compassion. She lay down beside him, willing, even after all this, to be with him. He reached out and touched her neck, thumbing the steady pulse that vibrated in time with his own.

You came, he wondered.

I told you I would find a way, she said.

Kat

Kat stayed with him, easing to the ground as he fell. His hand stayed tight around her neck – firm, but not choking – his thumb lightly pressing the carotid artery between her windpipe and neck muscle. Their hearts began to beat in sync, fused at his thumb. His eyes fluttered open and he stared blankly at her, as if observing her from an incalculable distance. She was not afraid.

"You came," he said.

"She told me to come. She told you she would find a way."

Tracker reached out with his other hand and Kat took it, interlacing her delicate fingers with his. His rough, dry skin was already growing cold. He tried to move, but she soothed him back to the ground.

"Be still," she said.

Tracker

Her delicate fingers felt fine in his. He tried to lift his body, pushing up on one elbow. But he could feel his life force draining and he fell back to the ground.

Be still, she said.

I loved you too much, he said, fighting now for each word, trying to fit a lifetime into a few syllables. *I couldn't…*

It's ok, she said. *You can let go now. We're together.*

He struggled to keep her in focus. Those green eyes. He had always loved her green eyes.

Do you remember your name? she asked again. *Who I said you were?*

My name…? he sputtered, confused.

Who you really are...

Kat

"I loved you too much," Tracker gasped. "I couldn't let go…"

"It's ok," Kat said. "You can let go now. You'll be together."

His pupils clouded from their edges toward the center, their inner light flickering faintly against the encroaching darkness. Vaguely she was aware that Jacob, Mother and Pepe had rushed over to help her.

No, she said to Jacob with her eyes, and her brother, comprehending, extended his arms to hold back the others. She could not explain her certainty, her sense of calm, any more than they could grasp it. She knew only that she needed to be near him in this moment, that everything had come to this.

"Do you remember your name?" Kat urged Tracker again in hardly more than a whisper. Their faces were so close that Kat could see the grooves of his lined face, her eyes surveying a craggy landscape of pain and endurance. His scar ran in a smooth river through the peaks and valleys of weathered skin. She traced her finger along it, caressing the expression of his pain, wiping it clean.

"My name…?" he sputtered.

"Who you really are," she insisted.

"My name is…" he started.

Tracker

My name is…

In a rush of memory, he could hear that sweet, slightly stilted voice singing to him in the dark as the world around them collapsed; could hear her insisting that he bore a great responsibility, that no matter what happened between them all as friends and lovers, that she knew in her bones that it would come down to him. They were alone that night, and her eyes shone brightly beside him in the bed, her silken hair fanned out around her face, her feathery skin soft against his own. She told him that she knew he needed to follow his own path, that she didn't understand it, or like it, but that she loved him, that she believed in him, that she knew he would do the right thing in the end. And she said that if he did, she would find a way to come to him, for them to be together again. He didn't believe her then, writing it off as another of her silly, superstitious ideas.

Tracker recalled the scent of her, vital and real. It mixed with the musky redwood and lingering pine as his vision faded here on the heights of his world. This was a place he loved to be: among the trees, in the high mountain air, close to the sky. From this vista, he could dimly see the possibility of something true and good – a new beginning, free from ambition and poverty and jealousy and greed. Above him, the expansive sky exalted in sunlight; tendrils of cloud opened and extended outward in welcome; no dust, no dirt, no heat; just cool, crisp, ethereal blue. As her scent melted into him, his failing eyes traveled the length of the trees, upward to infinity.

It's time, she said. *Can you forgive? Let go?*

I can, he rasped.

Your name? she asked, tears rolling now down her face as his grip released her neck and his hand fell limply to his side. A slow trickle of blood flowed from the corner of his mouth.

You called me…, he said, the faint hint of a smile on his lips. Then with his last breath, he said, *Masaw. My name… is… Masaw.*

Part VII

The Fifth World

Jacob

The first bombs fell that evening. Fighter jets roared overhead, wave after wave of American planes scorching the earth. Air raid sirens screamed unrelentingly as the L.A. basin filled with smoke and flashes of light, but the New California Air Force remained unable to respond, grounded by Bettina's lethal virus. Powerless to stop the Americans from pouring over the mountains, the New Cal army and air force began its slow-motion collapse after only a few hours. Ground fighting was fierce, especially in the north where troops had been built up over the preceding year, but it would only be a matter of time before they, too, surrendered.

From the junkyard, they headed north in the ragged truck Pepe had picked up in south L.A. Small as he was, Pepe handled the wheel with deft expertise. He wove through the growing throngs of fleeing citizens, most of whom were on foot, terrorized by the bombings. At one point, Jacob had him stop so that a family with five exhausted children could load into the back of the pickup. Before long the truck bed dipped with the weight of so many passengers that they finally had to turn people away. After hours of inching in and out of traffic, by early morning Pepe finally steered the vehicle clear of the City and onto the highway.

Jacob had sent Bettina a message when Tracker died, but he had been unable to reach her since then by phone. When Pepe told them about Hector, the three friends mourned him in each other's arms before climbing into the truck. But now, as Jacob surveyed the sad faces huddled near him in the truck bed, he knew that his losses only mirrored those of everyone around him – and his losses, at least, had been tempered by all that he had regained. Through the back window of the cab, he watched as Mother stroked Kat's hair, refusing to allow any physical distance between them. Hector's sacrifice, like Renard's, had enabled this reunion. For that, he would be forever grateful.

Just as his eyes began to close at last, lulled by the slow swaying of the truck as it chugged down the highway, his wrist buzzed and bolted him awake.

"You did it!" belted Bettina as he opened the call.

"*We* did it," he corrected.

"The Americans are everywhere. I've been monitoring all of it. There's heavy fighting up north, but it won't be long before they take L.A."

"Can you believe Pepe…" Jacob started.

"I can," she declared. "He's a street kid. After what happened with Rat, he vowed to protect Kat. I couldn't keep him here, so I sent him in before I wanted to. He waited three days for you at the rendezvous so he could take you to the mountains. I didn't know he had a gun, but I'm glad he did."

"You're a genius, you know that," Jacob said sincerely.

"I'm as lucky as I am smart on this one. But hey, I'll take it," Bettina laughed. After a pause, she said solemnly, "Hector…"

"I know. Pepe told us."

"He stayed behind in Cherry Hills to slow Tracker down. He did it for me, so I could escape." Her voice trembled with emotion.

"I was just thinking about him and Renard. And Agnes. The sacrifices they made for us…"

"Renard's plan worked. And now you're on your way to the mountains," Bettina said. "Just like Agnes always wanted. She knew."

"Yeah," Jacob grunted. "She and Kat."

"I'm glad you're with them."

He wanted to say many things, but he didn't know where to start. Finally, he asked, "You think it'll take long before Duke surrenders?"

"He'll never surrender. He'll sacrifice every man and boy he can if there's even a hope to stay in power. They'll have to kill him to end it."

"And how about you? What're you gonna do now?"

She hesitated. "I have to stay here. Renard's gone. Hector. Leo. Julius is going back to Mexico. Snake Clan needs me."

"Yeah," he agreed, unsure of what other option there might be, but unable to hide his disappointment nonetheless.

"What about you? You gonna stay with your mom and sister?"

"We're finally together again," Jacob answered. "I did all this so we could be together. And now we are."

"You said that's what you wanted more than anything."

"Yeah," he agreed. "It was."

She waited a moment, seeming to notice his use of the past tense, and asked hesitantly, "And your dad?"

Jacob gazed out through the pale night at the silhouettes of trees and shrubs and rocks. A world in outline. "Kat says... Kat says she saw him in a dream. Dying in the mountains. I guess he was trying to make it out of the country on foot."

"Maybe he's still alive," Bettina tried to reassure him. "It was just a dream."

"You never know, I guess."

"He'd be very proud of you," Bettina said.

Silently, Jacob fought back the welling of emotion.

"You know," Bettina said with effort, "we're gonna need people here in the City. Warriors. Leaders. We have a whole new world to build in California now. The *real* America."

Jacob held the phone away from himself as he took in a long draught of night air and exhaled slowly. With as much energy as he could muster, he said, "Warriors, huh?"

"For sure."

"Are you implying that I'm a warrior? I'm not sure that's how you would have described me when we first met."

She laughed. "I'm just saying, once your mom and Kat are safe, you could come back. I mean, don't get me wrong, I can do this on my own. I don't need you." The line hung empty between them for a long moment. Then, with more tenderness than he had ever heard her express, she said, "But I'd rather do it with you."

Kat

They drove as far as Visalia before the truck finally ran out of fuel. The refugees who had hitched a ride with them shared hugs, wished each other luck, and then parted ways. Some joined Kat, Jacob, Clara and Pepe on the slow walk north. At Three Forks, they discovered a dilapidated cluster of buildings along Highway 395. An old post office and blown-out storefronts were all that remained on the main road. One block back, on Shop Street, Jacob scouted out an empty room in an abandoned auto repair business. Rusted out cars and trucks decayed in the lot, missing wheels and half-covered in dirt. As they dozed in the room, wind whipped through the cracks and crevices, whistling them awake. But there was a roof, and plastic sheeting to reinforce the windows. Most importantly, it felt safe. Occasionally, small bands of refugees would pass by, hungry and weak, trying their best to make it to the camps they had heard about on the American side of the mountains.

After their restless night, they awoke early and hiked to the Kern River Valley. Each evening they would set up a scratch camp for the night: Jacob and Pepe scavenging for food, Kat and Clara building rudimentary shelters just as Jacob had shown them. They relished dinners of nuts, berries, and fresh-cooked squirrel. Over the open fire, they recounted stories of life in the favela and wondered what life would be like in this new world. Clara listened to her children with wide-eyed disbelief, unable to keep her hands from making contact with them, as if she needed constant reassurance of their physical presence to ensure that nothing would take them away again.

Four days into their journey, they reached the base of Mount Olancha and began their last, long climb. As they ascended, the California black oaks of the lower mountain gradually gave way to the pines – ponderosa, white fir, sugar pines. Dusk fell on that fourth night as they stepped into a clearing commanded by three giant sequoias. Rising toward the sky with unspeakable majesty, their roots formed a natural arbor, a shelter carved from the woods, as if expecting their arrival. A soft blanket of leaves and pine needles covered the ground. All of them stood in wonder, gazing up at the towering trees. Kat felt as if she had somehow been here before.

"We stop here," she asserted.

As the others set up camp, Kat wandered up the hill a short distance. A large rock stood in the middle of her path. She closed her eyes and inhaled the fragrant, tree-filtered air. With great care, she removed the amulet Agnes had given her from around her neck and placed it on the center of the rock.

Kat awoke. The sun had not yet risen. No breeze stirred. The sky blushed lightly purple with the advancing light. She touched Jacob gently on the shoulder. He startled awake with concern.

"They're here," she said.

Two men, tall and lean, emerged from the trees as Kat and Jacob rose. They kept their distance, remaining at the edge of the clearing. Extending a hand, one of the men dangled Kat's water jar charm before him. Kat stepped forward.

"Kikmongwe?"

"We will take you to him."

At intervals along the path, they were joined by other women and men, soldiers of the mountains, guardians of the community, who materialized almost magically from the trees and fell into line behind them. Soon, more than fifteen people, bows slung over shoulders, guns holstered to belts, faces dark from exposure to the elements, had become part of their ranks, forming a kind of elfin parade. Rounding a corner, the trees cleared to reveal a large plaza that gave way to open skies to the north. To the south gaped the mouth of a giant cave. One of the guardians cupped her hands around her mouth and blew, emitting a rich, bellowing sound. Moments later, a diminutive figure appeared in the cave entrance, a growing contingent of other community members behind him. He extended his hands in welcome.

"You have come at last," Kikmongwe said to Kat in a voice as ancient as the sequoias themselves. He lay his hands on her shoulders, eyes sparkling. "Just as my sister said you would."

Kat removed the water jar from around her neck. He accepted it, touching it to his lips. Raising his gaze to the sky, he rapidly whispered an incantation she could not understand. Then he returned the pendant to her.

"You must be the one to bury it, as the great legend tells us. Then the water will flow again to all the People."

Kat reached into her bag and produced the treasure chest from the terrarium. Opening the inner chamber, she revealed the four tubes of the Ecosystem.

"Water filters," she explained. "My father's invention. This is what Malcolm Duke wanted, and why my father tried to escape.

I am giving them to you. This is what my father would have wanted me to do."

"Four," he said reverently. "One for each direction."

He raised a hand and snapped his fingers. A young woman stepped forward from the lingering crowd and presented herself at his side.

"Take this. Once we have performed the ceremony – tomorrow, after the full moon – we will send the filters out with our runners. They will go to each corner of the world, to be shared with all people. Water. The gift of life. It belongs to no man, and to all men."

The young woman took the treasure chest, bowed once to Kat, and scurried back to the cave. Kikmongwe looked over Kat's shoulder at Clara, Pepe and Jacob.

"This is your family?" he asked.

"Yes," Kat said. "My mother. And my brothers."

Pepe's face shined back at her with glorious pride.

"Come," said Kikmongwe, a sorrowful look in his eyes. "I have something I think you will want to see."

They sat on beautifully carved wooden chairs in a large room deep inside the cave. Tunnels branched off in many directions from the main chamber, suggesting a vast, interconnected warren. Children and families hovered now at the edges of the room, materializing from the tunnels to observe the spectacle of this strange party of travelers and to listen to the great Chief speak with them. Kikmongwe called forward one of his scouts, a young man with long legs and a windblown face.

"Tell them," the old man commanded.

"A few weeks ago," the scout began, "I was walking in the ranges south and west from here – a long way away. A small group of refugees told me that a man had been with them for a few days and that they were worried about him. I followed their trail back, and I found him lying by the trunk of a mighty oak tree."

"Father," Kat whispered. Clara put her forehead on Jacob's shoulder and quietly began to cry.

"He had been taken by the forest many weeks before that. But the trees were singing for him, lamenting in their ancient tongue, caring for his spirit with their nurturing arms. His spirit is with them now, traveling among their roots across the mountaintops." He stepped toward Kat. "And I found this in his hand…"

The scout reached into his pouch and pulled out a small, bronze token. He handed it to Kat.

It was the American penny Father had taken from her room.

Angelfish

In the evening, the entire mountain community followed Kikmongwe a short distance through the pines, up toward the crest of a nearby ridge. Around a patch of soft, mossy earth, they gathered in a reverent circle around a ceremonial hole that had been carefully prepared by their elders. To the west, the sun fringed the horizon, spraying shards of lemon and orange into the dying blue. Pale and luminescent, the moon had begun its opposite ascent. A gentle breeze consoled them with remnant warmth. Clara's eyes were red from a day of intermittent crying, but she had composed herself during the short climb, comforted by having her children at her side, and by this new community that had embraced them. Jacob pulled his mother close, his heart as broken as hers; Kat clutched her hand fiercely. In a few days, Jacob would return to the City and to Bettina. Pepe would accompany him; for as happy as he had been to help his darling Kat, he was a child of the favela and longed to return to the bustle of his familiar world. Clara and Kat would stay with Kikmongwe and his mountain community until the war with America ended.

Kikmongwe made his way to the center and held his palms open toward the sky. When he did, four "runners" took their designated places at the cardinal points of the circle, each equipped with one of the precious filters in a pack, ready to depart at the signal of their Chief, eager to fulfill their mission of sharing this bounty with the world. The gathered crowd waited with solemn anticipation. Kikmongwe spoke in a deep, melodious voice that carried easily on the thin air.

"Our People have passed down a story through the generations. We say that Taiowa, creator of life, has had to re-make the world many times because of the folly of humanity. Each time he did this, he took a chosen few from among the People and placed them in the Kiva so they could emerge to begin the world again. The First World he destroyed with fire; The Second World with ice; The Third World with water. Legend tells us that he grew weary of the People's wandering ways. So for the Fourth World he named a Caretaker, a spirit who would be close to us, one of us – someone who could *embody* the evil and the darkness that we hold inside us, but also our potential for light and glory – for love. Taiowa knew that the Fourth World would not be destroyed from above, but from within. By us. By men themselves. And he could not bear it. So he left the burden to the Caretaker – to suffer for us and with us, to cause our pain and finally to relieve it. This Caretaker was called *Masaw*."

Kikmongwe turned to Kat. "Come forward, child."

Kat stepped into the circle and unclasped the chain from her neck. Kikmongwe took it from her, pressed it gently to his lips, then held it aloft. His voice rose again magisterially.

"The legend says that when drought plagues the People and the deserts reclaim their rightful land; when tyrants rise because of fear and hate and scarcity; when the frogs and the birds and the bees grow in unnatural ways and in unnatural places; when nature itself begins to collapse: these are the signs that the Fourth World is nearing its end. When this happens, what then do we do? Where do we go? How do we find hope, even in such darkness?"

Kikmongwe spun around slowly, meeting the eyes of every member of the rapt community. Holding the water jar aloft again, he continued:

"Taiowa bestowed a gift upon us, a vessel fashioned from clay. It is the source of life, and of hope. Each generation has passed it down, one to the next, since this world began. And when the world is ready to be renewed, so the legend tells us, the Chosen

One must bury the water jar – along with water from the sea, a feather from the wing of the mighty eagle, and a token of love. If we do this as the slow moon rises, then even though the land is dry, water will flow from the ocean, clean and sweet into every home, into every village, all over the world. And even though we are surrounded by violence and fear and death, that all will wane; and as it does, peace will rise from the underworld, climbing with the pale moon over the mountain to join the stars above us, awaiting the dawn of a new day.

"Today is the day of renewal. We have planned for this, hoped for it, suffered for it. We have trusted each other, believing that the Chosen One would find us with the water jar even as we were mocked, and rejected, and forgotten. We have a name for our Chosen One, who must now bury the jar with her own hands. We call her: the Water Bearer."

Kikmongwe signaled to the four messengers, who each took several paces through the parting crowd, waiting on the other side, ready to begin their long journeys down the mountain. The old man crouched down and scooped soil from the hole that had been prepared by the elders. Crumbling the dry powder through his fingers, he sang a beautiful song in a strange tongue. His voice merged with the wind and the dust from his hands, passing over the ridge, and across the valleys toward the setting sun. When he finished, he removed a small vial of water and a beautiful eagle feather from a leather pouch around his waist. Then he turned to face the Angelfish family.

To Jacob, he handed the vial: "To you, I give this: water, Mother Earth's most precious bounty."

To Clara, he said: "To you, the feather of the eagle, master of the air, who knows no boundaries and represents the great spirit that binds us all together."

He touched his forehead delicately to Kat's before extending the charm to her. "And to you, Water Bearer, I return the sacred jar."

One by one, the Angelfish family placed their objects deep in the ceremonial pit: the vial, the feather, and the jar. Kikmongwe dipped his head toward Kat.

"It is time," he said.

As the sun withdrew its last long tail of light, Kat placed Father's penny on top of the other objects. She extended one hand to her mother and one to her brother. Together they took fistfuls of soil and smoothed the hole in the earth.

Acknowledgements

The passage Kat reads in the bunker at the opening of the story are the first lines of Madeline L'Engle's *A Wrinkle In Time*.

Cover art and map designs created by Holly Sullo.

I first learned about the last group of Kayenta who left the Long House Valley from reading Jared Diamond's *Collapse*. The uncertainty of what happened to the Kayenta had, from the outset, been central to this story. Much later, after I had written an early draft, I wondered if there might be a way to tie the tale more explicitly to Hopi myth. Quite by accident, I came across the account of the water jar in the wonderful *Book of the Hopi* by Frank Waters. That legend eerily echoed mine, and I knew that I had found the title to my book. I subsequently took great liberties in rewriting the creation myth as described by Waters, adapting it to the context of Kat and Jacob's quest. For this act of literary license, I can only ask for forgiveness and understanding.

Kat's ability to perform echolocation is based on the remarkable story about Daniel Kish, as told by the radio program, *This American Life* in 2015.

David Spratt, my brother-in-law, read every draft, gave careful and wonderful input, and insisted at every turn that I keep going. There is no way I would have written this book without his support and encouragement. My own brother, Jeff, read versions early and late. An incredible writer in his own right, his edits were invaluable. And Aubrey Restifo provided wonderful editing and counsel in the course of getting this story over the finish line, and I am very grateful to her for the energy and enthusiasm she brought to it.

Finally, to Sam, who at a young age wanted me to tell him a story about "Jacob the Spy", and in so doing set me on this arduous path; and to Lily, whose blanket and guinea pig and gentle spirit were a source of constant inspiration – thank you both. I wrote this book because of you, and for you, and for your children. I hope you will read it aloud to them one day. Most of all, to Caroline – who has been with me at every step, and who has given me unimaginable gifts of time and love and advice and encouragement. All I can say is that this book is the least of things that would not exist without you. I just hope the ending doesn't let you down.